abattleagainstdemons.com

A BATTLE AGAINST DEMONS

Kjell-Vidar Åhman Teig

abattleagainstdemons.com

Author: Kjell-Vidar Åhman Teig
Cover design & layout: Kjell-Vidar Åhman Teig
Editor: Per Ivar Hjeldsbakken Engevold
Photo: Ida Charlotte Åhman Teig
Genre: Nordic Horror / Crime / Magical Realism
Edition: 1
Language: English
Number of pages: 366
Publication year: English translation 2024
(Original release in Norwegian 2023)
Translation: Music Is Everywhere
Publisher:
Music Is Everywhere / music-is-everywhere.com
ISBN: 978-91-527-9179-0

Thank you

A Battle Against Demons couldn't have been written without a life lived. People born, met, or passed away. It couldn't have been written without my family: Lotta (wife), Ida-Hermine (daughter), Nils Iver (son), Paprika (hamster), and Istella (cat).

A Battle Against Demons couldn't have been written without growing up in Båstad, a little village in the middle of nowhere in Norway, with a family that means so much: Terje (dad), Glenn-Øyvind (brother), Tonje (sister), and Hilde (new-mother). Thank you for believing in me.

A Battle Against Demons couldn't have been written without Tove (original-mom) and Odd-Johnny (younger brother). I'm sure you're both in a better place now.

A Battle Against Demons couldn't have been written without the help of beta readers, translators, contributors of all kinds, and my awesome editor, Per Ivar Hjeldsbakken Engevold.

Last but not least, thank you for reading this, whoever you may be.

Welcome to Øyerstad,
Kjell-Vidar Åhman Teig

Foreword

Horror and terror in written form have deep roots. In China, as early as 1500 BC, people wrote with reverence and awe about ancestors and the deceased. The Egyptians wrote about a spiritual world, beyond our own, filled with mystical and feared beings. In Roman, Greek, and Norse mythology, gods and heroes often fought monsters and evil spirits. Tales told around the campfire were written down and turned into stories that entertained, frightened, and transformed our storytelling traditions.

Modern horror literature can be traced back to the 18th century. Horace Walpole is considered to have written and published the first Gothic novel, *The Castle of Otranto*, in 1764. Gothic horror subsequently became very popular: stories of drafty mansions, haunted old castles, deformities, and hoarse screams in the night attracted a sensation-hungry and bloodthirsty audience. In the 19th century, the so-called Penny Dreadfuls appeared in England; mass-produced and serialised magazines with macabre stories of ghosts, demons, and vampires. These magazines set the standard for a new wave of accessible and recognizable horror that made adults draw their curtains and children shiver under their blankets at night.

Searching for Norwegian horror literature for adults, sadly, one has to search for a while. Although I've read horror literature for thirty years, I can't name five Norwegian horror authors. Children and young adults have a much better selection of such literature, but the grim reality is that horror literature for adults doesn't have particularly deep roots or a large audience in Norway. If one looks around, you will quickly find established names like Andre Bjerke (*De dødes tjern*) and Tom Egeland (*Ragnarok*). Fortunately, we also have some solid newer authors who have established themselves within Norwegian horror. Nikolaj Frobenius (*Mørke grener*, *Jeg skal vise dere frykten*) is one of them; T.H. Håvardsen (*Viktoriahavn*-trilogy) is another. There are also occasional factual books about myths and ghost stories, but genuine Norwegian horror books are surprisingly scarce.

We are a dark and cold country with a rather melancholic and despondent people. Why isn't there more Norwegian horror to be found? The reason is most likely crime fiction or Nordic noir. It's not as if the Norwegian people don't read, far from it. Few authors in Norway sell as much as crime writers. If the reader found themselves a place where a pack of gum could be bought, one could most definitely buy a crime novel there as well. Norwegian crime is very noir: some of these books are so dark, twisted, and uncomfortable that there is little difference between them and horror. Cases covered often include intricate and macabre murders. The limitation of crime fiction for horror enthusiasts is that these stories often draw from real-life criminal cases. They generally unfold from the perspectives of investigators, police officers, and forensic scientists. Unfortunately, a horror enthusiast may feel they're missing out, as this type of literature primarily revolves around scenarios that could actually happen. Where is the supernatural? Where is the mystery and the unexplainable?

Fortunately, there are several ways to publish a book. Norwegian indie literature, independent of the major publishers, is experiencing a modest resurgence. Now authors have a fair chance to publish their own books. I'm not an expert on indie literature, but what I have read of independent books has a rough charm that polished publisher books often lack. This is probably because indie authors have completely different parameters. They have greater creative freedom and control. You can write the book you really want.

An author who has taken charge of the stories he wants to convey, and the process of publishing his own books is Kjell-Vidar Åhman Teig. He has, including this book, published two books on his own. His debut book, *3 Steiner til Nøkken* (2020), is a very personal and emotional collection of short stories based on the author's lived life: here, stories from childhood and upbringing are intertwined with the fantastic, magical, and terrifying in a way I have yet to see other Norwegian authors do. The book simply hit me like a torch to the face and was undoubtedly my greatest reading experience in 2020. The first thing that struck me after reading *3 Steiner til Nøkken* is that it can be described as something as rare in Norwegian literature as magical realism, a literary direction where the fantastic, unreal, and supernatural are placed in a realistic and down-to-earth context.

With his writing, Kjell-Vidar creates a world of the nostalgic and macabre, the real and unreal, the witty and the absolutely heart breaking. Genre-wise, he places himself somewhere between horror, magical realism, and fantasy. This might be because he hasn't needed to fit into the often strict frameworks of traditional publishers. His texts are his own, and it's felt throughout the reading experience! *A Battle Against Demons*, like *3 Stones for Nøkken*, takes place in Øyerstad, a small community of the type found in many places in Norway. On the surface, Øyerstad resembles a typical Norwegian village. Underneath, it bubbles with stories whispered between the residents, shadows in the twilight, sounds in the night, good intentions, bad blood, and indissoluble ties that together make up a wild, beautiful, and sometimes pitch-dark community.

The people of Øyerstad battle against themselves, fate, each other, and most importantly, against demons...

Enjoy!
Henning Øverby Klausen
Skrekkruttskolen.no

A Battle Against Demons is loosely inspired by actual events, but none of the characters in the book are real people.

Prologue

The Circus

The entrance to the circus tent gaped widely, as darkness draped over me like the lid on a rusty charcoal grill. The canvas glowed and pulsated in shades of red, orange, and grey. Shouts of joy, laughter, and ecstasy mixed with frustration, panic, and crying. The abstractions that unfolded within the tent must have been the stuff of nightmares. A smell of sweets, popcorn, grease, and oil comingled with a stench of excrement. My throat pulled tight. I breathed heavily as my body slowly swayed back and forth. I heard feet, hooves, and claws against netting, bars, and metal. Heavy breaths in the darkness behind the tent. Yet, I saw no one.

I scanned the area from the tent, along the dimly lit stalls, and further into the darkness. The hypnotic melody of a steam whistle organ filled my heart with lead, pressing me to the ground. A movement in the dark, where the torches succumbed to the night, caught my attention. A figure, vague but familiar. A darker shade within the shadows struggled into the light. The light resisted.

If I stand completely still, maybe he won't see me? Goosebumps spread from the back of my neck. *Please, leave me be.* From the outside, I might've appeared apathetic, but inside, my blood was racing, my heart pounding.

After what felt like an eternity, the unease disappeared. The torches found new oxygen, and the flames flared up again. Darkness retreated, and the shadow followed it. I continued to sway back and forth. He was still lurking out there.

Robert

A lot has happened over my not-so-long life, and soon it will all be over. Just like that. My arms, held above my head, ache, and the rifle muzzle against the back of my neck feels cold. My knees against the wooden deck are sore. Even though the wind creates small ripples on the lake's surface, the raft is completely still, tethered to the bottom. It doesn't move. Neither do I.

I am, and always have been, proud of being from Øyerstad. Well, I have almost always been proud of being from that old stomping ground. Over the past decade, I've been a bit back and forth in that regard. I ran away some time ago to avoid going mad, or worse—I feared I would die if I stayed. Now, with my shoes firmly planted in my hometown once again, I wonder if I should have come back at all.

The pale underbellies of the clouds signal a change in the wind. A mild breeze caresses me with a scent of spruce and pine. It gently touches the spot on my head where they put the stitches less than a week ago. He presses the muzzle of his rifle harder against my neck, nearly causing me to fall forward. This wasn't how it was supposed to end. I had more important things I should've done. Things much bigger than that bastard with a gun behind me.

If he shoots me now, everyone I know and those who know them will be done for. None of us, I can guarantee you, will leave this world in a dignified or painless way. That's not how it works. Right now, only I can stop that from happening.

Soon, my face will be pressed against the wooden deck. Blood will ooze between the planks and into the water from a gaping hole in my neck. Maybe the blood will breathe new life into them? Them…

It's ironic that what ultimately kills me is a simple bullet.

A shot to the neck! Good Lord, it's way too simple. Especially compared to... all the other things that have happened. All the others who have…

Even though I knew this would happen, the shot still comes as a surprise, as if I hadn't truly believed he would actually pull the trigger. That it would all end here. The sound is deafening.

Øyerstad

Excerpt from the shelved manuscript: *The Witch of Mørkved, Death, and I - a Memoir by Robert Baastad.*

Rusty fenders scrape against the Volvo's tires, even though the father drives as carefully as possible over the speed bumps at the border crossing between Norway and Sweden. From Töcksfors to Ørje. According to the father, the customs service confiscates everything they can—pork, bacon, cigarettes, beer, wine, and spirits. They even take the kids' firecrackers if given a chance.

"I should've been a customs officer. Damn, life would've been good," he says, having yet another *snus*, a kind of chewing tobacco, after tossing a cigarette butt out of the window.

However, they're not stopped by customs officers, nor waved to the side for vehicle weighing this time either. They continue unhindered into Norway along the E-18 towards Ørje. They pass Hærland and approach Mysen. Before Askim, they turn right, away from the main road. They are not going to Oslo. Soon they pass through the dense forests and inner fields of Østfold. It's 1986 and Lionel Richie is "Dancing on the Ceiling".

In Skjønnsund, they stop to buy ice cream. The two kids each pick a "Kræsj Pink", an eighties classic with pineapple flavour, chocolate coating, and a chewing gum stick, while their parents choose ice cream cones with strawberry sauce. They drink lukewarm 7up, of which they have three crates in the car. As they drive out of Skjønnsund a few minutes later, the kids enjoy their chewing gum stick in the back seat. In the front seat, they drink coffee from a dented thermos, and light another cigarette. The windows are rolled down due to the heat, not the smoke. In the ten-minute drive to Øyerstad, they stop several times to observe elks wandering close to the road.

"Welcome to Solberg Camping," says a banner between two fir trees. It offers cabins, cosy tent spots, elk safaris with a money-back guarantee, and diving courses in Lake Øyeren. Then they pass a larger wooden sign where "Welcome to Øyerstad" has been, with a few bold pencil strokes, modified to "Welcome to Øyerstad - Rebel Town". Whoever added "Rebel Town" is likely referring to the many lowered Volvos with Confederate flags in the rear windows that burn rubber through the village. The youngsters—greasers, they're called—almost lying down while driving, often swing by the store where they buy pomade, steel combs, and bottled cola. They order their leather vests and pointy shoes from Sweden via post-order catalogues.

Like many others, these passing tourists won't remember Øyerstad. Ask them a bit later, say ten minutes or so, and they won't know what you're talking about.

"Øyerstad? No, never heard of it."

That's the case for most passersby. Øyerstad doesn't stand out, with its congregation of no more than about four hundred souls. In Øyerstad, everyone knows everyone.

The family in the car passes Solberg Camping on the left

without hearing about the "camping girls". Those who ruled the village until the "cabin girls" arrived and gave them competition. Every summer, the camping girls, and now also cabin girls, pop up outside the kiosk, on the pier at Øyervika, or on the raft up by Lake Mørkved. They speak different languages and have foreign dialects. Their clothes are colourful, have modern fits, and exotic logos. They talk about movies, bands, and artists that many in Øyerstad have never heard of. Some of them, the girls, return to the village year after year. Sometimes one of them falls for a local hero and decides to stay.

In the front of the car, rewind is pressed on the cassette player, as the kids in the backseat request "Dancing on the Ceiling" yet again as they pass Øyerstad Elementary School.

The passersby don't notice the children playing and cheering in too-short jeans and white tennis socks with coloured stripes. They don't see that Robert has Gene Simmons on his shirt, or that others have Iron Maiden, W.A.S.P., and Ozzy on theirs. The boys sing "The Number of the Beast" to the teacher's dismay, and they play soccer. They are Flying Dutchmen and English lions, they are Gary Lineker and Marco van Basten. Porn magazines are smuggled into the restroom as they dream about the gym teacher in tiny tights.

Over by the water fountain, the girls are playing hopscotch in striped Ball sweaters. Under towering crowns of permed or crimped hair, they scribble secret notes, while Linn stands alone in her corner, invisible. The family in the car sees none of this.

As they pass the church to the right, the mother notices all the cars outside but never sees the graveyard to the left. Neither of them sees how the 17th of May parade stops there every year to honour the locals who fell during the war. The courtyard behind the church where Kai lives, where everything eventually went to hell, goes unnoticed as well. They even miss Guro up in Sandåsen. That girl, who according to Robert, is more beautiful than all the others combined, even the cabin and camping girls.

The sign that tells them they are approaching the town centre goes unnoticed. It's not surprising considering a birch tree lays its branches around it every summer. The locals have long forgotten that they once demanded that the municipality cut down that birch tree. In the town centre, they pass Fina, the gas station that Kjell's father has run forever. It's not a big setup, but he has the locals on his side, and you must have that to succeed over time in Øyerstad. Locals stop by, fill up gas, drink coffee, and gossip.

Next to Fina is the house where Robert often sits on the living room floor and plays Super Mario Bros with his younger brother Fredrik. Robert was born in 1978. He turned eight in 1986 and is a year and a half older than Fredrik. Robert and Fredrik both have spiked hair. And a rat tail. In addition to the two of them, the family also consists of big brother Anders, who is three years older than Robert. Anders wears a leather vest and talks exclusively about motorcycles and cars even though he's far from old enough to drive either.

Robert's dad usually says that Robert's mom is like a meerkat—maybe because she has intense eyes, is small, slender, and has a pointy nose. Robert's buddies call her Kim Basinger on the sly, mainly because of her blonde hair. But most people in Øyerstad call her Mom. Her real name is Marianne.

Robert's dad takes up more space. Kjell, Robert's best friend, once said after they had seen the movie *Double Trouble*: "Terence Hill is cool, but he's no Bud Spencer. Come to think of it, your dad looks just like him. Like Bud Spencer!"

Kjell is partly right about that, except that Robert's dad doesn't go around hitting people over the head with his fist. Robert's dad is named Knut-Erik, but is mainly just called Dad.

Robert's grandparents live in the house next door. Then follows a small potato field, and after that the Øyerstad centre. *Øyerstad-cluster* would more fitting, since it's quite small. At the post office, Mom picks up bills and payment notices almost daily. In the bank next door, Robert's dad has loan applications and chequebooks rejected as soon as he steps through the door.

From the chapel on the way up to Kirkeåsen, a waffle and coffee-flavored steam rolls down towards the local store, accompanied by songs for Jesus. The store and its neighbouring kiosk proudly display an FM sign above the entrance. The presence of a chain store makes the residents of Øyerstad just a little bit prouder. The kiosk, a shabby shack, is balancing on a foundation of Euro-pallets a few metres from the store building. Huge posters tempt you with space burgers; with pineapple and crispy fries with cheese. Bazooka gum, Juicy Fruit, and other treats have found their place in the window too, next to a collection of handwritten notes about offers, missing and no longer missing cats, and other things that people have lost or found again. The family that bought ice cream in Skjønnsund doesn't stop there either.

The passersby don't see how the residents of Øyerstad help each other fix cars with flat tires or jumpstart dead batteries, how they adjust each other's TV antennas, and help paint each other's houses. The people of Øyerstad are helpful, and above all, they love coffee and chatting. You don't lock your house or car in Øyerstad.

The tower on top of Mørkved Hills has three red lights that shine over the village when darkness descends, yet it also remains unseen. The family in the car never swims in Lake Mørkved either, and soon they pass Texaco, the second gas station on their way out of the village again. According to Dad, they have crappy service. Therefore the Texaco crew struggles to attract the locals, and as a result, that station is the first to shut down a few years later.

The transient family remains unconcerned with these local intricacies. Their journey takes them past the skating rink, the old store, and the garage where Old Gunnar spends his days. As "Dancing on the Ceiling" winds down again, they leave Øyerstad behind.

One beautiful day, sometime in the future, at home in Kristinehamn, Sweden, the father might open the daily newspaper and read about the horrors that took place in Øyerstad, a village he could swear he had never seen or heard of.

In the backseat, Paul Stanley poses on the cover of some music magazine. The eldest girl daydreams of a life filled with glamour and grandeur as a sea of grain flows past the car. From the driver's side, another cigarette butt is thrown out, hitting the asphalt before coming to a stop against a pair of shoe soles. The figure on the roadside stands with his back to them. The sun glints off his helmet, making it difficult to see what he's looking at.

He suddenly jerks, turning to face the road. He stomps on the cigarette butt, twisting his shoe back and forth until the smoke disappears. He then gets on his moped, kicks the starter four, five times before it fires up. He glances to the left at the tourists and the car that passed by a short while ago. They are gone, heading towards the Akershus border. An ink-like liquid drips from his backpack and down his trousers. Either he doesn't notice, or he doesn't care. He turns his helmet towards Øyerstad, heading into the town centre.

Part 1

The Circus and Lake Mørkved

The Latter Half of the '80s

1

Robert

Our parents were terrified by the Chernobyl disaster and anxiously talked about Gorbachev (the one with the ink blot on his forehead), nuclear war, and AIDS. It sounded bad, but for us kids, around eight years old at the time, we had other worries. "Death" scared us more than all the evil that the adults watched on the news combined.

According to one of the stories, Death was born deep within the reactors of the Soviet's lethal jaws. In his youth, he fled to Øyerstad on a radioactive moped while eating AIDS patients, atomic bombs, and little babies along the way.

Now, Death haunted the village's children on a blood red, rusty Yamaha FS1. It rattled, screamed, and moved like an oversized metal mosquito. Fortunately, we could hear him long before he approached.

Some adults claimed that Death was human, but only for a couple of hours each day, running errands for the Witch of Mørkved. They said he scoured the ditches for roadkill, rats, badgers, deer, and any other roadside carcasses. He'd bring them back to the house up by Lake Mørkved, where he and the Witch... well, only God knows what they were doing up there. Regardless of which version you believed, it turned out that Death and the Witch had more to fear from us than we did from them.

Death's hair protruded from the helmet like a cloak as the dark knight roared through the village. His hands glowed milk-white against his pitch-black leather jacket, which likely concealed nothing but skin and bone. Fredrik and I rolled up our yoyos and ran, our ponytails flying straight out behind us when he approached on his vehicle.

"Don't go out on the road. What if Death comes and takes you to the Witch?" Grandma often warned, in a dialect as thick as the skid marks left by the local hot-rodders.

Grandma, or anyone else for that matter, probably wouldn't have used them as scare tactics if they had known what would later befall us, the village, and potentially the whole country. They'd instead have said, "Beware of the trucks! You could get run over."

Going to the kiosk, we took the path along the stream in the forest behind the house, up past the pond where we used to splash around and throw pinecones. Then we veered right after the treehouse. We looked down at our grandparents' house, which wasn't quite a skyscraper, but with its three storeys it stood taller than any other house in Øyerstad. In the middle of their lawn by the apple trees, there was a large scorched circle in the grass. Once a year, they'd take out the blackened cauldron in which they'd cook some sort of stew. I can still imagine it. One of my uncles, either Frode or Håkon, swinging an axe, beheading a turkey against a stump. They'd drink beer and laugh as the poor turkey ran its final laps around the house, blood spraying from the stump of its neck. The turkey then went into the pot with vegetables and all sorts of oddities they'd been cooking all day.

They started early, and the kids were welcome to the party, as long as it was bright out. Later, when it got dark, I'd lie in bed, listening to the screams and shouts of the merry-makers outside. The laughter and spectacle. Occasionally, I'd sneak outside and watch them dance around the cauldron in the glow, like witches and wizards in a magical ceremony. Some of them I didn't recognise, and some struggled to stand upright.

Fredrik and I had probably received a few shiny coins from our grandparents and, as usual, drove Nina at the kiosk counter mad. The older boys simply ordered "a bag of mixed" and intently watched as she leaned forward for the salty liquorice and twin cherries. Her pants tightened around her buttocks, and her shirt rode up, revealing the skin just above her hips. Fredrik and I, on the other hand, didn't care about such things, nor did we let her choose our candies for us. No, we chose our own: "Six red gold bears, four rock candy sticks, two chocolate cigarettes, one E.T. PEZ dispenser, and... wait, make that *one* chocolate cigarette and *two* rock candy sticks. And, can I get...?"

We maximised the number of items, and it took forever. Sometimes Fredrik would go a little bananas and order gummy bears for the entire amount. That'd give you a hundred pieces for ten kroner! My older brother Anders alternated between candies on the bottom shelf and a bag of mixed.

We were always cautious on our way to the kiosk, especially if it was just Fredrik and me. If we sensed the rumbling from Death's moped, we hid at the edge of the forest and spied down on the road. We didn't move until he passed, or until we were sure it wasn't him coming.

"Would you like anything else?" Nina asked, with admirable patience, as I picked up on the moped's frequencies. The sound was louder than it should have been. We had been inattentive.

"Would you like anything else?" she repeated.

She was barely audible.

"Do you think we'll make it?" I whispered to my little brother, glancing towards the forest's edge. He didn't react. "What do we do with the candy?" I asked a little louder.

We had trained for such situations many times. The protocol (a word we heard Kjell's father use once) was set, and we had a method. Any interaction with the kiosk's staff had to be interrupted. The prize, candy that is, no matter the size, had to be abandoned. Strict rules, but absolutely necessary. The written protocol under the bed read clearly: "Meeting Death face-to-face should be avoided at all costs. If he gets too close, run like hell. Run faster than Rijkaard and Van Basten combined."

Both of us stood stunned, and the sound soon peaked before gradually fading. The shadow on the main road never turned into the parking lot. Had he sniffed up some horrific accident further down the road, near the skating rink, or possibly by Old Gunnar's garage? It did not matter, because it meant we got away this time.

Nina handed over the candy bags, "I couldn't get through to you, so you got liquorice tops for the rest of your money." We took the bags, but she held onto them.

"Is it Death you're afraid of?" she asked.

The blonde fringe stood like a tidal wave on her head. Her eyes locked onto me like a rocket launcher in a video game, accentuated by the black makeup beneath them. I jumped when the bubblegum bubble she blew suddenly burst. Hubba Bubba with strawberry flavour.

"He comes to see me sometimes, did you know that?" she whispered, and looked around suspiciously.

We clung to the candy bags.

"It's not easy to hear him under the helmet, so once I asked him to remove it. You know what happens if you meet his gaze, right? If you see what's under the helmet? You've heard about it?"

A drop of sweat slid down my neck, and a mild shiver spread through my body.

"He first opened the visor slightly. 'If you're buying something here, get that thing off your head!' I yelled at him. Ha! Can you believe he took it off?"

Nina leaned out through the hatch. I could have kissed her, if I was quick, but now was definitely not the time.

"His hair. Sweaty, thick and sticky like black spaghetti. My God, his face! I promise you, ticks and leeches crawled under the pale skin. He had something in his crooked mouth. Something with claws and eyes on a stem. *Something. Was. Just. Totally. Wrong*!" The strawberry scent from her breath as she emphasised the last words was nauseating. I considered following the protocol, even if Death no longer posed a threat, when she exclaimed, "BOO!" She let go of the candy bags, and we both fell on our butts. She looked like one of the reptilian-like monsters in the series *V*, which Mom and Dad used to watch on TV.

"Death is coming. One, two, three. Death is coming for you and me! You should hide, you should run! You can't stop him with a gun. Death is coming. One, two, three. Death is coming for you and me!" she sang after us as we ran, terrified, through the woods, past stones, ants, spruces, and crows. We didn't stop until we were back at the house.

Like Tommy and Gina, Mom and Dad didn't have much. When Mom cried in the night, Dad whispered, "It's okay. Baby, it's okay." I guess they held on to what they had. And as long as they had each other, it didn't matter if they made it or not. Perhaps they were living on a prayer... though maybe not necessarily to God, but to someone who could help them put food on the table and get clothes for their kids.

Mom and Dad's red wine was brewed by Dad in the bathtub in the basement, in the stinky room. The fridge in the kitchen always felt too big. We would cut off the mould layer on the jam or brown cheese before eating what was underneath.

On Saturdays, we often took Dad's rusty, reverse-less Ford Escort towards ol' Ringstad's farm as the morning sun rose over the Haugen fields. The EU's vehicle inspection program later sent cars of that caliber into complete extinction. But during those early mornings when we set the course for those 'crazy eggs,' Dad's car was still a gem. And the eggs? They were cheap and therefore popular, even though most of them had cracked shells and some were soft, like little balloons of egg white and yolk.

Such a Saturday morning, the circus checked in at the Haugen fields for the first time. We watched it with wide eyes as we swung towards the house after our egg hunt. Mom stood outside on the porch, seeing the same as us.

"How many trays did you get? I assume you are ready for pancakes?"

"Pancakes and circus." Dad showed her the trays, received a kiss on the mouth and a pat on the butt. He was twice her size.

"Yes, we can eat on the terrace and watch them set up the tent. They're supposedly ready for a show in just a few days."

Mom took the trays with eggs and disappeared into the kitchen. Activity on the field was bustling. The tent practically popped up in the stubble field. People and animals moved together. Everyone knew exactly where they should be and what role they played.

That same weekend, there was a show. Smiling, expectant children pointed to popcorn wagons. Parents paid a fortune for lottery tickets and pony rides. The circus music reminded me of W.A.S.P.'s "The Big Welcome", and lay like an insulating layer under the sounds of laughter, cheerful voices, and the humming of the wheel of fortune. Judging by the queues at the ticket booths, I was alone in being a bit skeptical about the whole concept. Those clowns, what were they hiding behind that makeup?

Late at night and into the early morning, after the village had gone to sleep, the circus glowed out there over the trampled straw. I heard wild animals, loud acrobats, shouts, and yells in foreign languages. Drunk clowns. It smelled of hay, animal feed, and smoke all the way to my bed. The window was open. I didn't dare to get out of bed to close it.

2

Robert

Fredrik and I stood in the hallway while Mom was putting on her shoes, and then she opened the front door.

"Can we have a glass of Tropicana?" I asked, even though I already knew the answer.

"No, you can drink milk, but if it runs out, I guess you can have a glass of juice. And, remember to lock the door if you go out!"

As soon as Mom closed the door behind her, Fredrik and I rushed to the fridge.

"Five litres! There's five litres of milk in the fridge!" My brother shook his head.

"We can drink that, right? I can have three litres," I said.

"It's worth a try." Fredrik seemed optimistic.

"Yes, indeed." I opened the first litre and drank straight from the carton.

"That's a lot of milk," Fredrik said after a short while, with a milk moustache newly formed. "I haven't even had half a litre."

"Should we pour the rest out?"

"I was thinking the same thing," Fredrik said.

I poured my glass of milk into the sink, and Fredrik did the same. Soon after, two new unopened cartons sat on the kitchen counter. Fredrik hung his head and muttered, "Don't you think Mom will get mad if we put them all out? Shouldn't we just hide the rest instead?"

"Yes, that's a better idea," I replied quickly.

"Outside, under the stairs?"

"No, I know a better place," I said, lighting up. "We'll put the cartons under the winter clothes, at the bottom of our wardrobe. No one will look there until it snows."

"Clever," Fredrik said, and we executed our plan.

After burying the milk cartons under a pile of puffer jackets and hats, we were back in the kitchen, each holding a glass of Tropicana.

"Cheers," I said, taking a sip.

Fredrik also toasted, took two sips, then put his glass on the counter. "I'm not thirsty anymore. Want to play football?"

"For sure." I placed my glass next to Fredrik's, and we dashed out of the house, neither closing nor locking the door behind us.

A month or two later, the cartons in the locker could no longer contain their secret and exploded inside the wardrobe. Judging by the smell, old milk, given the right temperature and time, could evolve into something akin to the substances produced in the chain reactors of the aforementioned Chernobyl. Mom was livid.

"You do know what I have to do when you don't behave?" she exclaimed.

Sometimes, she threatened to take us to the Witch of Mørkved and Death if we didn't listen, got notices from school, or behaved in a generally mischievous manner. She had never followed through before, though. So, we were quite shocked when she sternly said, "Get in the car. Believe me, you'll stay in that damned house for the weekend, or until Dad comes home. I won't pick you up, that's for certain!"

Shortly after, we sat cramped in Mom's Volkswagen. The car sputtered and jolted but at least the reverse was functioning. We prayed it would break down before reaching the Witch's house. As the sun sculpted ominous shadows in the car, Fredrik's scar, which stretched from his right eye to his mouth, slowly shifted with the changing light. Kjell's dad, who owned the Fina station, waved at us from the pumps. We didn't wave back.

Soon, we took a hard left, following the signs to Mørkved Hills. Oscar from the sawmill was carrying a plank over his shoulder and nodded at us as we passed. His cigarette dangled lifelessly from his lip. He probably thought we were heading to the lake for an afternoon swim when we turned left again. As we drove past the bible house, where its owners had inscribed hymns in the concrete on the walls, we prayed for mercy.

Eventually, we entered the forest that bordered much of the village. Later, wide open fields came into view as we approached the crossroad. If Mom turned left, we'd continue on the same way, coming out on the other side of the village near the old store and skating rink. If she turned right, however, we were doomed. That road led to... The crossroad was crucial. Mom signaled right, towards the Witch's house. Could a mother really do this? Surrender us to a witch over some mischief? I don't think either of us took a single breath in the moments before she defied the turn signal, veered left, and continued towards safety.

Mom must have felt guilty upon seeing the look on our faces because, on the way home, we stopped for Hawaii burgers with fries and melted cheese at the kiosk—a treat usually reserved for when Dad got paid. We promised to behave, a promise we had made many times before.

Even though we feared the day when Mom would actually take us up to the house, we often ventured in that very same direction on our bicycles anyway. We turned right at the crossroad, then left past Svein-Kåre's turkey farm, continuing for a few kilometres on the gravel road towards Johnny

Mørkved's massive farm and gravel pit. Next, we would roll along the narrow forest road, nearing the Witch of Mørkved's house. Half a kilometre past her house lay the lake where we swam almost daily during the summer.

After the gravel pit, entering the forest felt akin to stepping into a cave. The spruce trees grew so densely they formed solid walls on either side of us. Above, branches intertwined like skeletal hands, creating a canopy that shielded us from the sun. We were zigzagging on our bikes, chased by mosquitoes and flies, while branches from mournful trees reached out for us like spiky nails. The air was probably filled with poisonous spores that would kill us if we lingered in this moist tunnel for too long. Despite all the dangers, we usually made it through the cave unscathed. On the other side, a reward awaited the brave who dared to traverse this port of doom: Lake Mørkved. The warmest water in the area, a raft, a diving board, and sun-tanned girls.

Just before the incline, where the forest thinned out to reveal the sky, a small passage opened to the right, leading to their house. For some reason, it reminded me of an old, dried-up apple. The roof, possibly with more holes than tiles, weighed heavily over the cracked walls that bowed inward, threatening to collapse at any moment. Loose paint flaked off the walls.

Sometimes, when our whole gang was together, we stopped at this turn, shouting and jeering from a safe distance. We teased the Witch for never coming out, and wondered if Death wore his helmet indoors as well, just because he was so ugly. Sometimes we flung more than words towards the house, throwing sticks, pinecones, and even a stone or two.

One of those summer days, sometime in the mid-eighties, Tony, one of the guys in our gang, managed a direct hit. The stone soared through the air before striking the kitchen window. The tinkle of broken glass pierced the air, and I froze mid-throw. My stone that was meant to follow Tony's softly hit the ground, and we all stood motionless. I could've sworn I heard the ants crawling around our shoes.

A dark shadow appeared in the kitchen, and soon the front door creaked open slowly. The moaning of the door hinges grew louder, and the Witch of Mørkved's gnarly fingers came into view on the doorframe. They moved up and down as if she was searching for a light switch outside the house. I briefly imagined she'd turn off the day and then swoop down on us when Fredrik shattered the spellbinding moment.

"You guys hear that?" He pointed towards the gravel pit, and we all realised at once that it wasn't the door making the sound we heard.

"Death is coming!"

Fredrik

My thighs burned as I pedalled up the hill. Even with Øyerstad's fastest BMX bike, I was way behind the others. My older brother, Robert, being a year and a half older than me, had more gears on his bike than the years I had lived. I was nine. I watched Robert reach the top of the hill, bathed in sunlight. As he looked back, his gaze shifted from me to something further back, his grin transforming into a gaping hole of shock. The monster was catching up to me, and my big brother showed no signs of slowing down or turning to help.

"Don't leave me! I don't want to die!" I screamed inside myself as my brain directed all the oxygen in my blood to my thighs. *Must go faster!*

Robert seemed to shout something, but all I heard was my blood pounding in my ears. At any moment, the creature's fingers would pierce through my t-shirt and tear out my spine. I'd seen such things in movies. Then I'd be dragged down to the Witch by my neck, leaving a thick trail of blood along the road and into the house of horror. In the kitchen, they would dissect me, boiling soup from the parts not barbecued. They wouldn't stop eating until the last of my bone marrow was sucked up. They probably loved bone marrow. The worst part was, somehow, I'd remain conscious. Feeling every bit of pain and smelling my own flesh cook until the very end.

When I was so tired that I couldn't pedal any longer, I surrendered to fate. I expected eternal darkness, but suddenly, daylight broke. I rolled into the sunlight on the parking lot, unharmed by radioactive vampire claws.

"Holy hell, did you see the witch in the doorway?" Kjell jumped on the spot. "She'd have killed us if she'd caught us."

"And what about Death?" Robert buzzed. "He came right after us. Had we not reached the parking lot, we'd have been done for."

Robert's smirk, as he shifted his gaze from Kjell to me, annoyed me. Why did we even stop by that house? We had no business there.

Robert quipped, "Looking a bit pale, are we?"

The others laughed, except for Rune, he seemed uneasy, like me. But soon, he too laughed at Robert's comment.

"You should've seen your face, little bro," Robert said, pausing for a moment. "Relax, Fredrik. Nobody followed us. I was just teasing. Death turned down by the house."

"I knew that," I lied, as the other boys giggled and danced around the parking lot. Soon, we discarded our bikes. Screaming with mock horror and delight, we darted between the pine trees, making our way to the beach.

"Last one to the raft is a three-legged pig!" I shouted, running right behind the others.

Robert

Not long after the bike race up the hill, we were chilling on the raft and showing off for the girls in our class.

"This is freakin' awesome, man. Damn, this is how we should spend the entire summer. Just chillin', ya know?" I remarked with as much swagger as I could muster, squeezing my bicep against my chest to make it appear larger.

Rumour had it that the lake was close to forty metres deep, and the big guys with chest hair often talked about it when we hung out there. It annoyed me. Why didn't they just try to dive down? Or measure with a rope and a stone? Again, I sat listening to their nonsense about how no one could reach the bottom of the lake.

That day, I did an extra run-up from the diving board and jumped higher than anyone had ever done from the raft (which is, strictly speaking, uncertain and hard to prove or disprove). As I was in the air, I straightened my body with my arms first, and pierced the water's surface like a straw through the top of a glass of Tropicana. The water barely reacted and soon air bubbles left my shorts and crawled up my legs. Below the surface, I shifted my body towards the underside of the raft. There, I grabbed the chain that held it in place—a metal guide to the bottom. Into the darkness.

It was just a week ago when I outdid the sixth grader, Asgeir, on a school trip to the swimming pool in Skjønnsund. He was the king of underwater swimming, achieving three lengths without taking a breath. They called him "The Shark".

Asgeir's reign came to an end when I swam four lengths and probably could've managed a few metres more.

A Maxim magazine at my dad's job contained an article about freediving. It detailed the physical and mental training needed to perform such an extreme sport. A Frenchman had reportedly held his breath for nearly twenty minutes, which I found hard to believe. After taking an extra look at the centrefold—Lisa twenty-four, from Oslo—I decided I was going to be the best in class at holding my breath. After diligent training in the bathtub at home, I managed three minutes and twenty-nine seconds. First, I held my breath for thirty seconds, then a minute. One minute and thirty seconds. It continued up to three minutes and twenty-nine seconds, a time I was very pleased with. I had to get into a meditative state and gain full control of my body. Even when my body began to twitch after a few minutes, I could still hold my breath for quite a while longer. Fredrik kept watch during my record attempts, after I once fainted in the bathtub. Fortunately, with that attempt, Fredrik came in and found it strange that I was sleeping in the tub with my head underwater.

Under the raft, conditions were different from those in the bathtub back home. The water felt heavy, pressing against my tightened skin, and the absence of light created an eerie feeling that someone might be watching me from within the darkness. However, the biggest threat was probably nothing more than a few medium-sized perch and the millions of tiny fish we used to catch with plastic bottle traps and bread when we were kids." But what if there were something more? What if something else lurked at the bottom? A pale creature watching me curiously, ready to take a bite of my foot at any moment. Then it would disappear. But not for long. No, it continued to follow me in the murky water. Waiting for the right moment to drag me further down into the darkness.

Damn you, Steven Spielberg. This is all your fault.

Nobody up there knew what I was trying to do. Thus, they'd never know if I succeeded or not. I could give up and swim back up.

Pull yourself together! Imagine emerging with a handful of mud from the bottom. Talk about being the king of the raft. Then you'd get the attention you want, from the ones you want it from. You'd never be forgotten, Robert. You can do this.

After equalising pressure several times and internally debating surrender, I thrust my hand into a soft mass, like cold porridge with lumps. The lake was deep, but not forty metres. Another troubling thought hit me: what if I kept pulling myself down along the chain? Through the layer of mud and clay, would a new world open up underneath? A dark and dystopic place, where everything that had fallen from our world came alive. Old slippers and forgotten towels resembling slimy snails crawling around endlessly while searching for a way back. Herds of animal carcasses. Some standing, others half-standing, and others crawling along the slippery ground as their rotting flesh came off their bones. The oldest ones were hardly skeletal, more like gelatinous figures on an eternal quest for something they once had. Layers upon layers of wails and screams creating a subterranean symphony of endless sorrow and despair. However, certain sounds stood out, like some kind of language, an attempt at communication. Something more than animalistic shrieks. Something human.

Reflexively, my body expelled the water from my lungs, and panic brought me back to consciousness when, without thinking, I had taken a breath. *Stay calm, Robert. Think of the bathtub. You can't panic now. You have to get up. A kick, one stroke at a time. The water is on your side.*

I fought my way up, and the water soon became warmer.

Black turned to a murky yellow.

As I neared the surface, it hit me that my neck would break if I crashed into the underside of the raft at that speed. Like a less graceful seal, I adjusted my course a few notches to the side, and soon I shot out of the water inches from the edge of the raft.

I trembled as I climbed up the ladder on the raft. *Is this how Dad feels crawling home after their drunken binges up on Kirkeåsen? Powerless, nauseous, and dizzy.* My throat hurt as I swallowed.

"Damn Robert, were you at the bottom?" Kjell looked at my hand, at the clay I had brought up.

"What do you think? The clay's real," I replied.

"Cool!" Kjell rubbed a bit of the clay between his thumb and forefinger.

"Was it deep?" Fredrik was also impressed.

"No, it wasn't as deep as I thought," I replied.

The chest-haired guys looked the other way. They said nothing.

For the rest of that day, and for a long time afterwards, people jumped more from the diving board than usual. They stayed underwater longer than they used to, but none of them ever came up with clay in their hands. They probably turned back when the light no longer followed them. Maybe I should've done the same, for my blood felt frozen for a long time after that dive. I swore I'd never do it again, but I had to break that promise several years later, in a far less innocent Øyerstad.

The Circus

Once, in another time, or perhaps in another dimension, eager children and adults would have frolicked among the many stalls outside the circus. Dart throws at balloons, air rifle shooting at plastic elks on a wire, a wheel of fortune, and many other oddities. But there were no ordinary people here. Not anymore. Only the phantoms remained.

One by one, they emerged outside the circus, standing and swaying, much like me. Milky white eyes. Limp, expressionless faces above gaping mouths. They never said anything and really didn't do anything wrong. Still, they scared the hell out of me.

The Witch of Mørkved and Death were phantoms too. They faced me from one of the stalls. Behind them, a wheel of fortune spun. It couldn't possibly bring anyone any luck. Death wore a large cauldron on his head, which in reality would be impossible to balance on his skinny body.

Next to him, the Witch of Mørkved's face pulsated in rhythm with the torches' wavering flames. Neither the counter in front of them nor the sporadically flashing wheel behind protected them from the pinecones, and occasional stones flying from outside the light's range. I could hear giggles and laughter somewhere out there in the dark. Even when pebbles hit the cauldron on Death's head with a clunk, they didn't react. They swayed, like seaweed on the ocean's floor. The Witch observed me, and I was certain that beneath the cauldron, Death was doing the same.

Then there was the one lurking in the shadows. His growl, a constant backdrop for the slow organ notes. I once named him Bingo-Bob to make him less intimidating. It didn't work.

Compared to a small or medium-sized dog, Bingo-Bob would seem quite large. More like a St. Bernard—think Cujo.

Bingo-Bob was black, making him hard to see as he prowled the outskirts.

Sometimes, a piece of darkness would detach, animate, and move into the brighter parts of the area, seemingly floating across the ground. As it came closer, I saw Bingo-Bob for what he was: fur, wet and tousled, stretched tightly over his skeleton body. Viscous goo dangled in strands from his mouth. His eyes were filled with a milky substance, within which his blue-grey pupils floated like drops of fluid. Slowly, he came closer.

"Uhm... hello? Does anyone own this dog?"

No response. A rumble from deep within the monster's belly echoed past his jagged teeth.

"Hello? Anyone? Could you come get your damn dog?"

"Listen, I haven't done anything to you, buddy," I said towards the monster.

His glowing gums were illuminated by the torches.

"Please, could you come get him now?"

If I stand still, maybe he won't attack? Isn't that what Grandma said to do if you encounter a bear in the woods? Stand absolutely still.

When he opened his jaws and lunged at me, I raised my arms to shield my face.

3

Robert

Hedgehog mushrooms and chanterelles hid beneath the first fallen leaves, while the activity at the anthill, a bit further from our treehouse, had waned. In the brook, water trickled slowly between the rocks and tree stumps, but that was soon to change. You could feel it in the air. The clouds were fat and seemed sad. Only many years later was I told that this was the day it happened. The incident that would slowly, but surely, affect so many of us in the years to come. Autumn of 1989. I was eleven.

Dag and Anitas' father liked to drink beer up by our treehouse after work. He probably wasn't allowed to drink very much at home, so he simply hid up there instead. The bottles he left behind were a fine extra income, in addition to our weekly allowance.

We were in the middle of a pinecone fight up by the tree house when Fredrik abruptly shouted, "Time out!" He pointed towards the other side of the stream. "What's that?"

"Rubbish!" I yelled, launching a pinecone that scraped his cheek.

"Time out, I said! That's not rubbish."

"Alright. Truce!" I emptied my pockets of pinecones and jumped down from the treehouse. Fredrik, Kjell, and Tony followed.

"Guys! It's a crate full of beer bottles," Fredrik said.

"All unopened," I added.

"Twenty-four bottles," Kjell said, giving me a look.

"They probably belong to someone. Perhaps we should

leave them?" Fredrik likely hoped I'd agree.

"What? Are you serious? Someone left them here and then forgot all about them. Let's cash them in. We could buy a lot of sweets."

I paused, seeing Fredrik waver, before he said, "Maybe we can open them with a stone or something?"

Fredrik tried prising a cap off with a stone shard. He jumped back when he broke the top off the bottle, getting beer splashed all over him.

"It's not funny." He wiped away the stains with birch leaves he moistened in the stream.

"We need a bottle opener! Hang on, I'll be back in a jiffy," I announced and darted towards the house. Dad was at work, and from the sounds of it, Mom and a friend were engrossed in *Jaws* again. Good, because then she wouldn't be concerned about what I was doing in the kitchen.

Back with the guys by the cabin, we popped open the bottles and then emptied the beer into the brook, causing it to foam and bubble. At what likely reeked like a local brewery for those familiar with beer, we left behind one shattered bottle and twenty-four caps. A bottle was worth one krone, so twenty-three bottles meant two hundred and thirty gummy bears! We relished the thought as we lugged the bottles to the shop.

Much of what they referred to as the past in the bigger cities was yet to come in Øyerstad. Deposit machines, for instance, were still a thing of the future. So, we accompanied Marit to the back of the shop where we set each bottle into a soda crate, counting out loud. We then got a handwritten slip that said, "Deposit: 23 kroner, approved by Marit Ness, 26. August 1989". With the note in hand, we sprinted out of the shop and to the kiosk.

Behind the counter, Nina probably enjoyed free gum,

given her employment. She blew bubbles as we clambered onto the wooden pallets, peering in through the window.

"A bag of mixed for twenty-three. Here, take the slip!" I said, tossing it at her.

"A bag of mixed?" Fredrik questioned as though I'd lost my mind.

"I reckon it's, um... faster, or... better. You get me?" I nervously glanced towards the woods.

Nina's chin dipped, her brows shot up, and she locked eyes with me. For the first time, my gaze trailed from her chin and down to her breasts. It was... something.

"A bag of mixed for twenty-three, then," she said, expressionless, and retreated into the kiosk.

Come on, hurry, I thought as a pang of dread swept over me. Death emerged from the woods, a broken beer bottle in hand. How did we not hear him approach? Where was his darn moped?

Behind me, Tony and Fredrik leaned over the counter, making sure they weren't cheated out of a single treat.

Death's hair jutted out like bat wings from under his helmet. His ghostly pale hands hung loosely as he nearly seemed to glide our way.

"Death is coming!" I finally choked out after several failed attempts.

"Quit kidding." Tony had noticed Nina's figure too.

"I'm not! He's headed this way."

"Robert, we're counting..."

Death came closer and lifted a hand to his visor. I can't recall who initiated the sprint, but before he could open it, we were already dashing around the kiosk, up the stairs, and back into the store. Going home was not an option since we'd have to pass him, and that was a risk we wouldn't take. We felt somewhat safer in the store, surrounded by others.

He wouldn't dare nab us with so many witnesses, right?

We huddled by the magazine rack, where vital decisions had been made for many years. Horror comics, *Conan*, or *Spiderman*? *Donald Duck* or *Top of the Pops*? Or perhaps the Nintendo magazine? Now, though, our eyes were glued to the entrance, not pondering what reading material to buy or nick.

To our surprise and relief, it was Nina who first emerged. She approached, and we hastily claimed—with decent credibility—that the bottles were from our basement. Dad had thrown a party over the weekend. Nina's eyes studied us intently, then trailed outside to the devil beneath the stairs. Was he pulling her strings? Were Nina and Death in cahoots?

"Stay put," Nina instructed, before vanishing into the shop. Soon after, she returned with a crate of beer which she bravely handed over to Death. He accepted without a fuss. They seemed to exchange a few words, and she rejoined us.

"If you find something that's not yours, leave it," she advised upon her return. She didn't seem mad. She seemed… Did she flirt with me? It wasn't completely far-fetched, as I saw it.

"He had to pay for his beer twice," she said.

I observed Death as he strapped the crate to his moped. For a fleeting moment, he didn't seem all that menacing. He never raised his head, hunched under the weight of his helmet.

As he roared onto the main road, we scrambled for the door.

"Hold on!" Nina yelled, and we halted mid-exit. She presented us with a bag of sweets. "He wanted you to have this."

No one said anything as we walked home with the biggest bag of sweets we had had in a long time. Perhaps ever. But we didn't open it. To think that we stole beer bottles from the village's (probably) only vampire, and then he gave us a bag of candy as a reward for it? Nina had both spoken to, and smiled at us. That day was special for us, and also for Dad, who was going hunting for the first time.

Dad

The staircase leading down to the basement was steep even when sober. It was there I crafted my moonshine. I made some good stuff in what the kids called the "stinky room". My fiery drops were always the best-tasting, strongest and most effective. Not too pure, and not too poisonous. Balance is an art.

Sometimes, I entertained the idea of venturing bigger into the distillery business. The stinky room was filled with enough alcohol to run a moderately successful enterprise in the heart of Øyerstad. If the moonshine baron over in Skjønnsund could make a living out of it, so could I. My spirits tasted better, and not just in my opinion.

A plastic container fell heavily towards me from the shelf, but I had it under control. A five-litre jug should be enough for the guys over the weekend.

The staircase was still steep on my way back up, and Marianne, of course, couldn't help but make a comment.

"Looks like the weekend's supply is sorted. Remember what happened last time?"

"Of course, I remember. Well, maybe not all of it. I'll take your word for it. If it's true, maybe it's better I don't recall. You look lovely today, by the way."

"Thanks, and nice subject change. Sure about taking a whole jug to the cabin? With those guys?"

"First of all, changing topics is my specialty, and I plan to skip the last five drinks tonight."

"Well, I've heard that one before. But that's not all I'm worried about."

"Kai?"

"Yeah. 'Half fox and half bat'. Is that how you described him?"

"Sounds about right."

"Do you think he dyes his hair?" Marianne teased with a playful grin.

"He doesn't strike me as the type to dye his hair," I replied.

"Who knows what he does in the bathroom when Helene's asleep."

"Come on!" I pulled her close, feeling the warmth of her belly through her cropped blouse. Her blonde curls smelled of shampoo. "Relax, darling. I'll handle Kai."

"A drunk Kai with a gun. Isn't that *why* you've been avoiding his hunting trips?"

"Well, maybe. But Kai isn't the reason I haven't hunted before. I'd rather not shoot at all. Neither animals nor a random berry picker."

I released her, striking a pose, mimicking Rambo from First Blood II. Only missing a bazooka. "Ever tell you about the time..."

"When you and Kai 'hunted' women on Hitra? Yes."

"It was *fishing* on Hitra. Someday, darling, we'll go there, all of us. You, me, and the boys."

"You fish but don't hunt?" Marianne asked.

"Exactly. Fish don't have feelings. Ever seen a cod cry?" I answered her question with a question.

"I haven't, but maybe that's because they're already wet when pulled up?"

"Well, it could be, but..."

"But what if you end up shooting something? An elk?"

"To be honest, I hope the rain comes sooner. Hopefully,

there won't be any hunting, at least not tonight. If there is, I'll make enough noise to keep wildlife at bay."

"Sounds smart. And another thing."

"Yes?"

"You stay away from Rakel, alright?" she said, with a mock-serious smile.

I found it baffling that Kai named his rifle "Rakel". It didn't give off good vibes. Playing along, since Marianne didn't know the details, I teased, "Rakel, huh? Picture her oiled up, and imagine me caressing her. Slowly and delic—"

"Stay away from Rakel!" Marianne said, feigning seriousness for a moment before breaking into her warm smile, the tip of her tongue briefly touching her upper lip.

"You don't need to worry about Kai, me, or Rakel. We're adults. Besides, Rakel is just a rifle."

I waved to Robert, Fredrik, and the other boys as they admired the pickup trucks with sweets in their hands. The first raindrop hit the cracked windshield of Kai's car.

As we turned onto the main road, dark clouds danced a slow waltz in the sky. Fredrik, Robert, and Marianne stood on the porch, waving us off. What was I thinking? I didn't even want to join the hunt. *Come on,* I thought. *Let the rain come.*

Robert

Indiana Jones had barely cracked his whip once when Mom refilled the popcorn bowl for the second time. The moviebox we rented suddenly stopped whirring when the house, and all of Øyerstad, plunged into darkness. Mom was quickly by the fuse box, but no matter how much she fiddled and banged, the power didn't return. The problem wasn't with us. Outside, the Fina sign was dark, like a cross above the soulless windows of the station building. Rain hammered down, and I hoped that Karianne, Petter's wife from the house across the street, had as many candles as we did. We didn't have much, but candles for power outages, those we had in abundance.

We played a couple of rounds of Yatzy in the candlelight, waiting for the movie box to whir back to life. *Indiana Jones and the Temple of Doom*. Surely, the electricity company would have a solution soon?

"They'll understand we couldn't finish the movie because of the blackout. We can probably return it later tomorrow," Mom comforted.

"But we were planning to watch it several times," I replied.

"At least three," Fredrik said.

"You can watch it several times tomorrow," Mom reassured us, the flickering candlelight reflecting in her eyes. She looked up towards the hills where Dad and his buddies were hunting. After three rounds of dice, we went to bed. Indiana Jones wildly cracked his whip over and over in my mind until sleep finally claimed me.

I jolted awake, either from the thunder or the bedroom light turning on as power returned. The alarm clock blinked 00:00, but it must've been later. My younger brother mumbled incoherently in the bed below. The streetlight near the trash cans, rejuvenated by the returning power, valiantly fought off the alliance of pouring rain and the night's colourless hues. Kai's pickup, the one Dad earlier filled with liquor, stopped abruptly under its glow. I recognised Dad's silhouette as he stepped out. The rain fell sideways.

He opened the gate leading to the house, then shouted

something to the driver. Unexpectedly, he took several swift steps back to the vehicle. The passenger door opened and Kai jumped out. The sky exploded. They were in the spotlight. They lunged at each other. It reminded me of a well-choreographed action movie fight, like those with Bud Spencer. I was unable to breathe.

Soon, one landed a heavy blow, leaving the other on the ground. Kai was the one standing. Whatever he yelled, his voice was drowned by the thunder as he gestured dramatically. After a while, he jumped back into the vehicle and sped off. My bedroom light flickered a few times before darkness returned. I felt sorry for the poor soul on duty at the electric company that night.

Shortly after, I heard Dad fumbling with the front door lock. He couldn't open it. When he started pounding, Mom's voice echoed from the hallway.

I don't know if Dad pushed her, but I heard Mom groan, followed by a thud. I'd seen Dad drunk before, but not like this. He was always merry, overly affectionate, and often sentimental. Never aggressive, especially not towards Mom.

Instead of heading to the bathroom or bedroom as he usually would, Dad opened the door to the basement—the stinky room.

"Leave me alone. Do you hear? Stay away!"

He then slammed the door and descended. When Mom opened my bedroom door, I pretended to be asleep.

"Robert? Are you sleeping? Fredrik?"

She let me feign sleep and gently closed the door.

Before I fell asleep, I faintly smelled hay, even though it wasn't the season for it.

The Circus

Kai sat in a chair behind a wooden plate carved into the shape of a car, pretending to drive a red pickup. Like in old American movies, Kai didn't need to focus on the road. In the back seat, gun barrels jutted out, and I assumed he was off to hunt by the lake. The streetlight above him looked exactly like the one outside my bedroom window. The difference here was that rain poured down on him from the light like a shower.

A few metres to the left of Kai, the Witch of Mørkved and Death still stood before the wheel of fortune, with its red and black squares and numbers. Tattered teddy bears and enormous Toblerone boxes hung around the wheel. A handwritten sign behind them declared, "Everyone's a winner!"

Either Death had shrunk, or the cauldron on his head had grown. Balancing precariously on his thin shoulders, I doubted his neck could bear its weight for long.

"Death, Death, sat on a wall, Death, Death had a great fall; All the Witch's corpses and all the Witch's men couldn't put Death back together again," we sang in childish voices, out in the dark, still pelting them with stones and pinecones.

In my peripheral vision, I could see a man in black and white striped clothing standing still—a mime. I'd seen him in a film when I was younger. His face was frozen in shock, fingers pointing at something in front of me. Looking down, I was horrified to see Bingo-Bob, the hound, clamped onto my forearm, his teeth sinking deep into my flesh. I felt more shock than pain. Soon warmth spread between my legs, and my throat tightened as I tried to breathe. I could not move.

Only when Bingo-Bob jerked violently did the pain set in—teeth scraping against bone in a Morse code of agony. Trying to pry his jaws open only made him bite down harder. The thought of diseases and filth entering my body through the gaping holes in my arm nauseated me.

"Please let go!"

He didn't.

"Is there anyone here who can help? Why doesn't anyone care?"

The cauldron on Death's head wobbled. As Bingo-Bob bit down harder, I wondered if the hound would ever release his grip.

4

Robert

The bedding had fallen to the floor, and the sheet was bunched up into a ball by the foot of my bed. I lay with my arms crossed over my chest—a feeble defence against forces that could tear me apart at any moment. My body tingled, and I felt nauseated recalling Dad, Kai, and that damned dog, Bingo-Bob. Thankfully, the skin on my arm showed no signs of damage, even though the infected teeth should have torn it apart. On the outside, I appeared intact, but inside, I felt as if something had broken.

Fredrik was reading a Tottenham fan magazine in bed, unaware of the nightmare I just came out of. I dreamed of a hound of hell. He was dreaming of a career at White Hart Lane. I have no idea where he got that from. The Red Devils from Manchester were my favorites; I got that from Dad. Our room's walls were adorned with the respective teams' colours. The posters of Blackie Lawless, Iron Maiden, and Kiss, which we squeezed in between the football players, were neutral territory. On my brother's side, there were posters of Arnold Schwarzenegger, while I preferred Mel Gibson: *The Terminator* vs. *Mad Max*.

The house lay silent, but a vague smell of coffee told me Mom and Dad were home—and awake.

"Should we call Kjell and Tony and ask if they want to play football?" Fredrik suggested, inspired by his white-clad heroes.

I jumped off the bed and posed next to a life-size figure of Mark Hughes, trying to shake off the last remnants of my dream.

"Let's roll," I said, mimicking the United legend.

As I opened the bedroom door, I sensed the aroma of fried fish pudding, rolls, and bacon—just like usual on such days. Mom and Dad often compensated for a lively night with a hearty breakfast. Good food can make one forget many things, but on that day, I wasn't particularly hungry.

Dad

Even my largest sunglasses couldn't cover my bruises. I was swollen, especially on the right side of my face. The cut on my lip probably should have been stitched, but I didn't care. That bastard landed a good hit, so it's no wonder Fredrik and Robert looked at me with wide eyes. Marianne too, for that matter.

I hardly remember how I made it to the kitchen that morning, and even less how I got into the house and down the stairs the night before. I slept in the stinky room, on the floor. I believe I deserved that. And the empty bottles next to me? That was enough liquor to drown myself in it. Still, I hadn't forgotten everything I tried to forget. Everything that happened before Kai knocked me down by the road in the rain was hazy, but not gone.

Fredrik might have bought my explanation, but Robert looked sceptical when Mom claimed that the hunt was called off because of the rain. She went on to say that I fell down the stairs because I couldn't see anything. It was all the power outage's fault. When I tried to back up her story, I quickly received a "shut up" glance. There was no sign of forgiveness in the way she looked at me. Her eyes looked cold.

The storm from the previous day still raged inside of me,

and I felt cold to the bone. No matter how much I told myself things would be okay, I knew it was a lie. We had done a lot of mischief over the years, but what we had done now could never be fixed. Not in a thousand years. We were all damned.

The fish pudding and bacon sizzled and bubbled in the frying pan. Neither Marianne nor I turned down the heat. I needed another drink.

Robert

Later that week, the people of Øyerstad began to ask themselves two questions. The first was quite common to ask at that time of year: "Where had the summer gone?"

The second question, however, no one in Øyerstad had asked before.

"It's been quiet this week," Hanne said at the store checkout to Karianne, who was paying for some tomatoes she had forgotten for her bean stew.

Karianne first looked at Hanne and then out towards the road. "You're right. The pressure after the rain hasn't really lifted."

"True. I keep feeling like something's missing," Hanne continued before asking that very special question: "Have you seen Death lately?"

Karianne and Hanne concluded that Death was probably lying in a ditch somewhere, decaying, like the roadkill he used to collect.

From the prayer house, tender whispers of Satan himself coming to the village to dispatch his rider spread like mould across the street, reaching towards the nearby houses and the grocery store. Some of the villagers over at the gas station claimed to have seen Death limping around in the forest.

Us kids, after all, had a strained relationship with the black rider, so we weren't particularly upset that he was gone. The rumours didn't say much about the Witch of Mørkved, but we wondered if she was gone too.

About a week after Death disappeared from Øyerstad, we passed Mørkved farm on our bikes. The playing cards in our bike rims, which made them sound like motorcycles, had been removed for the sake of our secret mission. We rolled our bikes into the forest tunnel. Then, on the other side of the road from the witch's house, we hid them under twigs and wormwood. They were invisible to passersby, yet close enough for us to make a quick getaway if we had to abort the mission.

All week, we'd been puffing ourselves up. Thinking about everything we'd find up there and what we'd do with it. We probably had to go to the sheriff and tell him everything afterwards. He would most likely be upset because we had put ourselves in danger by entering the house. But, when we showed him our findings, we would receive the police's bravery medal instead. The local paper would call us the Hardy Boys of Øyerstad. Everyone would admire us. Oh, what a commotion it would be.

At school that Friday, Guro couldn't keep quiet any longer.

"You've been babbling on about that house for a week now, but are you ever actually going to go up there?"

The question caught us off guard, or, at least me. If she hadn't said anything, we probably never would have acted on it, but now I sensed an opportunity to show bravery in Guro's eyes. To show her that I wasn't as lame as she might have thought. I made a plan with the guys to carry out the mission that weekend.

Come Saturday, we hid our bikes on the other side of the road. We didn't take the track down to the house this time, but snuck through the forest instead. Even though we (Fredrik, Tony, Kjell, and I) were no more than a hundred meters from the house, it was hard to see anything. Branches tore at our clothes as we trudged through the moss.

Fredrik broke the silence first. "Do you think they're home? Maybe we should head up to the lake instead? Check if there's ice?"

"Ice? At the lake now? There isn't even frost in the ground yet," Tony answered.

Kjell took two, three quick steps forward and soon he was backed up against one of the house's pale walls.

"Come on, the coast is clear," he whispered, using a kind of arm gesture like Arnold and the soldiers in *Predator*. We moved forward like highly trained killing machines on a monster hunt: quietly and elegantly.

We saw no one through the window and headed for the entrance door.

"Robert! Can you open the door a little more? I'll throw a pinecone to see if anyone reacts."

The door creaked softly, and images of the Witch's spider-like fingers in the door frame crept into my mind. Kjell sneaked up to the door and threw in the pinecone. He then pressed himself against the wall to avoid splinters as if he had thrown a hand grenade. After waiting a few seconds, with nothing but silence from inside, another arm gesture indicated the coast was clear. We snuck in.

"Damn, it smells worse than my grandparents' potato cellar in here," Kjell said, wrinkling his nose as we entered.

"Yeah, they could have aired it out a bit. Especially since they're having guests," I whispered.

We peered into the house through the hallway. "The bookshelf over there, see it?"

"Almost," I replied, following Kjell. The floor gave way

slightly but didn't creak like the door did.

"Where's Fredrik and Tony?" Kjell whispered as we sat with our backs against the bookshelf in what appeared to be a reading nook in the living room.

"Hey! Are you coming?" I shouted towards the entrance.

"Keep it down! Be quiet. What if they're home?" Kjell snapped.

"They haven't been home for weeks."

"We don't know that!"

"We thought we saw someone by the road," Fredrik whispered, as he and Tony entered.

"Is anyone here?" Tony whispered.

"I don't think so. But be careful. Don't touch anything. We don't want to leave traces."

"So, where do you think they hide the bodies? The ones Death picks up?"

"I haven't seen anything," Kjell said, letting his flashlight roam the room.

"I hope Death was allowed to take off his helmet inside at least. It's terribly dark in here," Fredrik continued, shining his light towards the windows in the living room. They were boarded up from the inside with planks and nails. All the windows in the house, except for the kitchen window facing the road. Maybe because they wanted to watch the bullies passing by up there.

"What about the jars over there? That's where they keep the body parts?" I pointed the flashlight at a row of glass containers in the kitchen. They reminded me of the displays at school where jars filled with pickled vipers, rats, and other creatures stood in a row.

There were no body parts, neither animal nor human, in the kitchen jars. None of the jars in the refrigerator containing pickled vegetables and jam were labelled with human names.

We didn't find cages with black ravens or stuffed cats either. The kitchen wasn't as scary as expected; I felt kinda disappointed.

"Think it's always been this cold here?" I asked.

"No idea. I'll let you know if I find the heater," Kjell chuckled.

"Yeah, or the fireplace because I don't think there's electricity in the house anymore," I said.

"If there ever was," Kjell replied.

When we finally dared to believe the house was indeed abandoned, we decided to expand our search area. I went alone. My first stop was the bathroom.

Yellowed newspaper and tape covered the mirror above the cracked sink. On the floor mat stood a wooden frame with its back turned to the room. I assumed it was also a mirror. Otherwise, the room was almost empty and so small that I could have jumped from one wall to the other. Yet, they managed to fit a bathtub between the mould-stained walls, set in the middle of the floor. It was filled to the brim with water as black as ink, and it seemed to swallow the light from my flashlight.

In movies, characters can easily tell how long a room has been vacant or how much time has passed since someone left a camp, simply by touching a coffee cup or feeling the warmth of a burnt-out bonfire. Temperature was a revealing factor. With that in mind, I approached the bathtub. I felt a need to touch the water, to dip my hand in it to see if it would disappear like the light from my flashlight. As I reached the tub, I hesitated, but then lowered my hand, almost against my will, towards the water. Slowly.

Robert, don't you stick your hand in there. You know what happens then. A hand, Robert! A hand flies up from the water, bloody and rotten. Grabs you and pulls you down into the bottomless tub. Don't do it.

I didn't listen to myself, and my fingers neared the surface. Five centimetres. Four. Three. Two. A centimetre from the water I stopped, when I saw the glow at the bottom of the tub, like cat eyes in the night. I leaned forward, and just as my finger touched the surface, someone shoved me from behind, causing me to fall.

Fredrik

This whole situation felt like a scene from a horror film, and I was quite surprised when the door slid open without a sound—no squeaking, no screeching. Not to mention the lack of cats. There were always cats in horror films, jumping at you just as you thought everything was safe and sound.

I stood in the doorway for a while, listening. Tony and Kjell were making a hell of a racket in the kitchen, and Robert went into the bathroom further down the hall. Why did we split up? Something movies taught me: you should never split up and wander off alone. Those who do rarely make it out.

A dresser and a bookshelf stood along the left wall. It was clearly water damaged. Black tentacles reached down from the ceiling, and the ragged wallpaper reminded me of sunburned skin, peeling off. Something that I assumed was a mirror on the right wall was hidden behind a stained blanket. The bed in the middle took up the rest of the space. I didn't see any reason to explore the room further, so I decided to head back to the others to gather the group, when suddenly, I heard a voice.

"Hi, Fredrik. Want to see something cool?" The voice behind me was sort of doubled, or tripled, as if multiple people spoke at once. Its tone suggested it came from far away, like from a dungeon deep underground. Under the bed.

"Stop messing around," I blurted, halting at the door.

"It's not a joke, or 'messing around' if you will," continued the voice calmly. "Relax, I'm not dangerous. I want to show you something."

"Tony?" I asked.

"No."

"Kjell?"

"No."

"Rob..."

"No. I told you not to be scared!"

"I'm not scared." My voice wavered. "Who are you?"

"I, we, are not so important. Let's focus on you, Fredrik."

"You know my name?"

"There's a lot that we know about you and your friends—all of them. Some would perhaps say we know too much? We know you like candy… and Tottenham. Oh, and we have lots of bottles for you guys. There's so much candy waiting for all of you."

"Guys, stop messing around," I said again, even though I had a feeling that none of them were actually hiding under the bed playing tricks on me, making crazy voices. I wanted to rush out of the room, but I stood still. I turned the flashlight towards the bed and saw tiny twinkling stars underneath. I took a step towards them. "Are you still there?" I got no immediate response. "Hello? Are you..."

"Yes! I'm down here. Under the bed. Under everything. Can't you shine the light a bit closer? I can't see anything."

"I don't know. I think I should go to the other guys."

"No, let them wait. I have a lot of bottles here. I promise. It's enough to buy all the candy in the store. All you have to do is shine the light for me. Help us up again. You see, we're stuck."

"We?"

"It's so tight here. You have to help us."

Had this been a movie, I would've jumped up from the couch and yelled at the TV: "Are you out of your mind?"

No one would've gone in there voluntarily. Now I realised people do stupid things in real life too. The floorboards creaked softly as I moved towards the bed, bent down and shone the light under it. The light had no effect underneath. I turned the flashlight to the wall to check if it was working. It lit up the room as it should. Back under the bed again. Still nothing. Dark. Again, I shone the light on the top of the bed, and the flashlight revealed a stained sheet. The pillowcase hadn't been white for a while either.

"Under the bed, I said!"

I jumped as the voice rang in my ears, followed by what could have been a warm breath brushing against the side of my face. I threw the flashlight under the bed, expecting to be face-to-face with a monster. But there was still nothing. Just darkness... Wait. It blinked again. Not stars, or cat eyes. Could it be... glass? Bottles? Yes, that was what it was. Hundreds of them. Maybe thousands. Wow, the guys would flip when they heard about this. They would...

"Love you because you found the bottles?"

"Yes, I... Wait! How can you..."

"Know what you're thinking? We know everything, Fredrik. We. Know. Everything."

Robert

I never saw who pushed me. As I tumbled headfirst towards the bathtub, I took a breath and closed my mouth, prepared to fall into the black water. But before I touched the surface, someone grabbed me by the shoulder, stopping my fall.

"Easily scared, huh?" Kjell shone a light in my face as I regained my balance. "Going to practise holding your breath in the bathtub again?" Kjell aimed his flashlight under his own chin now and said in a shrill voice, "Death is coming. Beware of the bathtub. Full of blood." Then he laughed.

I wanted to tell him to shut up, but he did have a point, after all. I was scared, and I probably would have done the same to him if he had been the one in front of the tub.

"Well, I felt a bit cold, so I figured maybe a warm, relaxing bath would do the trick," I answered as Kjell made eerie noises and waved his flashlight as he left the bathroom. He headed into the hallway.

My heart returned to its normal rhythm, and my knees stopped shaking as I turned back to face the room. The bathtub was still there, only this time, it was empty: white and almost rust-free. *Get a grip, Robert. You're seeing things.*

I considered dipping my hand into the tub again, just to check if the gooey water was still there. Maybe I just couldn't see it?

The plastic mat gave way beneath my feet as I finally eased out of the bathroom. The floor in the hallway also swayed gently. The walls sweated, and droplets shone like diamonds in the beam from my flashlight as I moved through the house. Even in the hallway, mirrors on the walls were covered with newspaper, carpets, and plastic. They hadn't skimped on the tape.

I pushed open the door to the room furthest down the

hallway. A strip of light penetrated through the planks on the window and revealed the bed that divided the room in two. Mould had crawled down from the wall and up onto the bedding. The full-length mirror in the corner hid under a sheet next to the dresser. Above it hung several pictures in a huge variety of frames, and I let the flashlight wander over the faded memories. In a wooden frame behind cracked glass, three people posed on a fishing boat. The cabin behind them was white with green and dark brown details. The sea stretched out in the background, and I thought of how Dad always spoke warmly of Hitra—the wind-battered island far out in the Trondheim Fjord, facing the open, endless sea. Maybe it looked like that there, like in the photos.

The older man must have been the captain of the boat, likely the father of the two children. Even though the photo was faded and out of focus, I could see how the sea had gnawed at the old man's face. He reminded me of the sailor on the Tiedemanns Tobacco poster Dad had on the wall in the stinky room. The two children, maybe seven or eight years old, posed with their fishing rods. One of them was the Witch of Mørkved. Those cold, grey eyes, and that... that sad look on her face. Even as a child, she didn't seem to have any light inside her.

In another picture stood an older version of the same woman. A young boy posed by her side. Skinny arms and legs. The hair was black, and ... I shone the light closer but couldn't quite make out his face. The ink had distorted the picture and smeared across the photo paper. Despite the, missing face, I understood who it had to be. In Øyerstad, he rode a moped until recently: Death. The Witch of Mørkved was perhaps Death's mother. Not that it was so strange, but I had never thought about it that way. That Death actually had a mother, or that the Witch had a child.

As I picked one of the picture frames off the wall to have a closer look, a piece of paper fell from the back of the frame. Newspaper pages hidden in secret drawers or, in this case, behind framed pictures on the wall, often contained revealing secrets. This was also the case this time, even if I didn't realise it until many years later.

On the paper, probably torn from a more extensive newspaper article, was a picture of three people. The young woman in the picture was the Witch of Mørkved. That same sad look on her face. The young man by her side looked like her, but I didn't know who he was. It could have been her brother. The third was a boy of two or three years, and also in this picture, the face was impossible to define. It had to be Death again.

The caption was in small italicised letters, "September 14, 1975. Ola..."

A scream from the room next door made the newspaper clipping fly out of my hands as if it suddenly caught fire. Then I ran.

Fredrik

Tony and Kjell stormed into the room first. Then Robert followed, stopping in the doorway.

"They were under the bed," I said, my voice choking with tears. "The floor swallowed my leg."

"Calm down!" Robert seemed relieved. You've stepped through the floor. It's all rotten. "It wasn't just the floor, Robert. It was…"

What should I tell them? That the crate of beer we stole from Death was under the bed? That it had grown thousands of times its real size, and was guarded by some kind of monster that spoke to me, and knew my name? All our names! Oh, and about those zombie hands that tried to pull me through the floor, and bit my foot?

"Calm down, Fredrik. We'll get your leg out and then get out of here," Robert said calmly.

Together, they grabbed my thigh, the part of the leg still above the floor, and pulled with all their might. But they didn't pull for long, my grimaces, tears, and screams stopped them. My foot was firmly stuck.

"Try to be quiet, Fredrik. We don't know who can hear us," Robert said, his face suddenly pale.

"We need to make the hole bigger," Tony said, and started wrenching the floorboards apart with his bare hands. The others joined in, and soon they were tearing away at rotting planks and splinters.

"Hurry," I whimpered.

Kjell cut his hand while pulling away a piece of wood with rusty nails in it. He was bleeding, but ignored it, and soon the pressure around my calf lessened. They continued working on the hole, and I glanced over at the void beneath the bed. If I had crawled all the way in there, into the darkness, I would've fallen seemingly forever before landing on the floor of hell. There were no bottles there.

"Holy shit, it stinks," Kjell said.

The stagnant air hit us as the hole around my leg widened.

"We should be able to get your leg up now," Tony panted, sitting back on the floor. They were all breathing heavily. Kjell winced as he examined his hand. Sweat dripped from their foreheads, like after a lunch break soccer match.

As we examined the hole, we all noticed the spiders almost simultaneously. Tony gasped and pulled his arms back. But even though the creepy crawlies seemed to be the size of our yoyos, it was the nails that scared us the most. They protruded from the top of my foot, glistening in the light from Kjell's flashlight.

"Damn," he exclaimed.

"Fredrik? What the hell?" Robert whispered.

"It's okay. Nails are fine," I mumbled, almost relieved amidst tears and spit. "Better nails than fangs and claws."

"Here! Bite this." Robert pushed a piece of wood into my mouth. Rambo! I'd seen him do it in a movie. I could handle it too.

"We need to get your leg free. This might hurt, okay?" Robert looked at me, then at the others. He blinked, wiping away sweat from his face. They counted to three, then pulled my leg again. The resistance wasn't too strong as the nails retracted through leather, skin, flesh, and perhaps bone. Out through the bottom of my shoe.

Kjell got up and rushed out of the room. He returned shortly with a towel, asking them to remove my shoe.

Soon, together, they wrapped the cloth around my foot, and before tightening it with Kjell's belt, Robert insisted I look at him. Still, I couldn't help but see the bloodstain growing on the towel. The room started spinning, and the pain faded. The warmth spreading from my foot and up my body was strangely comforting. Their voices dimmed, as if I had fallen through that hole beneath the bed after all. This was the beginning of the end for me.

Robert

Mom and Dad were told a story about a wild pinecone war up in the treehouse. Fredrik got too excited and did a "Mel Gibson", rolling around on the roof, throwing semi-automatic pinecones at the rest of us. Unfortunately, he didn't stop when the roof ended and landed on a pallet with protruding nails. The adults had no reason to doubt this version of the story.

The cops never found out that we'd been up at the cabin before them. Truth be told, I don't think they would've cared. As expected, they didn't make much of Death and the Witch's disappearance. The two oddballs had shown up in the village years ago without warning, and they left just as suddenly. Nothing suggested foul play. No one was reported missing. They simply returned to where they came from. Grandma claimed it was Blokksberg. And the sheriff? He didn't care.

5

Robert

The change in weather came on Monday, the last week of November 1989. The same week when the curse claimed its first victims. Jungle-Jim, our cat, was the first one to go. He was like most cats, loving and cute when he rolled in the gravel in the spring or curled up into a ball on the sofa in winter. Sometimes he more so resembled his relatives in the mangrove forests of India. Sneaky and dangerous. We laughed when he lunged at Dad's feet as Dad was coming up from the basement. Dad screamed and shook his foot, but the cat didn't let go. Sometimes he left half-eaten mice on the living room floor and decorated our sofa with puked-up hairballs. Cat things. We called him Jungle-Jim because he always played among the pinecones, bushes, and trees behind the house. I had never seen him anywhere near the front of our house, by the road. Never. Ever.

Since Death had disappeared, we walked along the road home, even though Mom and grandma still insisted we should go through the woods. Fredrik was fiddling with his yoyo, and I had my fist full of Mr. Freeze in all possible flavours and colours. We got them cheap, as no one bought ice cream in November. It was bitterly cold, but we were still heading home to challenge each other to a brain freeze competition.

Fredrik had attached the string to his yoyo and was winding it when Jungle-Jim came out of the gate. *What the hell are you doing?* I thought before he ran straight onto the road in front of a trailer. The truck driver showed no signs of braking before nor after he hit our four-legged friend and family member. Jungle-Jim exploded under the front wheel of the truck. Fredrik and I were left standing with splattered blood and cat-guts all over our shoes and trousers. Fredrik's yoyo fell to the asphalt and the string soaked up blood from what remained of our cat. For a while, time seemed to have stopped.

"I've told you to stay away from the road. What if one of you had been run over? Too bad Death doesn't scare you into the woods anymore." It was Mom. She set the world in motion again. She must have seen it all and came running through the gate towards us. She checked us up and down before guiding us towards the house. "Jungle-Jim, poor damn cat!" Mom was close to tears.

Soon a tub with green soap hit the floor in front of us in the living room, splashing water all over the parquet. We each got a cloth and were told to wipe off the blood. In the living room, my younger brother and I stood and watched Mom as she marched right back onto the road. This time with a bag and shovel. She didn't even notice the cars that braked abruptly to avoid hitting her. Some honked and shouted for her to get the hell off the road, but she didn't budge. She took her time. Scraped up as much of the cat into the bag as she could, then finally wiped up the blood with a towel. Jungle-Jim was not to be left on the road. He had to come home. Even this last time. Mom made sure of that.

I saw Mom shout something at a Swede who was shaking his fist at her. I don't know what the Swede said, but he quickly got back into his car and pressed the lock button as Mom stepped towards him.

Only when Mom was done did traffic resume through the village. Even though the situation was heartbreaking, Mom kept her head up. With messy hair and blood on her clothes and arms, she didn't care about those who honked or gave her the middle finger. She only cared about us. And Jungle-Jim.

Later there was a funeral, the first ceremony of that kind for me. It took place under the big climbing tree, a bit into the woods behind the house. There Jungle-Jim was buried in a shoebox with yellowed grass and leaves, two trembling hearts on a white paper, and cat food. "We will always love you, Jungle-Jim."

"He doesn't just disappear, you know," Mom said. "The tree by the grave, the grass, and the beetles. He becomes a part of all that. Jungle-Jim will always be with us."

Mom's words were comforting, and the thought of beetles with large furry tails, and a tree with paws and claws far out on the branches made me feel better. Mom read a poem, and we stood for a long time in front of the wooden cross we had made from spruce sticks and twine, Mom, Fredrik, and I.

A few days after Jungle-Jim left this world, we ventured out on new adventures. We trudged through the woods dressed in homemade balaclavas and camouflage suits made of white sheets and masking tape. As snow leopards, we moved silently through the woods on a mission: to play ding-dong ditch at Soldier-Ola's cabin, nestled in the woods behind the church. It was quite the walk, but it was worth it since he always got mad and chased after us. We figured that even though he was ex-military, he wouldn't be able to spot us in our new camouflage gear. We were a part of the scenary. We were snow!

The snow crust bore us both. I imagined the tree again, the only one in the world with reddish-brown fur and claws. My smile was cautious as we passed Kai's smallholding up in the ski trail, and we approached the cabin which was our target.

As we passed the main house in the courtyard, the exit door opened. Linn, Kai's daughter, stepped out onto the porch. The sight of her gave me a bad feeling in my stomach.

The beam from her flashlight brushed against the wall of the barn twenty metres from the stone steps she stood on. Then her light moved up to the trail, revealing snow-covered bushes that created ghostly formations. Fredrik and I threw ourselves behind a snow pile that probably hid a stump or two inside. Linn didn't notice us, and soon her flashlight returned to the barn.

Alarm bells were ringing in my head when Fredrik asked, "Do you think she's still upset?"

Ten Hours Earlier

The others laughed when I commented on the vibrating pipes in the ceiling of the old restroom beneath the school. "Damn, that sounds like Fredrik's butt after four slices of bread with chocolate spread and a litre of milk."

Fredrik covered his nose and nasally commented, "Your emissions in the back of the school bus aren't any better."

"Imagine throwing this away. We're lucky I found it in the ditch," Tony said as he pulled apart two stuck-together pages in the magazine he'd found on the way to school.

"Damn, look at those gigantic melons!" Kjell was ecstatic about the woman's attribute.

"That chick though… chocolate pussy," I said baffled. One spoke louder than the other until we were almost screaming.

"What if Principal Bergstein comes?" Fredrik glanced at the door.

"Screw it," I replied.

"She must be an acrobat. Look at how she's spreading!" Tony held up the magazine, and we studied the details.

"Hurry, flip the page," Kjell insisted.

"All of them are probably dating," I said when the next spread showed a pile of people all on top of, around, and inside each other. The women were in the majority. Heads, legs, arms, boobs, pussies, and balls everywhere. It was both beautiful and terrifying at once. Orgasms, screams, and unholy pleasure.

"Haven't you seen an orgy before?" Kjell looked at Fredrik, who was gaping.

"Orgies are cool, man," Tony said, pretending to know what he was talking about.

When the school bell rang for the first class, Tony lifted a ceiling tile to put the magazine back. There was something else up there. Tony discreetly pushed it aside and looked down at us. He didn't see that I noticed him hiding something.

In the classroom, the mood was tense, and my first thought was that Principal Bergstein had found the magazine in the restroom.

"Where have you put it?" he asked harshly.

"The certificate and the medal!" Miss Alvhilde prompted Principal Bergstein as they both stood with their arms crossed in front of the blackboard. Only then did I notice that the certificate and the prize Linn had won in the competition were no longer on the wall.

"Tell me where the prizes are now, or you will all suffer the consequences," Miss Alvhilde said, staring fiercely at us first, then at Principal Bergstein as if he should clarify what she meant by "suffer".

The principal hesitated briefly before exploding. "No one leaves the school until everything is back in its place. *No one*!"

I glanced at Tony who was fidgeting with his pencil case

when a collective sigh rippled through the classroom. Only Anne dared to say something. "But it's Friday. I have handball practice." She was chewing gum and smacking.

"No one!" Principal Bergstein reiterated.

"Come on, it was just a piece of paper and a plastic medal. Is it that big of a deal?" Anne was bold, you had to give her that, and many of the boys in the class admired her for it. In a way, that was good, because then I could have Guro to myself. Guro used less hairspray than Anne (I think), and she didn't laugh at her silly remarks. I wondered if Guro, under her messy hair, was also afraid of Anne? Maybe we had that in common? In fact, I was afraid of Guro too, but in a completely different way. What if she saw that I was looking at her? What if I said something stupid? Simply walking past her scared me. Legs all tangled up, I was afraid to fall.

Her stone-washed dungarees and shirt seemed like they had belonged to someone bigger—perhaps her mom when she was young. But I didn't mind. To me, she was perfect, no matter what she wore. She had been ever since the day Fredrik and I fed Terminator that last time. Rest in peace, monster dog.

"That's enough!" Principal Bergstein pointed with a trembling finger towards the back row.

"How could you do this? Think of our class. Our prizes, they're gone," Miss Alvhilde cried.

I wanted to ask her, "You mean Linn's certificate and Linn's medal?" But I kept quiet like the others, except for Anne.

"My dad won't like this," she muttered.

Four Days Earlier

Linn, undeniably the smartest in our class, participated in the school's big quiz, "Memorise This". Miss Alvhilde had named the competition, and perhaps that was why it meant so much to her. She was all red in her face the day she announced it.

The grand finale was broadcasted live from the Radio Skjønnsund bus, which was parked in the schoolyard for the occasion. The quiz participants sat in the bus with the chain-smoking quizmaster, answering questions about this and that. This was a big deal for us, even though the radio signals probably didn't reach far beyond Øyerstad and Skjønnsund. Those of us not actively participating in the quiz sat in the classrooms, with the radio volume turned up to the max.

Of course, Linn won without using the aids she was given to make the competition against fifth and sixth graders fairer.

On the final and decisive question, "Dovregubben, the troll king in Norwegian folklore, is notably associated with a famous piece of music composed by Edvard Grieg. What is the title of—"

"'In the Hall of the Mountain King'," she answered without hesitation. The class went bananas when the quizmaster announced that the answer was correct.

I sometimes wondered how she became so smart, since neither her mom, Hanne from the store, nor her dad, Kai, topped the list of rocket scientists and knee surgeons in Øyerstad. We liked them, but math, English, or social studies probably weren't their strongest subjects if they had ever decided to compete in any gameshow.

When the teacher hung up the certificate and medal next to the board at the front of the classroom, I caught a glimpse of what might have been a smile on Linn's freckled face for the first time ever.

We then celebrated loudly. We won! We hugged each other and cheered. Everyone, except for the one who had participated in the competition. She was never a part of us; she had never been. The smile I noticed didn't last long.

At some point during the celebration, Guro broke the circle to give the actual winner some attention. She grabbed Linn's arm and raised it into the air, as one does when someone has won a boxing match. No one noticed, or simply didn't care, and the arm fell limply back down when Guro no longer held it up.

After an extensive celebration, we sat down at our desks, and Linn stood by the board. Miss Alvhilde felt she had to direct a minute of attention towards her too.

The floor was Linn's friend, so she never looked up at the rest of us. The slump in her neck had become permanent after four years of elementary school. One could hope it was all the intelligence weighing her head down, but it was probably all the comments and mocking glances that made her feel so heavy.

"What? Can you speak up so I can hear you? And try looking at me for once. Or look at them! Let's have a proper victory speech," Miss Alvhilde gestured, first at Linn, then at us.

Of course, Linn was never going to deliver a victory speech, and we all knew it. The teacher knew it too. Giggles swept through the classroom again as she walked, head hung low, back to her desk.

Four Days Later - Friday

Hours before Fredrik and I snuck around the woods in camouflage, something dramatic had happened in the classroom. The certificate and medal Linn won in the competition were gone. If Linn had disappeared the same way, no one would have noticed, but the class's prizes being gone, *that* the teacher saw the moment she stomped into the classroom. She gaped at the empty wall before calling Principal Bergstein. As usual, we arrived late, having more important business in the locked down restroom.

No one confessed, and as the principal retreated back into the hallway, we heard someone shout, "How can you keep them at school over the weekend for such a trifle? Anne has nothing to do with this!" It was her father.

The prizes never reappeared, but we still left school when the bell rang for the last time that Friday. Linn sat in the classroom when we left.

Invisible.

Ten Hours Later, Snow and Ding-Dong Ditch

I was so used to seeing her in that old dress that it took a few seconds for my brain to register that she was barely dressed. Only a t-shirt shielded her from the biting cold. No shoes, pants, hat, or mittens. What the hell was she doing out in the cold like that?

As the light from her flashlight reflected in a mirror on the tractor, we saw the rope over her shoulder.

"Come on!" I leapt over the snow mound in front of us and wriggled in the direction of the barn. This was more exciting than ding-dong ditch.

"What the hell, Robert? What are you doing?"

"What *am I* doing? Are you seeing the same thing I am? Let's go!"

"I do see it, but I don't think we should get involved."

"What? Seriously? She's heading towards the barn, barefoot

with a rope over her shoulder." I chuckled as I spoke. "This is a real mission. We have to find out what she's up to."

"My foot hurts." Fredrik clearly didn't find this as thrilling as I did.

"Your foot hurts? From the nails in the house? That was ages ago. Snap out of it!"

"I swear. It's throbbing like hell. My shoes are soaking wet. I think it's blood."

Fredrik indeed hadn't been himself since he stepped through the floor in that house. Or, was "dragged through the floor", as he claimed. He had hardly played soccer or hockey since. His porridge portion on Fridays was getting smaller, and he always ordered a bag of mixed, as if optimising the amount of candy didn't matter anymore.

"Come on. We need to find out what she's up to."

Linn opened one of the barn doors and left nothing but darkness as she slipped inside. I took three quick steps towards the barn, but Fredrik still didn't follow. "Seriously, Fredrik?"

"Please Robert, we need to get home. Something is wrong here."

"Seriously?"

"Seriously... "

"Seriously. How about testing the camouflage instead? Stick to the original plan? Ding-dong ditch?"

"I can't. Maybe we can watch a movie? I have a bag of popcorn under my bed. We can share it."

"If I get to choose the movie."

"Ok."

The Circus

A new installation: like horses on a carousel, the truck slid in from the darkness—visible for a few seconds before sliding into nothingness again. Each time it appeared, I heard a slap before something hit my legs. A wet cloth. Not a cloth. Jungle-Jim. What remained of him after the truck tire did what truck tires do to cats crossing the road. I looked over at the vehicle disappearing into the darkness and then down at my legs. Heard the slap again. Looked towards the truck. The entrails slapped against my legs. The scent of hay and torches gave way to a sweeter smell, reminiscent of rotten beans.

6

Dad

Kai left wobbly tracks in the snow halfway into our yard. I put on my jacket and went out to meet him. Either he was up early, or he hadn't gone to bed. Not even his alcohol-scented breath could chase away the icy phantoms that danced from his mouth and nose.

"What are you doing here? I thought we had an agreement?" I said. "We weren't going to talk to each other ever again."

"Hey, Dad, long time no see. You look good." His words started soft but froze in the air.

"What do you want?" I asked.

"What do I want? Am I not welcome here anymore?" Kai opened his arms towards me and I smelled old sweat beneath the alcohol.

"We don't talk to each other."

"Oh, our agreement? That was a good one, but it doesn't matter anymore."

"What do you mean?"

"Come on, surely you've seen it."

"Seen what? You're drunk, Kai. Go home."

"The shadows, those damn shadows. The hole that sucks the life out of you? You've heard them, haven't you?" Kai suddenly sounded sober.

"Why are you here?" I asked, ignoring his talk about shadows.

"I needed someone to talk to." Kai spread his arms wide and suddenly screamed, "Can you hear me?" He looked past me towards the house. "I needed to confess my sins, and I'm not welcome in the church!"

"You damn fool, you're waking up the whole village. We keep quiet. That was your idea."

"The voices, it's the shadows talking." Kai continued, whispering again. A childlike laughter escaped his lips.

"Pull yourself together."

"The shadows speak: 'Everyone will die,' they say. Yes, you and I as well. We will die last. Because first, everyone we love will wither away. Everyone we love will die first. It's your fault."

"My fault? What happened to it being *our* fault? What about sticking together in this? If it were up to me, it would all be over by now."

"Over? We saved your ass! Damn it, don't forget that."

"Calm down," I whispered through clenched teeth. "Get your drunk ass out of here. For God's sake, stay away from us."

"Linn is dead." Kai's voice was so soft, that, as I turned away from him, the words were barely audible.

I stood there, all my weight on one foot while the other seemed frozen in the air. My breath stopped, and a voice from my dreams whispered to me, "You will all die, but those you love go first." Of course, I had heard them too. Slowly, I turned back to Kai, and he took a step forward.

His eyes were like bullets, seeming to want nothing more than to blow my brains out against the house wall. In the bedroom window behind me Robert stood watching us argue again.

"What are you talking about?"

"Linn is dead."

"Are you coming inside to talk?" Marianne stood on the terrace wrapped in a blanket, calling to us, "It's freezing out here."

"Everyone we love will die. Yours too," Kai whispered, ignoring Marianne.

Just as I thought he was about to lunge at me and stab me with the hunting knife he wore around his waist, he turned and followed his own tracks back across the snow-covered gravel. Out through the gate. I turned to Marianne, hearing the voice again— "Everyone you love will die!"

I wanted to hold her, hug her, tell her I loved her, like I used to. I wanted to ask her for forgiveness. But if I did that, would it mean she would die too?

"What really happened between you two?" Marianne didn't shine the way she used to.

"Linn is dead!" I snapped and walked right past her. I slammed the terrace door behind me.

Robert

The Monday following Kai and Dad's encounter in the garden, we skipped our usual distractions—like the porn magazine—and headed straight for the classroom. In the school corridor, the air was filled with the usual sounds of children shouting, laughing, and running. However, the mood in our classroom was anything but cheerful. Miss Alvhilde and Principal Bergstein were already there, standing rooted to the spot with their arms crossed. They neither smiled nor welcomed us as they usually did.

I walked to my seat, and for the first time, I felt that the posters at the back of the classroom shouldn't have been there. A blood-soaked Carrie and Freddy Krueger's knife fingers hovering over Nancy's terrified face. What made it even worse was a poster I previously hadn't thought much about. The girl featured on the April Fool's Day poster had her hair braided in a way that resembled a noose on her back. I hadn't seen the movie, but I considered walking past my desk to take it down. I didn't.

"Grief can make children do strange, selfish things," Miss Alvhilde lectured from the front near the blackboard. She stood with Principal Bergstein, and of course, they took Linn's death seriously. That's why they had organised a special memorial for the poor girl. Or rather, they had organised a special memorial about how sorry they felt for the rest of us who had lost a classmate. Not even in her own memorial was Linn the protagonist.

In my mind, I leapt up from my chair and ran to the blackboard, shouting, "Don't you realise we did this?" I jabbed a finger at our wrinkled teacher's face. She flinched as my words rained down on her. "It was you, me, and all of us. We did this. Linn believed us. She thought she was invisible! Now that she is, can't we at least acknowledge she was here?"

In reality, though, I didn't move. Anne was chewing gum, writing a note she passed to Kristin behind the desk next to her. Clearly, it contained something amusing. Kjell looked expressionless up at the blackboard, and Tony was still fidgeting with his pencil case, not looking up at anyone. Up front, Guro lit a candle next to a photo of Linn. Then she returned to her seat. I could feel the grief she carried in her heart, beneath her T-shirt with a picture of an elephant and pink letters spelling, "You're elephantastic."

The Circus

Linn stood in front of the booth near the Ferris wheel, where the Witch and Death now sold tickets. A rope dangled from her neck, trailing down her back and slithering along the ground like a snake. As when she was alive, she stared at the ground as if her head was too heavy to lift. She wore the same dress she always had.

"Are you worried you've forgotten your shoes, or what? Maybe it's that oversized brain of yours that weighs too much? Is that why you're always staring at the ground? Is the ol' blockhead too heavy?"

Those words slipped from my lips that day when Guro was supposed to be impressed that I too could hurl insults at the dullest mouse in our class. You know those moments when you should keep quiet, but the words spill out anyway? That was such a moment, and those were such words. They punched me in the gut as they came out, and I simply let them linger. Linn barely reacted, at least not outwardly, and I never apologised. I acted like nothing happened. Guro wasn't impressed.

The prizes on the wall around the Ferris wheel had been upgraded in honour of Linn, the new esteemed guest. Instead of teddy bears and chocolates, certificates and medals tempted the visitors to try their luck at the wheel. Linn extended a pale hand to the Witch and placed some coins on the cracked wooden counter. The Witch set a ticket beside her money. The coins shimmered as the Ferris wheel began to spin, at first, so fast that the colours merged into a yellow-ish glowing mass, then it slowed down. Colours separated, and the wheel stopped on black.

As with everything else in here, the scene repeated itself. Linn put coins on the counter, and the Witch of Mørkved handed her another ticket. "Everyone's a winner!" was written on the sign above them, but it wasn't true—Linn never won.

7

Robert

Mom's Christmas calendar was something else. It featured a brown cloth adorned with Christmas decorations and white plastic rings, from which hung twenty-four sets of chocolate pieces. The treats, individually wrapped in gift paper featuring elves and snow lanterns, were suspended from the rings by red ribbons. Each package was a Christmas hug from Mom, and there were twenty-four pieces for each of us.

Sitting at my desk, facing the Haugen fields, I contemplated taking the last treat from the calendar, as the clock had passed twelve. My pencil flew across the paper in short, quick strokes, bringing eerie figures to life. Fredrik was sleeping in the bed behind me.

I considered taking Fredrik's treat too. He had already given me all of his from the calendar so far. I had to promise not to tell Mom, Dad, or Anders. There would only be a lot of fuss and worry if they found out he didn't want his chocolate.

"Hey, ho, hey, brother. Ready for the pitch? I've got my jet-plane fueled boots on. See if you can beat me." You might think Fredrik was drunk when he spoke, but of course, he wasn't. He just wasn't awake.

"I'm ready. Should I bring diving equipment?" I quickly replied.

"Wonder if I should sign for Tottenham or some little league team?"

"Go with the little league team," I answered.

"That means pizza. I love pizza."

"With cauliflower?"

Conversations with my brother when he was asleep were often quite special. Rarely did his answers match my questions. I enjoyed coming up with one answer more bizarre than the next to see how twisted our conversations could become.

"Let go of me, I haven't done anything," he shouted in response to my cauliflower question, and suddenly sat up in bed. I had seen Fredrik behave strangely in his sleep before, but this was something else, and it kinda startled me. His bulging eyes locked onto mine. His head tilted back, and his mouth was open with the corners pointing downwards. The skin on his face and neck was so taut that the veins looked like they were creeping up over his face. A thousand spiders crawled down my back, down my legs, and out through my toes.

"Shit! You scared me," I said, rolling the chair away from the table.

"Let go of me, I haven't done anything. What do you want?" Fredrik seemed panicked.

"Fredrik! What are you talking about?"

"I don't know. But they… Over there, in the corner, they…."

"There's no one there. You don't have to be scared."

He scanned the room, and I must admit, I took an extra look too. Did something move underneath his bed? I leaned over in the chair to check. It was probably a shadow.

"Pass me the puck, I'm in!" Fredrik burst out, and then his face relaxed, looking calmer.

"Fredrik? Are you awake?"

"SHOOT!" He raised his voice.

Fredrik was still sleeping and I decided to engage in his dream match. "Alright, are you ready? Here comes the shot."

"Did I shoot you?" he asked, his face tightening again.

"What?" I responded.

"Isn't it cold in the water?"

"Fredrik?"

"Yes, I understand that it's dark down there," Fredrik said, laying back down in bed.

"Who are you talking to?"

"Hey! Cranky is coming. He doesn't look happy," Fredrik said, relaxing again.

"Cranky", the elderly man who maintained the ice at the skating rink, loved speed skating. You know those wimps in skin tight body suits? Fredrik, the hockey guys, and I had sticks and hockey skates. We considered ourselves much cooler than the others. Often, we hid in the woods next to the skating rink while Cranky finished up for the night. It took time to make perfect ice for the speed skaters. Us hockey players? He didn't care about us. He often stopped, took off his gloves, and stroked his hand along the ice. Was it perfect? No chips or unevenness? It had to be perfect. If he found any irregularities, he'd get back in the truck and take another round on the ice. Ten more minutes of waiting in the woods.

When he finally bent down, kissed the ice, wiped away a tear, and left, we jumped out of the woods with hockey skates, sticks, and homemade shin guards. We played for hours, sliding, hitting, and kicking.

Sometimes Cranky would come back to have one last look at his ice. He new there was imminent danger that we might sabotage his masterpiece. This often ended with us sprinting back into the woods, skates still on, while he shouted less-than-pleasant words after us.

A few days ago, Fredrik sat on the sidelines for the first time, watching the rest of us skate and tackle our asses off on the ice.

"Don't feel like playing today. Too tired," he said. He blamed his foot again, and not long afterward, Dr Larsen made another of his frequent home visits to us that winter.

"It must have hurt when you stepped on the nails, but it's healed nicely. The scars are almost gone. You're just fine. Eat an apple a day; it supposedly keeps the doctor away," Dr Larsen said during his last home visit.

Mom squirmed in the chair. "Are you sure everything is okay? He doesn't eat and looks terribly pale."

"Oh yes. He's a bit weak. But I can't find anything wrong. Let's see again in a week. Let's meet again over Christmas."

"You're probably right. It's been so much lately. Dad isn't himself either."

"Is he sick?"

"He's... I'm not sure what he's up to these days."

"Working all the time again?"

"Yes, that too."

"He just needs some vacation. Some rest would do you all good!" Doctor Larsen got up, grabbed his leather bag, and headed for the exit.

"Listen, Marianne, you don't have to worry. I agree that your boy seems a bit weak, but judging by all the tests he is perfectly fine. As for Dad, give him a shot of liquor and a week's rest, and he'll be back in business. It's been a long autumn. I wish you all a very merry and invigorating Christmas."

Dr Larsen left the house and slowly dissolved into the winter night.

The next morning, on Christmas Eve, I took my Christmas stocking and sneaked into the living room. There were two sources of light; the TV and the Christmas tree. Fredrik and Anders were already there. It smelled of pine needles and tangerines.

"Forget your stocking, did you?" Anders looked at Fredrik.

"Haven't forgotten it," Fredrik mumbled.

"Where is it then? Couldn't find it?" Anders asked.

We didn't get our candy in those red, fluffy Christmas stockings you see in American movies. No, we got our treats in Dad's work socks, which were the largest we had. Unfortunately, the socks also showed signs of their long service in his work shoes. We could only hope they had been thoroughly washed before Mom stuffed them with goodies.

"Seriously, is it still in your room? Don't you want it?" Anders persisted. "Should I go and get it? Hello, is anybody home? What's wrong with you these days?"

On the TV, little elves filled Santa's sack with gifts. They sang and rejoiced at the arrival of the festive season.

"You can have it," Fredrik mumbled after a while, not taking his eyes off the TV.

"You've seen that cartoon a hundred times before. It's not that good."

We always ate our candy together on Christmas Eve morning, watching the same cartoons and eyeing the gifts under the tree. We would wake up long before Mom and Dad, cherishing the quiet time. But this time, something was different, although I couldn't quite put my finger on it. Things just weren't as... cheerful; perhaps that was the word.

Dad had personally picked the Christmas tree, and it was only thanks to the presents underneath that it didn't attract more attention. If there had been a famous national TV show with an annual program called *Norway's Ugliest Christmas Tree* we would probably have been frequent contenders. Perhaps the show hosts would receive tips before the season from exasperated mothers or embarrassed children. Then they'd travel around in a van to report on the best candidates. The celebrity panel tasked with choosing the ugliest tree would likely have different favourites in the final round, but they'd come to an agreement in the end.

"No, I mean, I've seen a lot in my life, but that spruce in Øyerstad..."

"Yes, the one Dad had fetched from the forest. Did it even have branches on one side at all?" Bob Saget interrupts Johnny Carson.

"That one. That's my favourite. It was so crooked it almost went full circle," adds Oprah Winfrey.

"We probably all agree we have a winner." Bob Saget gets up to announce the winner of *Norway's Ugliest Christmas Tree*. "The Baastad family from Øyerstad!"

Later that morning, Dad ate anchovies and eggs for breakfast, we all ate porridge for lunch, and the day slowly moved towards *Donald Duck* on TV. The clock was approaching four, and it was an hour until dinner. That again meant that it was about three hours until gift opening.

"Those two packages there, the soft ones. Do you think they could be jerseys?" I asked Fredrik as the smell of food spread through the house.

"How would I know?" he replied uninterestedly.

"What if they are original jerseys?" I let my index finger roam over the paper to feel for revealing patterns.

"Are you two okay?" asked Mom from the kitchen, preparing ribs, potatoes, sauce, peas, carrots, sauerkraut, red cabbage, meatballs, those white sausages, and a lot of other stuff. When neither of us answered, she brought the scent of the ribs into the living room. She sighed exasperatedly as she felt Fredrik's forehead for the thirty-fourth time that day.

"I'm calling Larsen to be sure. Can you watch the potatoes, Dad?"

Dad slowly got up from the couch, mumbled, and dragged his feet into the kitchen. Mom went out into the hallway with the phone. She introduced herself to the person on the other end. She wanted to speak to Larsen. Again.

"I know I've called many times, but something's wrong with him. I know my boy well enough. My God, he barely cares about the Christmas gifts. He hasn't touched his candy."

On TV, a group of boys with big gaping mouths and white robes sang jolly carols. Fredrik watched them disinterestedly.

"We'll be there tomorrow at one." Mom didn't wish the person she spoke to a Merry Christmas before hanging up the phone. A bit harder, a bit more exasperated than usual. Was it "Give me the strength to survive this Christmas," she whispered before disappearing back into the kitchen?

With the evening came the opening of presents, and Anders read the cards with blessings and distributed gifts eagerly. He seemed to pick them at random, but maybe he knew what was in the two presents I considered particularly interesting. He held onto them for an unusually long time.

As an almost-twelve-year-old, I still found the number of gifts satisfactory. The pile in front of me was quite large when he pulled out the last two presents.

"Dear Robert. We wish you a very Merry Christmas, Mom, Dad, and Anders." Apart from "to Robert", the same was written on the package Anders handed to Fredrik after I received mine. The fact that the labels said "from Anders" in addition to "Mom and Dad" didn't strike me as odd at the time, even though Anders wasn't usually in the habit of contributing to Mom and Dad's gifts for us.

I tore off the paper in a flash, and soon my little brother did the same. It was the jerseys we have dreamed of, United and Tottenham, with accompanying socks and shorts. "Baastad" was written on the back of both. I had number 16 and Fredrik had number 7.

Grandma and Grandpa chuckled in the corner when they saw our smiles. Dad also smiled gently and Mom cried. Anders stood by the Christmas tree. He was the most upright and proud of the two. He nodded at me, and his lips moved. I think he said, “Merry Christmas, Robert.” Was he crying too?

That evening, while the adults drank coffee in the living room, my little brother and I played soccer in the kitchen for the first time in a long while. With the jersey on, he regained some of the energy and joy he once had. We laughed, fell, scored goals, celebrated, ate chocolate, and drank Christmas soda. We played for different teams, but that didn’t matter. We were both winners.

As the evening progressed, there was rice pudding, leftover ribs, more candy, TV, and happy conversations. The whole room smelled of Christmas: oranges and cloves. Even Fredrik rolled his eyes when Dad again talked about the size of the cod in the sea outside Hitra. They grew bigger every time he told his story. Mom went on about an episode of *Creepshow* where living, evil grass from another planet grew on a poor farmer. In the end, he had to take his own life. Anders struggled to see 3D figures that were supposed to jump out of the pages of the book he had been gifted. It was a perfect Christmas evening.

Grandma and Grandpa left just after eleven, and well past midnight, I found myself at my desk, drawing again. My pencil twitched and sketched a curve that mimicked the sudden rise in my pulse when Fredrik sat up in bed.

“Shit, are you awake?” I asked, erasing the unintended line.

“Yeah, I am. Did I scare you?”

“Nope. Just thought you were asleep. I’m testing the pen

set I got from Grandma and Grandpa. Drawing something for the *Horror Recruits Magazine*. Sooner or later they have to print one of my drawings."

"What are you drawing this time?

"A circus."

"Like the one at the Haugen field?"

"Yes, almost. Only, there are no ordinary people around—just a bunch of… I don't know. Some kind of demons, I guess. I call them 'the phantoms.'"

"Who are they?

"Not entirely sure, but I dream about them sometimes."

"Nightmares?"

"You bet."

Fredrik looked at me with wide eyes. "That one there?"

"A clown on a unicycle," I answered, not mentioning the time a juggler had approached me outside the circus when Mom and Dad had disappeared into the crowd by the Wheel of Fortune, leaving me all alone. Amidst the chaos, his eyes burned with a fire of blood-red flames. His lips, cut and gleaming, stretched into a too-broad smile, revealing dirty, jagged teeth.

"Are you there somewhere?"

"Well, I am, but I'm not... or maybe I am."

"Eh… what?"

"One of the phantoms. Maybe I am one of them? Always standing on the outskirts, a bit away from the tent. On the boundary between light and dark."

"Is it Øyerstad that lies outside there?"

"No, I don't think so. The circus area is more like an oasis, an island in a sea of nothingness."

"And those eyes there?" Fredrik pointed to two glowing dots in the dark.

"That's Bingo-Bob."

"Bingo-Bob? Who's that?"

"He... Well, he started everything, I think. He's in charge of it all. He´s... Nah, never mind. Anyway, go back to sleep. It's late."

Fredrik

When Robert asked if I was awake, I wasn't quite sure what to answer. Lately, I've had trouble even knowing for sure if I was awake or not. Often, I was somewhere in between. It began after our visit to the house up in Mørkved Hills. When I crashed through the floor. Since then, the doors between dreams and reality have been wide open. It all kind of blend together. Quite often I hear whispers and chatter coming from far beyond, deep down in my darkest dreams. Nightmares when you sleep are one thing, but when they don't go away once you wake up, it sucks.

Robert

Fredrik was probably awake. At least more awake than asleep, for we had a somewhat normal conversation. We often talked about our drawings, and gladly praised each other to the skies. It struck me that night how small and frail he had become. Pale.

Fredrik

The drawing he presented was good, and it didn't surprise me, because Robert was skilled at drawing. He used to praise my drawings too, even though I knew they weren't as good as his. Robert really deserved to have one of his drawings featured in *the Horror Recruits Magazine* someday. He had been sending drawings to the editors ever since we began subscribing to it. "Horror, terror, and sci-fi for young movie enthusiasts". Mom wasn't as enthusiastic as we were when Dad bought us a year's subscription.

"That entrance, it doesn't look like they have particularly cheerful shows in there?" I asked.

"No, I think the entrance is like a portal. A hole leading into something. Or a way out for those on the other side."

"And those marks? Are they some kind of letters?" I pointed to some symbols around the entrance.

"I think there is someone in there trying to communicate something, but we don't understand what they're saying."

"What do you think it is?"

"I'm not sure exactly what it is, as I don't speak demonic, but it's something scary for sure."

When he said that they're "trying to communicate something," I heard the voices again. Those that had followed me since I heard them from under the bed in that cursed house.

"What do you want? I haven't done anything wrong." I thought I was only saying it to them in my head, but I saw Robert react.

Robert

"Are you still asleep?" Fredrik's empty gaze drifted past me and out the window. His cheeks trembled, and his skin was as white as the snow outside. He reminded me of one of them—the phantoms from the circus. I wanted to run to Mom, but I didn't move.

Fredrik

Robert's drawing and the circus were one thing, but that entrance into the tent was something else. It reminded me of the darkness under the bed in that damned house, of the Witch of Mørkved. Of Death. Of the shadows that have followed me since the day we visited that place—shadows like the ones behind the TV this morning, or those pulsating around Anders when he handed out the Christmas presents.

They were everywhere and nowhere at the same time. They had swallowed the world around me, and Øyerstad was painted black. Sometimes I sensed more than just shadows. Something or someone lurked within them. Sometimes I imagined the Witch of Mørkved and Death floating around in there. Death probably wanted his money back for the beer we poured out. The Witch? She probably wanted us to stay away from their house. Stop throwing pinecones and rocks, or at least repair the hole in the floor we caused. Once, I saw something that resembled Jungle-Jim floating in there as well. His twisted face slowly emerged and receded, and his wailing pierced my heart.

Outside our bedroom, darkness pressed against the window as if it had consistency. Black mass. Antimatter. Oil. It seeped in around the window frame, in through the air vent and oozed slowly down the wall. The glass could give way at any moment.

"We shouldn't have broken into the house."

"What are you t… t… talking about?" Robert stammered.

"The Witch's house. Something followed us from there."

Robert

"I want them to go away. I can't take it anymore," Fredrik said with a trembling voice.

"Who should go away? There's no one else here," I replied.

"Yes there are, in the shadows. Out there."

"There's no one out there either."

"They want revenge."

"Revenge, for what? We haven't done anything." Maybe Fredrik was still asleep after all? This conversation was becoming more and more twisted.

I should get Mom.

Fredrik

The silhouette of the unknown man hanging, or floating in thin air outside the window, would normally have scared the crap out of me. But I was way beyond the boundaries of how much fear my brain could handle. Moreover, he actually looked more miserable and sad than scary. He swung slowly back and forth, as if he was hanging from an invisible rope. I felt that he would have thrashed and kicked violently with his arms and legs if he could. He seemed paralyzed. Bleak. Sometimes he was clear and visible, other times almost imperceptible in the stream of nothingness outside the house. Could it be a memory, or some kind of foreshadowing, or maybe even a warning?

"Are you awake?"

Robert's question brought me back into the room. Now he was different too. He sat in the chair, and dirty water streamed from his mouth as he spoke. Robert turned his head to the window, and I saw water flowing from his ear too. He looked out at the man outside and raised a hand towards him.

Robert

"It's best if you lie down and sleep. You're completely out of it. I'll finish the drawing, and we'll see what Dr Larsen says tomorrow. Fredrik, can you hear me?"

"What's happening? Robert, you're not yourself. That man out there, he… he…" Fredriks words where barely audible.

"You're not yourself! Pull yourself together." I raised my voice.

"But, Robert! The water—can't you see it?"

"Fredrik, it's time to sleep," I said.

Jesus, I hadn't seen Fredrik this miserable before. I mean, he looked really scared. Terrified. This was nothing like the corny conversations we had while he was mumbling in his sleep.

This has gone too far, I will tell Mom tomorrow.

Fredrik

When I woke again, the lights in our room were off. Robert had gone to sleep as well. I heard him breathing. The unknown man still hung outside the window and the voices spoke louder than before. Voices, wet and multi-layered, speaking to me from somewhere else—a different place, perhaps another dimension. Darker shadows within the shadows writhed like snakes in a mating orgy outside the house, and also inside the room along the floor and walls. They were strong enough now. The time had come. I gathered my things as planned and wrote the letter. Then I lay down in bed again to wait.

I woke to the sound of cracking glass. It wasn't long before the darkness outside exploded into the room. Glass shards cut my skin, and arms and legs broke like matchsticks against the ceiling and walls as I was tossed around like a ragdoll. As I opened my mouth to scream, a cold, slimy mass forced its way inside, sliding down my throat. Whatever it was, I felt it crawling inside me. Suddenly growing, threatening to burst out of my body. I wanted to vomit but my throat was blocked. Lungs compressed. My heart had no space to beat. My ribcage exploding sounded like a gunshot, and then the pain was gone.

Dear God, I don't want to die.

Robert

Snow crystals danced a quiet waltz after the truck that passed silently outside the house. The tension in my head was worse than before. It felt as if someone had placed a helmet that was three sizes too small on my head during the night. My pillow was damp, and the bedding clung to my body. I sat up and frowned. Bright.

You know when you've had a dream, and the echoes of it linger in your body, but you can't quite remember it? A feeling of unease that swims around in your head, and slips out of your grip when you try to catch it. Sometimes you see a glimpse, a hint of something, but too little to recall the entire meaning. After a while, you give up and let it drift away. That's how I felt that morning.

On the desk below lay my drawing. The lines were smeared across the paper in a black mess, as if I had spilled a glass of water over it. There was no glass on the table.

"Are you awake?"

Fredrik didn't answer. I leaned over the edge of the bed and looked down. He lay facing the wall, asleep. The sheet had been torn from the mattress and lay with the duvet at his feet.

"Are you okay?" I whispered. "Fre... have you packed your things?" There was a pile of stuff next to his bed.

The bunk bed groaned as I jumped down and landed softly on the carpet. I sat down on the bed edge next to the pile. On top of the Tottenham jersey was a handwritten note. Beneath that was the special assignment he wrote about Arnold. Then the "Movie Book" where he kept track of all the movies he owned. Every time he got a new VHS or recorded a classic from TV, he painstakingly wrote it down in the book, listing both the release year and the actors. Of course, it was also rated. We were generous back then, and movies like *Razorback* and *Cobra* were given top score. His collection consisted of thirty-four movies. Below the Movie Book lay other things he cherished.

The paper note made me nervous because Fredrik would rather eat Dad's meatballs than write more than he absolutely had to. My hands shook as I picked it up.

To Robert, Anders, Mom and Dad.

Robert, you're probably reading this first. Look, I know you don't support Tottenham. But you like football, so I thought maybe you'd keep my jersey for me? You can also tell Bjarte that I've quit football. If you want, you can wear my jersey, maybe once? I would like that.

The special assignment is for all of you to read, but Mom

can keep it. Please use gloves as the pages might become brittle over time. There are plastic gloves from Fina in the plastic pocket. You can use those.

Anders can have the Bruce Willis posters since he loves those movies. Dad can have the music posters; he likes those. Divide the movies by favourites, but Robert, you know this one: "You are not a God. Why don't you pull the trigger and find out?" That movie is yours. And what would Anders say? "Yippee-ki-yay, Motherfucker!" That movie is his.

All of these things… I won't need them anymore.

Love… you all. Maybe I'll see you sometime.

Fredrik.

I sat on the edge of the bed in my underwear, shaking. The letters blurred in and out of focus. A shrill ringing in my ears intensified, as if something invisible were squeezing my brain. If I sat as still as my brother lay behind me, maybe time would stop. If so, I would never have to turn towards him, touch him, or try to wake him up. Again, outside, snowflakes danced by the road as another trailer whizzed past. I waited. A little while. Then the letter fell to the floor, as I turned to face my brother.

Some time later I stood in the doorway to Mom's bedroom. Framed like a painting with the potential to become one of the most talked-about works in Norwegian art history. A picture Grandma would hang on the wall next to her copy of Giovanni Bragolin's *The Crying Boy*. I remember the artist's name from the label under the picture on their wall. You know the picture of the boy with tears on his cheeks, right? Grandma often spoke of how the picture was painted with sorrow and longing, but also with love and forgiveness. Grandpa, on the other hand, saw it differently. He called it cheap, tacky, and trashy.

In Grandpa's eyes, nothing could compare to Picasso's painting of the old man with the guitar. To him, that was real art. He imagined the impoverished life the poor troubadour must have lived. The painting's colour palette—blue, brown, white, and grey—sharply contrasted with the gold coins Grandpa hid in his mattress, or wherever else he stored his wealth. Even though Grandpa's painting was also a replica, we weren't allowed near when Grandpa admired his art on the wall with a glass of wine in his hand. Standing in the doorway, I felt a bit like both. Both like the pale, perhaps dead figure with the guitar and the boy with tears on his cheeks. I felt both invisible and present at the same time.

As long as Mom didn't wake up, she wouldn't have to face the fact that her child died in his sleep. Such an event could make her never want to sleep again—or perhaps she'd go to bed, only to never wake up.

I'm standing here, waiting for you to finish sleeping, Mom. Tough times are coming.

A hymn from my childhood surfaced through the sea of thoughts, images, and memories. Mom had embroidered the lyrics on a piece of cloth and hung it over my bed once in childhood. It might have been a baptism gift, and I had no idea where it was now. It no longer hung over my bed. "Dear God, I am well. Thank you for everything I've got. You are good. You love me. Dear God, never leave me. Look after the small and the big. God preserve Father and Mother. God preserve my family"

"Fredrik?" Mom spoke softly. I had put on Fredrik's Tottenham jersey, and it must have been that which deceived her. Her reaction gave me a faint, strange hope. What if she saw Fredrik? What if he was awake, and I was in my bed sleeping? What if I was just dreaming I was him? That I saw the world through his eyes. If so, this was just a bad dream.

"Mo… Mom…" I recognised the voice talking to her. It was mine, not Fredrik's.

"You can go back to bed, Fredrik. You sound like you have a cold, and it's still early." Mom yawned and lay on her side in bed again.

The ashtray next to the clock on the nightstand was topped with cigarette butts. The smell of stale smoke in the room suddenly became overwhelming. Most of the butts were from the night before, and maybe a few more had been added during the night. She hadn't had her morning cigarette yet. I thought about the circus and the torches.

"Mom, it's…" I had forgotten to breathe. I couldn't finish the sentence. I felt dizzy. Through the bedroom window, I saw another truck pass on the road. A circus resembling the one that used to visit Øyerstad appeared out on the field. An ice covered freak show from a remote place on earth, or even beyond. A frozen nightmare with dancing snow clowns, like the skeleton in grandpa's picture. Bingo-Bob covered in ice and frozen blood. I wanted to shield my ears and scream as the music, that damn circus music made my brain vibrate. Louder and louder.

"M… Mo… Mom… there, there, there's something wro…" I stammered, spittle flying.

"Robert? I thought it was Fredrik. Why don't you go back to bed; it's not morning yet," she said, without looking at the clock.

Winter's cold tongues had found a way into the house. Ice crept along the parquet floor through the hallway, over the threshold and up over my feet. Nailed me to the floor. I was an ice statue locked in this moment, for eternity. Here and now, forever.

“Did you become a Spurs fan last night?” Her voice barely reached me through the sea of ice in my head. My brain creaked and cracked.

“Not tired, are you?” She furrowed her brow, as if trying to focus.

“Mom. There’s something wrong…”

“Did you wet yourself, Robert?”

“Fr… Fre… Fredrik,” I said, unable to move. I didn’t hear what she asked me.

“What are you talking about?” She sat halfway up in bed.

I trembled as I took a breath, focused for a second or more, and then it came out: “Mom! There’s something wrong with Fredrik!”

When she finally registered how I looked at her and what I had said, she shot out of bed. Her eyes widened, looking straight through me, through the wall, and into the bedroom—at Fredrik. As she dashed past me and out through the hallway, she was chalk white.

Her steps were first heavy and fast, then lighter and slower. Soon, a sound came from the bedroom that reminded me of something from *The Living Planet* with David Attenborough. A dying whale, or an elephant at one of their very special graveyards. Then something heavy fell onto the bedroom floor, and I didn’t need to see to know that it was Mom’s legs that had given out. I knew how she felt. We weighed just as much as the whales or the elephants.

Her scream sent vibrations through the air, and the ice growing in me cracked. I tried to take a step back, wanted to go to her. My cry froze in my throat, and my chin twitched as I tried to breathe. Convulsive sobs. Music from the imaginary circus: the organ, the clowns, the unicyclist. Laughter. Screams. The animals hissed and chirped. Bingo-Bob was coming.

I felt the vibrations of Dad's steps as he came up from the basement. He didn't see me; Mom's scream pulled him in. She was probably lying on the floor—in our bedroom, Fredrik's and my bedroom. Dad's sounds were more like those you make when you get hit in the diaphragm and lose your breath. Sucking and wheezing. Then it all went silent.

Is anyone there? Please. Mom? Can you come and get me? Someone? You have to help me.

The ambulance sirens mixed in with the madness in my head, outside my head, pulling me back to reality, slowly but surely. Still, even after I thought I had regained control, I could not move.

In the movie, Superman flew so fast around the Earth that time went backward. I couldn't fly, but maybe I could continue to stand still? Super-still. So still that the whole world would stop. So still that not just I, but the whole world would freeze. Then no one could move again. Ever.

8

Robert

Mist pressed the dirty snow towards the ground on the day of the funeral, Friday, January 5th, 1990. A orange glow bled from the streetlamps, like watercolours on a stained canvas. It was one in the afternoon. Anders and I sat in the back seat of the Beetle, and Fredrik did not sit between us. We approached the church. Springsteen, The Rolling Stones, and Nazareth, who often entertained us via the car's cassette player, were absent. They probably wouldn't entertain us again. Dad either didn't notice, or simply didn't care that the windshield wipers were on, even though it neither snowed nor rained.

Mom took a long time in the bedroom before we left that morning, so the parking lot outside the church was already full. We parked along the road a few hundred metres away and walked the last bit. Mom's shoes seemed almost impossible to lift, and Dad's coat pressed him relentlessly down towards the wet gravel.

Below the church, Kai stood by his car. The news of Fredrik's death must have been hard for him too, after all, he lost his daughter just over a month ago. Kai nodded to Dad, but only I nodded back. A glow fell from the cigarette hanging from his lip. Mom's gaze shifted from one to the other. She must have wondered what had happened between them.

"You can probably watch Tottenham on TV in heaven too. Rest in peace, dear Fredrik. From Kai and Hanne."

The Tottenham jersey I wore at my first funeral stood in stark contrast to everyone else's mourning attire, and I think

Fredrik would have found that quite cool. Fredrik and I believed in it. He would play at White Hart Lane, and I at Old Trafford. Seriously, everything was possible for the two of us. We had all the time in the world—until we didn't.

Tears soon spread like melancholic melodies over an instrumental version of *Wish You Were Here*. Church bells, marking the beginning of the ceremony, dutifully followed the organist's prelude. Mom wanted them to play that song. I think Dad liked it too, even if he didn't show it.

I turned around on the bench and saw all the weary eyes. Handkerchiefs, snotty noses, and tears. Children, adults, and the very old. Everyone cried. Except for me. I didn't want anyone to see me break down, to see me as weak. I didn't want their sympathy or their pity. This wasn't about me.

I'm strong for you today, like I should have been that night. I should have told Mom you were sick. I could have called Dr Larsen myself. Anything, and now you're gone. I hope you don't think it's all my fault.

The coffin in front of us bathed in a sea of floral wreaths, one of them from Kjell and his family. They sat four benches behind us. Kjell didn't see me looking at him. They cried too.

"We're sure you'll get free hot dogs in heaven too! Rest in peace, dear Fredrik. From Mari, Harald, Gustav, and Kjell."

Miss Alvhilde sat to the left of them. I wondered if her tears were genuine, or if she was sad because she had to be? Was it somehow part of her job description?

"In the event of the death of one of the school's students, as a representative of the educational institution and as part of its focus on building stronger belonging and trust among Øyerstad residents, you are to show your utmost sympathy by attending the deceased's funeral. You must show the highest degree of compassion, even if the deceased was a student you didn't sympathise with in your daily work."

Our eyes met, and I turned back to the priest and the coffin.

"You were a good boy. Rest in peace, dear Fredrik. From the staff of Øyerstad elementary school."

The priest spoke about God, Jesus, and the forgiveness of sins. Linn was also mentioned before he summed up Fredrik's life in a few short minutes. He said nothing of Julius and Colargol, about the treasure in the woods by the cabin, or Dad's charred rubber boots. Things that only Fredrik and I knew about. My little brother and I.

Outside, during the ceremony, the hounds of hell awakened and their froth lashed against the colourful, yet fragile windows. They scratched and gnawed at the church's outer walls. The closing ceremony by the gaping hole out in the graveyard was going to be cold and heavy.

On a couple of occasions, I made cheeky remarks about the priest, or the ceremony itself, to Fredrik next to me. I, the thinking Robert, knew well that he wasn't there. But my feelings, the autopilot, the habits and routines, they hadn't caught on that the world was a darker place now. A place with more space. A place with an empty seat.

Your brother is in that coffin over there, Robert. He can't answer you anymore. You see that coffin with those flowers, right?

"What did you say?" Anders whispered.

"Nothing. I just... Forget it". Anders wiped away tears with the handkerchief Mom handed him, and looked back towards the coffin.

"Thanks for everything, little brother and best friend! Anders and Robert."

Soon, the priest made the sign that activated the pallbearers. Anders and the others chosen got up and walked to the altar. Soon, they each grabbed a handle and lifted Fredrik's vessel, carrying it with them to the launch site. This was my little brother's last journey, into something completely unknown.

"I'm sorry, Robert, but the coffin is too heavy for you. It's better if the adults carry it," they said when I volunteered as a pallbearer earlier in the week. Clearly, they didn't have the same faith in the strength between brothers as the Hollies did when they sang, "He ain't heavy. He's my brother."

As my little brother's spaceship neared the exit of the church, a gust of wind flung open the doors with a crash. I hardly flinched as we walked single-file straight into the monster's gaping maw. I sang to myself, "Hey Satan. Payin' my dues. Playing in a rockin' band." Quoting "Highway to Hell" in church—Fredrik would have loved it.

After we crossed the main road, which was blocked by church servants in yellow vests for the occasion, my uncle slipped in the mud and lost his grip on the coffin handle. He took a couple of steps aside not to fall, and as a result, the other bearers lost their balance. On pure reflex, I lunged forward and grabbed the handle at the very back, the one no one was using. Together, we managed to keep the coffin upright. My uncle regained his footing and met my eyes, thanking me silently. I had prevented them from losing the coffin.

"Fredrik, you were always so kind, helpful, and happy. We will miss you. Greetings from aunts, uncles, cousins."

I gripped the handle as tightly as I could, lifting until my arm hurt. The coffin was heavy, like the adults had said. But my job was to carry my little brother through heaven and hell, and that's exactly what I was doing now. *Don't be afraid. I've got you. No matter what, we're always together, right? And if you can't rest where you are going, you can always come back.*

I was snapped out of my trance when my uncle put an arm

on my shoulder. "It's time to let him go, Robert. You've done your job. Your brother would've been proud of you. It's time to say goodbye."

We stood by the six-foot-deep hole, and the others had taken one or more steps away from the coffin. My hand, still gripping the handle, had turned pale and cramped. Soon, Mom also whispered in my ear, "You need to let go. You have to let Fredrik move on."

Rain lashed my face as my uncle pried my fingers off the handle. I was afraid my fingers would shatter. Soon, they guided me back to the others, and I stood between Mom and Dad. Anders stood right behind me, placing a hand on my shoulder—holding me up rather than pressing me down. The priest quickly finished the mandatory routines associated with this part of the ceremony. The spidery ice crystals crawling on our clothes were indifferent to the holy words that the wind whisked away.

"You are dearly loved and the void will be immense. Thank you for everything, dear little boy of ours! From Mom and Dad."

After the ceremony, our family gathered in the church hall, where they served roast beef sandwiches, soda, and coffee. My uncle sat with his head hung low, his finger wrapped in a blood-stained towel. He looked at me again. "You were strong, boy. Without you, we would have dropped the coffin. You saved us. Thank you."

The ice on our clothes melted quickly, creating small puddles on the linoleum floor. The atmosphere was initially hesitant, but then the "party" began. People soon gossiped and chatted about all sorts of things. They laughed as if they had forgotten why we were here. The scale of merriness shifted from funeral to wedding, baptism, or birthday in four point three seconds. Soon, it was only their clothes that revealed they were here for an unhappy occasion. Had they forgotten Fredrik already? Was this really how it was supposed to be during a memorial?

As all the adults, who were talking so loudly, poured themselves coffee, I wondered if it was some kind of magic potion. Perhaps it could chase away the cold that clung to me. And so, I had my very first cup of coffee, it didn't taste like Tropicana. I mean, how could they willingly drink that stuff? I barely managed to finish the first cup, but still I had a *refill*, as the adults neatly put it. The second cup possibly tasted a bit better. Caffeine was uncharted territory, and likely the reason for the increasing tingling in my body. After one roast beef sandwich, a soda, five cups of coffee, and a Danish pastry, I felt sick to my stomach. My head spun so badly that I had to grip the chair.

On a sofa at the other end of the room, Mom lay with her head in Grandma's lap. Grandma ran a hand through her hair while the other lifted the coffee cup to her wrinkled lips. Dad sat at a table farther away. Aunt Kari talked to him. He didn't respond. Dad's hair had turned from a light shade to entirely grey in a week. Behind them, Inger, an older cousin, laughed so hard that bits of the Danish pastry and coffee splashed across the tablecloth. The others at the table laughed too, along with her.

They better be talking about something funny Fredrik did.

Sugar and coffee surged in my stomach.

Grandpa got up from the table behind me as I ran towards the toilets in the hallway. I slammed the door shut and locked it. I never managed to lift the toilet lid before vomit erupted from me. Over the toilet, up the walls, and onto the floor. I let it out, pushing to expel every last drop, until I lay exhausted on the floor in a pool of vomit. My little brother's

Tottenham jersey was soaked in half-digested soda, coffee, Danish pastries, and bread. A design that would likely not be approved by the football club's design team or fans. All the actual shit, anxiety, and torment that I really wanted to throw up did not come out with the rest. I felt darker than ever when there was a bang outside the door. A bomb.

Dad

No one else reacted to the shadows that trailed Robert as he sprinted towards the toilet. Like black tentacles, they snaked forward in the parts of the room where the light didn't quite reach. I had seen the same with Fredrik. Yes, actually, it was a bit like that with everyone around me these days. Especially those I cared about. The shadows were particularly interested in them. That no one else seemed to see the same as I did, indicated that this was all in my head. That the shadows were a manifestation of my own wretched guilt, creeping and whispering in nooks and crannies among cobwebs and dust.

I stood up and followed Robert out to the corridor. Marianne, who was lying on the sofa with her head in her mother's lap, didn't see me.

Marianne, you should be lying in my lap right now. You should have found comfort with me, and I with you. But I can't give you that. I can't accept that. I don't deserve it. All of this is my fault.

Marianne wore the same tense expression she had by Fredrik's bed just over a week ago. Eyebrows furrowed and knitted together like a clenched fist in the middle of her forehead. Eyes bloodshot and barely visible behind pinched eyelids. Her mouth was a simple line beneath her nose. She wore a mask crafted from grief. The image of her hand in his would never fade. She, vibrant and full of life. He, pale and lifeless.

Sweat droplets balanced on my forehead when her scream first pulled me out of the nightmare and then out of bed that morning. The voices in my head, slowly fading as I stumbled up the stairs, had become part of the headache, anxiety, hangover, and all other damn things that weighed me down. The taste of spirits lingered in my mouth when I reached the hallway and saw Robert with his back to me. He stood in the doorway to our bedroom where Marianne and I once shared a bed. Her screams came from the boys' room. Before I remembered that Anders had spent the night at a friend's, I was afraid he would come running too. Thankfully, he was spared from seeing what I was about to see.

The shadows were, of course, there too—stronger and more alive than ever. They pulsed in and out of the corners, and I wanted to shout to Marianne, "Do you see them too?" But I didn't, and I even hesitated to enter the room. *It's just your conscience showing itself. Get in there now. Marianne needs you.*

The shadows receded as I entered the room, hiding in more natural places like under the bed and behind the wardrobe door. Marianne knelt by the bunk bed.

He's dead because of what we did. We've lost our little boy because I, we didn't... Pull yourself together, man! This has nothing to do with it. It's nonsense!'

My knees gave way, and my fall was halted by Robert's desk. Soon I sat on the floor, watching them. Marianne and our son. Only one of them moved. Only one made a sound.

I sat there, my head in my hands, until the wail of ambulance sirens broke the silence. I still don't know who called them. *All of this is my fault.*

Jens-August, a banker and the children's grandfather, was

heavy as he lunged at me from behind. We both slammed into the toilet door Robert had just closed behind him. On sheer reflex, I turned around and threw a punch at the one attacking me. A jolt went through my arm as I hit his left cheek. The damage from the punch was probably minimal, and he countered with his weight once more. Marianne and I often joked that he weighed as much as his fortune—and his fortune was substantial.

"You first steal my daughter, then you take her child away from her. What the hell is wrong with you?" he screamed. Like a madman.

In a way, it felt good. I could finally let my anger out. A much-needed vent for all the crap I carried within. And the pain? It was deserved.

"I've done everything I can for my children," I yelled. We danced around like two wild bucks, and soon we slammed into another wall deeper in the room. Then another wall where his head went straight through the plasterboard. He should be thankful that the walls in the church room weren't made of concrete like the vaults at his workplace.

"Everything? You've done everything? You haven't done a damn thing! We could have given the boy the best doctors and the best hospitals. You gave him Dr Larsen? Dr Larsen! How could you let it be up to him? A damn quack from a shit village full of yokels and inbreeding." His mouth spewed blood as he screamed at me. His breath smelled of chemicals, like rotten meat.

"Your money would never have made us happy, or healthy for that matter. Not even your own daughter wanted it! Do you hear me? We gave Fredrik all the help he could get."

Now it was raining blood over his face too. It came from my snarling mouth.

"Your pride killed the boy!" was the last thing the old pig

squeezed out before I hit him again, right across the mouth. Maybe it was bones in my knuckles that cracked, but more likely it was his teeth that gave in.

"Marianne didn't want your money. We didn't want it," I said, kneeling over him. "You have no damn idea what it's like to hide on the floor when the bailiff comes knocking. What it's like to ask your kids if they want to play the 'we're-not-home' game. 'Just lie down on the floor with us; let's see how quiet we can be.' Even after having to steal shoes for our kids, when I suggested asking you for money, Marianne refused. She'd rather steal bread from the store than ask you for a dime. Your money wouldn't have made us better people. It wouldn't have made us kinder or more loving. It wouldn't have saved Fredrik." I felt myself almost collapsing from exhaustion. "You miserable old man. We had love. We had everything we needed."

Marianne's voice was distant when I stood up and towered over her father. His shirt looked like a flag in the closing scenes of a World War II movie. Bloody and torn. Marianne's screaming, her crying, were louder than the others'. We were both trapped in this mess, all of us, and the worst part was that the old pig was right. Fredrik's death was my fault.

Part II

Darkness Descends

Hitra - 1972

Excerpt from the shelved manuscript: *The Witch of Mørkved, Death, and I - a Memoir by Robert Baastad.*

They couldn't foresee the consequences of what they were about to do. Was it really so bad, that they ran away that day? So bad that people had to die?

On a sea like shimmering silver foil, the boat bobbed just off Ramsøysundet, a narrow sound protecting the mainland from the ocean's waves. Deep inside the sound, under the gentle rays of the morning sun, lay the cabin they rented through Old-Gunnar at the garage in Øyerstad. He knew someone who knew someone, so they only paid five hundred kroner for the cabin and boat for a whole week. The perfect deal for three unemployed guys from Øyerstad.

The lines dangling from the deep-sea fishing rods, which were secured over the railing of the nineteen-feet-long boat, were designed for heavier fishing than what was being done that day. They preferred braided line over nylon because it didn't stretch at great depths. Even with two hundred metres of line extended, you could still feel the sinker as if it were just below the surface.

They used to say that no psychologist in the world could compete with a lukewarm beer in one hand, a cigarette in the other, and a fishing rod firmly planted between the legs. It didn't matter if you were sitting upright or lying on the bench with your legs dangling over the railing. All that mattered was that you gave the rod an occasional jerk, engaged in aimless chatter, and simply allowed yourself to be as you were. If you had asked any of them when they last showered, or changed underwear, the answer would have been, "Before I went to Hitra." When did you last brush your teeth? Same answer. Even time seemed irrelevant on these trips, as it never really grew dark in the evenings or during the night. None of them could tell what time it was that morning. These trips were therapy for their souls.

The small fishing boat didn't take them far out that day. If they'd leaned over the gunwale to look, they could have seen the crabs and sea stars at the bottom. It didn't matter; none of them were focused on fishing anyway. A real downer for the screaming seagulls that circled above the three unusually silent men in the boat.

Kai was the first to speak as he picked up a beer can from a previous fishing trip. "We should stay away for a while."

He wiped away coagulated fish blood and seaweed with a cloth before opening it. The can sighed heavily and fizzed over, but Kai didn't seem to even notice it.

"You sure?" Dad asked after Kai had emptied half the can in one gulp.

"Sure? The folks here are fucking insane," Kai said.

"Insane? Are you sure about that too?" Dad asked.

"You know as well as I do that she's lying."

"Maybe. But the timing fits pretty well. And… why would she lie about it?"

"She wants to get out of here. She's told us a hundred times—her father and all. As for the timing, well, it's more than—"

"The timing is damn good if you ask me," Petter said, who wasn't sleeping after all, so Dad handed him a clean beer can from his backpack.

"Nope. I think I'll wait a bit. Thanks anyway," Petter replied.

"Chicken? Come on, you pussy. Have a beer!" Kai looked at Petter with a mocking gaze before continuing. "Regardless of timing, or what's true or not, we can't—"

"We?" Dad looked at Kai, who shifted his gaze to the sea.

"We can't stay here any longer. Finish your drinks and reel in the lines," Kai said.

Dad halted the beer can before it reached his lips. "Are you serious? We can't leave now. We have several days left."

"I don't give a damn. Reel in the lines." Kai had that look again.

"You should talk to her." Petter spoke to Kai, but looked at Dad.

"Reel in the lines, I said! We have to get the hell out of here."

1

Early '90s

Mom

At Fredrik's funeral, it was as if shadows fell from the church ceiling, and circulated above his coffin. Later, they swirled around us in the fog outside in the graveyard, like ghosts from the many graves. As soon as the rain-covered coffin was in the ground, the shadows settled over me. At first, I thought they were figments of my imagination, a result of malnutrition and sleep deprivation. Those vague shapes led their own lives, moving slowly at first, but soon they spun faster and faster. Twisting into each other to become one entity. A spiral grew, not upward into the air, but downward into the ground, swallowing everything in its surroundings.

They're still here, the shadows, stronger than ever, and I stand on the edge. Up on the ridge of the roof. My bare toes are cramped against the wood. The wind pulls at my nightgown, and my hair sticks sideways across my face. Far below me, the spiral spins, an all-consuming hole in the ground. If I move, I fall. If I fall, I die.

The child beside me wasn't there a moment ago. At first, he resembles Anders, who through tear-filled eyes transforms into Robert. Robert wants to say something, but when I blink away the tears, it's Fredrik standing there.

Fredrik.

Believe me, I'm not dumb; I know my son is dead. Torn away from me, from us. Yet, in that moment, all I can think is that he's alive after all. That a miracle has occurred. That everything before was just a bad dream. *At last, I am awake again and my son lives!* I grab the collar of his sweater so tightly that the veins bulge on my arm. We need to get down from the roof. I must tell the others that we've been blessed with a gift. A second chance.

As I try to take a step back, my foot bumps into something invisible. A glass wall of some kind is preventing me from getting down from the roof and taking my son to safety. I search with my arms, but there's nothing to hold on to. My body slowly tilts forward.

"Mom?" The wind carries Fredrik's tears like a harbinger of rain onto my arm. "I'm scared."

"Don't cry, my boy."

"Mom, I don't want to fall."

"Don't worry, darling. I won't let go of you. Shall we play a game?"

"A game? Mom, I—"

"Let's play Freeze, and see who can stand still the longest. Just you and me. We start right away. One, two—"

"Mama, I can't—"

"Three!"

He falls silent. For a short while. "Can't we go to bed? It's so windy."

"We can't go to bed. If you want to see Anders and Robert again, you have to hold on, okay? You have to be strong, like your Dad. You're a master at balancing; I know that. I've seen you at school."

"Mama? Don't let go of me."

"My darling, I'll never let go."

"But you—"

"Relax, I will... Fredrik?"

The expression on his face as he falls over the edge is more one of bewilderment and surprise than of fear and dread. “You pushed me, Mom! You pushed…”

“No, I will never…” *What is going on?* I’m no longer holding onto his collar. Instead, I find myself clutching something white made of plastic—a small white box with contents I know all too well. A pillbox, offering safety and peace. I look at it. Hate it. Love it. Then my gaze shifts back to my son. What the hell have I done?”

“Mama!”

I let go of the box, and it seems to hover for a moment before nearly freezing in mid-air. Time itself has slowed. The hole beneath us churns sluggishly, consuming everything in its wake. Time is shattered and gravity broken as I reach out for my son with my fingers, powerless. He’s falling ever so slowly backward, yet I still can’t hold him. The fear in his eyes. It’s all my fault. Shadows, like black tongues, move from the wound in his foot, up through his leg, stomach, and chest. He lifts his arms and claws himself bloody as the shadows reach his face.

“Mama, you let them take me. You pushed me.”

“No! I… didn’t mean to.”

“It’s your fault, Mama. It’s your fault that I—”

“Fredrik, you were sick. It’s all that damn cancer’s fault.”

“I didn’t have cancer, you know that!”

The wind pulls at me again as the world returns to its regular speed. Then he falls quickly. Down towards the hole, which again spins, gapes, snarls, and roars. Into the hole. Gone. Forever.

Should I jump after him? Maybe I can catch him. We can fall together, Fredrik and me. I don’t want him to be alone. He’s just a kid. My Fredrik. I should jump! No, wait. Think about Anders and Robert; they need a mom—maybe now more than ever. And what about Dad? Maybe he needs someone too.

Fredrik. No, I can't jump. My family needs me.

My chain of thoughts is interrupted by a scream. I turn around without a thought to keep my balance. "MARIANNE!" A stench of decay washes over me, as I see the heavily deformed face. It's reminiscent of a pair of inflated pig lungs I once saw in school—a balloon of veins with a mouth as bottomless as the hole beneath me. The eyes are barely discernible beneath the skinless mass. A wave of bottomless grief engulfs me as the figure stands motionless on the edge, while I too fall. Into the darkness.

The devout people at the chapel believed that these dreams were the work of the devil and part of a grieving process that would last for a long time. They said things would improve someday, but first, you had to go through all the phases in a year, experiencing everything for the first time without the one you love. First, you have to live through a day unlike any you've ever experienced. It's the first day of life after losing your child. Breakfast is a forgotten word. Lunch? Don't think so. And dinner? Dinner is something other people have. You don't do much that day—or the days that follow. They come and go. Dressed in grey.

A week goes by, and you realise that nothing will ever be the same. When another week has passed, the others around you have moved forward. Baby Steps. They have that chocolate they crave and play a song that makes them feel better. Gradually they speak more than they whisper. You, however, faint for the first time due to a lack of everything your body needs to keep running. Sleep, food, rest, peace of mind, love, and all that.

After weeks comes a month. Then comes your lost child's first birthday. He is still missing. April 18, 1990. That day, you lie in bed and cry while others light candles by his tombstone.

Faith, hope, and love are engraved on the stone, but you find none of that. The birthday card you've written, and placed in a plastic bag to guard against rain, is never laid by the grave. With time, it disappears into a drawer, never to see the light of day again.

After his birthday comes a new day, a new week, and a new month. A new holiday is to be celebrated. The first Christmas, you get out of bed, but you don't cook. You barely get dressed. You do not respond to the smiles from your other children, from your husband, even if you'd like to. You've lost that ability. Your unwashed hair hangs in thick strands down your face. That smell of sweat must be from you.

Credit to those up at the chapel, though. They were right, everything is hardest in the beginning. And over time, the burden gradually lightens as one year turns into two, and then into even more years. While it never becomes easy, astonishingly, your zest for life does strengthen with time.

According to the report that finally arrived from Fredrikstad Hospital, my son had an extremely aggressive and rare form of cancer. It likely began as a lymphoma on the outside of the stomach and then spread to the lymph nodes. The same document also stated that there were contradictions between Dr Larsen's conclusions and the development of the cancer during the period when he examined Fredrik in the winter of 1989. Dr Larsen's accounts showed no signs of illness following the examinations he conducted. Well, apart from the accident with the nails in his foot, but those wounds had healed without complications. Nor did Dr Larsen's blood tests show, in the best or worst case, any irregularities. This was also verified by experts at Askim Hospital.

The report from Fredrikstad Hospital, on the other hand,

concluded that the cancerous tumour must have been so extensive that the patient should not have been alive when the local doctor treated him. The discrepancies were impossible to explain. At the time, I too believed that Dr Larsen was to blame for the cancer never being discovered.

"Fredrik (10) died as a result of malpractice by a local doctor." The picture the local newspaper printed for the story was taken at Grandma and Grandpa's cabin many summers earlier. That day when we swam down by the cliffs was special. His laughter was light, and his smile radiated childish joy.

Dr Larsen withdrew from his job after the uproar, despite never being convicted of having mistreated Fredrik, or any other patients. For me, it didn't matter; our boy was gone regardless.

2

Robert

As the '90s unfolded, elementary school in Øyerstad morphed into middle school in Skjønnsund. The first couple of years passed by quietly—they're nothing but a blur in my mind. By the time I reached ninth grade, the writing desk in my bedroom had become my confidant during late nights and evenings. The bunk bed was still the same, and Fredrik's bed was always neatly made up with Tottenham bed sheets. They didn't need making every day like mine—not that I really made my bed either. Fredrik no longer talked in his sleep while I sat at the desk. I had turned fifteen. Fredrik would have been fourteen.

I didn't draw much after Fredrik passed away. I had no one to impress, no one to share my stories with. I mean, who would encourage me to submit them to magazines or to show them off to the world? Who would tell me that I could become a famous artist one day?

Instead, I began to write—poems, songs, and stories. I made multiple drafts of what I hoped would become world-famous novels. I wrote about living in a vacuum, in isolation and darkness. About circuses. About demons. About being haunted by death and sorrow. Occasionally, I also wrote about love, but rarely about happiness. Lonely wolves howling in the night, bleeding hearts, and rivers of tears became recurring themes. Jon Bon Jovi would probably have been proud of some portions of my lyrics. However, the first text I wrote was a poem for Fredrik, even though he would have probably preferred a hard rock song.

My Little Brother
by Robert Baastad

In silence, we linger, side by side,
may this path to home, be your simple guide.
Always there is someone. Always someone new.
Always someone you might know, emerging into view.

A step is taken forward, a journey just begun,
his story's written shortly, his final days are spun.
Always there is something. Always teary eyes.
Always someone has to go, always someone dies.

Now I'll tell you his story, all I need is time.
A story built with laughter, beyond the perfect rhyme.
If you listen well, to what I say,
New memories will find you, day by day by day by day.

I speak for you now, we're no longer, side by side,
Darkness growing thicker, it was a joyful ride.
Always there is someone. Always someone new.
Always someone has to go, emerging into blue.

Perhaps the urge to create came from a need to prove that I was still alive. If I created things, then it must mean I was still here. If I too were to die, which I assumed could happen at any time, I had something to leave behind. A song, a story, a poem, or even one of my old drawings. Something that could be picked up and looked at after I was gone. Like Fredrik's special assignment, the one about Arnold, the Terminator. Like the letter he wrote.

I bought my first guitar after cleaning toilets at the retirement home for fourteen hours a day, all summer long.

It was a crappy summer job for sure, and the pay was bad. However, I did get paid, for the first time in my life. My well-earned money introduced me to a new six-stringed friend—a Fender by Squier (a cheap Fender copy), which came with a rattling Roland amplifier. I wasn't sure whether the amplifier was broken, or if it should have sounded the way it did. I learned to like it, though. From the library, I borrowed—and stole—books about learning to play the guitar. I taught myself chords, blues scales, and pentatonic riffs. That autumn, I didn't do much else but play on what Kjell called my "Øyerstad fiddle". I eventually became quite good, and we dreamed of starting a band, Kjell and I. We wanted to be famous.

It was winter the day I opened the window and placed the amplifier on the windowsill. With the volume on my amp cranked up to ten (it didn't go to eleven), I played the living hell out of it. The racket must have gone on for an hour, long enough for the glass of water on my desk to freeze solid. Had anyone seen or heard me, they would have thought I was insane. But no one seemed to notice. Nobody saw me. Nobody heard me. No one was outside. No one was home.

Even when there was actually someone at home, in our house, things weren't as they used to be. Not even the most ingrained rituals survived. Saturdays at 4:00 p.m. I set my pen down on the desk and noted that it was almost time. Football and pizza.

The TV wasn't on when I entered the living room, even though it was minutes before the match was set to start. A sweet smell lingered in the room. It was not pizza. Alcohol and cigarettes

"Hasn't Anders arrived yet?" I asked, glancing at Mom and Dad who were sitting at opposite ends of the sofa. There was no conversation between them. No music or radio playing.

"Haven't seen him," Mom replied, staring blankly ahead.

After Fredrik passed away, Anders largely disappeared, too. He was rarely home after that. You could say I lost both my brothers at once—one to death, the other to grief.

I thought about asking if we could order pizza, but refrained. Instead, I picked up the remote and turned on the TV. United was playing Tottenham, and the match had started. Dad poured himself another drink, not stopping until liquid spilled onto the table. Mom took a sip of her beer. No one said anything.

It was nothing I had planned, but after a few minutes, I went back to my room and put on Fredrik's Tottenham jersey. It was a bit tight. Back in the living room, I sat down in front of the TV—a further attempt to reach out to their shut-off faces. Mom said nothing as she got up and left. Dad stayed a little longer before he sighed, "That was fucking unnecessary, Robert." He left the room, walking in the opposite direction from Mom.

Shortly afterward, Mom returned, but she simply picked up her beer bottle and retreated back into the kitchen. She didn't see me cry. I heard the flick of her lighter as she lit up another cigarette. I watched the match alone—without pizza, without cola, without a family. Tottenham won 1-0, and later that evening, Mom announced that she and Dad were going to separate.

Anders finally arrived. He said nothing about the match and barely greeted Mom, who had returned to the living room sofa. Dad wasn't home.

"I didn't mean to get upset, I'm sorry," she apologised. "That jersey, it..." She lit a new cigarette. She held the first puff in her lungs for what felt like an eternity. She'd worn the same t-shirt yesterday, and the day before that.

"Dad and I are getting divorced," she finally said. No one

responded, so Mom continued, "I'm moving into an apartment in the house of fishmonger Olsen, across the road from his shop in Skjønnsund." It won't be long. He's promised I can rent it cheaply. You guys will stay here with your father for a while. At least until..."

She grabbed a beer bottle from last night and shook it. Empty. She reached for another one, but it too was empty.

"Fuck…" she whispered, continuing to lift the bottles from the table. By the time she got to the seventh or eighth bottle, she found one that was only half-empty. Her smile was as thin as bleach.

"It's probably best if you stay in Øyerstad." She took a sip from the lukewarm beer.

"Yes, I... we think it's best that way." This time the smoke left her lungs through her nose.

"You'll come to me every other weekend, so we'll still spend some time together."

Anders picked up the TV remote, changed the channel, and turned up the volume. The evening news—definitely not his favourite program.

Mom's hand was cold when she took mine, but it felt good anyway. "It will be ok," she said, addressing Anders as well, though he didn't look at her.

"You don't have to get divorced. Can't you work it out?" I said.

"I don't think..." she stopped mid-sentence.

"Don't think what?" I asked.

"I don't believe..." Her whisper was so faint I barely heard what she was saying. She glanced at the wall behind me. I turned around but saw nothing there.

Mom

They say that good relationships are built on communication, respect, and understanding of each other as individuals and as a couple. Dad and I had all of that. We shared information with each other—just ordinary, practical things. "Remember to take out the trash tomorrow, and don't forget that fishmonger Olsen is coming on Friday. We're having cod for dinner."

We talked about our feelings and often said "I love you", truly meaning it. When we were sad or felt down, we shared it with each other. We talked about us, about what we could do better for each other. We had plans, together. Maybe we weren't perfect, but we were proud of what we had built together. Relationships like ours, what we had, they never fall apart. We had everything under control, until we didn't anymore.

The decline began that night when Kai and Dad made a racket outside the house. That weekend they went hunting. Dad never was the same again. And then, when Fredrik passed away, everything simply collapsed. Dad more or less vanished into his work, even sleeping at the apartments in Oslo. I took to sleeping on the living room sofa, drawn to wake up closer to the bottles on the table. In the end, maybe my father was right; perhaps I should have taken his money...

My mother, father, and I may have been the first outsiders, specifically from the posh side of Oslo, to build a cabin so deep in the woods of Indre Østfold. Øyervika was, after all, fantastic, with small sandy beaches and cliffs leading down to the Lake Øyeren. An occasional beaver would fell a tree while perch, pike, and roach nibbled diligently on bait and hook. Yet, I hated Øyerstad, and my father, who forced me there. I loathed his Porsche and the constant stench of champagne. I detested lobster, scallops, and all that crap. As for Mom, I suppose I hated her mostly because she was married to my father. Actually, I hated just about everything during that period of my life.

The day my parents announced the "big news" was no different from other Thursdays on the finer side of town. Father, Jens-August, had opened a bottle of red wine that Mom fetched from the wine cellar beneath our house. Frédéric Chopin's "Waltz in E Major" flowed through the living room. Welcome to our home; it's Amarone Thursday. Mom's anxious eyes were in place as she buzzed around, straightening things that weren't askew. She always did that when there was something unsettling afoot.

I struggled to focus, searching for a headache tablet—or maybe eight. By this time, I should've already been to school and back, especially since father was home. He was a director at the bank, a fact he relished sharing with anyone crossing his path.

"Marianne, would you come into the kitchen? We're going to hold an extraordinary family meeting." Father's lips met the expensive crystal as he sipped wine that surely cost more than an average monthly salary in Øyerstad. He swirled the glass a bit, as if he could discern whether the wine was good or not. "Lovely secondary bouquet," he exclaimed. My God, what a poser.

"A family meeting today? Why? I got home last night, didn't I? I can't deal with this bullshit right now." Despite my objections, I appeared in the kitchen (the headache tablets were in there). Once they'd decided on a family meeting, that's what happened, no questions. My protests were a waste of energy. My father always got his way.

"Oh, a *whole* glass of wine? Not the usual half? Serious

matters coming up?" I glanced towards Mom, who was also swirling her glass. I suspected she didn't even like wine and felt like shouting it at her.

"Father has decided that we are going to make some changes. Right, Jens? He has..."

"Enough!" He cleaved Mom's sentence in two. "You can't continue this nonsense. It's not proper."

"Not proper? For whom? Ah, you're talking about 'family honour' again? That I'm not behaving the way your money wants me to?"

"We... you... have a responsibility: to uphold our family's reputation, our dignity. Call it 'family honour' if you like."

Family honour? What bloody honour? We don't have anything like that. None of us do, not my father, nor my mother, not me. Not our fancy friends at the Hotel Continental. Caviar and lobster. I mean, who the hell serves truffle dreams to a seven-year-old who wants a Kinder Egg? Honour? We have money!

This was exactly what my rebellion was about. The upturned noses, the cigars, the injustice. Should being born on the "right" side make me better than everyone else? We were a bunch of over-consuming jerks, ignorant of what was happening in the real world around us.

"Were you at school today?" Mom asked.

"I've been sleeping."

"Overslept?" Father straightened up and tilted his head back so that he could look down at me. I noticed drops of red wine in his grey, well-trimmed moustache. He had more hair in his nose than on his head. "You should have been at school; registration was today."

"That school is not for me. Those aren't my people."

"Your people? I, uh, we, are not paying for you to be with 'your people'. We're paying for you to get a proper education."

"Sorry, 'my poor people...', that's what you call them during your gentlemen's nights at Theatercafeen, right?"

"My dear, I don't understand why you want to go to that school. You'd rather go to a regular public high school? They simply don't have the resources to provide an education good enough for youngsters who want to go far in life," Mom said.

"That school is good enough for me. Regular people are good enough for me. A regular high school is good enough for me!"

Truth be told, he had a point when he claimed that the public school system was the source of my troubles. That bothered me because it was indeed in a regular high school that things went south. I found myself among the radicals, the far-left outliers. People weren't wrong when they called us punks, anarchists, or communists. Many were squatters, and we'd happily throw eggs at the police near embassies and shout insults outside the parliament building. I smoked weed and got wasted, mainly because the upper crust said I shouldn't. That I had to consider my family's reputation.

"You're going to a private school. It's the best school in the city. You start tomorrow."

"That's absolutely out of the question."

"It doesn't matter what you want."

"Yes, it..."

"We've bought a cabin in a place called Øyerstad, and we're going there on weekends from now on." Mom squeezed the words in between us.

"Øyerstad? Are you going there on weekends?" I sensed some hope.

"*We* are going there on weekends," father said, emphasising the first word.

"What the hell are you talking about?"

Red wine splashed out of Mom's mouth as I swore at the

bank director to his face. I was also shaking, but not because of what I said. I felt sick from all of it.

"Look at you, Marianne. You're not doing well. You have to stop taking... whatever it is you're taking. It's not good for you. Drugs have no place in this family. We've established that multiple times."

"I haven't taken anything. Not since..."

"No? Look at you; you're pale, red-eyed, trembling!"

"Yes, and you're slurring your words, Marianne, don't you think?" Mom's voice was puny, and she looked like a mouse in her chair.

"You sound like a junkie!" The old man shot back, and I feigned shock.

"Junkie? What the hell are you talking about?"

"We're going to the cabin tomorrow. After you've been to school."

"No, we're not. I'm meeting Morten."

"We're leaving for Øyerstad after you've been to school tomorrow." Father gulped down the rest of his Amarone and set his glass down so hard that the wine Mom was sipping spilled across the table. He shot her a malevolent glance too. He probably wanted to say something about not wasting precious drops, but he remained silent.

It should be said that Øyerstad wasn't as bad as I wanted it to be. My hatred slowly softened and soon shifted towards the other end of the spectrum, towards love. After all, it was more sustainable and better for my health. Sounds hippie-ish, right? That's fine, because, strictly speaking, I was a hippie at the time.

Øyerstad perhaps saved my life back then, and later it gave me the love of my life. That it was just a fleeting stop in a land of happiness, I didn't know at the time.

The "Beetle Gang" (as in Volkswagen) in the village had a

fondness for moonshine and the Camping Girls who, until we came along, had monopolised their attention. With my 1.68 metres, blond curls, and fairly shapely figure, the locals claimed I was the most beautiful Cabin Girl in the market. That I was also the first and only one didn't bother me much. Cabin Girls were the new moonshine.

Dad, as everyone called him, was quite stylish as he buzzed around in his Beetle (which was built for smaller guys than him), often with a splash of liquor in his system. He talked about fishing trips to Hitra and how to brew proper moonshine.

My father was not impressed by Dad's cigarettes or his tight jeans with flares. My old man hated the Hep Stars and Pink Floyd. I, on the other hand, loved that music. Especially 'Wish You Were Here", which must have been released a year after the cabin in Øyervika was completed.

"Dad? What kind of nickname is that? Is he already a father? Is he able to care for you? What do his parents do for a living? Potato farmers? How is a kid from such a family supposed to support his own?" My father's voice squeaked like air leaving a balloon as he criticised Dad and the locals of Øyerstad. I realised I didn't hate him anymore, my father. He was pathetic, trying to lock me away like I was his Rapunzel.

In September 1975, I became the mother to a wonderful boy: Anders! His skin was velvet against my lips. One first goodnight kiss turned into an infinite number of others. When he smiled for the first time—eyes so innocent and dependent. He needed me, my best self, and I wanted to give him everything. Every touch extinguished a bit of the ugly fire that burned within me. Soon, there was nothing left but hope and love. First Øyerstad, then Dad and soon Anders gave me all that I wanted and needed.

You could never get Dad out of Øyerstad. So, moving to

Oslo was out of the question. Not many years after I arrived in the village with my hatred, I settled there permanently. Voluntarily and full of love.

Dad's parents halved their potato field so we could build next to them. A free plot helped a lot, and we barely had time to put the key in the door of our new home before Anders was born at Askim hospital. The house was relatively large, and we, of course, wanted more children running around on the parquet. More love. We had become addicted.

Still, it took three years before Anders got a little brother, Robert. Fearing it would take just as long again, we didn't waste any time. Only a year and a half later, Fredrik arrived. The family was complete. We named the house "Gledesbo" (House of Joy) with a simple toast in moonshine. The name fit well in the beginning, but considering everything that happened later, we might as well have named it "Helvetesbo" (Hellhouse) right away.

Robert

Mom had been quiet for a few minutes before I finally asked, "Are you okay? You're shaking."

She eventually answered, "Yeah, I'm fine." She paused again. "It's a bit much right now. Would you grab me a beer from the fridge, please?"

"Sure." I got up and headed towards the kitchen just as Anders changed the channel in the living room. I recognised the soundtrack from *Poltergeist* immediately. Carol Ann and that clown in the chair. They still scared the crap out of me.

3

The Circus

The circus tent stood heavy in the mud, its entrance curtains swaying gently, as if the organ music wafting through was a cat slipping past. The cadences crept beyond the ticket booth and along the wooden walls of the stalls, which stood in a row like the teeth in a monster's maw. The muffled tones didn't invigorate or colour the scene. The overpowering smell of excrement dominated everything.

Kai remained pale behind the cardboard backdrop as water streamed down from the lantern above him. Jungle-Jim was crushed by the truck, over and over again. Linn continued buying new raffle tickets from the duo at the Wheel of Fortune stall, still winning nothing. The Witch of Mørkved and Death had never been the jolliest couple around, but now they seemed paler than before. Dirty, damp, and bloated—as if they were absorbing the mire and moisture from the ground.

The cauldron must have been five times larger than Death's head by now. It should have fallen off or pushed him into the ground long ago. His frail body could not possibly hold it up. So for the first time, I saw the iron chain. It shot up like a spear from the nape of his neck, passing straight through the roof of the stall and disappearing into the empty void far above us. Something was different. I got this feeling that something was off-balance. As if something from the outside was intruding into my most personal space. Something beyond my control.

Further in, to the left at the boundary between light and dark, stood Bingo-Bob. A piece of Fredrik's torn face dangled from his jaws.

Øyerstad, 1985

Robert

You know the kind of summer day you think of when you say, "Everything was better back then." You scarcely knew what a worry was, and the sun stood high in the sky. Shorts were your only defence against the spray of water from the sprinkler. Death and the Witch of Mørkved were nowhere near. Momentarily out of our minds. A beautiful day.

Mom, Dad, and the other adults laughed and told tall tales, the mood lifting proportionally to the growing number of beer bottles on the patio table. We kids ate ice cream and drank Racing Cola straight from the bottle. Yet again, dinner and a party were in full swing at Kjetil and Torill's house, Guro's parents, who lived in one of the houses furthest up on Kirkeåsen. To the east, one could glimpse Lake Øyeren beyond the fields and forests, and to the west, the view stretched over Øyerstad. Down at the Haugen field, workers at the newly arrived circus were diligently preparing everything for the first show. From up on the hill, it looked like a genuine little flea circus. Mom had promised us that we'd attend one of the shows while it was in town.

Guro's dad looked much like a barbecue sumo wrestler, somewhat reminiscent of John Candy. He kept checking the heat on his colossal grill. The folds of his neck glistened above his translucent t-shirt. As the smell of steaks, summer chops, sausages, and corn began to spread, no one cared about his sweat sizzling when it rained onto the charcoal. His wife, his female counterpart, handled the sides and kept things simple. "The one with chives is so delicious," she declared as the plastic tub of potato salad landed heavily on the Respatex table.

Guro sat at the end of the table, drawing. I wondered if her parents ate all her food, for she wasn't particularly hefty. She sat there and didn't mean anything special to me. That would all be flipped upside down in about half an hour. One of the worst, and at the same time, one of the best experiences of my life was about to unfold.

Dinner was consumed well before the sun was set to descend from its throne up in the sky. The adults were enjoying themselves, and so were we kids. During the meal, Torill handed Dad a clear bottle to make a "drink to go with the food."

She herself filled a kitchen glass from a bottle labelled "Campari." Anders glanced up from his *Transformers* comics every once in a while, helping himself to the feast. Guro kept drawing.

"Have I ever told you about the time we tried to have a child?" Torill was already deep into her glass. "Yes, before you, my darling," she said, patting Guro on the head, making the flesh on her forearms wobble.

"You've mentioned it," Mom said, laughing. The other adults joined in.

"We really wanted a proper child, even though we already had Terminator." She blew a flying kiss that took a scenic route around the corner of the house, down the stairs past the flower beds, across the courtyard, and over to the tree where their monstrous dog was chained.

"You know what? We trained every single day. Kjetil gave his best, for sure"

"That's right. And not only did we train—my God, Torill stood on her head too. Can you imagine? It's not easy getting that body to stand upside down against a wall," Kjetil winked at his wife.

"Yeah, not that I understood what good that would do," Torill added. They all laughed again. Every single one of them.

"But, despite all the effort, no eggs appeared in our nest"

"So, we went to see Dr Larsen, and he didn't really find anything wrong either. At least not initially."

"Except that he said we looked a bit… well-fed."

"He wondered if weight might be a factor, yes," Torill chimed in.

"But my guys are in order," Kjetil said, looking down at his pants, dropping a piece of potato salad from his mouth.

I thought to myself that he probably hadn't seen "his guys" down there in quite a while.

"The problem was something else," Kjetil said.

"So what was the problem?" Dad chimed in, as if he had never heard the story before.

"I WAS STILL A VIRGIN!" Torill shouted, causing Campari to spurt from her nose. Laughter rippled around the table. Guro put on her pink headphones.

"We apparently had a slight contact problem," Kjetil finally said dryly. "Despite diligent training, I never quite made it to the finish line."

"I tried to lose weight; we tried to lose weight, probably for about a week. But we quickly got a hankering for a BBQ," Torill said, piling another sausage onto her plate, topping it with a scoop of potato salad.

"You're probably still a virgin," Kjetil said, and Dad laughed so hard that his drink splashed over his plate.

"Thank goodness they can fix things like that in Denmark. Sausages, beer, and test tubes. We like that. Right, Guro?" Guro continued to draw. "And then, of course, we have Terminator," Torill added, giving Kjetil a kiss on the cheek that left a good helping of mustard and potato salad behind.

Later, we collected the leftovers of the meal into a plastic bowl. Fredrik and I were given the honour of feeding the monster. Mom always reiterated the rules; she couldn't help it.

"You do not go up to Terminator. Stop at the stump and throw the food from there. Okay? You do not even attempt to pet him. Stay at the boundary."

We had heard the rules many times and adhered to them. Although it was exciting to feed the dog, to watch him gnaw and crunch bones, we had respect for this four-legged not-quite-man's-best-friend. Mom had naturally informed us of the consequences of falling into the claws of a Doberman of this calibre. He wasn't the size of a car, as Mom claimed, but these stories did have a tendency to exaggerate a bit.

New waves of laughter followed us from the other side of the house. We approached the boundary by the stump. Between the tree and the dog, the chain was stretched tight, possibly on the verge of breaking. The face of the canine was taut, and his ears pointed towards us. Bulging muscles overlapped each other beneath the fur. Teeth gleamed beneath his lips, and he growled softly. If Satan had a dog, it would be this one. Minus the chain around its neck, of course.

The area between the stump and the two metres leading up to the dog was no man's land. Just like Mom had instructed, we always threw the food from there. The first chop landed well within Terminator's territory. The rumble from deep within the dog's stomach increased in volume as he opened his jaws and sank his teeth into the meat. Bone cracked. The second chop disappeared even faster than the first.

On the third throw, things went wrong. Fredrik miscalculated. He launched a sausage that landed in the no man's land. No matter how eager the dog was, he couldn't reach it, and he didn't like that one bit.

Fredrik looked at me first, then at the sausage, and then back at the monster. What if the dog managed to tear up the tree, break free, and attack?

"Forget it," I said, throwing a new piece well within the dog's reach. Then everything happened at once. The chain fell to the ground as Terminator chased after the piece I'd thrown, and Fredrik took two to three quick steps into the forbidden zone. Just as he picked up the sausage and was about to throw it into enemy territory, he tripped and fell flat on his face.

The adults laughed again, far away. Maybe Dad was telling the story about the time Kjetil tried his car (sumo wrestlers and VW Beetles are a problematic combination). Someone shouted "CHEERS!" as the frothing jaws turned towards us. The sausage was hardly the target as the monster lunged towards Fredrik with his jaws wide open.

For once, I reacted quickly, lunging forward as the bowl of food scraps flew through the air. Before it hit the ground, and before the adults had ridden out their last wave of laughter, I grabbed Fredrik by the scruff of his neck. He was heavy, but I had temporary super-strength, and hurled him to the side. He landed safely beyond no man's land just as I swung my right fist through the air. I struck the attacking dog on the side of the head, near the ear, but not hard enough to deter him from making me his new target. Without hesitating, I swung my fist once more towards the dog, who was now lunging at me, mouth wide open. This time, I hit the beast in the eye. The animal howled, and I hoped it was from pain as I pressed on, feeling my thumb grow warm and wet all the way to my palm. We rolled around in the gravel, Terminator and I. My grip was locked, and it would stay that way until the adults arrived. Terminator was not going to touch my little brother.

When we finally stopped, we lay still, both of us. The dog had a gaping hole where his left eye should have been. My thumb was dislocated after having spun several rounds deep within the monster's skull. It didn't particularly hurt. Adrenaline probably spared me most of the pain.

Mom, Dad, and the rest of the gang finally came running, horrified. But when they saw that Fredrik had only minor scrapes, and that I was more or less whole, their mood improved. I had saved my little brother and killed a Doberman with my bare hands. The adults couldn't praise my heroic efforts enough. Word spread. I became a local celebrity, received a medal at school, and even got a full-page feature in the local paper.

No. Unfortunately, that's not how it went down. There was no fight. No escape. When I should have saved my little brother, I didn't lift a finger. My blood retreated towards the most vital organs, protecting me against an impending attack. Protecting me! Not Fredrik. It wasn't even me who was being attacked.

A groan escaped Fredrik as Terminator's jaws clamped over his face, tossing him to the ground like a ragdoll. There was no fight. Fredrik offered no resistance. He simply lay on his back, trembling, his arms limp at his sides. The monster's jaws were clamped over his face, like a gas mask with teeth. Fredrik soon stopped shaking, but Terminator did not release his grip. Growling.

Mom's scream pierced through me, even though my skin felt as hard as armour. The ground vibrated beneath Kjetil's footsteps. Blood oozed thickly where the dog's jaws were latched onto Fredrik's face. Perhaps the hellhound thought it was too easy, or maybe he was just asserting his dominance when he jerked my brother's head. Sporadic spasms pulsed through Fredrik's body, and his skin split near his left ear. For the first time, I saw human flesh and bones. His face began to detach from his skull.

Kjetil finally arrived, grasping Terminator's jaws to pry them open. At the same time, Dad raised an iron shovel above his head. He swung it with remarkable precision, striking Terminator squarely across the neck. After a muted "clonk", which must have instantly snapped the dog's neck, the creature slumped to the ground. The monster lay on Fredrik's belly. Kjetil still held onto the jaws even after they released their grip on my brother's face. I stood in the eye of the storm, doing nothing to save my little brother.

Fredrik was quiet at first. A long time passed before he finally cried. Before he finally screamed in pain. A good sign. Dad, who had been drinking quite a lot, didn't hesitate to fetch the car. Alongside Mom, he carried Fredrik towards the backseat. They left behind a trail of blood. Mom sat in the back with Fredrik; his face seemed to hang loosely on one side. Dad jumped in behind the wheel. I think Mom yelled to Kjetil, Torill, or Anders that they should watch over me, but that might be something I've invented afterward. Kjetil and Torill sat beside Terminator's body and cried. The blood on their shoes was not from the dog.

Despair pulled me towards the precipice. Just millimetres from the edge, seconds before I would plunge into madness, I was unexpectedly pulled back. I didn't see her approaching, but when she took my hand, she filled me with enough strength to resist jumping off the cliff and into the abyss. Maybe there was still some kind of hope? Some kind of relief.

Standing still, facing her weeping parents and the lifeless monster, I experienced bottomless terror and overwhelming love simultaneously. Guro held my hand.

4

Back to the '90s

Robert

After the divorce, Mom moved to Skjønnsund, which, in addition to Øyerstad, wasn't exactly the centre of the universe. Geographically, it was a little over ten kilometres away. It seemed many small towns suffered the same fate throughout the '90s. As for Øyerstad, both the post office and the bank relocated towards Skjønnsund, wanting to establish themselves in more central areas.

The municipality spokespersons used words like "efficiency" and "centralization". As commercials appeared on TV and *Mortal Kombat* and the *Super Nintendo* replaced prayers to the ones above, the singing at the prayer house gradually faded. Winter darkness swallowed the aroma of coffee and waffles, while paint peeled off the church walls. The kiosk was torn down, and Nina started working behind the cash register at the store. Meat Loaf sang about doing anything for love but not that one particular thing.

Mom turned up the volume in the Volkswagen as we skidded back and forth along the snow-covered road leading up to Lake Mørkved. A snow plough had recently cleared the way, but the road was still barely distinguishable from the fields on either side. Mom claimed that the winter tyres were on, but that wasn't necessarily true. Tyres were probably not high on her list of priorities. I doubted whether or not we'd make it to the cabin where Kjell was waiting.

The cabin furthest in, on the other side of Lake Mørkved from the beach, belonged to Kjell's parents. We, the youngsters, had it for the entire weekend. Kjell was already there, and I was on my way in Mom's car. The other guys were coming later.

After a scant six months in high school, we too had to start partying if we were to keep up with everyone else at school. Two half-litre bottles of liquor had been purchased for the occasion. We paid ninety-nine kroner for a half-litre of Polish smuggled liquor. Enough "jet fuel" (Øyerstad slang for alcohol) to kill an entire circus, elephants and all. We were going to get wasted. Big time.

Mom

Robert leaned forward in the passenger seat, peering out through a hole in the ice that covered the windshield. If it weren't for the snow stakes, I wouldn't even know where the road was. I made a mental note: snow stakes and summer tires are not an optimal combination.

"The cable TV is working now. They messed up the bills again. It'll work the next time you come. I promise. Won't that be great?" I noticed my hands were almost blue on the steering wheel. I should've been wearing gloves.

"Yeah, that'll be nice." A frosty breath billowed from Robert's mouth as he spoke. I hoped he wasn't s not too cold.

"Hey," I said, putting my hand on his knee, and only then did he look up at me from under his cap. "Have you seen anything of your dad?"

"He's probably at work."

"Did he fill up the fridge before he left?"

"Nah, maybe that's why he's not coming home? He gets

free meals at work. Or maybe he's just avoiding us. He barely even says hi these days."

"So, he hasn't improved then."

"Nope! Something's off, for sure."

"He's not watching soccer anymore?"

"Nope, at least not with me."

"Robert, losing a child isn't easy," I said as the glow from the cigarette lighter set the tobacco alight. My hands trembled.

"He hasn't had it easy, Dad."

"Well, losing a brother isn't easy either. Besides, he was acting weird even before Fredrik passed away," Robert added.

"Yeah, that might be true," I responded.

"He's been more or less a mess since he fought Kai. Those blows hit harder than we thought." Robert glanced down at his backpack between his legs.

"Thirsty?" I asked.

"Huh? What are you talking about?" He wasn't very good at playing dumb.

"Are you thirsty? You're keeping a close eye on that bag."

"Oh, my God, Mom. It's soda and snacks."

"Good," I replied with as little conviction as possible. He smiled, perhaps a bit embarrassed, as I winked and tousled his hair. I loved that smile. "Drink plenty of water, and you won't get as hungover as your dad. Also, it's about time you got a haircut."

"If you're paying, I can get a haircut for sure" Robert replied.

"And what about Anders? Still working at the dog food factory?"

"As far as I know. I don't see him much, either. He mostly keeps to himself. Anyway, he said he'd fix the oil leak on my moped, so you don't have to worry about it. Money saved."

"That's good," I blurted out, maybe a little too cheerfully.

Unfortunately, it wasn't the fact that Anders could fix his moped that made me glad. It was the fact that we'd avoid the expense. At the garage, they wanted 2,500 kroner to fix it. It's a freaking moped. The whole thing doesn't even cost that much.

If I hurried, I'd be back in Skjønnsund in half an hour. Then I could go to Sørensen and pick up the package anyway. Maybe I could get some sleep tonight after all. A few hours without their incessant buzzing. I could still make it.

"Wonder what really happened to Death and the Witch?" Robert looked out at the crumbling house on the side road to our right.

No one had set foot there since the police put up the caution tape, which still hung from the bushes and trees surrounding the house. It had been many years.

"They just disappeared. Gone," I answered.

"We weren't very kind to them," Robert said.

"You were kids. And we told those stories to scare you, to keep you away from the road."

The house gave me an uncomfortable feeling, and my hand in my pocket didn't find what it was looking for. I needed to stop by Sørensen's.

As we pulled into the parking space near Kjell's parents' cabin, smoke rose from the chimney. Kjell waved from the kitchen window. Robert was eager to get inside, so I mustered up the courage to say what he likely wanted to hear. "I'm sorry about how things turned out last weekend. I promise it won't happen again."

"It's okay, Mom."

"No, it's not okay. I… we can't keep doing this when you come over. It's just that sometimes it's too much for me, and then…"

"It's too much for you? You could stop inviting them.

They're drunks, Mom. You're not like them."

"Not them."

"Who then?"

"I… I meant everything that's happened. I'm not well when I'm alone. I'm sorry. Next weekend will be different. It'll be better. We'll be by ourselves. I promise."

"Ok. Kjell is waiting."

"But you will come next weekend, right?"

"I'll come."

"Thank you," I said as he turned towards me and kissed me on the cheek. "Thank you, Robert."

"Robert?" I called after him as he trudged towards the cabin, snow up to his knees. "I got a job! Isn't that great? I'll get paid this weekend; you'll get your birthday money back. Think about what you'd like us to eat. Anything you want."

"That's good, Mom," he replied, waving without much enthusiasm. For a moment, I thought about skipping Sørensen and saving that money for something better. Just for a fleeting moment.

Robert

Later That Night

Silence, darkness, and freezing cold. I lean forward. The edges squeezing my waist are sharp, cutting into the flesh of my arms, which are pinned tight against my body. I don't know where I am, or why. I think my eyes are open, but I can't be sure. Everything is black. I have to get out. I can't. What the fuck happened here? It's like I'm trapped in a snare of some kind. Stuck in an oversized fox trap. Waiting for some hunter to come and shoot me. Maybe he'll bash my head in with a wrench? Skin me and eat me. I HAVE to get out. Now.

The first signs that I'm not alone don't come from the outside. No, something stirs inside me. In my stomach. I clamp my mouth shut. I dare not, cannot open it. A thick, slimy snake, a gigantic eel, crawls around deep in my gut. It coils, swells, squeezes, and writhes. It wants out. From the stomach, it pushes up into my throat, and I can feel how large it is. I try to swallow, but it's stuck. Finally, just as I can't keep my mouth shut any longer, a jolt strikes my legs. I clench my teeth so hard they crack, seal my lips, and kick wildly. Whatever is happening, I can't let them pull me further down into this hole. I make myself bigger, wedge myself even tighter. The struggle doesn't last long before I manage to land a solid kick into something heavy. Whatever it is, it gives way. Then it stops. Just as abruptly as it came. Was that a voice I heard? Did someone speak? No. Only silence is left. That thing in my stomach, is it still there?

You need to calm down, Robert. There's no one else here. Stay calm. Think.

After a while, I manage to relax, and only then do I notice the clumps on my face. In my nose, mouth, and on my chin. Ice.

Then it comes again. The snake inside me. I don't open my mouth in time, and it bursts out of my nose first. Clumpy, thick, and acidic. Then through my mouth. I vomit. The world spins. I vomit again! I am heavy and weightless, up and down all at once.

A short time later, I find myself hanging with my legs on one side and my upper body on the other of whatever it is that's holding me fast. I try to straighten myself, but my back muscles don't respond. I have to get free. I try kicking with my legs. Again. But they're so heavy that I can't move them.

My arms are still stuck. Goddamn it, I can't take this anymore. Not now. Please. Let me loose. I can't breathe. I try jerking myself out of the jam, but nothing happens. I'm too weak. My thoughts are fuzzy. I wait. Wait for a relatively quick, but painful and panic-stricken end. Occasionally, I twitch, more spasms than realistic attempts to free myself. I collapse inward, into myself. I twitch again. My nose is blocked by vomit that freezes on my face.

Just when I think it's all over, I vomit again and ice creeps down my throat as I draw breath. It tastes sour.

"K...K...K...jell?" The words are mine. No one answers. What the hell is this? I was in the kitchen with him a moment ago.

Earlier That Day

Kjell stood in the hallway waiting for me. "Didn't think the damn car would make it up here," he said.

"Neither did I. You forgot to clear the road? Didn't want any visitors?"

"Forgot? I was busy, you see." Kjell pointed to the empty glasses on the kitchen counter in the next room. Behind them sat a bottle of Coke. "Are we ready to rock?" He formed a sunburst with his fingertips under his face and grinned mischievously.

"Hell yeah," I replied, giving my backpack a pat. I soon handed Kjell a bottle. He poured a generous amount of liquor into the glasses, then topped them off with Coke. The glass he handed me was lukewarm, but I didn't complain.

"What ever happened to Tropicana?" I asked.

"Hard to say. Coke will have to do."

"And the liquor?"

"It's about time," Kjell responded.

"Soon we'll be on par with the guys in that shithole Mysen," I said, my tone dripping with irony. Yet we both knew there was a grain of truth in it. "Cheers to new times. To drinking, smoking, and making out."

"And sex. Just like the cool guys," Kjell added with a wry smile.

"Sex?"

"Why not? That's what they do in high school."

"Fair enough. Cheers, to the whole damn thing then."

The Coke did a poor job of masking the taste of alcohol, and I thought about the adults—how they willingly gulped this down. They even seemed to like it. "God, that's good," I said, wrinkling my nose.

Kjell laughed. "Yes, that hit the spot!" He walked over to the freezer and fetched a tray of ice cubes.

"Good thing you didn't bring those right away," I said.

"No room in the glass," Kjell quickly replied. He must have been thinking the same thing I was—that the drink was lacking something.

The ice made the drinks more bearable, and by the time we reached the bottom of our glasses, it no longer tasted that bad. The lead weight in my stomach lifted as the floor gently swayed. "Another?" I extended my empty glass towards Kjell.

"To sex again?"

"Let's have one for friendship this time."

"We deserve it," Kjell responded, mixing another "grog" as my dad and the others used to call it at the campground in Askim (outside Göteborg, that is). He started with ice this time. "To friendship and women."

"To friendship, and Guro," I raised my glass.

By the time the others arrived, Robert and I had a good head start. We were ready to rumble long before they were, and I have vague memories of us continuing to sing long after everyone else had stopped. At some point, it was just Kjell and me, alone again, with only a paraffin lamp and the glow from the cassette player for company. The others must have gone to bed. We were never going to end the party. No matter what happened to us, we were best friends. We were kings, rulers of our lives.

Again and again, we sang about when we were eight years old, running with a dime in our hands to the bus stop to pick up a paper for our old man. We sang about how we'd sit on his lap in that big old Buick and steer as it went through town. He tousled our hair and told us to take a good look around. This was our hometown. Øyerstad was our hometown. Our hometown.

Back in the Cold

Something is pressing against my head now, pushing it downward—forceful and tight. I want to stop it, but my arms won't move. The edges of the frame I'm somehow stuck in cut even deeper into my arms. I tremble uncontrollably. Then, I hear the voices.

"H-H-He... hello?" I stutter.

My face feels heavy, as if laden with lead. My nose is congested and my eyelids are thick and sticky. Ice from vomit and tears. I make another attempt to free myself. Gathering strength, I prepare for battle. I steady my breath. Searching for inner power—enough to burst free. *Are you ready, Robert? This is it. 1. 2. 3...* Then, suddenly, I see my left arm in front of me. It's free, as if it has never been trapped at all. As far as I can tell, it's not injured either. No cuts. No blood.

With my arm free, the pressure around my torso lessens. The frame that I'm stuck in seems a bit more spacious, but my body still won't cooperate. My arm is difficult to manoeuvre as I try to wipe the filth from my face. It tugs at my eyebrows and skin as I tear away the ice. Then, I catch glimpses of light. A forest hides beneath white pillows—snow and moonlight. I see the path up to the cabin and catch sight of the log walls next to me. I'm hanging out of the bedroom window—a small window. No wonder I'm stuck, wedged between the window frames. My head no longer feels as cold. Someone has put a hat on me. My body also feels warmer, and I see the blankets covering me. But my face is still frozen solid.

I am calmer now, feeling the floor beneath the soles of my shoes. Just as I'm about to wriggle back into the room, I see them out on the snow-laden ice. First, a lamp or a torch. Some source of light, at least, swinging gently back and forth. In the contours of the light, I see movement. Maybe it's one, or several people, lurking out there. They float through the snow in various shades of black and grey, intertwining with each other. Slowly, as if they are dragging something behind them. I want to shout to them, but my voice is pathetically weak, tasting of bile. Sour and icy. Are they really there? Or are they ghosts wandering through the forest in search of something they once held dear? Forgotten family members or pets. Is it an echo of summers past? Is it us on the raft? Summer days filled with swimming and fun. It could also be a time that is yet to come. Could it be something nice? Must everything always be so damn dark?

Something is moving by the spruce tree to my left. A shadow glides past, just at the edge of my vision. I turn my head towards the movement, and my sight only gradually catches up. Layer upon layer focuses in, and soon, I can see clearly. Of course, there's no one there. The world spins.

Damn it, Robert, don't move like that again! Slowly, I turn my head back towards the lake. My vision lags behind.

They're still circling out there. "H-h-hello? What a-a-are you doing?" Something important is happening, and I can't do anything about it. "H... h... hey, y-y-y-you must..." The bang comes so suddenly that I slam my arm into the wall, hard enough that I'm sure my elbow is shattered. My hat falls off as I hit the back of my head against the windowsill above me. A gunshot.

The sound of a shot fired in drunkenness around here isn't unusual. There are some cabins up here, after all. But it is the middle of the night, I think. Out on the ice. On the lake. No, it's not entirely reasonable that there'd be shooting right now. The moon seems to sense my unease and retreats behind a layer of clouds. With that, the light also disappears. My arm is throbbing like hell, and that's when I sense movement again.

"Damn it, watch where you're puking!" The voice comes from below, and I recognise it well. I don't dare look down. I won't. Because if I do, I will never be myself again. Because if it's him, he's not what he once was. He must be all decomposed and rotten by now. He... "Fr... Fr... Fred...rik?" I bend my head down and find myself face-to-face with my dead younger brother.

The Day After

I woke up to the smell of bacon, and for a brief moment, it actually smelled good. The others were bustling around in the kitchen when Kjell walked into the room.

"Good morning, darling," he chirped. "Bucket, cloth, and brush. For you."

"Fredrik?" I said, as if it were a continuation of a dream.

"Nope! Just me, and the others in the kitchen."

"C...c...co...cold last night!" I shivered.

"It was fine for a while," Kjell replied, "until you opened the window."

The smell of bacon thickened in my throat as I transitioned from a more or less unconscious state. I looked at the bucket.

"Cleaning ourselves out?"

"No, but we are doing some cleaning nonetheless." Kjell hummed some cheerful tune from a cartoon, one I couldn't place. He jumped back when I retched. Hanging over the side of the bed, I saw yesterday's dinner on my pillow. On the floor lay a pile of sausage bits I didn't remember eating. I followed the vomit trail across the floor, up the wall, and out the window.

"I hope it's okay that I helped you open the window when you tried to puke through it?" Kjell looked at me somewhat seriously.

"Uh, I...it's okay," I said.

"You don't remember much, do you?"

"No. It's pretty much… nothing."

"You were babbling like crazy last night. Not that I'm an expert, but I know what my mom would say—'Robert's having a panic attack.'" He mimicked his mother, who, despite being one of the locals, had a very posh and fine dialect.

"Huh?"

"Yeah, panic attacks are apparently vogue these days."

"I..."

"You... we were pretty wasted, dreamed about the circus again?" Kjell moved closer, almost whispering. "You were hanging out of the window, and we thought you'd freeze to death. We tried to pull you in, but you went berserk. You shouted out across the ice."

"At the lake?"

"You seemed to see someone out there. Bingo-Bob? And

then you spoke about Fredrik."

"Damn, I don't remember shit."

"How's your arm, by the way?"

"My arm?" I barely got the word out before I felt the pain in my elbow.

"When we tried to pull you in, you slammed your arm into the wall so hard the picture above the bed fell."

"The gunshot…"

"No, the elbow. Against the wall. Painful."

I plucked a piece of food out of my hair. "Did we have sausages yesterday?"

The other guys were in the kitchen eating when Kjell and I finished sanitising the bedroom. Tony pointed out that I probably didn't handle liquor as well as Dad while munching on bacon. Grease dripped unnoticed down his chin.

"Yeah, you might be right," I said, glancing at Kjell. "Thanks for the help, buddy."

"You're not done yet," he grinned, beckoning me. He put on a pair of shoes and walked out onto the porch in his long johns. He dumped the buckets over the railing, and rising steam turned into falling ice crystals.

I slipped into a pair of wooden clogs and followed.

"My guess is fifteen below," Kjell said, shivering. He then pointed towards the outside of the bedroom window. "After you'd thrown up all over the room and the window, you continued puking through it."

With a mix of horror and fascination, I studied the column of vomit from the window down to the ground. In the middle of it hung my hat, which had fallen off when I hit my head on the windowsill. The ice sculpture reminded me of something from *The Thing*, in the middle of some sort of transformation from one creature to another.

"I think you need to buy a new hat." Kjell was enjoying himself, and I managed a small smile too.

"We'll talk about that later. You need bacon and a drink," he said.

I wanted to refuse. To keep my distance. To go home and bury myself. Never see anyone, never eat or drink again. I thought of Mom and Dad. The booze. Dad always said that "a hair of the dog" was the best cure for a hangover. That you just had to force down another glass. Or more. Never stop. I thought "no", but said "yes". It scared me.

5

Robert

Somewhere in the '90s, I traded my Yamaha for a rust-red Volvo 240. Anders fixed it up for me for a mere few thousand kroner when I turned eighteen. My hair grew wild over dirty t-shirts with rock motifs. Down below, I wore short jeans and white tennis socks with one red and one blue stripe. We often partied up at Kjell's parents' cabin. We were *Harley Davidson & the Marlboro Man*, especially once we started smoking—just like the cool guys did.

When we weren't getting drunk at the cabin, we partied in Mysen and enjoyed ourselves with the ladies in the "big city". We were kings and queens, standing on the steps leading to the old gym. We smoked and downed the last drops of moonshine and beer before heading to *Valdis*, the disco. One evening, Kjell splurged and bought a joint from a shady passerby. You should have seen me on the dance floor that night. I was Jim Morrison, or really more like Val Kilmer acting like "the lizard king", as I spun around with my arms in the air to Mariah Carey. Later, I made out with an unknown girl who insisted on having a threesome with her friend. That, of course, never happened. Not that I could remember, anyway.

On a Saturday in August '96, we were back on the raft by the lake. It sat lower in the water than it had when we first claimed it in our childhood. I was soon going to do something I had once sworn never to do again.

Even though we were hung over, we flirted recklessly with the girls from class who also were there. Guro was one of them. She was the funniest and most charming girl on the raft. Why more guys hadn't noticed her was beyond my comprehension. My flirting was mostly directed towards the other girls; they meant nothing to me, so it was easier. Safer.

"Does it hurt?" Kjell looked at the tattoo on my shoulder.

"I'm good," I said nonchalantly.

"Has it been ten hours since you got it? You shouldn't be swimming with it yet, right?"

"Probably not, but you should know. You're the one who tattooed it."

"Well, yeah, but I was drunk," Kjell chuckled.

"Damn, remind me that we shouldn't play with tattoo guns the next time we drink. The idea was good, an "F" for Fredrik. That's fine. But what's around the letter? Is that a dragon?" I asked.

"Eh, I think so... Damn, that tattoo is so hot," Kjell laughed.

"I'm sure Fredrik would've been pleased."

"I hope so because better tattoos have definitely been made. But I'm happy. It's a genuine 'Kjell'—your first and likely last tattoo job."

The mood on the raft was good as we reminisced about the previous day's party and experimentation with needles and ink. I didn't mention the girl I had kissed or her proposition. Guro was also quite impressed with Kjell's tattooing skills.

"It'll at least be a nice memory and a good story," she said, and she was probably right.

"Heard Kai was at your place again?" Tony lifted his sunglasses and looked at me. "Out on the lawn as usual?"

Fina had become Shell, and Kjell's dad had expanded the family empire by adding a motel and pub to the gas station. The pub had become a popular addition to the village, especially on Fridays and Saturdays. Before, and often long after closing time, local heroes stood in a line along the highway, peeing onto the tips of their shoes. Some took the opportunity to vomit a bit while they were at it. Others stuck their tongues into each other's mouths and went home with people they probably shouldn't have. Then, of course, there were those who argued and fought over trivial matters. The local police often came by to clean up.

"I bet your dad's pleased. Kai probably drops a good amount of cash at the pub," I said, glancing at Kjell.

"Since Linn…" Kjell looked around, then lowered his voice, "hanged herself, yeah, he's been on quite a few benders."

"A good, old-fashioned alcoholic, then," I said.

"Dad kicked him out last Friday," Kjell added.

"Was that before or after they played ''Who the Fuck is Alice?' for the three thousandth time that night?" I inquired.

"Not sure, but it could have been after," Kjell replied.

"I would have gladly been thrown out myself. Can't your dad just ban that song from the pub?"

"I'll ask him. But Kai, on the lawn… Tell me."

"Oh, he showed up after the pub on Friday night."

"Wobbly as usual?"

"Of course. When he finally managed to crawl over the fence, he stood on the lawn and started shouting again." I stood up on the raft and imitated Kai. "'Hey, I know you're in there!'" I shook my fist towards those on the beach. Everyone on the raft laughed.

"For a moment, I thought he was shouting at me, but of course, he was after my dad. 'I'm talking to you, hear me? You're keeping quiet, aren't you? We must keep quiet.'" I continued my imitation of Kai.

"He was literally fighting an apple tree, and honestly, I thought it would win before he got to Dad's window. 'This is the price to pay. We have a pact, you hear, Dad?'" My imitation persisted.

"He tried to light a cigarette but eventually gave up and cursed as he threw the lighter away. 'We've been through enough shit. All three of us. We don't need any more. If we talk, it will only get worse, you understand?' He put his finger to his lips and blew."

"Been through enough shit, yeah. Well, you all have been through some, he's right about that," Kjell said, stretching out on the raft.

"I wonder what really happened between my dad and Kai? They sure have done something stupid once or thrice, but how bad could it have been? A night at the hunting cabin goes south and ends with a fight in the car outside our house. And then, all this..."

"Must've been pretty bad."

"He called my dad 'superhunter,'" I said.

"Wow, never heard that before." Kjell sat up, and Guro also looked in my direction. "'Superhunter! I'm talking to you. You and Petter are no better than me. One talks, all fall.'"

"Ah, he dragged Petter into it, too?" Tony was paying attention.

"Yep, everyone's included," I replied, continuing. "Kai turned towards the house on the other side of the road. 'This goes for you too, Petter! You sanctimonious bastard. It goes for us all'. Then he was back at my dad again. 'Superhunter, watch where you're shooting, is all I'm saying.'"

"Watch where you're shooting? Wow," Kjell remarked as he studied Elisabeth on the other side of the raft. "Watch where you're shooting," he repeated, while the sun scorched my skin.

"Did he talk about the shadows again?" Tony was curious for more.

"He mentioned them, too, before he threw his arms up and staggered back towards the gate. 'If you don't shut up, demons will be the least of your worries. I'll personally make sure you each get a one-way ticket to Satan himself. Remember that! Keep quiet."

Lying in the sun on the raft, I had decided to finally ask Guro. Once and for all. Plain and simple. I had psyched myself up and planned to ask her if we could swim over to the cliff on the other side for a private talk. I was interrupted when a couple of older guys with cut-off denim shorts, tattoos (fancier and not as fresh as mine), and full-fledged rockabilly hairdos joined us on the raft.

"Supposed to be forty metres down to the bottom," said the one in the black denim shorts.

The other lifted his sunglasses. "Forty metres? That's no problem. I've dived deeper than that, let me tell you. But you know, coming straight from the barber, don't want to mess up the ol' hairdo." He shifted his gaze from his friend to Guro."What do you say, darling? You don't mind getting a little wet, do you?" He winked cheekily while his friend giggled like a teenage girl.

"We'll save the diving for another day. There's more to see up here than down there, I guess." The taller one set his eyes on Elisabeth and licked his lips. Kjell noticed it too. We looked at each other.

The lion tattooed on the side of the taller one's belly and up over his chest seemed to stretch as he lay on his back. The predator's eyes were red and glowed over the gaping jaw. Without much subtlety, he put his hands behind his head and his right elbow over Guro's thigh. They'd been here just a few minutes, and already he'd touched her more than I ever had.

What the hell? Why doesn't she move? Does she like it?

Some monkey in my head was jumping up and down as I

wanted to tear him apart. Of course, I did nothing of the sort. Instead, I stood up, took long strides up the ladder, and planted my feet on top of the diving tower. "Afraid to ruin your hairdos? Nah, don't think so. You don't have the guts to do it!" I leapt over the tattooed idiots and into the water. Again, the dive was decently elegant and the splash minimal. Under the surface, I angled myself towards the chain anchoring the raft and followed it downwards. As the water transitioned from lukewarm to icy cold and the daylight bid farewell, I remembered why I said I would never do this again.

The water soon felt thicker, slowly churning around me. The pressure in my head increased. Bubbles crawled over my body like ants. Yet, I wasn't as scared as last time. I'd grown accustomed to the dark, the unseen.

It didn't take long to reach the bottom this time either, and I felt more in control than last time, despite years without training in the bathtub. The expectation, of course, was that my hand would plunge into the mire below. But something else happened. A jagged object latched onto my hand, piercing my skin. It seemed the more I struggled to free myself, the more tightly I was ensnared.

Surrounded by nothing but black, my mind filled the visual void with images I would rather be without. Flaps of decaying flesh hung from Fredrik's skull as he burst towards me like a pimple squeezed from the underworld. His form barely held together. My stomach erupted in a frenzy of burning butterflies as his face approached mine.

"Robert, you have to help me. I can't be here anymore. Why didn't you save me?" His eyes were filled with crawling leeches, water beetles, and dragonfly nymphs. His hand, sharp as crab claws, tightened its grip on my wrist.

"Be careful, you're hurting me. My hand, it..." Fredrik squeezed harder. Soon, I felt splinters of bone penetrating my skin, like knives through a glove. Screaming down here was as impossible as resisting the urge to try.

"You must find us! If you don't, this will never end. Never!" His skeletal jaw moved, but the voice seemed to emanate both from within and outside my head simultaneously.

Pull yourself together, Robert. That's not Fredrik. It's all in your head. He's dead and buried.

Of course, it wasn't Fredrik. And just as suddenly as he had appeared, he was gone. However, my hand remained ensnared in whatever it was that held me.

Take control of the situation. The bathtub. Hold your breath. Stay calm. Don't waste oxygen. Lower your pulse.

For a few seconds, I hung suspended, my heart rate slowing. I pulled myself towards the object that had me ensnared. It was round and hard, with jagged edges. At least it wasn't Bingo-Bob who had latched onto me, a small comfort despite the looming threat of drowning. Planting my feet against the object, I pushed away, swaying back and forth. The edges cut deeper into my hand. Don't panic now, Robert. Try again. Once more, I tensed my muscles and pushed. Just as cramps seized me, and I was on the brink of giving up, a strip of skin tore away, and my hand came loose. I was free. I had to get back up. Fast.

As I fought my way to the surface, my arms felt heavy, like lead. The blood from my hand was warmer against my skin than the surrounding water. Luckily, it didn't really hurt. It felt like forever, but it probably wasn't long before my body burst through the water's surface, mere inches from the edge of the raft. My friends greeted me, understanding what I had done. However, the state of my hand put a damper on their celebration. They helped me onto the raft while I looked for the two older idiots. Where the hell had they gone?

This time, no one was concerned whether I had reached

the bottom or not. My friends gathered around me, pondering what to do about the gash in my hand. It bled profusely, but the wound didn't look as severe as it felt. Guro used a hair tie to patch it up as best she could. When she made contact with my hand, jolts shot through my body. Not pain. Something else. An electric sensation.

She touched me.

"You need to keep your hand above the water and swim to the shore."

"Yes, I—"

"What the hell were you doing? You could have died down there." She wasn't impressed this time either.

You've done it again, Robert. Well done. Very well done.

I swam for the shore, hand aloft, and the ache began to intensify. What had caught me down there? Could it be the concrete blocks anchoring the raft? I had this feeling that… it was something completely different.

6

Almost a Year After the Dive

Robert

The scar on my hand, with which I now held a pencil, served as a memento of my last dive into the lake.

"If only you'd stay on the surface for once," was Mom's initial comment when she met me in the parking lot.

I had my hand well-wrapped in a towel, which I got from a startled lady, during my climb up the hill from the beach. Mom took me to the emergency room in Askim, and all the details from that visit remained clear. The dive, on the other hand, was much more diffuse, a memory I was reluctant to revisit more than necessary. Nonetheless, the scar was sort of cool. It stretched from the tip of my index finger and along the upper side of my palm, resembling a road, on a map—a hidden pathway to buried treasure. Something concealed.

The text I wrote that evening dealt with matters entirely different from hidden bounty and ominous dives; it evolved to become more than a poem, as it was initially intended. After hours of writing, the result lay before me on my desk: two and a half handwritten pages. Documentation. Evidence that Guro had asked me out on a date earlier that day. At least Kjell was convinced that was the case.

At that moment, I felt quite pleased with the text and wondered if it might be the beginning of a book—a memoir of Robert from Øyerstad. I envisioned myself at a book signing for the English edition, perhaps at a convention in Las Vegas or maybe San Francisco. People would line up for hours to secure a signed copy. The most zealous had even camped out in tents from the day before. I'd read aloud from the book, sign copies, and take photos with my admirers for hours on end. The queue would seemingly never dwindle. Guro, to whom I would be engaged with by then, would finally announce the end of the book signing. Now it was her turn to have a piece of me. All I needed to get there was to write something people would actually want to read and then get it published. Oh, and to get engaged to Guro, of course.

Excerpt from *The Witch of Mørkved, Death, and I - a Memoir by Robert Baastad*

Robert's employment at Øyerstad Saw and Planing Mill, also known as 'the mill,' was need-based. However, there was always enough work, so Robert was happy to work long shifts with only one day off a week. Sometimes, he worked on that day as well. Fortunately, he lived only ten minutes away, so the early shifts weren't too bad. He was often the first one in, sitting in the kitchen area of the warehouse with the old refrigerator humming in the background. Coffee in hand, he would look over orders from local artisans. Robert kept busy and appreciated the banter among the guys on the floor. He was one of them now, just like his father always had been. A working class hero.

On one of these days, Robert had finished loading a truck that was headed to Hølland with a load of two-by-fours. He was standing behind the counter in the shop, just as he pressed print on the order sheet, when Guro appeared in the doorway. Snowflakes nestled in her hair. She resembled a slightly bewildered penguin as she shook the snow off her oversized jacket.

Robert, in his mind, swiftly moved forward and hugged her while saying something clever. In reality, things remained as they always were. Guro was enchanting, and Robert was nervous. He made no advances.

Neither screwdrivers, allen wrenches, hammers, nor the new spirit level for only one hundred and ninety kroner caught Guro's attention as she walked towards Robert behind the counter.

What the hell is she doing here? Should I sit down? No, I'll stand. Maybe I should lean against the counter? Come on, think of something smart to say. Think!

"Hi," Guro said.

"Eh…morning," Robert said, as he fumbled, looking for a place to put his hands.

Guro got straight to the point: "Doing anything in particular next Saturday?"

Robert thought of Lady, the dog who shared a meatball with Tramp during their romantic dinner at a Italian restaurant in the Disney cartoon.

Guro picked up a pen on the counter and appeared to study it. Was she nervous too?

"I, eh, no, I don't have plans. I think?" Robert knew full well that he had accepted a shift at the mill that weekend, but was nonetheless pleased with his answer.

"Was that a yes or a no?" Guro asked after a while. She had put down the pen and was now fiddling with the zipper on her puffy jacket. She bit her lower lip and looked anywhere but at Robert.

"That was, no. I mean, in terms of, I don't have plans for Saturday."

"So, you want to hang out?"

She looked at Robert and opened her mouth cautiously.

"Yes, definitely. I'd... I'd love to hang out."

"A movie?"

"In Mysen?" I asked.

"No. Oslo."

"*Men in Black*?" I asked.

"No. *Titanic*," she said.

They didn't talk long while she was there, but what was said felt just right—the perfect amount of words, no more, no less.

The bell above the door rang with an optimistic jingle as she tucked her head down in her collar and went outside. Robert was left trying to wrap his head around what just happened. Was that an invitation for a date? With Guro?

Kjell, who was further back in the shop and had been spying on them, had no doubts.

"Oh hell, man! You nailed it. Finally! It took you nineteen years to get that date. What took you guys so long?"

"Well, I don't know. A date? It might not be what she meant."

"Robert! *Titanic*? With Guro? Seriously, mate. I don't know about Guro, but you've just hit the jackpot."

"Relax, man. Friends go to the movies too."

"Friends? Robert! Guro didn't invite you to Oslo to watch that ship sink."

"Maybe she did? She does like Leo, you know. Remember him in *Romeo and Juliet*? I believe she said she loved him..."

"Robert, Leo may have stolen your dream girl once. A long time ago. Now it's your turn."

The night after I wrote the first pages of what would become the manuscript for the novel *The Witch of Mørkved, Death, and I - A Memoir by Robert Baastad*, I had a nightmare. Well, not really a nightmare. It was more like watching a movie—a damn realistic horror movie where all senses and dimensions were present. In some strange way, I *was* my older brother Anders, experiencing everything that happened to him as if it were happening to me. The cold doorknob as he closed the front door behind him felt as real as the windshield of the car that exploded when he flew through it.

I wasn't even aware I had fallen asleep when I saw Anders fasten his seatbelt. He turned on the heat and switched on the radio. Elton John lit a candle in the wind for the millionth time that year, and my brother switched the frequency a few times before hitting play on the CD player. Iron Maiden's "Be Quick, or Be Dead" filled the car. The bass speakers in the trunk made the rear view mirror, trash, and bottles on the floor dance and shake as Nicko hit his drums and Harris' fingers galloped on the strings of his bass.

The headlights of the car and the street lamps along the gravel road were the only sources of light as he passed the skating rink. In my mind, 'Cranky'—that's what we called the old-timer who fixed the ice when we were kids—chased us away from the rink and into the woods. Perhaps Anders saw the same, for his gaze lingered on the darkened rink for a moment. We liked hockey back then. Fredrik did too.

When Anders, a short while later, turned towards Lillestrøm at the intersection by the old store, I noticed orange work clothes in the passenger seat. On the clothes lay a metal lunchbox like the one Dad always had. Anders was on his way to work, and I was along for the ride as a mute observer in his mind.

As we passed the closed-down store, I caught a glimpse of a figure standing on the porch, facing us. Had I gotten one more second, I'm sure I would have recognised him. However, Anders turned his face away to keep the car on the road.

Anders might have noticed the same thing I did, for he turned his gaze back to the porch, but by then, the figure had vanished. One more second and I would have...

Soon we crossed the border between Østfold and Akershus, entering what must have been Northern Europe's most winding commuter road. Passing lanes were, and still are, as rare on that road as sober people at a party in Øyerstad.

That night, there were no other cars on the road. The asphalt slid by while Iron Maiden sang, "Hell ain't a bad place, hell is from here to eternity". After many years of working in Oslo, every turn was mapped onto Anders' mental GPS. He knew exactly how fast one could drive through every single curve without ending up in the ditch.

Once, when our whole family had been on a trip to Åråsen to watch a soccer game, a moose tumbled down from a slope and onto the road in front of our car. Dad miraculously managed to stop before we hit it. It was a small consolation for the elk, who broke both its front legs upon landing on the edge of the asphalt. The poor creature soon lay in the middle of the road, flailing wildly, sending tufts of hair and deer lice flying. Since Dad's car couldn't go backwards at the time, we sat motionless in the middle of the road while the moose kicked out the left headlight and turn signal. Before long, a line of cars stretched for miles in both directions. Eventually, Kai arrived with his rifle, Rakel, and delivered a well-placed shot to the moose's skull.

Anders probably thought of the same event when he looked up towards the slope where the moose had come from. However, something else caught his attention this time. It wasn't another suicidal moose that moved outside the car. The object was more diffuse, like a figure in a 3D book—those types where you stare at an apparently random pattern until an object seems to float up from the page. Once you've seen it, it's hard not to see it again. My first thought was of a… a black hole. An entity so dark and obscure with gravity so strong that not a single ray of light could escape it. I remember reading once that it's actually impossible for humans to see black holes—no light, nothing to observe.

This, however, was not actually a black hole, at least not the kind I had read about. Because, unlike those, I could see this one. In front of me, in front of us, gaped a black spiral—a vortex suspended in mid-air beside the car as the cliffs raced past. Anders should have looked forward at the road, but didnt seem to able to take his eyes off the anomaly. At first, the hole was just black, but soon I noticed tiny blinking lights deep within the void—twinkling stars. At first faintly, then with increasing intensity, as though they were drawing nearer. Accompanying them were darker, tentacle-like shadows that swiftly emerged from the hole. Death worms seeking souls, and Anders' was their current target. His spirit would be torn from him, leaving his body empty, brittle, and lifeless.

Centipedes crawled in my stomach, and I wanted to flee this hellish vision. I wanted to yell at Anders to turn around and go back home. I wanted to scream at myself to wake up, but the movie unrelentingly rolled on.

Where they came from, or what they were, I couldn't say. But they had to come from somewhere—from some other side. From a place that Christians would threaten you with if you didn't believe in the same God as they did. A portal that had an opening at both ends. A door from life to death and from death back to life again. However, whatever lurked inside was not here to make pottery with Demi Moore. These ghosts, these demons, harboured a darker intent.

The music on the stereo sounded as if I were underwater in the bathtub—muffled and thick. Anders still wasn't looking at the road. The hairs on my body stood on end as the death worms moved into the car, floating through glass and metal. The glittering stars in the vortex paired up like cat's eyes, and I could make out the outlines of the figures that carried them. There was someone there. Yes, there bloody well was! Two, or perhaps several figures. Anders leaned closer. He lifted his hand as if to touch the shadows. Look at the road, Anders! He didn't hear me. The vortex consumed him. There was definitely someone there. Someone who—

LOOK AT THE ROAD, ANDERS!

After what seemed like an eternity, he broke the trance. The echo of my voice still resonated between the walls of the car as the music returned to full volume. The tires screeched as he swung the car around a sharp right turn. Again he flipped his gaze from the road, this time more quickly, to the thing on the right side of the car. It was gone. I didn't see it. He didn't see it. The rear view and side mirrors revealed nothing out of the ordinary. But, when he looked forward again, it was there, in the middle of the road. Right in front of us. He couldn't brake in time, and we drove straight into the blackness. The noises that followed, as the car twisted around, over, under, and past the obstacle, still give me chills. Screeching and scraping metal, being crumpled up and torn to pieces.

Even though I could have sworn my brother fastened his seat belt outside the house, he lifted off the seat and flew through the windshield. Unlike the car, Anders (and I) passed through the hole in a storm of glass, snot, and blood. I felt only a chilling cold within it before we emerged on the other side. Anders continued hurtling through the air towards the cliff that rose beside the road. Again, I was powerless on the sidelines, unable to do anything to save my brother. Again, unable to stop time.

The Circus

Anders' car appeared outside the stall area. Close to the border where light turned dark. Maybe no more than thirty metres from me. The blood around the hole in the windshield looked almost black, while smoke from the engine spread like ghosts dancing a waltz. Anders was likely lying crushed and shattered somewhere out in the field, soon to come crawling back—crumpled, broken, and bent, like a human spider.

The cauldron on Death's head was so large that it pressed against the walls of the stall, making the planks bow outward. The chain still held him up, but soon the cauldron would rip his head from his body and land in the muck with a splash. Very soon. The Witch of Mørkved stood next to him, her head tilted slightly to the side. She was shorter than Death.

Again, I followed the chain up from Death's neck, and for the first time noticed something else above us. Way up there, probably twenty metres high, a square plate balanced on the end of the chain. I thought of a juggler with plates balancing on a stick on his forehead. There was movement up there. Figures that leapt off the object, hit some sort of a surface before they scrambled back on. Not unlike children and teenagers on a raft, seen from below.

Robert

My thoughts—*now we die*—merged with Anders' scream as I came to my senses in bed. When the phone rang in the living room, my heart sank deep into my stomach.

Don't answer. If what the voice on the other end has to say is never said, perhaps it never happened.

An eternity seemed to pass, and the phone kept ringing. I held my breath when the ringing finally stopped, but it was only a matter of seconds before it returned. Dad was still sleeping in the stinky room; hopefully, he hadn't heard the phone. Or had he already left for work?

"Hello?" Dad's voice was subdued. He must have been sleeping on the sofa, as if it was meant for him to answer this particular call. He spoke in single words. "Okay. Yes. What?" He ended the call with, "We're coming!"

Two days after we arrived at the hospital, I finally got to speak with my brother. He was connected to a network of machines, each emitting its own set of noises and blinking lights. Tubes inserted into his body were filled with various liquids, some leaving, some entering. Bags of IV fluids hung next to his bed.

"Hey, havent got anything else to do, than to wait for your old brother to wake up, huh?" Anders' first words to me after the accident were feeble.

"I guess I have to when you go around crashing cars like that. They say you flew six metres. Had you not landed in the ditch, you'd be dead. You were an inch away from hitting the cliff, you know."

Anders coughed. His eyes were barely visible due to the swelling. "Good thing Kai didn't come and shoot me, then."

"Yeah, I stopped him, you know. He was going to put you down too. But I told him some people might be offended if he put your head up as a trophy on his wall. Fortunately, he agreed and left you alone."

Anders might have tried to smile, but I wasn't sure. He went quiet for a while before he said, "I didn't fall asleep."

"Asleep?"

"I've heard what they're saying, that I fell asleep and crashed into a tree."

"The tree was better than a cliff," I replied.

"It wasn't a tree. I didn't sleep, and I was wearing my goddam seatbelt," Anders said.

"They claim you weren't wearing one," I said, visualising him fastening his seatbelt as he got into the car, just like in the dream I had.

"I did. I swear."

"I believe you. But it doesn't matter now. Does it hurt? You look like Cranky finally caught up with you. Kicked your ass for trashing his ice".

Anders winced. Perhaps he tried to move, but his body remained still. The bandage wrapped around his head had dark stains, contrasting with the yellow-white cast on his forearms and the bruises on the rest of his body.

"Scrapes, bruises, broken arms, crushed ribs, and a fractured skull... You sure go all out when you crash," I said.

"Yeah, I guess my modelling career is in jeopardy. I should probably look for something else..." His lip twitched in an attempt at a smile. It was short lived. "Mom and Dad?"

"They're outside."

"Smoking?"

"Smoking."

"So, they think I fell asleep too?"

"Maybe, but I don't think they care."

"True, they haven't cared about anything for a while."

"I know you didn't, though"

"You do?"

"Yes, I saw it all."

"You saw it?"

"Yes, you crashed in my dream."

"Uh, okay. Into a tree?" he asked.

"Not a tree," I answered.

The sponge in the bowl on the table next to us, meant for moistening his lips, lay unused. It seemed so insignificant compared to the injuries he'd sustained.

"Some really weird shit happened that day, you know. Something was following me, before it blocked the way," Anders said.

I sat silently, while Anders told me about what we had both seen. I thought about Fredrik, what he said happened when we snuck into that house, and how Anders spoke of similar things. That something was following us.

Why would anyone do that? We haven't done anything wrong, have we?

Anders had fallen silent, and for a moment, he looked as though he had deflated. Panic struck me as I feared he might be dead. But, the machines kept beeping and no one came rushing from the corridor. His chest rose and fell slowly but steadily. My big brother was still alive.

Mom

Dad didn't say much as we stood outside on the concrete steps, protecting the embers of our cigarettes from the drizzling rain. We both should have quit smoking by now. We should have cut back on the alcohol as well, spent our money more wisely, and hung out with better people. There were plenty of other things we should have done better too, but changing habits was hard. Why is it that you do one thing even when you know you should do another? Doing the "right things" always required so much more effort. I mean, sinking is easier than flying. Even though I tried to fly from time to time, and sometimes lifted a few metres off the ground, I fell as soon as I took a break or faced any resistance. I tried love over hate. I loved my children. I loved Fredrik. I loved Dad. And Anders. But you see the same pattern as me, right? Where did love lead me? Straight down the drain. Love only gave me things that could be taken away. Indifference is easier. It demands nothing from you. And you don't have to do anything. Just let it embrace you.

Indifference.

"Sorry I woke you," Dad said.

"It's the least of our problems," I replied, taking another drag of the cigarette.

Being woken up in the middle of the night was not a part of the plan when I passed out on the sofa after a bottle of wine and medication from Sørensen last night. My head was still pounding, and only now, out on the steps with Dad, did I register the pain between my index and middle finger. I had fallen asleep with a cigarette in my hand again.

"Think you'll manage the electricity bill?" he asked, sounding like he cared.

"What?" I responded with a condescending tone, as if whatever he was insinuating was completely off-base.

"It was so dark that I thought..."

"You came in the middle of the night. People's houses are dark then."

"But you didn't have..."

"It will be fine. I'm getting paid soon."

"Good. Let me know if you..."

"Do you think he'll make it?"

"Yes, he will. He has to, because I'm afraid this accident is my fault as well," Dad said, and flicked his cigarette away, the ember hissing against the wet asphalt. Hunched, he shuffled towards the reception in his oversized clothes. He had barely hit forty, but he looked like he was eighty. I probably should have felt sorry for him…

Individual snowflakes stood out in the drizzle as my cigarette followed the path of his. I turned towards the reception as well, and soon we were walking silently through the corridors.

It's not uncommon for parents to feel guilty when they lose a child. When you nearly lose another one, it doesn't get any easier. People say things like, "It's all my fault," regardless of whose fault it actually was. Most of the time, it was no one's fault at all. No matter what anyone had done, the outcome wouldn't have changed. But what if it actually was his fault? What if he had killed Fredrik and tried to kill Anders too? It was, of course, not true, but what if he had committed some other act he shouldn't have, something that led to all of this? What if... Snap out of it. We've been through this before. None of you are at fault here. Not you. Not him. This is shit that happens. Fredrik getting cancer overnight, Anders crashing into a tree—these are things you can't control.

Midway down the corridor, Dad stopped and turned to face me. His gaze was empty beneath the heavy skin of his face. He opened his mouth. Was he about to tell me something? Was he offering me an explanation for his behaviour? And then, right there, for the first time in a long while, I saw Dad. My Dad. A small opening into the chamber where he hid his former self and his love for his family. One. Brief. Moment.

"First, we took Fredrik. Soon we'll have Anders too. Who will be next? What do you think?" The voice, or voices, speaking were not Dad's—I knew that much. They came from a completely different place. From someone else. Dad just stared blankly ahead, lips unmoving. He did not make a sound.

I wondered if he had heard them too, as we stood facing each other. I wanted to ask him, but waited for him to speak first. His lips moved. Finally, now he would explain everything.

Nothing happened, and I wanted to scream at him. "Say something, Dad! If you know anything, talk to me! Tell me you heard them." Not a sound. The old, familiar Dad faded away. He shook his head, then turned away and trudged further down the corridor.

I used to quiet the voices that spoke to me with mental firewalls, positive affirmations, and meditation. And, of course, alcohol. But that was a long time ago, before they grew as strong as they are now. These days, I have stronger stuff to silence them: medication against the demons. It works, but only until the effect of the pills wear off. Then the voices return, louder and harsher. The cruel words. The haunting whispers. Until I take the another dose.

Dad stood in the doorway to Anders room. Robert sat beside the bed. Dad and I looked at each other for a second, and the love I had sensed a short while ago was gone. His eyes were like smoke inside glass orbs. He neither hated nor loved me; he simply didn't care.

A chill ran through me as my fingertips brushed against an object in my left pants pocket. Small, round, and hard. I hurried to the bathroom, locking the door behind me. "The voices aren't real," I whispered. In the bathroom mirror, I met my own eyes, popped the pill into my mouth, and swallowed. Then I waited for it to take effect. The medication. "It's all in your head," I murmured. "The voices just in your head."

7

Robert

We took the bus from Øyerstad to Skjønnsund, Guro and I, where we switched to another bus headed for Askim. From there, the train would take us to Oslo where we would watch James Cameron sink the *Titanic*. Guro insisted on buying one-way tickets to Oslo, even though purchasing a round-trip ticket would have been cheaper, but I didn't make a fuss about it. After all, she was usually more thoughtful than me, and I didn't want to reveal that I was more or less broke.

"Is your brother okay?" she asked as we sat down on the train. She held my gaze. "And, are you okay?"

"Yeah, he's getting by. Came home from the hospital yesterday. He's going to stay with me and Dad until he's feeling better."

"So, living with you, in your dad's house?"

"Dad's not wearing out the floorboards, no."

"That's cool, though. I've been thinking about getting my own place as well."

"In Øyerstad?" I asked so quickly that I feared she'd see right through me.

"Don't know. It would be nice to get away from this hole. I mean, if tumbleweeds were a thing in Norway, that's where you'd find them: in Øyerstad."

"I guess, but…"

"I don't think I want to be a cashier forever."

"No, but you could…"

"Work at the sawmill? I'll pass. I have coffee at home. We'll see. But back to your brother: how's he doing?"

“He doesn’t talk much about the accident. He still claims he didn’t fall asleep, that he hit someone who was standing in the middle of the road.”

”Right. I can see why some do not believe him. People don’t usually hang out in the middle of the road at that hour. And especially not that road. In the middle of absolutely freaking nowhere”

“Maybe it was another psycho moose?” I suggested.

“Another one with a death wish?” Guro looked at me. “If so, I guess it’s time for them to have someone to talk to in those woods.”

“Yeah, maybe an owl or so; they’re supposed to be smart and could make good shrinks. Anyway, he is a bit confused these days. Reminds me of Fredrik,” I said, unsure whether to talk about the dream I had—the one where I was Anders.

“Reminds you of Fredrik? Yikes,” she said, gazing out at the trees speeding by. God, how I wanted to hold her hand.

“Cancer sucks, and possibly Dr Larsen as well,” she added.

“I don’t know about Larsen. Or Fredrik. He was acting weird before he passed away, and now Anders has the same tendencies. What if it’s the same shit?”

“That sucks,” Guro replied, and continued, “It will be nice to see *Titanic*, though. I hear it’s uplifting. Supposedly the ending is great.”

“Yeah, I’ve heard the same. What about Leo? Still in love?”

“A bit,” she smiled.

If her face were a map, I could have drawn every road, mountain peak, and trail blindfolded. Her canine tooth was still slightly crooked compared to the others, and the small freckle on her cheek below her left eye was still there.

“Do you know something weird about the *Titanic*? About the pool on the ship?” Her eyes lit up.

“The pool? No, I am not too familiar with that, to be honest.”

"After all these years, it's still full." She sat still for two seconds before bursting into laughter, nearly crying. The joke was hardly a knee-slapper, but her reaction sent me into fits of laughter along with her.

Trees and green fields gradually gave way to roads and houses as we neared the capital.

"You never went to Elisabeth's party?"

"Nah, had to work late, and up early the day after."

"There was a guy from Hølland there," she said as we got off the train at the central station.

"I see. You kicked his butt? You know we beat up people from Hølland, right?" I posed like a fighter as we walked past Oslo City, the shopping mall.

"Yeah, I know that. But we didn't fight."

"No? What did you do then?" As I asked, a knot formed in my stomach; I stumbled as my legs got tangled.

"Well... We... We kissed, I guess, but it wasn't serious or anything."

No, no, no! Why did she say that? I knew it. Why did I even get my hopes up?

"So, is something going on between you two?" I asked, as nonchalantly as I could, wondering if she could hear my heart breaking.

"Don't think so. I barely know his name. Stuff like that happens when you're out, right?"

I had obviously been with a girl or two myself along the way, and it didn't always stop at a kiss. However, they meant nothing to me. But Guro telling me this could mean only one thing: she and I were just friends. Why else would she tell me? We were simply two friends going to the movies.

"Lise isn't home this weekend. So we can use her apartment if we want. I need a shower before we go. There might be a beer in the fridge if you're thirsty," Guro said after a while. I wondered why we needed an apartment to go to the movies. Couldn't she have showered before we left?

The fridge in Lise's apartment contained not just one beer, but also white wine, grapes, and a small basket of strawberries. I grabbed a beer and sat down on the sofa, impressed by Lise's fine habits. I popped the cap off with a knife on the table and let the beer calm my nerves.

"Did you find something to drink?" Guro shouted from the bathroom as she turned on the shower. The door was slightly ajar.

"Yeah, I did. All good," I hollered back, but she didn't reply. I leaned back on the sofa and surveyed the room.

Is this the type of place Guro dreams about? Moving to the big city? What if she leaves Øyerstad? Get a grip, Robert. You can think about that later. Now, she left the door open. You saw her, she did that on purpose... What are you waiting for? Do something!

I sat on the sofa, considering my options. I could get up and knock on the door. I could just smile and walk in... She was all quiet as steam filled the bathroom, and condensation started climbing the mirror in the hall. Maybe she was waiting for me... Maybe. No. What if I was wrong? I would die if I made a move and she didn't mean what I maybe thought she did... I didn't move, and eventually, she emerged from the shower. I could make out the outline of her breasts and a black bra beneath her half-open shirt. Her underwear had a tiny ribbon at the top, near her stomach. She buttoned her pants as she walked through the room.

"So, when does the movie start?" I asked, mentally slapping myself on the forehead.

Stupid question.

Guro stopped buttoning her pants, and our eyes met. Then

I did something I never thought I'd do. I stood up. Without breaking eye contact, I walked over to her. I wrapped my arms around her, and for a moment, we swayed together in the slowest waltz anyone had ever danced. Our bodies fit perfectly together, her head tilted up to meet mine. We said nothing, and I trembled as she laid her arms around me. She was so warm. It could be from the shower, or more likely, it was the special connection between us. Electricity. Her hair smelled of strawberries, as her shivering breath warmed my neck. Just as I closed my eyes and parted my lips to kiss her, she murmured, "It starts in a couple of hours..." I was still sitting on the sofa, and Guro had finished buttoning her pants. I did nothing, and soon we left for the movies.

The movie coloured us all in a potpourri of opulence, luxury, melancholy, love, and above all, sorrow. The circumstances were optimal for being romantic, and again, I failed to make a move.

I thought about the time she took my hand. When Fredrik was attacked by Terminator. When she showed me love during one of the worst moments of my life. Now I could have done the same as Leonardo (spoiler alert) let go of the raft and sank into the sea. Everyone in the theatre was crying. Maybe Guro was too. I didn't dare to look. Perhaps I moved my clammy hand two millimetres towards hers, but we never made contact.

Imagine what could have happened if we'd had a microsecond of contact. One finger touching another. We would have exploded right there. I'm sure of it. We would have gone back to that apartment and stayed there forever. Just Guro and me. We would have kissed. We would have connected in ways we had never done with anyone before. But I'm afraid *Titanic* could have sailed across the universe without sinking, rolling across the screen for weeks without me making a move. In a way, I had told Guro that I didn't want her, without even realising it myself. I guess I didn't deserve her anyway. Then again, after all, it might have been for the best. Because if we had fallen for each other that day, she would have marched right into the same misery as me.

Soon we bought the return tickets for the train home. The ride home was quieter than the ride in.

8

The Circus

Teeth protruded like rusty nails from Bingo-Bob's speckled gums as he lunged at me. As his jaws snapped shut over my face, I heard a crackling noise, and overwhelming pain surged as teeth cut through skin and into bone. My scream seemed to feed the creature's frenzy as it clung to my face.

Robert

I was sitting upright in bed when I woke up. My heartbeat thrummed all throughout my body, as the contours of the nightmare retreated into the corners of my consciousness. At first I was confused. Then scared. And finally, somewhat relieved. It was only a dream. Another night with that damned dog. Sweat stung my eyes, and the bedsheets felt like sandpaper as goosebumps rippled across my skin. The room around me initially seemed blurry, as if I were underwater or behind a shimmering wall of light. I wiped away the sweat, and my focus sharpened, but things still didn't quite add up. Again, I rubbed my eyes and blinked a few times.

Sure enough, my bedroom had fewer posters than when Fredrik and I shared it, but some soccer players and rock bands still clung to the wall. The walls in the room surrounding me now bore no posters of any kind. They were colourless and bland.

The window facing the Haugen fields wasn't in front of me as expected. Instead, the sun's first rays streamed through a window to the right of the bed. I didn't see the fields through that window either. Just a couple of trees and another house I recognised but couldn't place. The clock on the nightstand, an old-fashioned alarm clock with two bells on top, wasn't mine, and neither was the nightstand. I didn't own any of these things. The bed I woke up in was not the one I had gone to sleep in.

I became aware of the pain in my toes, curled beneath the blanket. Cramps spread from my toes through my feet. I tried to relax my foot, my legs, but the muscles were taut. Soon the muscles on the back of my thighs were cramping as well, and I was afraid the cramp would crawl all the way up to my heart and stop it. Lock it in place until I fell backward, down through the unfamiliar bed in the unfamiliar room, never to wake up again. Where the hell was I, and how had I ended up here? It hadn't been that many hours since I wrote the last line in *my* manuscript at *my* desk and went to bed. My bed. In my room.

I lay there for a while, pondering, and soon it occurred to me that the room was not as foreign as I first thought. The house outside the window was familiar, even if the angle from which I viewed it was different than usual. The clock on the nightstand—I recognised that too. Before they separated, it stood in Mom and Dad's bedroom. Even before that, a very long time ago, it stood in Grandma and Grandpa's cabin in Øyervika on their old dresser. These days, it stood by Mom's bed in the house in Skjønnsund. The room I woke up in was Mom's.

An arm reached for the pillbox standing next to the clock; the arm wasn't mine. The scar above the watch on the forearm, I hadn't noticed it before, glowing gently in white. Raised tissue cast small shadows under the creeping rays of the sun. I recognised this scenario. This type of dream or illusion. If it was like before with Anders, then I was seeing the world through Mom's eyes.

Mom grabbed the plastic box and shook it – silence. The last pill had been taken the night before. As she sighed, an unsettling feeling crept through my body – a craving, a burning desire, a hunger. There was something I needed. Quickly. There was still hope to make the world a little better again. A little safer. A little quieter. She sat up in bed and stayed there for a while, the room swaying as if we were in a boat. The floor was ice-cold against her feet. I still had cramps in my toes.

She got up, and I recognised the neighbour's house outside as she floated through the room. For a moment, she stopped by the mirrors on the wardrobe. Even after I closed my eyes, I saw her body. She was wearing only underwear. I wanted to leave; I had no business being there, but somehow I knew I was meant to see this. I opened my eyes.

She was as pale as the bedsheets and the wall behind her, like a zombie I'd seen in some uncensored doomsday film. She appeared distant and didn't move. However, her eyes seemed to focus on a slight movement in the corner where the sun's rays had yet to vanquish the shadows. There stood a figure, one I had seen before on the steps of the old store the night that I "was" Anders.

A solitary tear on Mom's face turned into a stream. The observer in the shadows reminded me of someone I, or we, had loved more than anything else in the world. As if he had heard me pray for him to come back. As if he had heard that I didn't want to be here alone. Mom had probably prayed for the same. A chill rushed through me as she stuttered "F... F... Fredrik? Is that you?"

When I hoped that my little brother would step out of the shadows and declare it all a terrible joke, Mom twitched.

Then, as if someone had kicked her in the back, she slammed against the wardrobe mirror. Her face hit the glass so hard that I feared her eyes would pop out.

I recoiled as her face met the invisible barrier separating us. A force in the room pressed her against the glass until it creaked. My head creaked. Her body creaked. Cramps spread through me once again, deep into my brain, while she was being crushed against the mirror. A muffled snap followed the give of her nose against the glass. Her skin seemed suctioned to the mirror, and I stood powerless on the other side. Just when I was certain she would be pushed through the mirror, drowned in a flood of blood, glass, and mucus, she was yanked back into the room. The mirror was stained with blood, and the fog from her breath slowly receded from the glass.

As if possessed, she remained standing, staring at her reflection with eyes like smouldering torches. Her lower jaw twitched in spasmodic movements. Again, I thought she tried to say something, but the sounds were indecipherable. She hadn't stood that way for long before something invisible tightened around her, as though she were wrapped in plastic film. Her hair plastered itself to her skull, and her arms bent inward towards her torso. She hissed as her skin tautened around her skeleton, as if a vacuum had formed inside her. Her skin grew so tight that I expected it to rupture and be absorbed into her body. She vibrated as the force that gripped her lifted her into the air— an inch, several inches, almost a foot. What the hell was going on?

This can't be happening. She can't fly. This is just a dream; wake up, for God's sake, wake up now!

She remained, suspended in the air before the mirror, perhaps half a meter above the ground while blood flowed down her body, dripping from her toes onto the carpet.

Her pupils seemed locked onto the figure in the corner as a gurgling sound erupted from her throat. Maybe she was trying to communicate, attempting to speak to me, or maybe she was cursing the demon holding her in its grip. Maybe she was just trying to breathe.

Her toes still didn't touch the floor as she began to move again. She swayed gently side to side, first to the right and then to the left—the entity holding her seemed uncertain of its next move. However, the indecision didn't last long; her movements quickly became deliberate. A sudden twist rotated her body forty-five degrees to the right. It happened so fast that I feared her neck would snap, her head lagging behind. Now I saw her from the side as she began to float through the room. She brushed against the half-open bedroom door as she vanished into the hallway. A ghost.

"Wait. Mom... Stop!" She showed no signs of hearing me. Of course, she didn't. She couldn't possibly know that I was there, that I saw everything. A streak of blood on the floor trailed her through the hallway and into the bathroom. Like a pig carcass hanging from a hook in a slaughterhouse.

As she passed through the doorway into the bathroom, she must have broken the spell, even if only for a brief moment. She grabbed onto the doorframe, clinging with all her might. However, the force surrounding her showed no respect for a mere human body and its frail composition. Her nails snapped off abruptly, leaving red marks on the inside of the doorframe. My throat felt sore as I tried to swallow. What the hell should I do?

Soon, I saw Mom's face in the bathroom cabinet mirrors. She slumped and seemed to shrink as the force that had held her up let go. I didn't see her feet hit the floor, but I felt something pressing against my toes. They were still clenched in spasm. With her feet on the ground, the grip around her loosened. Her hair spread out to the sides, grew larger, and her arms extended away from her body. Her lungs had room to expand, and her skin possibly regained a hint of colour as she drew a long breath. Blood circulation.

Please, leave her alone.

At first, I thought it was the sweat in my eyes, or maybe Mom's, causing it. That it was an illusion when ripples, like rings in water, spread from various points on the linoleum wallpaper behind her, at the other end of the room. The wall resembled the surface of a pond, perhaps the Nøkken Pond up in Superman Hill behind the house in Øyerstad.

"We were once just like you," a voice began. At first, I assumed it was Mom speaking, but her lips didn't move. The voice wasn't hers. It was more like multiple voices combined into one. It came muffled and wet, filling the room all at once.

"My child was once alive too," the lighter of the voices asserted.

"But not for long," interjected the darker one.

"No, not for long. Not for any of us, right?" The teasing tone of the lighter voice sent shivers up my spine.

"Oh no, they're all gone now," the darker voice responded, with mock sorrow.

"And soon you'll join them," said the lighter voice, speaking directly to Mom.

"It's your turn now," the dark voice declared, cold and emotionless.

"You shall all die!" the lighter voice suddenly shrieked.

I took a step backwards. Unlike me, Mom, was unfazed by the scream. How could she not react to that? Perhaps she had heard them so many times that she no longer cared.

Resigned.

She opened both doors of the bathroom cabinet at once.

Fredrik's toothbrush in the Transformers cup was gone. She had brought it when she moved out after the divorce and put it in the cabinet in her new house. As if Fredrik might show up one day and need to brush his teeth. It had been there for years, but now it was replaced with pillboxes. The same kind as on the nightstand. I just knew that if you removed the first stack of pills, you would find another stack behind it. Behind the second stack, you would find a third, and so it would continue, in an endless array of pillboxes.

"Everyone has to pay," the voices spoke as one again.

Mom's hair moved damply as the voices caressed her. The scar on her arm was wet and irritated as she grabbed the first box. Liquid oozed from the wound and trickled down her arm. Mom didn't care about it, or the loose nails on her blood-red fingers, as she popped open the lid of the box. Then she poured its contents into her mouth. All of it. She closed her lips, chewed, and swallowed. Gagged a few times, and swallowed again. Soon, white foam oozed out between her lips. My jaw muscles burned as both Mom and I clenched our teeth so hard they could crack at any moment.

In the manner of dream logic, she suddenly had a Coke bottle in her hand. The cap was off, and she poured its contents into her mouth. It was clear. Not Coke. No, of course it wasn't. Not in Øyerstad. Clear liquid in Coke bottles was either bad moonshine or smuggled alcohol. Strong stuff. Still, she gulped it down, taking big swigs to wash away the foam. No one could drink liquor like that. Not half a litre.

The fire set my throat ablaze, seemingly in sympathy with hers. I shuddered, kicked, and flailed wildly, so forcefully that it must have been when I fell out of bed. Without waking up. Mom took another box. More pills. All at once. This time the foam came immediately.

Mom never touched the doors of the bathroom cabinet

that closed on their own, allowing me to see her face in the mirrors. They wanted me to see her. They wanted me to see the wall behind her. The wallpaper was no longer like the surface of a calm pond. Instead, it resembled an angry ocean that bubbled and surged in and out of the room. God knows what sort of hellish things circulated in its depths. Mom breathed spasmodically. Her nose bled under her bloodshot eyes, and her lips seemed to have disintegrated. Blood, alcohol, and foam oozed down her chin.

If it weren't for the fact that she was standing upright and actually moving, she might as well have been dead. Beyond all possible contact. But then, for a moment, I could have sworn she saw me. Somehow, we connected.

"Rrrrrrrrrrrr," she tried. "—Rob b.b.bert... You, it's..." With each syllable she uttered, blood sprayed across the mirror. The sound she made through clenched jaws was like that of an impact drill. "Rrrrrrr... Rob b.b.b.b..." Then the pressure became too much, and I heard her teeth give way.

"Robert, you need to wake up. You need to wake up and get to Skjønnsund. Now!" I screamed to myself. Over and over. Louder and louder. And finally, against all my expectations, she reacted. I think she heard me. The world was put on pause. We connected.

"Robert?" she managed to say at last. Almost effortlessly and clearly. She knew, and I knew that this was the last thing we would say to each other.

"M… m… mom?" I wanted to tear down the wall between us. I wanted to fight, bleed, and die. For her. "Mom, I lo—"

I hope she understood what I was trying to say before the invisible force seized her again. She was lifted up—hard, fast, and brutally this time. She shot up into the air and hung there while her arms and legs snapped in all directions. She was a ragdoll that someone was playing with. Then she was thrown back through the room. She, I, we, flew towards the wall, and it swallowed us as we hit the surface. I had time to think that this was the end, that we were going to be crushed against the plaster and beams. It didn't happen. The splash and pressure reminded me of when I jumped into the water up at Lake Mørkved. So did the darkness' clammy embrace. The low rumble and the cold that brushed against my body.

I have no clear memory of what was inside the wall when we fell through it. For me, it went dark. Perhaps we lost contact for a brief moment. In many ways, it was liberating, as I no longer saw her tortured body and face.

Through a filter of blood, spit, and tears, I glimpsed the sofa to the right, the lamp, and the TV. We were no longer in the bathroom. The lamp used to stand on the living room table, but now it lay on the floor beside her... beside me, with a shattered shade. At irregular intervals, the exposed light bulb sent jolts of light through the room.

Knives cut into my body as Mom moved.

Please, don't move. It only gets worse if you do.

Broken glass and wooden splinters were scattered all around us. Somehow, Mom had fallen through the bathroom wall and landed on the glass table in front of the TV in the living room.

The light flickered, seeming to synchronise with Mom's blinking. Tiny ripples spread through the pool of blood she lay in—a ripple for each heartbeat. The time between each wave grew longer and longer.

"Just relax, Mom," I silently urged. "I'll wake up soon, and then I'll get help. Just lie still. Don't move."

"Are you still there? I have your address logged and we're going to send help to Major Myhrvold's Way in Skjønnsund."

"..."

"Are you still there? Are you having trouble communica-ting?"

"..."

Mom focused her gaze again, and I made out the contours of the phone on the floor in front of us. I think she tried to answer, but the sounds she produced made no sense. Blood-red foam painted abstract patterns on the floor towards the phone as she coughed and gagged. I stood on my side of the nightmare, shouting as loud as I could, but the person on the phone, of course, couldn't hear me.

Glass shattered somewhere else in the room, followed by a dragging sound. I felt a faint vibration on the floor. Foot-steps? Someone was approaching. I thought of elephants, and soon I saw a pair of feet, wet and caked in muck. They somewhat confirmed my thoughts about the large mammal. Here and there, I made out pale skin and veins. The fingers of the hand that picked up the phone were swollen and almost translucent. They looked like overcooked and burst sausages.

"If you can hear me, know that we have a car on the way to Skjønnsund to check on your situation. It won't be long before they arrive, and I'm going to stay on the phone and talk to you until you have..." The phone crashed to the floor with a bang, and then it went quiet. Until the strange voices spoke again.

"One by one, slowly but surely, you will all pay. First all who are loved, and lastly, the one who loves." The vile creature spat the words with contempt as everything went black again, for Mom, and for me as well.

I was sure that Mom was dead, and I wondered if I was too; but when I opened my eyes again, I was sitting on the floor next to the bed. In a room I knew well. My bedroom. In Øyerstad.

Dad and I stood in silence as the headlights of the car that swung into the driveway set us ablaze. Anders soon stormed into the living room.

"Are you awake? I wonder if Mom..." He trailed off as soon as he saw us, fully dressed.

We hurried towards Anders's old Volvo, idling outside the house. I settled into the back, with Dad and Anders up front.

"Still hurting?" I asked when Anders winced as he sat down on the driver's side.

"I'll be fine," he replied, as he swung onto the highway and stepped on the gas.

The CD magazine in the back seat, which could hold thirty-five discs, and the homemade bass box in the trunk sat unused. Neither Stray Cats nor The Blasters felt appropriate for the moment. Without music as a backdrop, the lingering scents of yesterday's farts, Wunderbaum, and cigarettes became all the more pronounced. In silence, we drove towards Skjønnsund.

If Dad was a North European champion in Teletext, my brother was the same in speeding. He might have been the one person in Øyerstad who had lost his licence the most times despite being only twenty-three years old.

"I drive just as well without a licence," he often announced before speeding off. That night, however, I was more concerned that we weren't going fast enough as the car headlights sliced like shards of glass into the night, past the church, the school, and the campground. Halfway to Skjønnsund, the heavens opened up on us.

As we finally neared the centre of Skjønnsund, we took a sharp left at Gundersen's bakery. A couple of hundred metres later, we passed the fishmonger on our right. Mom's apartment was on the left. The car came to an abrupt halt on the parking lot, and the two in the front bolted out towards the front door. They flew up the stairs and frantically rang the doorbell. No one opened or answered their calls. My brother ran a lap around the house, pausing to look in through the windows as he went. The house was as dark inside as the night was outside.

I had a feeling that if this was anything like what had happened when Anders crashed, Mom would be lying in the living room amidst shards of glass and splinters of wood. Her mouth filled with blood and foam. Maybe that's why I stayed in the car for a while. I didn't follow the others.

I jumped when Anders opened the car door, fished a set of keys out of the glove compartment, and disappeared again. The door was left ajar, and rain poured in. Soon, they both slipped into the house, which gradually lit up one room at a time.

It wasn't until they turned on the light in the living room that the figure in the kitchen window caught my attention—the room they had just passed by. There he was again, a silhouette of a person against the kitchen window. A silent observer. The entity Mom had called Fredrik in her dream.

With my eyes fixed on the kitchen window, I got out of the car. By the time I reached the stairs, I was completely soaked. I paused, trying to focus. The watcher was still there, yet at the same time, he wasn't. Like a shadow or a translucent decal.

The kitchen was only a couple of metres away, and whoever it was wouldn't be able to get out before I got in there. So, I dashed into the hallway, and two seconds later, I was standing in the doorway to the kitchen. Of course, no one was there. Nothing.

Get a grip. You're seeing things!

I saw Dad and Anders standing with their backs to me in the living room, through the opening on the other side of the kitchen. I knew what lay on the floor in front of them, even if I couldn't see it from where I stood. *Dear God, or whoever the hell is in charge. This can't be happening. Not now. Not ever. Please.*

I floated through the kitchen and soon I was standing in front of her, with my remaining family—Dad and Anders. Our wonderful Mom had fought bravely, but in the end, she frayed at the edges and gave in. I was certain she loved her kids, and on some level, she still loved Dad as well. He must also have loved her somewhere deep down inside. He had to. A thought gripped my heart as I stood over her in a puddle of blood, glass, and wood splinters—what if she never knew that we loved her too?

9

Robert

Initially, they wanted to bury Mom in Skjønnsund. According to regulations, she was to be buried by the church of the municipality in which she died. Grandpa insisted that Oslo was the only proper place, but not even his credit card could make that happen. After much back and forth, including a petition from the local residents of Øyerstad, we finally got our way. Mom was coming home to Øyerstad.

A little over a week after her death, we were sitting in church again. Friends, as usual, were on the left side, and family on the right, facing the altar. At the front stood the coffin, surrounded by wreaths with white ribbons and heartfelt messages. My thoughts scattered as I tried to wrap my head around what all this meant for Dad, Anders, me, and everyone else.

The sheriff was also present, partly on duty and partly as a resident. He was the first official to tumble into Mom's house the night we found her.

"It's the sheriff! Is anyone there? Identify yourselves!" he yelled before bursting in.

He made one hell of a racket as he kicked a pile of junk in the kitchen. We didn't answer, not even when he insisted we put our hands up. We did nothing.

Shortly after, the paramedics arrived. Anders and I stepped back when they asked, but Dad didn't listen, nor actively resist, yet it took three of them to pull him away from Mom's side. They carried him through the room, placing him at the other end, close to the kitchen. He did not move.

Soon, the paramedics focused on Mom. They did what they had to do, but she was already gone. All three of us knew it, yet they proceeded nonetheless. It seemed to go on forever. Apparently, protocol dictated that efforts should continue for up to an hour, but I don't think they persisted that long that evening. I believe they gave up when Kyrre, the priest, arrived. He said something to Dad. Dad said nothing in return.

Later, after Mom was taken away and the house underwent further examination, they found a single box of pills in the bathroom. Not thousands, like I had seen in my... dream. One box, combined with a bottle of liquor, was more than enough to kill a woman her size. They said she had likely taken the mix of pills and alcohol, then changed her mind. That's why she went to the bathroom, to throw it all up. Failing to do so, she stumbled down the stairs to the living room, where she called for help. Weakened, she lost her footing and fell through the glass coffee table. She never rose again.

Later, the local newspaper coined it a "family tragedy" when covering the event. Everyone knew what they meant by that, and it was bullshit. Mom loved us too much. She would never give up like that. She was stronger than she had been in a long time—on the rise. She had even landed a job. The local press also wrote that she was alone when she died. More bullshit. Someone was there with her, and they had been there with Fredrik too. And Anders, who barely survived. Sitting in the church, I was convinced of one thing: whatever was chasing them was now after me. I was the next name on their list.

The priest sat on a wooden chair to our right, and a man in black sat down at the piano on the left. As his fingers soon danced between white and black, a beautiful melody wafted gracefully and gently through the church. In front of the piano stood a guitar and a microphone stand. On it, hung a hat that Mom had once given me. Grandpa gave it to her a long time ago. It was supposedly a lucky hat, and I always wore it when performing for others. I had decorated it with various pins, bracelets, and pieces of cut-up fabric. "Tour Young" was written on one side, the letters cut out from a Neil Young t-shirt. Further down on a hook from Ikea, attached with duct tape, hung a harmonica holder with a G major harmonica. On another hook hung a worn Tottenham jersey.

Partway through the funeral, the priest nodded towards me, and my throat tightened.

Stay on your feet now, Robert.

My pulse pounded beneath my tie knot, and I fought the urge to run out and throw up. My breath stuttered like an old LP needle, and the air halted at the top of my lungs.

You need to calm down. Breathe with your stomach.

I don't remember standing up, but soon I found myself at the altar, like a deer caught in the headlights of a truck. That truck. Jungle-Jim. The truck was approaching quickly, and I froze with my eyes wide open.

Come on Robert, this is for Mom. Get yourself together.

On the guitar stand hung my beloved Martin 000-18, a guitar my grandparents gave me a year ago when I turned eighteen. Dad never said much about it. He probably wished he were the one giving it to me.

The strings, ranging from 0.11 to 0.56, which usually felt soft and familiar, now seemed hard and foreign against my fingertips as I strummed a chord. My hands were trembling so much it must have looked like I was trying to shake the notes out of the harmonica when I wrapped the holder around my neck. Pink Floyd didn't use a harmonica in "Wish You Were Here", but I played my own version of the song. Mom often sang along while cooking: "We're just two lost souls swimming in a fish bowl."

After a shaky harmonica intro and the first line of lyrics, I wanted to give up and step down. How in the hell was I going to get through this?

Did you see Robert when he fell from the altar in the church? Couldn't handle the pressure. No, it hasn't been easy for him. Well, when you mention it, isn't that kid a bit odd? He's always been a little quirky.

Eventually I managed to calm myself down. Shifted my focus from the song to all the people who had come to say goodbye to Mom. Dad sat next to his parents on the left side of the family bench, while Mom's parents sat far to the right, as far away from each other as the bench allowed.

It surprised me that Kai wasn't holding a beer, sitting on the friends' side. I mean, if he drank a lot before Linn passed away, his drinking heavily intensified afterward. When his wife, Hanne from the store, also crossed over, he drank even more. He found her frozen in the yard one winter night, stumbling home from the pub. It must have been half a year ago. She had apparently slipped on the ice.

Kjell, Tony, and the others were there, Guro as well. We hadn't spoken since the *Titanic* sank a month earlier.

My song was nearing its end, and I took a step back. My right foot snagged on something, and I lost my balance. As I fell, my eyes swept over the people in the hall, up along the walls, and over the majestic church organ. Beyond the paintings on the ceiling. Everything happened fast, but I had time to think that the floor wouldn't catch me. That I would fall right through it. Just like Mom had fallen through the wall in her bathroom. Now, it was my turn to step into the shadows, into a nightmare from which I'd never escape. As expected, when I should have crashed into the floor with a bang, I fell through it, into the darkness. The light from the church shrank smaller and smaller until it was the size of a peephole, like the one on the door at Grandma and Grandpa's city house.

Then…

Everything…

Black…

"Robert, are you alright?"

"Fredrik?"

"No. It's Anders. You fell."

"Fre..."

"It's Anders… What's going on? You're soaked in sweat."

"I... I don't really remember. I think I tripped."

"Yeah, you could say that. All of a sudden, you fell backward. Crash!"

"I... I tripped over a cable or something."

"Well, it doesn't matter; it was a dramatic ending to the song, to say the least. Nonetheless, you nailed it! Mom would've been proud of you."

Anders helped me to my feet. His smile and strength made it easier to walk upright back down from the altar. Murmurs buzzed throughout the hall. The congregation likely wondered if I was capable of carrying the coffin, if I was strong enough this time around. I wondered that myself. I felt their eyes; they were all watching me.

Dad

We found ourselves in the church house for another memorial service. Once again, he was there. "I'm sorry for everything," the bank director squeaked as he lurched towards me. Silence fell over the room. Everyone looked at him. He looked at me. "You had nothing to do with Fredrik or Marianne's death. No more or less than the rest of us, at least. We have all made mistakes. We... I have behaved poorly. Isn't it time to put this behind us? If not for ourselves, should we do it for the kids? For the future, if there still is one out there?" He spoke loudly.

Shadows were pulsing in and out of nooks and crannies all over the room. Fully visible one moment, only to disintegrate and disappear back into their corners the next. Seconds later, they would emerge again. Something in them, in the shadows, wanted to come through. I heard voices from deep within them—gnawing at my conscience and whispering bleak prophecies.

As Mom was gone, Robert became the centre of their attention. I wanted to comfort my son, of course, but I couldn't. I wanted to love him, but they wouldn't let me do that either. At the other end of the room, Grandma watched her bank man with a furrowed brow.

"Can you forgive me?" The bank man extended a hand.

"I should have protected them. They were my responsibility," I whispered.

"Do you hear what I'm saying? I'm asking... Are you okay?" The bank director leaned over, and his breath reminded me of mould.

"It's my fault. They're dead because of me," I blurted out and stood up. "I have killed them all!"

Cups and plates rattled as I pushed my way through the tables. Then, out in the hallway, like Moses, I parted the gathering of guests, their mouths agape in shock at the spectacle I was causing. Their crying grew louder as I approached the door, and faded again as I left the house. That was the last time I saw most of them. Forgive me. Dear God, you must all forgive me.

The Circus

Mud clung to her bare legs as she stood with her back to me. In front of her, the bathroom cabinet floated in mid-air, and I saw her foggy eyes through one of the mirrors. With a trembling hand, she opened the cabinet doors and picked up a box of pills. She popped off the lid and swallowed its contents. All at once. She chewed mechanically, like a machine, until blood-red foam bubbled from between her lips. She was one of them now. One of the phantoms, forever caught in a loop of pain.

The cauldron on Death's head kept growing. Linn stood by the wheel of fortune, but this time the Witch didn't take her money. She was busy with something else. A large, black lump lay in front of her on the counter, and malevolence was painted across her face as she regarded it.

What the hell was going on? None of the phantoms had ever acted on their own before. They didn't decide what actions to take. Once they were here and became one of the phantoms, that's how they were. Like wax figures in a house of horrors. My house of horrors. My fears, my dread, and my imagination. Whether I liked it or not. All in my head. At least, that is what I thought it was.

Bingo-Bob lay paralyzed in front of her; he might even be dead? Her fingers, thin and crooked, moved in jerky motions and soon pointed down at the mutt. She observed him for a moment before digging her claws into his fur. The dog twitched and whimpered; he wasn't dead yet. His lips pulled back, revealing his teeth before he snapped his jaws shut. Several times he tried to bite her while she tore and pulled at him. The sound of his jaws clamping together grew increasingly faint. Soon, all I heard was the wet sound of her claws tearing into his belly. She slowly withdrew one hand and blood ran thickly down her arm. She studied her hand for a moment before plunging it back in. Higher up, towards his neck this time. Then once more, towards the head. His skull almost split in two, and blood sprayed across Linn's dress. Unaffected, she observed the chaos with her measly coins in hand. She wanted a new ticket.

Don't get me wrong, I was afraid of The Witch and Death, but Bingo-Bob had always been worse. Now he was gone. Slaughtered by the Witch. She took command, and I couldn't understand why it was happening. Why now? How? How could she even do this? The Witch of Mørkved and Death had disappeared ages ago.

Part III

The Witch of Mørkved, Death, and I, - a Memoir by Robert Baastad

Robert

Perhaps writing was a kind of therapy, but it wasn't conscious on my part. Occasionally, I fantasised that all the words would become a book, a memoir, but it likely wasn't interesting enough. I mean, who would read about the rather insignificant life of a guy from Øyerstad? For now, the manuscript is named *The Witch of Mørkved, Death, and I - a Memoir by Robert Baastad.* It lies beneath a pile of other scribblings, tucked away in a drawer. In the context of this book, certain parts of the manuscript are suitable to shed some light on my time away from Øyerstad.

Part III of this book consists of a range of excerpts from the shelved manuscript: *The Witch of Mørkved, Death, and I - a Memoir by Robert Baastad.*

Hitra - 1972

Olav

Back then, the weak light from underneath the door was accompanied by laughter and folk music from the living room. Playing cards smacked against the table amidst protests, discussions, exclamations, laughter, and cheers. Games of Bridge and Whist unfolded. Stories were shared. Yells and toasts filled the air. Mother, Father, aunts, and uncles, and surely a neighbour — possibly even a random passerby or two—all joined in. The smell of cigarettes lingered.

Olav peeked out from under the duvet in bed. Pale light sneaked into the room like tentacles, seeping through cracks in the walls along the floor and ceiling. Where had the loud and cheerful atmosphere in the living room gone? Nowadays, Olav's father was the only one there. He whispered stories of sailors, posed uncomfortable questions, and cried silently. Olav's duvet did not protect him, even though he tucked it under his feet. Sleep was far away.

They had been out with *Hitrakrabba*, his father's fishing boat, earlier in the day. As usual recently, Olav's knots were too loose, the saithe too small, and he damn well had to learn to handle the crabs. After all, he was fourteen years old now. Almost grown up. When his father took Olav's hands, it was not to warm them. He squeezed them hard, as punishment, even though the ropes were coiled up in perfect lengths, just as Olav had done a hundred times before. His father stank of spirits, as was usual when they swayed out at sea. Once again, he lay in bed hoping he would never have to go out on that boat again. Mother had said good night to her husband, but he didn't seem to notice. He hadn't in a long time. He didn't speak while she was awake. They didn't touch each other. Sitting at the kitchen table, Olav's father talked to himself again.

"It is a problem and it needs to be fixed," he murmured.

"We can't wait for it to solve itself. We have to do something about it. It's not too late."

"But, can't we leave it be?"

"No, we can't. Think of what will happen if..."

"Yes, I am aware. But she is just a child."

Olav must have been closer to sleep than he thought, for the words spun around in his head like living letters in a crab pot. Sharp and hard.

She is much more than a child now. Old enough to do as she wants. Old enough to decide for herself, Olav thought, while his father continued mumbling. He continued to talk. To someone who wasn't there.

Towards the End of the '90s

22: Concentration Camp for Crabs

Olav Aksnæs' eyes were as light as the summer sky beneath his blond fringe. With the moustache under his nose, he could have slid right onto the album cover of any cheap country record. According to statistics, he was roughly at midlife when he turned off at Berkåk and set his course for Hitra. Boisterous voices from suit-clad gentlemen in Trondheim's stately hotels and restaurants swirled in his head. With money in their eyes, they talked extensively about the crab hotel that was to be built outside Værnes, the local airport. It was supposed to be even larger and better than the one near Gardermoen, the airport a good distance south of Oslo. Olav liked the idea, but not the representatives who crawled out of their holes to make money whenever such projects popped up. Hitrakrabba AS was Hitra's largest employer and exported nearly five thousand tons of crabs in a season. Since Olav was the majority owner, he was an important piece to get on board. The interest was there, but many details still had to be clarified. The crabs' last stop before they were shipped out to boiling pots around the world. A concentration camp for our shelled friends.

I need to change the windshield wipers tomorrow. Firstly, I can't see a damn thing, and secondly, if the rubber falls off, the windshield will be ruined. Olav took off his tie and tossed it onto the passenger side floor of the old Mazda. A grave voice on the radio announced that the American embassies in Kenya and Tanzania had been subjected to terrorist attacks. Al-Qaeda was identified as the culprit. Over two hundred were killed and more than four thousand injured.

"At least I only kill crabs," Olav mused, watching the loose piece of rubber drag itself back and forth across the window. It was going to come off soon.

"Damn wipers!" he burst out, swerving the car to the side. He exited the 50-zone and narrowly avoided hitting the hitchhiker's arm. Luckily for the kid on the roadside, his headphones had reflected the car lights.

It might have been the rain on the windshield and the wind sneaking in from the north that made him consider stopping. That, and perhaps the fact that he had nearly killed the poor soul. Olav didn't like hitchhikers, or any other freeloaders for that matter. Especially not those outside Hitra. He didn't need endless monologues from random folks at the roadside to keep his mind occupied. However, out on the island, things were different; there, Olav had a brand to uphold. There, it was about marketing, an opportunity to talk in cheerful gatherings about the tourist facility at Karskjær (which he also owned). But the mainland? No, that was far beyond his area of responsibility.

"What the hell am I doing?" Olav slowed the car down, and he'd barely stopped before contemplating driving off again. But seeing the hitchhiker running in the rear-view mirror, he couldn't bring himself to do it.

If I have to listen to a poacher all the way to Hitra, I'd rather have him shoot me. Olav watched the hitchhiker in the mirror. Poachers rarely wore Metallica t-shirts. Maybe a drug addict, but not some freeloader. Olav rolled down the window and quickly concluded that the hitchhiker wasn't a drug addict either, even though he looked worn out.

"Headed to Hitra?" Olav asked.

"Eh, I think so," the hitchhiker replied.

"You think so, huh. Well, I hope you figure it out because

that's where I'm headed. You're hardly dressed to walk the whole way."

"I didn't have..."

"Get in the car, so I can close the window. The seat is getting wet."

A few hours earlier, Robert Baastad had left Øyerstad with a fragile psyche, some cash in his pocket, some clothes, and a far-too-small Tottenham jersey in his backpack. First, he headed south towards Skjønnsund. Aerosmith's "Don't Want to Miss a Thing"— the soundtrack to *Armageddon*—skipped and jumped as the laser in Robert's Discman struggled with the well-worn CD. He had seen that movie four times in the cinema with Kjell that spring.

Steven Tyler had barely warmed up when a heavily-loaded trailer, heading north in the opposite direction, began to slow down. The truck driver, a sturdy fellow with "Honk If You Love Bacon" printed on his shirt, asked him to hop in. Robert did as he said, thereby saving himself from the contemplation of what he would do if he had to walk past the church. Would he visit Fredrik's gravestone, or stop by the wilted flowers on Mom's mound to murmur a goodbye? He might find himself regretting his decision, potentially not leaving at all. It would be so much easier to close his eyes. To cease caring. To flee from it all. Without thinking. Without uttering goodbyes to anyone.

The truck driver, Steinar Flataboden, also cheered for Tottenham. Well, "*Toten*ham", as he pronounced it. Yep, that's right. He hailed from Toten, a rather small place tucked away in the middle of nowhere in Norway—somewhat like Øyerstad—and he didn't cease chuckling at his own joke until they passed Elverum. After a hot dog and cola stop there, they took the E6 north through Østerdalen. About ten miles before Trondheim, they passed a sign indicating Berkåk just a couple of kilometres ahead. In Berkåk, a turnoff led towards Norway's largest island. "A fantastic place with incredible nature and fishing spots" as Dad would have said. Hitra. Robert smiled, thinking of how Dad used to be. "You know, the island has Norway's densest deer population? We should go there sometime, the whole family."

"Hey, it'd be great if you drop me off in Berkåk. I believe I should head west, towards the sea"

Oh yeah? Like the Village People? To the West? You think life is peaceful there?" He laughed, briefly pausing before continuing, "I thought you were riding with me up to Trondheim?

"I thought so too, but there has been a change in plans..."

In Berkåk, as the taillights of Flataboden's truck disappeared northwards, Robert continued west along Highway 700 on foot. The more miles he put between himself and Øyerstad, the source of all his misery, the more the buzzing in his head subsided. Thoughts separated from one another and his brain became clearer. The lump in his throat and the stones in his stomach shrank and diminished. For the first time in a long while, he felt kinda free, even though Chris Rea was singing "This ain't no technological breakdown, this is the road to hell" from a greatest hits CD. As the song neared its end, the first drops fell.

Okay, Robert, for the first time in your miserable life, you've managed to get out. Away from everything old, away from that cursed place, and... you should have brought a rain jacket. And a flashlight. Soon it will be pitch dark. Soon you'll be damn wet.

Olav cleared away old newspapers, a book, *Beyond Good and Evil* by Friedrich Nietzsche, some crumpled chocolate wrappers, and used coffee cups from the passenger seat. The tie stayed on the floor.

"Excuse the mess, but I've been on the road for a few hours. Didn't expect to have guests, you see."

"I understand. I don't hitchhike that often either. Not around these parts, at least."

"You travel light. You're not on the run, are you? Robbed a bank? Or a post office?" It was over two hours to Hitra, so Olav went ahead with a handful of basic questions.

"To be completely honest, in many ways, yes. I mean, I am on the run, but I haven't robbed anyone. As a matter of fact, I don't really know what I'm running from, just that if I don't get away, it will kill me. Just like it has the rest of..."

Olav scrutinised him. "...the rest of?"

"My family." Robert didn't hold back.

"Family issues?" Olav asked, not taking Robert's statement about his family being killed literally.

Robert twisted in his seat before answering. "You could say that. My kid brother died a few years ago. We buried Mom yesterday. Dad's gone mad and my big brother is half handicapped. Family issues all over the place, I guess." Robert looked at Olav. "Sure you want to hear more?"

"Uh, we've got time. I don't have any other plans," Olav replied, keeping his eyes on the road.

After an hour in the car, the sun once again revealed itself over the island to the west. An orange velvet carpet unfurled over the Trondheimsfjord, as Olav asked, "I wonder how they are feeling, your family, now that you're gone too?" His eyes remained fixed on the way ahead.

Robert had shared most of what happened in Øyerstad, omitting smaller details like the circus, butchered dogs, black holes, and demons.

"Dad probably doesn't care. And Anders? He's better off by himself."

"So, do they even know where you are now?"

"I left a note for Dad saying I'd be gone for a while. But I didn't say where. I didn't even know myself when I left."

"And now you're headed to Hitra."

"Yeah, I guess so. The old Dad would've liked it. Not sure about the new one, though. Maybe I can tell him about this sometime." Robert's gaze followed a flock of frantic seagulls down to a fishing boat passing by out on the fjord.

"When your dad and his pals were here, they must have taken the ferry over there," Olav said, pointing towards an abandoned ferry terminal. "These days we are using the tunnel, a six-kilometre-long expedition underneath millions of tons of water. Cod, crab, anglerfish, and all sorts of other weird stuff swimming above our heads."

Robert sank into his seat as they descended into the underground. As they approached the bottom, Olav brightened.

"Down here," he said, pointing ahead and to the right, "Norway's most lucrative speed camera! Tourists are a bit scared of the depths, you see. So, as they near the bottom, they hit the gas just a little bit harder to build up enough speed to get up on the other side. They wouldn't want to be caught down there. And then they all get photographed. 'Smile!' Olav grinned. "The picture arrives in the mailbox a while after their vacation, along with an invoice for varying amounts. It's the only money that they leave behind. They arrive with their cars loaded with diesel and food. Then they live on the island, filling their trailers with fish and crab, before heading back home. Some tourists are fine, but the Swedes, oh, and the Poles, they're the worst."

Olav slapped the steering wheel with the back of his hand. "If I get the chance, I encourage them to really step on it down in the tunnel, so they can make it up on the other side. I tell them speed limits don't apply in the tunnel. We can't risk having a pile of tourists stuck at the bottom, blocking traffic." Olav glanced at the camera as it flew by and then continued, "Between you and me, I don't always pay taxes on everything either. So let this be my contribution to the prime minister and his friends." His laughter was louder and more resounding than Robert's.

"I guess you haven't planned where to stay when you arrive at Hitra?"

The question itself didn't surprise Robert as much as the manner in which it was asked. Olav's accent was gone. He suddenly sounded like one of the locals over at the gas station in Øyerstad, chit-chatting about all sorts of things! Robert looked quizzically at Olav, before commenting, "You're quick with picking up dialects, huh?"

"Excuse me?" Olav didn't seem to understand the question.

Robert had heard that many merchants often mirror their target audience in both speech and body language to appear credible, to close the sale, but this was just odd. "I just thought… Never mind. No, I haven't figured out a place to stay yet."

"You can stay with me. I have a vacant fisherman's hut. But it won't be free." His accent was back.

"I see. Well, I'd be happy to borrow it, but I'm kinda short on cash. You need help with anything? I'm hardworking."

Olav remained silent, staring straight ahead, as if he hadn't heard what Robert said.

"Sorry, I didn't mean to be pushy."

"Pushy? No, it's not that. I'll find some work for you... I'll find some work for you," he repeated, mostly to himself, thoughtful, savouring the words as he seemed to be far, far away in his mind.

The ocean lay to their left as they navigated the winding gravel roads. Sometimes the view towards the horizon was open, other times shielded by weather-beaten pine trees and extensive moors and bogs. Glowing houses, worn hamlets, and farms were sporadically positioned between them and the sea. They reminded Robert of monuments, or gravestones memorialising old days of glory, when generations of fishermen brought life to the island.

Things had changed here as well, not unlike Robert's Øyerstad. The younger generation didn't care about the farms and houses. They couldn't get away from the island fast enough, heading towards the hustle and bustle of the big city, stress, and ulcers. Things here were different from in Øyerstad, but also much the same. Nostalgic in many ways.

With every metre Robert rolled along with Olav, he moved further away from Øyerstad than he had ever been. As they approached Karskjær after just under an hour, it was not possible to get any further away without switching to a boat.

"There are more deer than people here," Olav said to Robert, who was watching a buck in a meadow they passed by. "Over five thousand of them. They mostly stay inland on the island, while the people of Hitra reside near Fillan, out on the west coast. That's where I have my factory, Hitrakrabba."

Soon they veered off the main road towards Olav Aksnæs's red-painted kingdom nestled within a small bay. The sky was ablaze above the collection of houses and boats down by the pier. Robert thought about the postcard on the refrigerator at home. It could have been the same place, although all such places probably looked exactly the same up here.

On one of the two gas pumps under the "Welcome to Karskjær" sign, hung a smaller poster. Olav had probably made it himself from cardboard and plastic foil. "Super cheap gasoline and diesel!" Next to the pumps was a wooden hut with a corresponding sign; "Kiosk and gas station."

"This is my place, Robert! The most beautiful place on

Hitra. In all of Norway, or the world, for that matter." Olav spoke in awe.

"It is beautiful. It really is." Robert said, and meant it.

"Over there, to the right," Olav pointed towards a small house past the intersection. "That's where my mother lives. She's holding up well even though she's not as quick on her feet anymore. You'll probably run into her on a stormy day. At least if you stay here for a while."

Further ahead, out by the docks, a row of fishing boats gently swayed. The old fenders and woodwork creaked. A scent of seawater and diesel swept into the car as Olav opened the window, seemingly to give Robert the full experience.

Beyond the dock was a shop where Olav sold fishing gear, groceries, and beer to tourists, who frequently scrutinised their receipts in disbelief after paying. This was Olav's island, and these were his prices. Above the fish receiving station, a bit further from the shop, lay "Olav Aksnæs Delicatessen and Catering", a restaurant which also was overpriced but, after all, served exceptional food.

The Karskjær boat harbour was well-shielded from the open sea by hundreds of small islands. If you were to take one of the many boats along the docks, it was about forty-five minutes out to open sea, between Hitra and the neighbouring island of Frøya. After that, it was either England, Iceland, or the USA next. It depended on the direction you took.

Olav handed Robert a set of keys and pointed him towards a numberless fishing cabin.

"You can sleep there tonight, and tomorrow I'll find some work for you."

"Are you sure it's okay? I really don't want to be a burden."

"It's fine. Just, take the key now. A few hours in bed will do us both good."

As Olav turned to leave, he once again said something that

made Robert halt.

"Last one to bed is a three-legged pig!" he said in perfect Øyerstad dialect.

For a microsecond, Olav paused. He seemed to freeze. Was he also wondering where that phrase came from? Robert only knew two, maybe three people who used that phrase, a three-legged pig. One was Robert himself, Anders might have said it, but Fredrik owned that expression.

"... a three-legged pig," Olav repeated quietly, as if he was searching for the source of what he just said. Robert considered asking what he meant, but refrained as Olav started walking towards the house again.

Once inside the cabin, Robert tossed his backpack onto one of the two beds. They were tightly placed together in the tiny bedroom. The mattress was firmer than the one he had had in Øyerstad.

Anders, Dad, Mom, and Fredrik, you should have been here now. The dream of an impossible family reunion accompanied him towards sleep. That night, Robert experienced the most rejuvenating sleep in ages. *You should see me now, Dad. I'm on Hitra.*

24: Like a Dream

It didn't take many hours by the sea before the memories of Øyerstad began to fade, to crumble and fall apart like a sea star washed ashore on one of the many stony beaches. The Witch of Mørkved, Death, and whatever might have remained of Bingo-Bob did not appear—neither in dreams nor visions. Not in daylight. The circus quickly transformed into faint memories of a nightmarish playground, a domain for everything he had once feared. The grief, hanging like lead with hooks in his heart, lightened after a few days. Robert saw Mom smiling again, and that's how he wanted to remember her. Forever.

27: Coffee in a Plastic Cup

For Robert, the combination of coffee in a plastic cup, the scent of the sea, and the low-hanging sun to the east was pure magic. He met first-time visitors on the pier at five in the morning to teach them to navigate among the islands. Once out at sea, it wasn't always easy to find your way back and many rocks lurked beneath the surface. Olav, tired of rescuing tourists among the islands, offered all newcomers a free guide on their first trip. An introduction to maps and compasses. The introductory tour took three to four hours, visiting spots where the tourists could catch almost unlimited pollock, cod, and maybe even a halibut. Some threw in a few extra kroner and also received a lesson in slaughtering fish, or as Olav reminded Robert on several occasions, "It's not slaughtering fish, you damned southerner. It's gutting fish!" Olav praised him for the job nonetheless, possibly exaggerating a tad, likely to avoid the dirty job himself. Later in the day, Robert helped out in the kitchen. He peeled potatoes and cut vegetables.

"Today, you must get those damn cherry tomatoes right. Remember, people eat with their eyes!" The head chef, who had many years behind him at top restaurants in Oslo and around Europe, had also been on the national cooking team, participating in the Bocuse d'Or. He barked orders and commands as he prepared a fennel purée for the halibut at the other end of the kitchen. The first of ten courses in the tasting menu they assembled once a month. "Folks, today we're making food that'll fuck in their mouths! Make me proud."

Robert lifted his knife above his head and joined in the roar along with the other chefs. He also spent many hours behind the cash register in the store, often followed by a trip to Hitrakrabba, the factory in Fillan, where he fixed malfunctioning conveyor belts and changed lightbulbs. Together, Olav and Robert ensured the pumps down at the pier had enough gasoline and diesel, and that the cabins were ready to welcome new guests after the old ones said their farewells. In addition, a heap of small tasks filled any gaps in the schedule. They painted and sanded boats and repaired jarred engines. They also assisted half- and fully-drunk tourists who had lost the keys to the cabins in the sea. No matter how large a wooden piece Olav attached to the key ring, someone always managed to lose them. Olav also caught Robert one evening with one of the guitars that gathered dust in the bar, leading to sporadic live performances in the pub. Robert protested at first, but of course, succumbed to the pressure. Towards the end of the summer season, he played for the last of the tourists, and then into the autumn and winter, he entertained the local heroes with overplayed classic songs.

Robert also liked standing in the kiosk up by the fuel pumps. Not to charge for gasoline, no, it was for the candy. On Hitra, Robert was the one who picked candy for the kids and helped them rent movies while their fathers were out fishing. Robert could almost see him, and sometimes even thought that it wasn't entirely impossible that Fredrik too might wander in and order "super-salties for ten kroner."

When the evenings came, Robert was so exhausted that he didn't even turn off the light before falling asleep. Therein likely lay the key to how he so quickly shed everything he carried with him from Øyerstad. There was no time to brood. No time to think. *Keep busy, Robert.*

Hitra - 1975

Dinner with the Aksnæs Family

They sat in silence as Olav's mother served veal steak, potatoes, and broccoli. She was humming a somewhat minor-key version of "Love Will Keep Us Together". The original, which was incessantly playing on the radio, was in a major key. Her eyes nervously skipped between her guests. Jesus, they had grown up. Olav, her lovely little kid, wasn't so much a kid anymore; at seventeen, he had started working on his blond mustache. That serious look on his face. And Rakel. She had been through more than most locals went through in a lifetime, even though she was only twenty-two. *I should have protected her,* the family mother thought. Protected her from him. Her eyes moved over to Knud-Olav, her husband. He sliced his steak so forcefully his knife screeched against the porcelain plate. His movements were mechanical, programmed for a plate three millimetres lower than the one he was now eating off. Clanging, tinkling, and jingling. Olav was irritated by the sound of the cutlery, but he despised the smacking even more. *Can't you just shut that dreadful mouth of yours?*

How had his father managed to persuade Rakel to come to dinner, anyway? What had he said to her? They hadn't had dinner in the same house since she announced her pregnancy. That was years ago. After that, she was no longer welcome. Driven away from her family by her own father, and now, all of a sudden, they were sitting in the same room again. Olav and Rakels mother glanced down at her potatoes. She held a fork in her hand. She said nothing. She did not smile. Maybe she knew what Knud-Olav were up to?

Knud-Olav Aksnæs, Olav's and Rakel's father, was a wealthy and powerful man, to the extent that one can be powerful on Hitra. Politicians, businessmen, and fortune-seeking women wanted to be seen in his company. He often brought some of them out on his boat. The women, that is.

"That's a business partner and friend," he had said to Olav last time they were out, just weeks ago.

His wife never said anything, even though she must have known what was going on. Was she afraid of what might happen to her if she did talk? She only needed to look to Rakel, her own child, to see the consequences of not keeping quiet. She would be treated as an outcast for the rest of her life. Not only by her husband, but by everyone on the island. He would make sure of that.

Again, the knife screeched against the plate, and the gathering around the table made corresponding grimaces. Knud-Olav cast an accusatory glance at Rakel. She turned her head towards the stroller where the baby was sleeping.

Three years after becoming a grandfather, Knud-Olav still hadn't gotten over the shock. The humiliation. His own daughter, his blood, Rakel, wasn't married. Not engaged. She didn't even know who the father of the child was.

"Must have been some tourist, I guess," she had said, shrugging indifferently when confronted by her father. Olav was still astonished that Knud-Olav didn't hit her that day. Nevertheless, he did not spare his words. A bastard child was not fitting for an Aksnæs. The daughter of the Crab King. He had a reputation to maintain. What would people say about them now? What would they whisper into each other's fat-chewing mouths at the gentlemen's clubs when he turned his back?

It didn't help anyone that the child needed extensive treatment due to severe deformities in its face. Knud-Olav had become a grandfather to a child whom he, and many on Hitra, referred to as "The Elephant Kid". The crab throne was to be inherited by genuine men, not a freak. "That kid belongs in a damned circus!" Knud-Olav was merciless.

Of course, he tried to persuade Rakel to get rid of the child. As long as she kept it, she wouldn't get a penny from him. He was trying to smoke her out. Stop the supply of water, food, and air until she agreed to his bizarre demands. Rakel's mother helped her with money for rent and the child's treatment for a while without Knud-Olav knowing. When he found out, he hit her for the first time.

Now, Knud-Olav's robotic arm stopped mid-air when the doorbell rang. The ringing mimicked huge church bells and echoed throughout the living room. Rakel looked again towards the stroller. Knud-Olav signalled to the others around the table to remain seated. He stood up, wiped his hands on a cloth napkin, and then threw it onto the table.

They could hear him conversing at the door. It felt like forever before footsteps resonated in the hall. He did not return alone.

"Is our boy in there?" a woman's voice said, as she stepped in with her shoes on. She looked first at the stroller, then at Rakel. The joy in her face. Sheer joy. The man behind her, whom Olav assumed was her husband, also looked satisfied, albeit a bit more reserved.

"Our boy?" Rakel said after a few seconds, looking at Olav. Then they both turned to their mother, who looked down at the food she hadn't touched. Finally, their gaze shifted to their father, and they realised what he had done. He had put the boy up for adoption! Sold him, or maybe even given him away. The estranged couple were here to collect the child, Pål-Ottar.

The hopeful couple stood expectantly in front of the dining table. They had found a child they intended to live with and love for the rest of their lives. From their appearance, it seemed they had been searching for a long time. Knud-Olav had fulfilled their deepest wish. However, everything was merely an illusion, as the child's mother knew nothing about the deal he had struck with them. It did not take long before the glow in the stranger's face cooled. No words were exchanged between her and Rakel. They simply looked at each other. A telepathy between women.

It was unclear what Knud-Olav had expected, but Rakel's plate, which exploded against the wall just centimetres from his head, took him by surprise. The man, presumed to be the husband, lunged towards his wife, pulling her down to the floor as a plate of Brussels sprouts exploded over their heads. Rakel probably wasn't aiming at them.

After Knud-Olav's immediate reaction had settled, he lowered his forehead and directed his focus towards the stroller. Then he flew across the room, hissing, "This is for everyone's best." His wife, the child's grandmother, pushed herself away from the table, stood up, and blocked the way. At the same time, Rakel was on her feet, heading towards her baby. Mothers protecting their children, you don't mess with them. They'll do anything. Dead or alive.

Knud-Olav's hand struck his wife's face with such force that she tumbled over the dining room table before hitting the floor. He paused for a brief moment, casting a glance at her as she lay still on her stomach. A scream from the unknown lady brought him back. He continued towards the child. First, he was going to get Rakel out of the way, and then the strangers were going to take her child with them. No matter the cost. Again, he raised his arm, this time against his own daughter.

Olav did not react as quickly as the women in the family, but eventually, he too awoke. He grabbed a fork, pushed himself away from the table, and lunged after his father. At the same time, he swung the fork through the air and hit the seaman in the neck before he reached Rakel. The fork conjured a scream fuelled by fury, not pain.

Knud-Olav staggered backward while trying to get a grip on the fork stuck in his neck. Then Olav hit a person for the first time in his life. His father's jaw yielded as the knuckles hit him squarely in the face. Knud-Olav kept stumbling backward and tripped over his wife, who was still lying on the floor behind him.

"You've gone too far," Olav screamed in fury. "Get out! That goes for you too! You'll find no child here today. Not here. Never!"

The innocent couple scuttled back through the hallway, hurt and shocked. Leaving their dreams and hopes, smashed into a thousand pieces, behind them. Knud-Olav crawled backward along the floor, and Olav followed. His father was still muttering that this was for the best for everyone.

As they reached the front porch, Olav screamed, "You'll never set foot in this house again." The injured captain got to his feet, straightened his shirt, and regarded Olav with a puzzled expression. Knud-Olav was not merely hurt and angry; Olav thought he might have seen a trace of pride in his look…

Back to the End of the '90s

29: Who the F*ck is Alice?

We had emptied a bottle of Laphroaig, and Olav's speech resembled the sounds of a beached orca. Still, he insisted he wasn't drunk. Robert, struggling to focus, leaned in closer to catch the rest of the story, doing his best to filter out the noise from the others in the pub.

"He never came back?" Robert asked.

"Nope. Neither he, Rakel, nor the baby, Pål-Ottar." They disappeared. Poof! Gone." Olav gesticulated with his arms how they evaporated into thin air.

"Huh? All of them disappeared?"

"Yeah, well, after I chased my old man out of the house, I stood on the porch for some time, just in case he would come crawling back. He never did. After a while, I went back in and found Mother on her knees in the living room, scrubbing the floor. She didn't seem to notice me, nor the blood dripping from the cut above her eye. 'Where is Rakel?' I asked. She didn't answer, just scrubbed even harder. 'Mom! Where are Rakel and Pål-Ottar?' Still, she said nothing, glancing towards the terrace door, which stood wide open."

"They left through the back door?" Robert shifted his attention from the glow of his cigarette back to Olav.

"Yes, and I couldn't find them. Not in the garden, nor down by the road. I screamed and shouted like a madman, but got no answer. So, I took the car. I drove around all night, but still nothing. They vanished into thin air."

"So, you think your father got hold of them? That they went with him on the boat?"

"It's the only sensible explanation. Father and his boat disappeared, and so did they. He must have snuck around and waited for them. If he just got hold of the child, Rakel would have done anything to get him back."

"You must have talked to someone? The cops? They couldn't help you?"

"They tried. Trust me, we searched for a long time. The whole damn island was involved. At least in the beginning. Then Danne, Olderø, and I continued long after most people, the police, and the coast guard had given up. It was so strange, I mean, when people disappear on the sea like that, you always find something. A buoy, a can, a rope, or barrels bobbing against a beach nearby, or damn far away. They always leave something behind."

"But not this time?" Robert looked at Olav with wide eyes.

"Not this time," Olav repeated.

"My God, what a mess."

"At least the local paper got a real story to write about. Finally, they could use those big, dramatic headlines. Most articles were about Father, the fishing boat, the factory, and then his family. In that order. They portrayed him as some kind of saint—a great loss for the local community. Everyone wondered, 'Where did he go? Why wasn't there a single trace of him?' Nobody asked about Rakel and her child, at least not that I heard. 'What would happen to the jobs at the crab factory?' Shit, they even named a street after him.

National newspapers covered the case as well. Some of them even wrote about Rakel and Pål-Ottar. Hell, even I appeared in one of the pictures. That newspaper sat on my desk for ages, always open on the same page. Rakel, Pål-Ottar, and I on Father's boat. That picture… It was… I'll dig it out someday. You should see them. They were beautiful."

Robert emptied his beer, and foam ghosts sank with open

mouths to the bottom of the glass.

"For most people, life simply went on," Olav continued. "People took the bus to work, missed their appointments, and ate fish pudding served with dill in tart shells. People still ate crab—more than before. I took over the factory, even though Rakel probably would have wanted us to let it rot and die. But the locals needed jobs. A future. Mother and I could still give them that."

Robert placed a hand on Olav's shoulder.

"You did what you had to in order to protect your family. My God, you knocked out your own father! Not many can say they've done that. And then, you kept the factory running for the community. You've given them all of this." Robert lifted his arms and gestured for Olav to take a look around.

"Yeah, I guess it turned out okay in the end."

"I think Rakel would have been proud of you. All the things you've done."

"I hope so." Olav emptied his beer too and waved to the bartender.

"It seems we have quite a bit in common," Robert said as two new freshly tapped beers arrived at the table.

"Yes, we've had our struggles. But we've managed fairly well nonetheless. We're sitting here, aren't we? That's something."

"You know, if I had stayed in Øyerstad, I would have snapped."

"Well, going through what we have, it leaves its mark. You had your demons to fight, and I had mine. I think I inherited mine from my father when he was no longer around. His spectres suddenly haunted me. He posed many questions in the night, and soon I did too. Could I have prevented it all? Was it my fault? What if Rakel died cursing me for siding with Mother and Father? Could I have done more to stop them? To stop him?"

"You couldn't have known what they were planning. No way! But, what about your mom, do you think she knew anything?"

"I think she knew something was happening, but not what."

"You never asked her?"

"No, I never did. I might have planned to, perhaps even wanted to, but we kept pretending as if everything was fine. We never discussed it, kept it all bottled up. At first, it seemed okay, but then something toxic started to grow within me. Something cancerous, frustration and resignation building up. Still, I pushed through, filling my days with work. And when I wasn't working, I drank—a lot. A relentless cycle of distractions, work and poison, poison and work, all to avoid confronting my thoughts. More poison. And then, when you've finally hit rock bottom and accept that the way you live is... well, shit, it's too late. Failure is a part of your system, and you can't get up. Like with your brother, right? Fit and healthy until suddenly it's over."

"Well, it is…"

"… One negative thought might seem harmless, but when one arrives, others usually follow. They take root here." Olav pointed to his head. "The pain then seeps into your stomach. Before long, you resort to self-medication and wallow in self-pity. More dark thoughts... You try to persuade yourself you're strong, that you don't need anyone. You don't talk. You don't share—until one day, you lose control. I've been there. As you said, I could have snapped too."

"But you got out of it," Robert almost stated.

"Yes, I guess I did, but it took time.

"What happened?"

"I guess, in a way, you could say a book saved my life. Psychology, philosophy, big thoughts, and nonsense." Olav leaned forward, clenched his fist, and placed it against his forehead like a Greek philosopher. "Knowledge begets knowledge," he declared with a dark voice and looked up at the ceiling.

"Now, that's deep," Robert commented with a smile, and took a drag of his cigarette. A gulp of beer. "Now you simply need a white sheet and an olive branch in your hair."

"Deep stuff, indeed," Olav said and laughed. "All joking aside, I actually stumbled upon a book that turned things around. Made me aware of some stuff. Got me to try to live a bit more like the person I really wanted to be. If you did that, things should start happening gradually. Better things."

"And it worked? Mr Miyagi-style?"

"It sounds stupid, I know. But think about it, what if you forced yourself to find and focus on the good things, no matter what kind of shit you've gotten yourself into. Most people can't do that because they don't know. They think they are their thoughts. They don't know that they actually can change what they think, and how they act upon their thoughts, if they really want to. Instead, they let themselves be swept away in a downward spiral. They give up as soon as they meet enough resistance. But you can't give up, because, believe it or not, slowly but surely, something happens to you. You start to see solutions instead of problems. A little more light instead of a lot of darkness. You just have to pretend long enough."

Olav was no longer embodying the role of a Greek philosopher, and Robert pondered: were Bingo-Bob, the circus, the Witch of Mørkved, Death, and all the rest just figments of his thoughts? A cancerous growth in his mind? *No*, Robert shook it off, *there has to be more to it.*

Just as Robert felt the urge to hug Olav, a familiar song blaring over the speakers interrupted him. Still not realising how drunk he was, Robert jumped up and belted out, "Alice, Alice, who the f*** is Alice?", like he meant it. Olav paused, wiped away his tears, and then, with a hint of a smile, joined in.

31: Robert Didn't Hide

Robert hadn't really planned on hiding on the island. He just didn't tell anyone he was going there. By the winter of 1998, after living in the fisherman's cabin for well over six months, he hadn't been in contact with friends, family, or anyone else for that matter. There was nothing about his grand disappearance in the national press or on teletext either. That was somewhat positive, after all. No one had reported him missing. No one was looking for him.

—

Robert wrote letters and postcards to friends and family but never mailed them. It was for the best, because even if just a tiny speck of his DNA ended up in a mailbox in Øyerstad, they—Death, the Witch of Mørkved, and everything else that haunted him—would trace him back to this place. It was best not to take any chances.

—

It's often said that it takes ten years to replace all the cells in your body, effectively becoming an entirely new version of yourself. Yet, time on Hitra seemed to elapse more swiftly than elsewhere. After a few days and weeks, Robert felt like a new person. He focused on good things, meaningful work, and had a boss who really cared for him. The co-workers, no matter where he turned, smiled and were so pleasant that Robert occasionally envisioned the crew at the Karskjær complex as a sect. Their Messiah was Olav "Christ" Aksnæs, and they all drank his blood from his cup.

The pressure in Robert's head was gone, and he slept well at night. Occasionally, he got the feeling that things were almost going too smoothly. As if someone or something wanted him to forget where he came from. He still remembered Guro, Dad, Kjell, and Anders, but he didn't long to go back all the same. He didn't often think about Fredrik or Mom either. Life before Hitra seemed pale and transparent. He missed nothing of it.

—

The person in the mirror smiled back as he walked out onto the terrace with his coffee cup. "Good morning, Captain, you're looking sharp today." He said it without a hint of irony, even though his beard growth was probably Hitra's, and possibly Europe's, slowest. But stop shaving, and stubble will eventually appear. On Robert too. Out on the terrace.

17th May 1999 was still a couple of weeks away, and while the wind was cool, it was not cold as it brushed against his face. The water was calm, and the sun mirrored itself in the windows of the boats and the red-painted houses. The seagulls made a hell of a racket as a fishing boat chugged into the harbour. The captain of the boat waved at Robert, a bottle raised high in the air. Then he went straight into the doorframe as he was entering the cabin, to dock. The scent of the sea. A light taste of salt and spring on his tongue. In the kitchen of the restaurant, they were preparing lunch. Baked halibut with bacon and cod omelette.

From the terrace, green glass spheres and ropes hung,

while a fat sea urchin balanced on a rock below the water's surface. The dried sea urchin shells his Grandpa had hanging on the wall of the cabin in Øyerstad sneaked into his thoughts. Robert wondered if Dad ever stood in Karskjær and saw the same things he did. Like now. Breathing the same air.

As the drunk skipper and his boat were finally docking, another, faster boat approached the docks. A speedboat filled with harpoons, wetsuits and oxygen tanks. Divers. They came in from the left, inside Helsøya, which shielded Karskjær from the open sea. The boat was tied up at the dock, and Robert found himself wondering about the eye colour of the brunette at the front. She glanced in his direction, but he doubted she really saw him.

—

Half-Swede Danne, the owner of the diving shop in Fillan, was always eager to share not only tips, advice, and tricks on diving but also insights on how to connect with people to influence their decisions. After all, he owned the most successful diving shop on the island and seemed to have a kid around every corner. However, there was still no sign of a wife, at least as far as Robert knew.

"When you greet new people, be open and smile broadly. Approach them and extend your hand. First, notice their eye colour. Repeat it in your mind. When they introduce themselves, weave their name into a memorable story, maybe from your childhood or a movie or concert. You look them in the eye, shake their hands, and you remember their names. People like that.

—

Robert was snapped back to reality by Olav's honk from the other side of the cabin. Grabbing his backpack, he headed for the door, murmuring, "Thank you for now, dear cabin. It's been a pleasure." He stepped outside, locked the door one final time and climbed into the idling car. He handed the keys to Olav and tossed his backpack onto the back seat.

"I'll bill you for the rent, sometime before Christmas," Olav said, smirking.

"Ah, well, you know what happens then. I'll take off, and never come back," Robert replied.

"So, where will you run to this time?"

"To the Bahamas. No, actually, it'll be Poland, because you won't look for me there."

"You know me well, In Poland, you'll have to fend for yourself." Olav laughed and reversed out of the parking lot. Soon, they were leaving Karskjær, heading towards Nordbukta, about ten kilometres from the centre in the direction of the tunnel.

The smooth, sloping coastal rocks lay bare under the spring sun, while the short-statured heather basked in the warmth. Seaweed was exposed by the retreating sea as they turned onto a gravel road, leaving the main road behind after ten minutes. They followed it for a few hundred metres, and when they passed the farmer's house, Olav greeted the woman in the window. Then they passed the barn on the left. In front of it, down by the water, was the house. It stood sturdy with its two stories and a footprint of no more than maybe eighty square metres. The house bore many scars from its battles against the harsh sea climate. White paint flaked off the walls, the gutter hung loose, and the living room window to the left appeared cracked.

Olav got out of the car while Robert sat for a while, observing the Volvo parked in front of the house. The paint was heavily rusted, and the bumper hung loose on one side. In Øyerstad, this was a real gem.

Robert got out of the car as the farmer, Odd-Johnny, came strolling down to the yard. He wore a John-Deere cap and rubber boots with dignity. His arms, reminiscent of a TV antenna, flailed as he pointed out the nearby boat, barn, house, and the small mountain peak in the distance—the only place nearby with cell phone coverage. Robert didn't have a mobile phone, so it didn't matter much to him.

After a while, the farmer extended a pair of keys towards Olav.

"It'll be nice to have some permanent residents here for a change," he said, a hint of weariness in his voice. "My wife and I have longed for that. We can't keep renting out to all these companies. You just can't trust them. You never know who's going to show up, and when something gets damaged, they never fix anything. What's worse, their employers don't seem to care either. They end agreements on a whim and pay whenever they feel like it, if they even pay at all. I'm sure you'll take better care of this place, Olav."

"Ah, no, the keys are for him." Olav pointed at Robert, and the keyring soon flew through the air towards him.

"Figured as much. Didn't expect to get fancy people like you out here," the farmer said, looking at Olav. He then turned to Robert. "There's a key for the house and one for the car."

"It's a long walk to Karskjær. You need a car," Olav said with a certain pride.

Robert stood gaping.

"Yeah, you need a house too. What else are you going to do with a car? You've earned this, kid! A place of your own."

"We should go in and check it out," Odd-Johnny said, taking the lead. A smiling Olav followed him, with Robert trailing behind in disbelief.

To the right of the hallway lay the living room, where a framed map of Hitra and its adjacent waters hung above the sofa. Pine panelling adorned the walls. On a small, round table, beside a larger living room table, stood a travel TV. The type Grandpa used to have at the cabin, equipped with the world's longest antenna. Atop the TV were two dried sea urchin shells and a couple of troll dolls.

A massive, untreated pine cabinet with black iron details stretched from the wooden floor almost up to the ceiling. It must have been built in place, as there was no way they could have gotten that behemoth through the doors. On the upper part, there were two cabinet doors. *Classic liquor cabinet*, Robert thought.

At the bottom was a cabinet door where he assumed board games and a cabin guest book or two were stored. On the plate in the middle of the cabinet lay hunting and fishing magazines, a Yatzy pad, a couple of well-worn decks of cards, and a ballpoint pen in a copper bowl.

The bathroom featured a plastic tub with a shower curtain protecting the toilet when in use. The linoleum floor was pastel green, complemented by yellow plastic wallpaper that framed the rest of the room. A picture of the Swedish royal couple hung on the wall above a shelf, which held only one book - "The Big Toilet Time Spender," bursting with jokes about Swedes. Above the toilet, a ceramic tile displayed an image of a guy peeing on the floor with the words "If you can read this, you're close enough" written in sufficiently small script.

The wallpaper in the kitchen resembled a scene from a Boney M music video, bursting with pastels. A solid kitchen table took up much of the floor space, surrounded by mismatched chairs. Up the stairs from the kitchen, there were three bedrooms accommodating a total of eight beds.

Later, after touring the house, Robert watched as Olav's car disappeared over the hill behind the barn. Turning his attention to a cabinet in the living room, he wasn't surprised to find a stack of magazines, filled-out Yatzy sheets, and cabin guest books. In total, he counted sixteen books, each differing in shape and colour. The most recent entry dated back to August '97, while one of the earliest was from the mid-70s.

I wouldn't be surprised if this was the cabin Dad & Co. stayed in. I escape from Øyerstad and end up in the same place Dad has talked about my entire upbringing. It wouldn't surprise me one bit..

33: The Divers

The final notes of "Wish You Were Here" lingered in the air as Robert took a pause before "Wonderwall" opened the last set of his gig. Outside the pub, in the May twilight, he stood with a Lucky Strike dangling from his lips, conversing with Heinrich and Liza, whom he had seen earlier that day on the boat with the divers. Their initial exchange was in German, somewhat halting on Robert's part.

"*Sie kommen also aus Hamburg*?" Robert asked, only to realise he had no idea what they answered. He admitted that was all the German he knew, apart from "*Ich habe Angst*," and so the rest of the conversation shifted to English. Robert immediately fell for their German accents, particularly Liza's.

Heinrich, Liza, and their fellow divers travelled the world, seeking the most exotic diving destinations in Thailand, Australia, New Zealand, and more. When Robert asked what on earth brought them to the cold north, they regarded him with bewildered glances.

After nearly a year on the island, Robert was aware that people came there to dive, but he evidently hadn't grasped how sought-after Hitra was as a diving destination. The Germans used words like "world class" and "amazing" (preferably read with a German accent) to describe it. Underwater visibility was apparently exceptionally good. Especially in autumn and winter, one could see up to thirty metres. In spring, visibility of around fifteen metres was expected. While there were only a few wrecks, most were easily accessible, even for beginners.

Liza suggested that Robert join them for a dive the following day since her "crew" as she referred to her friends, had planned a dive to the *MS Kletten*. Even amateurs could reach the wreck, according to her. Heinrich clarified that he intended to get properly drunk, thus getting up early to teach Robert to dive was out of the question. Liza, however, thought she could squeeze Robert into one of their dry suits and undertake a morning session with him.

After wrapping up the evening's gig with "Rocking in the Free World" and "Summer of 69" as an encore, Robert arranged a time and place to meet with Liza for diving lessons. However, after some back and forth, they agreed that it would be simplest if she accompanied Robert home to his new house. That way, they could get to know each other better before their first dive together.

Not as early as intended, they stood at the water's edge outside the fishermen's cabins in Karskjær the following morning. Liza was an inspiring, hungover, and pretty hot instructor, and the concept of diving came naturally to Robert. They hadn't splashed around long before Liza deemed him ready to join the others. Alternatively, she might have simply grown tired of playing with him in the shallows.

MS Kletten lay forty-five minutes by boat from Karskjær,

and the mood was cheerful on the way out. Sea spray enveloped them as they sliced through the water, drawing white lines in their wake.

"You know why divers jump backwards into the water?" Liza yelled, doing her best to drown out the engine noise. Without waiting for Robert's reply, she shouted, "Because otherwise they would land in the boat!" Her laughter and smile kindled something he hadn't felt in a while. A pleasant warmth travelled through his body. Heinrich winked mischievously. Robert returned the smile, then gazed down at the dive tanks at the bottom of the boat.

Upon reaching the wreck site, after some final instructions from Liza, they lined up, backs to the water. A flicker of old memories brushed Robert, bringing with them a mild discomfort that slightly dampened the good vibes. Vibrations from beneath the raft on Lake Mørkved.

It was no more than eighteen metres down to the wreck, so he should reach the bottom without any problems. But what if he didn't? What if the Witch of Mørkved and Death awaited him down there?

"Are you ready?" Liza took his hand and pulled him backward. She didn't wait for an answer.

They fell together.

Robert's inaugural dive to MS Kletten took place merely hours after he first tried on professional diving gear. This was probably nowhere near best practice, but Robert didn't care.

The wreck was a thirty-two-metre-long cargo ship, commissioned by the road authorities to transport asphalt during road construction on Hitra in the mid-80s. The vessel sank near Skoldflua to the northeast of the island after striking a reef. Since then, the boat rested on the sandy seabed, cloaked in dead man's fingers, peacock tail anemones, and seaweed branches.

Robert was in love again, with the ocean. Here, he could fly. Be weightless and innocent. The ocean allowed him to be himself, and the love between them was unconditional. Having Liza, following the ocean currents by his side, certainly didn't detract from the experience. However, once at the wreck, the German mermaid halted Robert as he tried to follow the others inside. There were limits to what one was allowed to do after merely splashing around on the beach for a few hours.

In the final days of the divers' visit, more of them slept in Robert's shack than in the cabins they'd rented in Karskjær. The nights were late, filled with plenty of drinks and the occasional joint that the Germans had cultivated on their terrace back in Hamburg. Liza slept in the double bed alongside Robert, and he felt serene with her. He was not afraid of rejection or of embarrassing himself, clearly because he knew they would only be there for a week. They would soon leave, and he would never see her again. Perhaps it was also because he didn't tell himself that he didn't deserve this. Occasionally, in bed, after they had done more than talk about exotic diving destinations, his thoughts wandered towards Øyerstad.

I wonder who Guro is sharing her bed with now?

35: Es ist vorbei

"Es ist vorbei, es ist vorbei!" Some of the German pub visitors lay on the floor, writhing in pain. Screaming. Others sat with their heads in their arms, some crying. Robert and Olav, however, did not cry. They stood on tables made from old cable reels, wrapping their arms around each other. Bottles, glasses, and chili nuts flew through the pub as they jumped up and down, danced and sang. Ole Gunnar Solskjær had just slid on his knees towards the corner flag at Nou Camp after scoring the winning goal in the Champions League final on May 26, 1999. After more than a year and a half on the island, Robert had become one of them. The locals.

Earlier in the day, he had assisted the kitchen crew in preparing fish and chips that were, by his estimation, thirty-eight times better than what they would get served in England. The German "*bier fisch*" posed no challenge for the kitchen staff either. The Champions League menu that Olav and Robert had assembled was simple, yet it was the perfect pre-match stomach filler. However, Robert chose whole grilled chicken, or *poulet grillé* (as the head chef preferred to call it), with garlic and rosemary, instead of the two national dishes. Olav had fish and chips.

Most Germans sported Bayern Munich's colours, but Olav and Robert wore Manchester United jerseys for the occasion. Robert's love for the Red Devils had been passed down from Dad. Also, there was something about that red devil in the logo that captivated him. It fit well with his passion for hard rock and horror films, as Robert had explained earlier during dinner.

Somewhere deep inside Robert's mind, Dad sat alone with a bottle of booze, watching the game. The glow from the screen cast shifting colours onto a face that betrayed no joy when Sheringham equalised to 1-1. Dad didn't even cheer when Solskjær made the Germans cry by netting the winning goal three minutes into stoppage time. He simply marked the victory with another sip from the bottle, raising it towards the TV in a quiet toast.

"Where did you go?" Olav asked, emptying another glass after they'd toned down the celebration a notch. He squinted.

"I'm here now. Just thought about something, but it doesn't matter," Robert said.

"You ok?" Olav looked at him with those compassionate blue eyes.

"Yeah, I'm ok. We won, didn't we? Beat the Germans"

"We did! Speaking of Germans…"

"Those Germans?" Robert nodded towards the table where a group of Munich fans sat crying.

"The divers. They've slept more at your place than in the cabin they rented."

"I guess they did. Wasn't really planned that way, but it's been an interesting week."

"And Liza?"

"What about her?"

"What colour were her eyes?"

"Olav, I don't do that…"

"No?"

"They were green."

"Bloody hell! Can you tell Danne they were brown? I bet fifty kroner on it."

"Sure, if I get ten percent."

"You've learned to negotiate, I see. It's a deal. They left today, right?"

"Yep, early this morning."

"Good, so you'll finally show up to work on time again?"

Olav looked slyly at Robert.

"Well, not tomorrow. I'll be hungover."

"You will be. But on Friday, we need to get the kiosk painted. Ok?"

Olav and Robert each raised a glass and toasted.

"You played a great gig today. I think the Germans appreciated it. Before they learned you were a red."

"Yep, it was fun. They were pretty good singers."

Ash fell from Olav's cigarette and softly landed in a beer stain on the table. Robert paused, glass halfway to his mouth, as Olav talked about a dream where he was diving out by Blåskyskjær.

"I'm sitting on the edge and I fall backward. Instead of water, I hit something else, soft like an old mattress. The taste in my mouth is the worst part. When I open it to breathe, my mouth fills with something heavy. Slimy. Innards. My throat is blocked when I try to scream. I can't get out of the water. I flounder around in the remains of clothes and… what's left of them. Every single time. Every time I fall backward towards the water, I land on their corpses. Father, Rakel, and Pål-Ottar. They're so rotten that I fall right through them."

Olav's face paled, cigarette smoke streaming from his mouth, as he glanced over at Robert. He opened his mouth as if to say something but then turned away. Robert's gaze shifted to the Munich fans, and for a fleeting moment, he felt something reminiscent of sympathy. That lasted only a second before Olav began speaking again.

"I haven't told you the whole truth."

"Ok...?"

"Earlier, I gave you the official story about Hitrakrabba. That version doesn't say anything about the boat actually being found. Danne, your Swedish diver buddy, and I, we found the boat."

"You found it?"

"Yes, we did..."

"And, what about..."

"We only found the boat."

"Empty?"

"We don't know. We never got inside it."

"What? Danne's not afraid of a wreck dive, is he?"

"First of all, Danne, Olderø, and I, and now you, are the only ones who know about this. Not even Mother knows this. Actually, we were down by the wreck on multiple occasions. Near a ravine. Parts of the boat were, or are, right at the edge. Even Danne backed off when Hitrakrabba moved while he was trying to get in. We couldn't risk anyone going down with the boat into those depths. We planned more dives and even considered having the wreck raised, but it never happened. I started questioning whether finding them would change anything? I mean, they wouldn't have come back anyway."

"So, you are saying you don't know if they're down there?"

"Strictly speaking, I don't, and it's probably one of the reasons why I chose not to try again. If I didn't know they were down there, they could be alive, both of them."

"All three, you mean?"

"Well, Father must have taken the boat so he's probably there. But Rakel and the kid might not be. They might never have gone out on the boat."

"Well, that's... Have you never been out there again? You must be wondering?"

"No, I haven't, I had to let that go. And now, a dive like that, that's not suitable for old men." Olav chuckled and raised his glass. "I do well on the surface. Cheers to not knowing. It keeps hope alive." Olav's gaze wandered back to the windows, and he whispered, "It's probably best to stay on the surface."

“You have to show me where the wreck is. I mean, if it’s still there, it’s not going anywhere anytime soon.”

“No, I… That would be a sight for sore eyes. This body, in a wetsuit!” Olav patted his belly. His United shirt was stained from the food we ate earlier, as well as the booze we’d been downing during and after the match.

“When do we dive?” Robert raised his glass, but Olav was still laughing at the image of himself in tight Lycra. He didn’t raise his glass to cheer this time.

“I’m glad I picked you up, boy,” he said later.

“Me too,” Robert answered.

43: Rubber Boots and Newspapers

The rain descended in a torrential downpour, and the wind tried to haul the fishing cabins into the churning sea. Water splashed and wires screeched as the boats tried to free themselves with help from the wind. The air hung heavy, evoking the scent of slaughtered—pardon—gutted fish. On such days, the store where Robert stood behind the counter was often quiet. Most tourists were inside playing Yatzy and drinking coffee with a dash of something stronger. The sound of the raging rain outside amplified as the bell above the door chimed. Raindrops splattered from the umbrellas of the family hastily entering the store.

“Hurry up!” A man held the door while, what probably was his wife, slipped in first, followed by two children.

They didn’t really stand out in any way, but something about the latter child triggered something in Robert. A salty taste in his mouth. Not sea salt, but a bit sweeter, akin to liquorice, or some other kind of candy. From somewhere inside his head came voices and images he hadn’t heard or seen in a long time. He saw himself leaning against a motorcycle parked outside the Fina station in Øyerstad. Robert and his buddies used to do that when they were kids, checking out their top speed. The faster, the cooler. As Robert felt the itch on his left leg, he was reminded of the sound of his skin sizzling against the hot exhaust pipe when he had accidentally pressed his leg against it. His mother's expression, seeing the burn right above the boot's edge, was full of pity.

How she managed to get to the store, buy ointment and bandages, and return home in such a short time, Robert still couldn't understand. Her hands trembled as she applied the ointment. She was probably afraid Robert would fall apart if she wasn't careful enough. She first stuck the bandage tape to the table to remove some of the adhesive so it wouldn't hurt as much to remove later. Then she bandaged the leg, tightly enough that the bandage wouldn't fall off, and loosely enough not to put too much pressure on the wound. After things had calmed down, she went to the store again. She had more time this round. She bought ice cream. For the whole family.

Standing in the store on Hitra, Robert suddenly felt safe and cared for as the taste of vanilla and strawberry replaced liquorice. A memory, several memories, came to him from Øyerstad, and they weren't of the unpleasant kind. Goosebumps rolled over his body as Fredrik's laughter enveloped him. He remembered that time when they put Dad's rubber boots on the… Rubber boots! It was the boy's rubber boots. They had triggered this avalanche of memories as he ran into the store. Dark blue and white. They could only be bought in one place, as far as he knew anyway; "Viking Gummi" in Askim. The factory was shut down a long time ago under quite sad circumstances. All the employees were apparently poisoned by solvents, including several of the elderly in

Øyerstad who still told stories of working conditions in what they called the melted rubber pit.

Even inside the retail part of the factory, it stank of rubber, and my God, how they searched. Mom, Fredrik, and Robert. First, they passed shelf upon shelf with boots and shoes in all possible shapes. Raincoats, rain jackets, and rubber trousers. All the beautiful colours and popular patterns. The Baastad family, though, stopped first at the enormous plastic containers filled with B-grade products. These were rubber boots with defects, faulty seams, and holes, and there were heaps of them. Hundreds, maybe thousands of pairs. They rummaged, sought, and searched for treasures. Mom approved or rejected the boots as they were held up pair by pair. Those that could easily be fixed with repair kits at home got a thumbs up. They repeated this treasure hunt every autumn, for as long as Robert could remember. If the haul was good, they sometimes celebrated with spring rolls at the Chinese restaurant next door.

Back home, Fredrik and Robert kicked a football around while Dad retrieved the patching supplies. Those black and orange rubber patches, a small piece of sandpaper, and glue. It worked as well on rubber boots as on bicycle tubes. Together, Robert's mother and father ensured dry feet for their children throughout autumn—all for a low cost, and with a good dose of love and creativity. They needed nothing more.

The cash register drawer clicked shut behind Robert as he walked out into the store, past the shopping baskets, and around the snacks and candy display. He followed the wet boot prints on the floor.

A man's voice further in the store used words like "damn weather" and "damn overpriced fishing gear". He wasn't the first customer Robert had heard cursing aloud after seeing

Olav's homemade price tags on the lures and everything else in the shop.

As Robert moved towards them, around the corner, he felt a twinge of that old familiar anxiety again. A tickling feeling in his stomach and slight dizziness.

Relax, Robert. This isn't Øyerstad. Just old memories resurfacing.

The father was holding one of the larger metal jigs in his hand while the mother helped one of the boys off with his rain jacket. The kid's rubber boots were red and white, not a brand Robert recognised.

"Good day, do you need help?" Robert exclaimed as he searched for the second child.

"These prices don't exactly make for a good day," the father muttered.

The mother smiled apologetically, and said, "We are on our way to Fillan and thought to buy a new pilk for the little one." She glanced down at the child by her side. He was all wet.

"That's great. There are excellent fishing conditions here for both children and adults."

"Little Hendry is going to try fishing with an adult rod and jig. Right, little guy?" She pinched the child's cheek. "You've become so big now. Do you want to try the adult jig? It's huuuuuuuge. Do you? Hmmm?"

The kid seemed disinterested and didn't answer.

"You might want to look at some lighter jigs," Robert interjected, meeting the man's gaze. "They're cheaper and more suitable for your children."

"Well, it'll be only one jig," said the mother. "Little Hendry won't be fishing much, right?" She was about to pinch her son's cheek again, but met his eyes this time and restrained herself. "He's easily bored, you see."

Robert was still searching for child number two when the

bell by the door chimed once more, signaling activity at the entrance.

"I... excuse me for a moment," Robert said and jogged back through the shop.

The second child had left the shop and was headed down the stairs. Robert quickened his pace, calling to the parents. "Your boy has gone out into the rain!"

He yanked open the door and peered out into the gloom, and all he saw was a wall of grey hammering down onto a handful of parked cars and the kiosk's roof. *Where the devil did you go?*

He looked around the corner and down towards the dock on one side, then down towards the fish receiving station on the other. Nothing. He stood in the door until his feet got damp, then closed it again. Inside the shop, the family waited by the register. A two-hundred-and-fifty-gram metal jig lay on the checkout belt along with chocolate, soda, and a package of hot dogs."I'm sorry. Did you call us?" the mother asked.

"Yes, your child, the other one, walked out of the shop. Maybe he went to your car?"

The father looked even less pleased, but the mother replied, "Little Hendry is here. It must have been someone else's child you saw. Our little treasure doesn't go anywhere without telling Mommy. Right?" She pinched him on the cheek again.

"Eh, ok, but I saw him coming in with you, so I thought that... "

"Thought what?" the father cut in sharply.

"Eh, nothing" Robert said, although he really wanted to ask if they were sure they only had one child. It was a foolish question, and deep down, Robert understood that it wasn't their child he saw.

"If it weren't for Hendry, we wouldn't have bought a jig at all," the father said.

Ramsøy Lighthouse and the mountains inland no longer stood as powerfully as they did days ago. Robert felt uneasy, and the saltwater stung a cut on his finger. It wasn't the first time he had spent a few idle hours on the boat out there. His focus was on anything but the jig, which he kept still in no more than five metres of water. His thoughts wandered to the boy in the store the day before. To his boots. Light ocean waves provided no solace, and the seagulls were merely annoying as he replayed the event over and over in his mind. He felt frozen to the core, and there was nothing the peaked sun could do about it. He had this feeling that something sad had happened. Something ugly, hidden and suppressed crawled with oily tentacles back into the light.

He sat hunched over in the boat, watching the fishing line descend into the water. *What if it was actually him? What if Fredrik was there in the store? What if he tried to reach out to me in some way? But how? And why now?*

Robert didn't react as usual when the rod jerked against the boat's rail. His reel started screaming. He was near what he had come to call Olavsgrunna, named so after Olav always seemed to get snagged when they drifted over it. This time was no different. Robert cursed and reversed the boat, trying to free the jig from the rocky bottom.

Although the fishing was not particularly focused, one rarely came ashore without a catch. So this time, too, there was fish in the box. A saithe of around two and a half kilograms eventually ended up in the kitchen sink while Robert remained, peering out towards the barn through the cracked kitchen window. He leaned forward against the glass and squinted up towards the birch tree between the forest and the plank fence. If he relaxed his eyes and stopped focusing, he glimpsed a figure standing among the bushes. Like the creature in *Predator*, it was almost invisible. A camouflage expert from outer space. Fredrik loved that movie. Now, as Robert focused more intently again, he could have sworn it was moving. It reminded him of…

A heavy thud in the living room snapped Robert out of his trance. He stumbled forward, hitting his knee on the cabinet door beneath the kitchen counter. You know the pain when you step on a Lego brick or kick a door frame? It hurt that much. He narrowly avoided cutting his thumb off on the knife that dropped into the sink with a clatter.

"Fuck, that hurts!"

He stood for a while, holding onto the sink. He chuckled at how much it actually hurt. He looked down at the knife in the sink while something dark lurked on the edge of his consciousness. Muted tones from an organ he hadn't heard in a long time. Smouldering torches. Dark figures and funerals. He had forgotten that these things existed, and now they spread in his head. Images, movies, tastes, smells, and feelings ebbed and flowed. Some in black and white, some in colour. In slow motion and fast forward. It smelled like strawberries and then shit. Something rotten. The scar on his hand ached again. That dive when he got stuck, he hadn't thought about that for so long. Fragments from another life. Again, he looked past the barn and up towards the forest. *Someone is standing there. The same figure as...* Another thud sounded from the living room. Robert twitched at the sound and instinctively seized the knife from the sink, limping his way through the kitchen.

"Odd-Johnny, is that you?" No respond.

With just a metre left to the living room door, another thud echoed, making Robert step back. It sounded like someone was hurling objects—stones, large ones, against the wall. He paused, taking a deep breath. The air smelled stale and felt damp. He heard echoes of kids laughing, chanting something about a witch, as he launched himself into the living room, knife raised. Then it all went quiet. No one was there. Everything was as he had left it in the morning. *Almost* everything. The door to the pine cabinet was closed when he left. In fact it was always closed. Now it was open.

The farmer did, indeed, drop by occasionally. Both when Robert was home and when he was away. Although Robert was not a big fan of him snooping around the house when he was not home, it didn't matter much either. Olav also dropped by for various errands, but he usually didn't enter unless Robert was home. After all, it wasn't Robert's house, and he didn't have much to hide anyway. One of these days he was going to ask the farmer for his spare key, but it wasn't urgent because he didn't lock the door anyway. No one did that at Hitra, unless you were paranoid, or actually had some skeletons in your closet (not necessarily literally). Somewhat like in Øyerstad.

However, the farmer didn't usually hide. Quite the opposite. He would gladly stay for a cup of coffee, preferably spiced up with something stronger. Robert never had the heart to chase him away. Not until darkness crept in, at which point he could cite an early meet-up in Kvenskjær as an excuse. Yet even then, the farmer might press for one final cup—a fortifying sip for the morrow. Robert was fairly certain it wasn't the farmer who was here, or who had been here.

He was about to close the cabinet door with his knee but bent down and used his hand instead. Locked the door with the key. Checked an extra time that it was properly secured.

It was only when he turned back towards the kitchen that he noticed the newspaper on the table. It rested on a woven cloth of brown, orange, and white that adorned the coffee table. The newspaper was slightly yellowed, and atop it lay a sheet of paper and a ballpoint pen.

The boat was gone, so I guess you're out fishing. Bet you're coming home with a saithe or five. I dropped by to show you the newspaper, the one I talked about at the pub. It's been a while since I saw it myself, so I got a bit fired up. Might be good for you to have seen both the boat, Rakel, and Pål-Ottar before tomorrow's diving adventure. Then you know what we're up against.

Note! Don't use the newspaper as toilet paper if you run out, because I'd like it back. Flip through carefully.

Olav.

Robert limped into the kitchen, without touching the newspaper or the letter. Opened the fridge. Took a can of beer and downed it in one go. Took another can and limped, slightly less, back to the living room. He sat heavily on the sofa and had to stretch to reach the newspaper. The paper was thin and brittle. It would hardly have worked well to wipe oneself with. Olav needn't worry about that.

The front page told of how Harald "Dutte" Berg had been pivotal when Bodø/Glimt secured their place in the soccer semi-final, triumphing over the mighty Viking. The footballers' beards that adorned the front page were precisely as they should be for players in 1975. The second item revealed that Albert Norden, from the bourgeois party, lost in a friendly game against the Labour Party's girls' team. The smaller notices at the bottom reported on various events: over three thousand dead in an earthquake in Turkey, Hegnar threatening someone with police intervention, and a family of three still missing on Hitra.

Robert opened the newspaper, not stopping at the football news or the piece stating that the seat belt mandate appeared to be a successful venture. He elegantly flipped past the page with "celebrity crude jokes for children."

"The Sea Swallowed a Family of Three". The headline was dramatic, but it was the picture that hit Robert hardest. Olav had talked about the picture, but Robert couldn't in his wildest fantasies imagine it was *that* picture. That picture! A semi-hysteric laugh escaped Robert, and blood immediately withdrew from less essential parts of the body. His fingers blanched and soon bore tiny translucent droplets. A drop of sweat dripped from his forehead, and the paper absorbed it. Robert tried to swallow, but it ended with a series of jerks in his throat. That picture…

A tornado of memories whirled through his head. Faster this time and more chaotic. However, it did not take long before a particular memory engulfed him and spat him out again in another place at another time. The Witch of Mørkved and Death's house. The room next to where Fredrik crashed through the floor. Back then, the same newspaper article fell from behind a picture on the wall. In the Witch of Mørkved's bedroom in Øyerstad. It must have been ten years ago, but now he was standing in the room again. Then, as now, the young woman in the picture was still a young version of the Witch. The child was still Death. Perhaps two or three years old.

In a few seconds, Fredrik would scream in the room next door. Robert knew it because he was there when it happened.

The third person in the picture. Next to the Witch of Mørkved stood the figure he didn't know who was back then. The one Robert wondered might be the Witch's brother—it *was* her brother. It was Olav. That meant the Witch of Mørkved must be...

The echo of Fredrik's scream in the room next door sliced through the house back then, and now it flew through Robert's mind. His skin tightened. Armour. Sitting on the sofa, he jolted and inadvertently tore a rip through the newspaper article. For a brief moment, he thought of discarding the paper and fleeing—leaving the house, abandoning Hitra, and never looking back. Kinda like what he had done in the Witch's house when he dropped the picture and ran to the next room, from which Fredrik's scream had come. This time though, he ignored the screaming and looked down at the words beneath the picture. Olav must have read them thousands of times, but Robert read them now. For the first time. The photo caption.

September 14, 1975. Olav Aksnæs (17) (left) Pål-Ottar (2) (centre) and Rakel Aksnæs (22) (right) on the fishing boat Hitrakrabba, before mother and son disappeared following a shipwreck off Hitra. Captain Knud-Olav Aksnæs (37) (not pictured) disappeared in the same incident. They are deeply missed by family and Hitra residents who have not given up hope of finding them.

Rakel was the Witch of Mørkved. Olav's sister. Death's mother. The Witch of Mørkved! Robert's brain raced, synapses crackling and sparking as electric bursts sought the right connections. The old sailor hadn't kidnapped them. Rakel and Pål-Ottar never went out with him on the boat. Hell, she might not even have known her father left with his boat that night. Instead, she'd fled the island, eventually finding her way to Øyerstad for some strange reasons. My God, she likely only learned of her father's death from that newspaper.

Robert retched as the TV flickered to life on its own, the room echoing with the tones of the Evening News. Droplets of sweat felt like insects scurrying down his legs. Air evaded his lungs. He couldn't breathe.

"We are live following a shooting incident in the village of Øyerstad, in the inner part of Østfold County. Through the local newspaper, we have a journalist on the scene." The reporter on the TV spoke eagerly while flies buzzed about the fish in the tub in the kitchen.

"There are reports that a person has been shot and killed in his home, on the other side of the road from the local gas station and pub. Behind me, you see the house where the crime is alleged to have occurred. Unconfirmed information tells that the act took place last night, a number of hours ago. Nonetheless, the ambulance was not called until late morning today, around eleven. The police are searching for the perpetrator, who is still at large. They are following up with several persons of interest, and one of them is said to be a local person closely related to the victim. They are urging all potential eyewitnesses to get in touch with the police immediately. More detailed information has not yet arrived."

The reporter then turned toward the house where the police, fire department, and medical personnel were doing their thing.

"The wife of the deceased alerted the police. She has explained that the ambulance was called as soon as she came out of the shock she was in after the incident took place. Several shots are said to have been fired, but only one person is confirmed dead. The deceased is said to be a man who has been a long-time resident of the village. We are not releasing names as the information has not been verified by the police."

Pausing again, the reporter put a hand to his ear. Then he

looked back into the camera. "I have received a message that we will get an exclusive eyewitness account of last night's events. As the only channel, we have been allowed to enter the house, to give you a more detailed overview of the situation. Exactly as it happened last night." The reporter, clearly exhilarated, took a deep breath, like a boxer before entering the ring.

"Dear Robert," said the reporter, looking into the camera.

On the sofa in front of the TV, Robert couldn't move as their gazes locked. Eye contact is impossible to make from so many miles away. Impossible to make through a TV.

"I must warn you of graphic images. Remember, Robert, you are only seeing this on NRK!"

47: Hitrakrabba

The beer can on the living room table toppled as Robert jerked awake. He hardly noticed the tones of the steam-whistle organ fading away, their echoes slowly stirring cobwebs and dust. A lone lamp stood its ground against the lingering night, casting a dim glow across the room. The reporter was gone, and the TV screen resembled a dark void—a portal to an unknown realm. The room was spinning as he squinted and brought a hand to his forehead. It felt as though a colony of bullet ants was marching and gnawing on his brain.

"SHIT!" Robert sent the beer can hurtling across the room. It burst upon impact with the cabinet, then spun on the floor, hissing and fizzing like a beer fountain. "Damn! DAMN!" Robert struck his head. Once. Twice. Several times. Even more. "FUCK!" Hitra had stopped working. The shadows from Øyerstad were back. "Not now, please not now!" Again, he pounded his fists against his head. If he could just crack open his skull, maybe he could tear out the damnation once and for all.

Shapes darker than the night itself shifted and swayed around him in the room. Dull and terrifying creatures moving slowly, overlapping one another. The beer can continued its spin on the floor, splattering its contents on the walls. Robert rubbed his face, tore at his hair, and massaged his temples so intensely that the muscles in his forearms bulged.

Slowly, in time with the beer can losing its momentum, Robert also calmed down. Eventually. To breathe. He swallowed. Paused. Looked down at the floor. Closed his eyes. Tried to gather his thoughts. Sought connections. Then the sound was there again. This time it thumped right in front of him, so hard that the sofa vibrated. Robert looked up and into the room, and without thinking he said, "Fredrik?"

The newspaper clipping still lay on the living room table, where Olav had been quite literally torn away from his family. A piece of tape on the yellowed paper would hardly reunite them. They were gone for sure, but not in the way Olav thought.

Robert's body ached as he pushed himself up and limped onto the living room floor. Still alone. Beyond the outcrop with mobile coverage, the sun's rays wrestled with the night's gentle shade, creating a twilight dressed in pink, purple and orange. Light would triumph sooner or later; it always did, even if just for a fleeting moment before darkness reclaimed the sky. The perfect balance. Night and day.

Robert sought something in the orange-purple sky when he heard that sound again. Behind him. Thud! In the cupboard. The boards vibrated under his feet as something heavy fell to the floor. The cupboard door was open when he turned around. He rubbed his index finger against the thumb, as if trying to remember the feeling of a key in hand in the last few seconds. Nothing. He had not unlocked it. He didn't even know where he had the key.

Cautiously, Robert knelt down and peered into the open hatch. Everything inside, he had seen before. The cabin guest books, the old brass mugs, and magazines. The bowl with pens and the deck of cards. Again, he was about to close the cabinet door when the banging on the wall outside the house sent him backward onto his buttocks. Muffled scraping sounds and several thuds followed, as if someone was tearing and pulling at something. Instead of getting up and looking out the window, he lowered his head to the floor. The wood panelling was warm against his ear as he peered under the cabinet. He expected a fat rat to jump out and bite his nose, but that would be alright. If it was all just a rat.

The dice underneath the cabinet certainly didn't freeze where they hid under blankets of dust. Popcorn kernels and old bottle caps too found refuge, nestled amidst cobwebs. There was nothing else under there. He was about to get up when another thud made the windows clink in their frames. Whoever was banging had grown weary and hit with all their might. After the big bang, a smaller one followed, and something moved behind the cabinet. Robert pressed his head to the floor again, and saw a square shape that hadn't been there seconds ago. Something that had to be a book balanced on the wall trim behind the cabinet. It must have been wedged between the cabinet and the wall, and whatever was banging had caused the book to fall. Someone wanted him to see this, but they didn't make it easy. No matter how hard he pressed on, or tried to lift the cabinet, he couldn't get his hands under it. He tried from the sides. Too narrow. The cabinet had to be moved. Robert groaned as he braced his legs against the wall and pulled with all his might. At first, it didn't move, but on the second or third try, he managed to move it an inch or two. Up on his feet again. Out in the hall. The crowbar.

As Robert finally managed to extract the object from behind the cabinet, the sun's rays sneaked into the living room. A wedge, crowbar, muscle power, and a good deal of will did the trick. It was another cabin guest book. It might have weighed a hundred kilos, for Robert could barely carry it to the sofa. He sneezed as he brushed the dust off the cover. The numbers 1970-1976 were printed with surprisingly intact gold lettering on cracked leather. Robert had studied the other books without finding a single signature he recognised. Now, considering how he found this book, he was sure he was going to find something. Nothing here was random. He glanced at the newspaper clipping. The three looked back at him. Olav torn from the other two. Robert opened the cabin book.

By page eight, he found what the other books had lacked: a signature he recognised. It was one he had replicated many times before—on absence notes and report cards from his school days: Dad's. Both Petter and Kai had also left their marks. Ghosts of the past emerged from the pages. In July 1970, Dad had jotted down notes about bountiful fishing, delicious food, heavy drinking, and notably, about the women at the Fillan pub. "They party like crazy, even wilder than back home!" Sketched onto the paper was a beer bottle and a pair of lips—big, thirsty, and distinctly in the style of The Rolling Stones trademark logo. Robert had had his own encounters with a few girls on the island, so he could imagine how they must have felt back then.

Robert flipped forward, lightly skipping random entries and drawings of boats and fish. As he approached the summer of 1971, he slowed down again. June. And there they were—

those same signatures. The first entry began with an account of their wild drive, ending with their arrival at the cabin, ready for new adventures. Subsequent entries showcased various handwritings—some long and feminine, others short and masculine. Most of the time was dedicated to partying, with only occasional mentions of fishing. It was essentially a party diary. Robert scanned the first couple of entries before halting at a more extensive one written in careful cursive. Acid reflux stung his throat.

Hello, there! I guess it was about time I wrote some words here too. It's late at night. No, more like early morning. I like this. Everyone else is sleeping. It's just me here, the glowing, growing, blood red sun. The deer out on the grass, on the field in front of the house. I'm surprised we didn't scare them away. Kudos to the Øyerstad boys. They sure know how to party.

I mean, we had the first drinks out on the boat long before dinner. Right out in the bay. My God, we drank so much that I think even my father would have been proud. For once. And believe it or not, we actually did some fishing as well. We caught quite a bit, cod, saithe, and herring. Ha, I think Dad, as everyone calls him, had a fish on the line for an hour without noticing... I mean, we tried to tell him, but he was too wasted to get it. You should have seen his rod, it was bouncing like crazy. We eventually got through to him, though. It wasn't much of a fish when he finally reeled it in.

We had grilled fish and pork chops when we got back to the shack. We hung out there by the fire, drinking and playing music, singing, until the old farmer tried to put an end to it all. He wasn't too happy, claiming we scared his cows, so we brought ourselves inside. And the party continued. Dad danced on the table and sang "Mama Weer All Crazee Now" and "All the Young Dudes". The rest of us sang too, for a really long time.

Then, as the night wore on, they dropped off one by one. Dad and Petter are sleeping upstairs, the others have gone home.

One of the Øyerstad boys, no names mentioned, insisted that I stay. So I did, and I don't regret it. So far anyways. He's lying next to me on the sofa, sleeping. I like the contrasts. First the noise and the silence that follows. Kiss and make up. I've always done that, liked being alone with my thoughts. For a while. Gather them, charge the batteries before the next lift.

All alone in here!
The world is silent, fast asleep,
On front row, I'm in too deep.
In my heart, a new black tear,
I am all alone in here.

Summer night hides the light,
See, the stars shine so bright,
Deep in my heart, I hide my fear,
I am all alone in here.

So many, a part of history,
Are you the answer to the mystery?
You seem so calm, you have no fear,
Yet, I am all alone in here.

Warm breath, like a summer breeze,
If I stay, will my pain ease?
Can I go with you, my dear?
I no longer want to be alone in here.

Oh, that's deep. I guess it's a fitting end to my entry. There must be room for that in a guest book, right? Anyway, I need some sleep as well. I'll crawl onto the sofa next to my new friend. I think we're going to lie there for a long time, well into the day, and then I am sure we'll go at it again.

Thank you so much for the stay.
Rakel.

Robert repeated the last meaning to himself, "Thank you so much for the stay. Rakel." If Dad and Petter were sleeping upstairs, it must have been Kai lying on the sofa with her. They knew each other?

The rest of the entries that week were even more party reports. The notion that Kai and Rakel were almost a couple was further solidified by several subsequent posts. With trembling fingers, Robert jumped ahead by about a year, searching for their next visit to the island. He found it halfway through the book. It was the last one in the book, abruptly cut short. He glanced at the picture in the newspaper.

The last entry was in Dad's handwriting.

Things turn quickly on Hitra—not just the weather. We had planned to stay here forever, but now even this has come to an end. Seems we caught more than we bargained for, at least some of us did. From now on, we'll be fishing inshore. Anywhere but here. The choice is easy when it comes to it. We do prefer a bottle of spirits to a bottle of milk. So, we thank you, dear fish, deer, gravel roads, salt, Hitra, and even the locals. It's time to head back home to Øyerstad, fast as…

The text ended there with a line drawn across the paper and off the page. No one had signed the entry—the last in the book.

He looked at the newspaper clipping again. Olav, Rakel, and Pål-Ottar—the child's hair, the slender body, and the sharp, albeit malformed, face. Kai's rifle. He called it... Rakel?

"Rakel!" Robert said her name out loud, still seated. Soon he repeated it, a bit softer this time, "Rakel." He let it linger, "Rak..." And then it hit him. "He looks just like his father," he whispered. *Death looks just like his father.* Kai is Death's father! He must have gotten Rakel pregnant back then, and when he found out, he left everything behind. That was why they had to leave, and why they never returned. Rakel lied when she told the old sailor she didn't know who the father of her child was. She knew all along. Kai, Petter, and even Dad left the pregnant girl behind. With her crazy father.

His arms were bloodless and heavy when he noticed the deer in the meadow near the barn. Were they the same deer that Rakel had seen back then? Standing in the meadow's grass, they had no worries. Nothing to fear. He could have sworn the deer were looking back at him through the window. They made eye contact, and like delicate puffs on a dandelion in the wind, the pain in Robert's head lifted. His pulse slowed, and the ants' infernal eagerness for human brain subsided for a moment. The deer had grass, and they had each other. They had their place on this island, and that was all they needed. Imagine being born into the world as one of them instead. A deer.

Of course, it was only an illusion. Not the deer, but the calm and safety. They didn't stand there long before they too became aware of a danger approaching. A sound from up the hill. A car came speeding on the road behind them. Their ears perked up and they froze for a moment before they bolted into the woods. A flight for life. The ants sank their teeth back into Robert's cerebral cortex. He put his head in his hands as the car sped past the barn. Olav was out of the car almost before it stopped rolling.

Robert shielded his eyes from the sun as they stood by the car.

"Rough night?" Olav asked. "You look… tired." Without warning, he threw a backpack at Robert, making him take a couple of steps backward, barely holding onto it. Olav returned to the car and fetched the diving tubes.

"No, it's fine. Slept terribly, that's all." Memories of a dream lingered in his mind. Millions of crawling ants.

"It is… uh, I heard about Øyerstad on TV yesterday. A shooting? The radio now said the guy who was shot was named Petter. Petter Slorafossen. Someone you knew?" Olav's brow furrowed.

The question at least confirmed that the TV broadcast itself wasn't merely a crazy dream.

"Wasn't he a friend of your father's? The one who was here on Hitra?"

"No, that's another Petter," Robert said, without really thinking. Of course, it was the Petter Olav referred to, Dad's close friend, but it didn't feel like the right time to delve into that. Robert's mind was already overloaded. "I mean, I know who he is, was, but I didn't really know him," he added. "Dad didn't hang out with him often.

"Tragic, regardless," Olav said.

"Listen…" Robert squinted at Olav. "There was only one person killed, right?"

"Should there have been more?"

"I thought... Never mind. It doesn't matter."

"Just one as far as I know. And hey, did you see the paper?"

"Huh?"

"The newspaper and the note on the table?"

"Yeah."

"And? You didn't use it as toilet paper?"

"Didn't you write that I should?" Robert smiled. "Kidding aside, I saw it, and it was quite an article."

"I guess it was time you got the full picture."

"Yeah, I got it," Robert said, searching for the camouflaged observer by the trees beside the barn. There was no one there.

"We'll talk more about it on the boat. You ready to dive? At least the weather gods are on our side."

Robert observed the pennant up by the farmer's house hanging limply beneath the rising sun.

Listen, Olav. Your sister never went out on the boat, and neither did her kid. No, they went to Øyerstad to search for Kai—the same Kai who came here to Hitra with Dad and Petter. If you ask me, I think Kai shot Petter last night (yes, it was that Petter), maybe to shut him up, I don't know. And Kai, he was the one who made your sister pregnant. He is Pål-Ottar's father, did I mention that?

You know, we didn't call your sister Rakel. No one in Øyerstad knew her real name. We called her the Witch of Mørkved. And the kid, Pål-Ottar? We called him Death. Because of his looks. So much better than "The Elephant Man", right?

We didn't treat them well. No one did. Did they do something to us? No, of course not! We told stories and were mean anyway. A simple villager needs something to do. After all, they weren't like the other locals. How could they be? They weren't from Øyerstad, even though they'd lived there longer than many of us.

Did I tell you that they disappeared without a trace from Øyerstad almost ten years ago? That we broke into their house after they disappeared? Do you know what I saw there? The picture in your newspaper. I've seen that picture before. I saw it but was interrupted so abruptly that I forgot it. It didn't make any sense back then. Your sister, Rakel, saw the newspaper articles too. She read about Knud-Olav and Pål-Ottar's death. Her own death. How they all drowned that day. She probably saw a chance to start anew in Øyerstad. Completely anew. And your paper, I think I might have torn it apart.

Listen, I have one more little thing. About them somehow coming back. No, not as regular people. More like... demons. I'm thinking that maybe they killed my brother. My mom, too. And a bunch of others in the village. They were the ones who made me run, and then I ended up here. I thought I could hide from them. But now they've found me.

And they must be strong, because they tore Bingo-Bob to shreds. As if he were a filthy ragdoll. The thing is, Bingo-Bob, he was my demon. The boss. He came to me after he almost devoured my little brother years ago. Almost bit his face off. That scared the living shit out of me. Then, he got tangled up with that damn circus. And the clowns. Shit, I really created one hell of a place. In my head. It was all just in my head. I think.

Rakel, or the Witch of Mørkved, and Pål-Ottar... They appeared there too, at the circus. I called them phantoms, those that showed up. But they had no real power in there. Not like Bingo-Bob.

But somehow, they grew stronger, the Witch and Death. They're so full of rage that they spread out like a cancer. Took over the whole place. I couldn't control it. And the weird thing is, I don't think they're actually my demons. Kinda crazy, huh? I have no idea why they're chasing me, or my family. It would be one thing if they were after Kai, but what did we have to do with it?

I was supposed to run away from all of it, and then I ended up here. With you, the brother of the Witch of Mørkved. And now, the two of us are going to search for them, even though they definitely aren't there. A peculiar situation, wouldn't you say?

"Was it near where you grew up?"

"Huh?" Robert jumped out of his mind and looked over at Olav. "The guy who was shot. By the gas station. Wasn't it around where you grew up?"

"Yeah, the house was across the street from us."

Olav's gaze left a passing seagull, wandering towards the windows of the house. He probably expected to see a girl in the window. "Did you have company last night?"

"No. I wish," Robert replied, accepting the swim fins. He started walking down towards the boat but soon turned back to Olav again.

"Are you coming? Hello? Are you there?"

Olav reacted slowly, as if coming out of a deep thought.

"Yeah, I just thought I saw someone in the window. You...?"

"There's no one there," Robert answered.

"I see. Maybe I need to get myself some glasses."

"Well, you're no longer a young man," Robert smiled.

"Maybe not, but I still look good in a wetsuit."

"We'll see about that."

Just before they entered the boat, Robert asked, "Nervous?"

"No. Or yes. A bit."

"You'll be ok down there?"

"Yes. It's time to get this out of the system once and for all."

"Do you think they're still there?" Robert didn't look at Olav.

"There can't be much left of them in that case. The boat likely crashed down the ravine a long time ago." Olav tossed the equipment into the boat and continued. "If this goes shit, remember that you talked me into it." Then he laughed and gave Robert a pat on the back. "Blåskykøya."

"Out by the island?"

"A bit to the north of it. By the ravine. That's where Hitrakrabba sank."

Robert had dived out by Blåskykøya many times before. The conditions around the main island were perfect, and tourists loved the underwater lagoon. Once, Robert and a group of

Danish divers ended up in a shoal of sharks and swam with them for what felt like an eternity. Of course, these were not the bloodthirsty kind that haunted Chief Brody outside Amity Island. No, the gurry sharks, even though large in size, preferred their meals in smaller portions: minor sharks, eels, flounders, and sculpins. Rumour had it that one once ate a polar bear, but that was not confirmed—at least, not to Robert's knowledge. Robert's newfound Danish friends were so impressed that they brought him bottles of whisky after the dive. They wanted to go out there again.

"So, what did you do with them out there? I haven't seen them that happy before — divers, I mean. They brought you whisky? After a simple dive, eh? Good job," Olav was impressed.

Little did Robert know at the time, while he was dancing with sharks, that Hitrakrabba was close by. Directly north of the main island, Blåskykøya, lay Blåskykskjærene—a gathering of rocks breaking the surface. Further out towards Iceland, at a depth of about twenty-five metres lay the wreck of Hitrakrabba. Like a secret monument perched on the edge of the drop towards the Skråskjær Ravine. A ravine that descended 1300 metres down into the abyss.

About fifteen minutes after leaving the dock, they headed north, passing Hallarøya to their right and Lya Island to their left. In between lay Ramsøysundet, peaceful under light blue skies. Coming out of the sound, they continued towards Sæbu Island. Past Skår Island, the distance between the islands and islets began to increase. Soon the open sea bid them welcome. *Get back home to Øyerstad as fast as...*

They anchored not far from Blåskykøya, the island. Once again, Robert felt overwhelmed by its vastness—the ocean. In one moment, he could see the mountains and islands of the mainland stretching out in the distance; the next, a mighty wall of water swelled towards the sky. It blocked the sun and threatened to swallow them alive, tear their boat apart, and pull them down into the darkness. Just as the sea had done so many times before. The sea gives, and the sea takes.

The oxygen tank on Robert's back felt heavy. His diving mask was too tight, and the valve was dry in his mouth. His flippers squeezed, causing his toes to cramp. *Screw it!* Then he fell backward, seconds after Olav had dived in.

The length of the dive was estimated to be forty-two minutes, and they planned to stretch the three-stage rule a bit. A third of the time to dive down to the wreck, a third in the wreck, and a third to get back. Assuming the wreck was where it was supposed to be, it would not take long to get there.

As they began their descent, a school of herring circled them a few times before disappearing into the blue. Way below, in the sand, crabs paraded among dead man's fingers, shells, and seaweed. Robert admired the sea urchins in their fixed positions near the shallow coral reefs. The beauty of the ocean was evident, and one was entirely at its mercy.

Soon, the cutter that used to sail through the Trondheim Fjord and out onto the sea appeared like a ghost ship in front of them. According to Olav, she was the first, bravest, and most eager cutter in Knud-Olav's army of boats. This despite her modest forty-eight feet. She always took the lead in the hunt for the finest crabs. Now the sea had made the former majesty a part of itself.

The bow was easily accessible, while the stern hung over the edge towards the ravine. Like a sea within the sea, a shadow in the shadows, the ravine opened behind the wreck. A portal to the underworld.

Robert and Olav circled around the front of the wreck a

few times before they approached the cabin. The wood was barely visible beneath layers of algae, snails, and coral. In front of the cabin, a large black hole gaped, as if a cannonball from the heavens had fallen through the boat.

Way back, when Olav had been down there with Danne, they only made it as far as the wheelhouse before turning back. He remembered well why they had stopped, why he turned around and insisted that Danne follow him back up. It was more a thought than the actual fear of the boat tipping off the cliff. What would he do if they found them down there? If he saw them, their dead bodies. Then everything would be over. His father was one thing, but Rakel and the child? No, he couldn't live with that.

Now, Olav felt the urge to stop again, to pull Robert up this time, to run away once more, and to never speak of it again. Back up on the surface, with his feet on solid ground at Karskjær, he would wait. Wait for that day when they would appear by the store or the kiosk.

However, Olav didn't stop this time. He grabbed the door frame, dragging himself into the cabin that had seemed so much larger when he was a child. Sometimes he would lie flat and sleep on the shelf in front of the instrument panel. The cabin was as large as a house back then. Now, all these years later, it had shrunk. It could collapse at any moment.

The helm in the five- or six-square-metre cabin resembled a spider's web, draped in algae and snails. The compass, having not guided anyone for nearly thirty years, likewise reflected its abandonment, as did the instrument panel. Nevertheless, Olav could visualise how it once was. All the buttons, arrows, and gauges, back when he and Rakel actually enjoyed being out at sea with their father. Before the phantom sailors found him. Megalomania and liquor. Olav also recognised the radio and the old sea charts.

I should have drunk more water, Olav thought, his mouth ironically so dry he could hardly swallow. Perhaps he should head back up after all, just to have a drink. There surely wasn't that much of a hurry; the wreck had remained here for all this time, so it shouldn't be going anywhere anytime soon.

The cabinet door loosened when Robert pulled it. Olav indicated he didn't want a taste when Robert held two bottles towards him. The liquid appeared brownish as Robert rubbed off the algae and shone a light on them. Either they were discoloured from their time on the ocean floor, or it was good old-fashioned whisky inside. They rummaged around for a while amongst planks, ropes, and metal scrap before Robert signalled that they should move down below deck. The water in the cabin had turned turbid, clouded with swirling algae that resembled smoke. Millions of particles danced around them like in a surreal, underwater ballet. Choosing to ignore Robert's signals, Olav occupied himself by fiddling with some metallic device he had picked up from the floor.

Right now, they could still be alive, and I still have the opportunity to let them remain that way. If I find them down there... I am killing them. It will be all on me then. Why would I do that? Do I really need to know what happened? Does it truly matter?

The cabin Olav had lent to Robert had stood empty since being built almost fifteen years ago. It was a special place, meant for Rakel and Pål-Ottar, should they ever come down the road towards the tourist facility, perhaps in need of a place to stay. Why Olav had decided to lend it to Robert, he couldn't quite explain. No one had ever stayed there before. Something had made him, something outside his control.

Robert continued to signal to Olav, who eventually followed him down below deck. Some of the sea's more elusive inhabitants were concealed there, having remained in darkness since the ship's fateful sinking.

Olav attempted to swallow once more, blinking in an effort to regain focus. *I should have brought a larger flashlight.* They semi-floated through the cabin as planks and debris dangled precariously from the ceiling and walls. What might once have been beds now lay in a chaotic heap on the floor, draped in algae and coral. Pots, plates, and cutlery were strewn about, lying next to what seemed to have once been a dining table. Buoys, ropes, barrels, tanks, bottles, and glasses.

Then there was the large hole in the middle of the boat. They both looked up towards the surface through it, noticing that the weather seemed to have changed up there. Night had come early. They exchanged glances hastily before the room was abruptly engulfed in a blinding light—a flash, reminiscent of a Hitra-Posten journalist capturing the intense emotion of their dive. The light faded as quickly as it came, and Olav wasn't sure if he saw what he thought he saw. In the corner furthest towards the wall, huddled down in a corner. Was there someone there?

There was no time to think or contemplate what had just happened before the wreck moved. Robert wouldn't have been surprised by some minor, subtle movements—as if the old wreck simply wanted to stretch a bit. However, this was something entirely different. Something seemed to lift the wreck and toss it around. The ensuing chaos was so unexpected and extreme that Robert thought this might be one of those hyper-realistic dreams, like the ones he had with Anders and Mom. The type that rarely ended well.

Like clothes in a washing machine, they tumbled around in a chaotic whirl of flashing lights, bubbles, mud, wood, and metal. Robert flailed his arms, trying to grab onto...

something. But everything he touched seemed to crumble or give way. Panic overwhelmed him as his mouthpiece was yanked from his mouth, leaving him unable to breathe and certain that he was about to die. Yet, surprisingly, he managed to regain enough composure to catch the mouthpiece and bring it back. However, his relief was short-lived. Soon he struck his head against something hard, and sounds, flashes of light, pain, and even his fear, all began to fade. He was in freefall, descending into the hole beneath the bed that Fredrik had spoken of.

Just as he resigned himself to his fate, accepting that this was the end, he was suddenly hurled back towards reality at high speed. Emerging from the hole, it felt as if he was opening his eyes after being gone for a very long time. The chaos had subsided, and everything was quiet except for a constant ringing in his head. A blood-red shadow moved in the light from the lamp hanging from his arm. The water was murky, and visibility was almost zero. A heavy burden, something more than fear, weighed against his chest, making it hard to breathe. His skull pounded, and his field of vision expanded and contracted with the pulsating pain.

Robert tried to focus. Regain control. Nevertheless, his vision continued to come and go. He lifted his head, but the rest of his body remained motionless, afraid of what he might discover if he moved. A broken leg, a fractured arm, or, worse, that he was impaled by the scrap that had cascaded through the boat earlier. The pressure against his chest did not let up, and he became aware of the wooden beam holding him down. He assumed it would be stuck firmly, but even though Robert barely had any strength left, it moved slightly when he tried to lift it. Still, it was not enough for him to get free. He needed to rest a bit. Gather a little more strength. Just a few more minutes. Maybe forever.

The light kept flashing.

Olav? Where the hell is Olav? Robert jolted back to reality as a disturbing thought struck him; perhaps it wasn't his vision that was coming and going. Could it be Olav's lamp flickering in the murky water? A signal? Maybe a cry for help? Quickly, Robert grabbed his lamp, casting light on an obstacle course of metal, wood, and scrap lying between him and the other source of light.

If the beam that had pinned him down had struck with its full force, there would have been no way for him to break free. He never would have regained consciousness. Fortunately, that wasn't the case; the beam was partially propped up against the wall beside him. Summoning all his strength, Robert made himself as compact as possible and pressed downward towards the floor, desperately seeking some space between himself and the beam. Just a tiny bit. He squeezed and shifted until the pressure on his chest eased. Cautiously, he dragged himself along the floor until only his head was still trapped. Panic surged again when his mouthpiece hit the beam, coming loose and filling his mouth with seawater.

Don't panic, Robert. You've trained for this. In the bathtub. With Liza, and with Danne. You've got this, Robert. Stay calm.

Robert let the mouthpiece fall, pushed his head under the beam, and wriggled free. He then found the mouthpiece again by following the hose from the oxygen tank on his back. When he finally moved towards Olav, his body burned, his muscles stiff and powerless.

Perhaps I should slow down? Catch my breath a bit? I'm not in a rush, right? Besides, if I lay down and rest for a while, I'll return even stronger.

Robert's primal instincts drove him onward. The light, rhythmically flashing, was drawing closer. *Be careful, Olav. Maybe you should stop flashing? What if she sees us? Fredrik,*

I told you to stop flashing the light! If she sees us now, it's over. Pull yourself together, Robert. You need to reach him and help him.

Something black trembled and shifted next to Robert, suddenly lunging towards him. A ghost, a phantom from his past. They had caught up to him. Skeletal fingers reaching out, grabbing, aiming to tear him apart, to devour him. To... No, not a ghost. A large piece of wood, possibly a locker, which had come loose from the wall and was falling towards him. Rather than crushing him, though, the object struck one of his flippers. After a brief struggle, he managed to free himself, although his flipper was lost in the process. Robert continued forward.

Why don't you chill a bit, Robert? Sit at the desk and draw a little. It's getting late. Robert! The light. Fredrik? The power's out. Is Kai and Dad there? With you? They're after you now. Olav. You must help him. Help who? Fredrik?

Catching sight of Olav across the room had an immediate impact on Robert, akin to the effect of smelling salts or whatever it was they used in movies to swiftly bring the hero back to consciousness after a heavy punch. Robert found himself regaining a semblance of control. His thoughts became clearer, his strength somewhat returned, and a sense of relief filled him at finding his friend alive. Eagerly, he reached out to grasp Olav's diving vest, intending to pull him upright, but Olav resisted. Looking closer, Robert saw the reason why: a metal rod or perhaps a wooden pole, something sharply pointed, was jutting out from the upper part of Olav's thigh. The blood spreading from the wound was minimal. Could the tightness of Olavs dry suit actually be a benefit after all?

Okay, this is easy, Robert. Remember Fredrik up in the house of the Witch of Mørkved and Death. Fredrik's foot. Simply pull as hard as you can. Straight up.

He grabbed a hold of Olav's leg just before a new roar shook them and the wreck moved again. Robert felt the edge of the ravine draw closer. Soon they would fall.

Despite Robert's efforts, Olav's leg remained trapped. Gathering his strength, Robert braced himself and pulled harder. As he did so, Olav started bleeding more heavily. *Hurry! Get him the hell outta there.* Robert made yet another attempt, this time trying to break off the rod that was impaling Olav's leg.

Once again, without warning, another flash danced through the wreck. The roar that followed was louder than before. Then, the inevitable happened—the boat snapped in two. Instinctively, Robert grabbed Olav's arm as they, along with the stern of the ship, began to slide over the edge. It didn't really happen fast, but still time was critically short. If only Olav had been free, they might have been able to swim to the surface through the opening above. If only he had been free.

Robert once again launched at the rod impaling Olav. *Come on, damn it.* Nothing. *I won't give up, even if I have to go down with you.* Nothing.

Again, Robert seized Olav's leg, placed his feet against a beam behind them, and pushed with all his might. They were going to the surface, both of them, no matter what. His muscles cramped, and stars danced before his eyes, yet despite his efforts, nothing happened. *How is this even possible?* Preparing his body for another attempt, Robert finally saw the situation for what it was. The object impaling Olav's leg wasn't a metal rod at all.

The bony fingers sticking up through the hole in Olav's thigh, locking it in place, were familiar. He had seen them before, in the doorway by the house up by Lake Mørkved.

When they were kids throwing pinecones and rocks at the windows. Now, he also saw the figure huddled behind Olav. The Witch of Mørkved. She wore fragments of Bingo-Bob's crushed skull as a macabre mask over her face. She had found Robert, but she probably didn't realise she was about to kill her own brother. Blind with rage. Still Robert refused to let go. There would be no more running.

I'll be damned if I give up now.

Zero Seconds

Whether the oxygen tank had broken, or it was empty, didn't matter. Robert couldn't breathe, so he let the mouthpiece fall yet again. The Witch of Mørkved did not let go of Olav's leg. Robert did not let go of Olav's hand.

Ten Seconds

Robert had given up hope of freeing Olav. Olav had given up hope of breaking free from the Witch. If any of them were to survive this, she would have to be the one to show mercy. For some reason, she would have to choose to spare them.

Fifteen Seconds

The beam from Robert's lamp, the only source of light, trailed behind them like a comet's tail as they descended toward the abyss. What was in reality merely seconds felt like an ocean of time passing. It was as if they were floating around in a vacuum, a black hole — the three of them, all alone. But that moment didn't last. For soon, another light appeared. A sort of glimmer. Something far down below. Down there. A faint glow radiated from several elliptical objects. Slowly, they grew brighter, casting a lazy shimmer over the landscape beneath them. Robert didn't really consider the illogical nature of these lights in the deep. He didn't reflect upon the fact that such lights often served as death traps for those who ventured too close. Nonetheless, Olav and Robert continued their descent towards the bottom.

Rocks and underwater cliffs soon rose majestically around them as their descent neared its end. From the nearly invisible ocean floor, stalls that Robert recognised from the circus emerged. Soon they stood spread out like gravestones, draped in algae, shells, and corals. A row of torches along the aisle leading to the tent flickered as glowing jellyfish danced in sync with obscure seaweed species. The tent's canvas sprawled along the bottom like a gigantic manta ray. The entrance gaped at them with dirty teeth. Robert couldn't do a damn thing. They kept falling towards the monster's mouth. Closer.

Please stop! Please don't make me go in there. Please. I beg you. I can't enter that place. That thing. There must be some other way... Robert knew that nothing but bottomless horror awaited inside. He tried spinning around, jerking and tearing loose, yet never letting go of Olav. As they drew closer, the urge to throw up surged, his body tingling and burning as if on fire. There was no way out. No way back. Soon, they passed the jagged, rusty metal teeth, plunging into the monster's belly, into the stomach of the circus.

At first, there was nothing. Not a sound. No taste. No smell. No pain. Even Olav and the Witch were gone. Robert was alone in the belly of the beast, in the darkness. No fear, no joy, no sorrow. Not even nothing.

Then, seconds, minutes, hours, days, or maybe even years later, things changed. Out of nowhere, the surroundings exploded in a fireworks display of emotions, senses, and events. It was like the kaleidoscope he used to play with at Grandma and Grandpa's cabin, except the mirrors didn't reflect plastic pieces in every conceivable color, but memories spinning around in a somewhat controlled chaos. All experiences, known and forgotten, dark and bright, formed an archive, an account of life. Complete and unfiltered.

Robert was the centrepiece, floating in the midst of this cascade of memories. He wished to linger longer on the memory of Guro in her pink t-shirt on the swing at elementary school, but he was abruptly thrust into another. At first, it was indistinct, like the old movie nights at his uncle's house in Sandåsen, where it always took some time to bring the projector's image into focus. First blurry, then sharp, then blurry again. Ceilings and walls came into view. Posters with familiar colours and patterns began to emerge. Those posters. He remembered them well as he had seen them a million times before. Flags, scarves, and banners. Iron Maiden, Ozzy Osbourne, and Kiss. Van Basten, Rijkaard, and Lineker. They all appeared on the walls and ceiling around him. Blurred. Semi-sharp. Blurred. Sharp. Sharp!

Robert was home. In the house in Øyerstad. Back when things were so much easier. In another time. He was sitting at his desk in the bedroom. The pen in his hand switched from dark blue to black. It had always been black, the pen he used the night Fredrik died. Christmas Day, less than ten years ago. Ink spread across the paper, resembling the blots psychologists used in movies.

"You have to let go!" Fredrik sat on the edge of the bed. He was the same age as when Robert saw him for the last time. It was him. He was back! Robert wanted to shout with joy, but something blocked his throat.

"The special assignment is for you. I don't need it where I am going," Fredrik fumbled with the stack in front of him, pointing to the assignment he wrote in school about

"Arnold—The Terminator". The drawings and scribbles weren't the finest the world had seen. The images were unevenly cut. It didn't matter. It was the effort he had put into it, the passion. That was the only thing of importance. His smile, the day he came home from school. He, Fredrik, had received praise at school. Mom had barely believed him, and when he asked why she was crying, she blamed something in her eye.

Now he placed the special assignment on top of the pile in front of him and picked up the jersey.

"You have to be careful with this, even though it's Tottenham," Fredrik said.

Robert coughed, tried to speak, but ended up nodding his head instead.

Fredrik, listen to me now. You can't go to sleep. Not tonight! If you do, you won't wake up again. It's so damn empty here without you. You hear me?

"Will you take care of my stuff, or what?" Fredrik looked at Robert, folding the jersey and placing it on the stack. "I didn't want to die, you know. Not Mom either. But the ones in the hole, the Witch of Mørkved and Death, they did. I think they laughed when I died. After all, we were mean to them, but were we really that bad? I mean, I only threw pinecones, and... Why are they after all of us?"

Some thick fluid gurgled in Robert's lungs, and the words he coughed up were impossible to interpret. He jerked and shook as if someone was trying to start him with faulty jumper cables. Fredrik continued, seemingly unaffected by Robert's behavior.

"I wanted to help you. Get you away from Øyerstad. The truck driver, you remember him? I made him stop. And then there was the sign, the one pointing towards Hitra. Dad always talked about that island, you remember? I think

I got Olav to stop too. Your new friend. I don't know how I did it though. It just happened when I wanted it to. But I couldn't help you all. Anders and Dad, I couldn't get through to them. Or maybe I did, but if so, they ignored me. I've tried to protect them too, but I can't anymore. I don't think they can hear me like you do.

The Witch of Mørkved and Death, they're not sorry anymore. They're angry, boiling with fury."

Robert noticed the water on the floor. It was rising slowly, soon lapping at Fredrik's toes before covering them completely. The water kept rising. "I followed Anders on the night they made him crash..." Fredrik's fingers twisted his rat-tail. "I tried to show you, and you did see me, didn't you? On the stairs of the old store? The Witch and Death weren't very strong back then, so I managed to stop them."

Fredrik gazed at Robert with sunken eyes, reminiscent of those black holes, shadows, spirals, or whatever they were. His face was pallid, and frosty breath accompanied his words, drifting through the room. "I found Mom too, but I couldn't save her. I really tried to wake you up, to save her. I tried to stop them from hurting her. I… They had become way too strong by then, and they said they would take you too. So, I had to get you away. You couldn't stay in Øyerstad and I thought you'd be safe on Hitra. But they found you anyway."

Like a scene in a film, we jumped forward. Seconds or minutes into the future. Gary Lineker was cheering on the duvet while Fredrik struggled with pen and paper. He didn't look up from the letter, the one he wrote so many years ago. He continued to speak.

"I think Mom went straight over to the other side. I think she did, because I haven't seen her. When I... when I died… there was only one way to go. Along the streetlights. I think something nice is at the end there, but I couldn't go all the way. Not yet. So I found a way back. I pictured myself jumping off the school bus one stop too early. It was actually quite easy. I was not ready. I had some things I needed to do, even though I didn't know what it was. Wonder if they felt the same, that they had things they needed to do too? The Witch of Mørkved and Death. What if they're dead like me, and they jumped off the bus too? What was it that they had to fix before they could go all the way?

You're not safe here anymore. They have found you. And your friend, you can't sacrifice yourself for him. If you both die, I don't think we can stop them..."

Fredrik looked past Robert and out the window towards the road that lay beyond the lawn outside the house. Øyerstad was submerged. Only a quivering glass pane kept the room from being crushed by the world outside. Out in the Haugen Fields, the circus tent emitted a mild glow, shifting slowly with the underwater currents. To the right of the field lay Karianne and Petter's house, shrouded in darkness. Police tape fluttered like seaweed caught in the ocean's sway. In the window farthest to the left, in the bedroom, there was a flash, and the silhouette of a person appeared. Gunshots? Petter being shot to death. Same event that was spoken of on the news hours earlier.

"That was Petter and Kai," Fredrik said. "And Kai? He is on his way here. To the house. To Dad. You have to get back to Øyerstad, Robert. But you have got to hurry. You can still save Dad. You can still save them."

Three Minutes

Outside, along the road, beneath the streetlights, they gradually became more visible: an army of the living dead.

Everyone who meant something to Robert was there. Mom, Dad, Anders, Jungle-Jim, Linn, and others. Side by side they stood with pale, sunken eyes and open mouths revealing nothing but darkness within, like the phantoms at the circus. Facing the house, they swayed back and forth. Slowly. Guro was there too.

Above the parade of death, Olav hung, slowly spinning towards Robert. His eyes seemed forced open by fear and panic. As he jerked, air bubbles found their way from his mouth, trailing up his face. Muscles in his neck, cheeks, and arms appeared to bulge as if he were trying to break free from a spell of paralysis. Again, he jerked violently a few times before he seemed to regain some control over his body. Extending an arm towards Robert, who returned the gesture, he made a silent plea. Although Robert was seated a bit away from the window, his hand continued forward through the room as if distance didn't really exist in this place. His hand didn't stop at the glass. It just faded slightly as it passed through it, without resistance. Rings spread through the glass like those in water, ebbing out before they reached the windowsill.

"You have to go back to Øyerstad, Robert!" Olav spoke with Fredrik's voice. "You have to stop this, otherwise, so many more will die."

Three Minutes and Forty Seconds

The window pane yielded, and water surged into the room with immense power. Robert was thrown off his chair and crashed into the wall behind him. Fredrik and his bed were lifted from the floor and tossed around the room. A water tornado was unleashed, showing no mercy. There was nothing one could do but follow the water and hope not to be crushed or impaled by the debris.

In the midst of chaos, Robert felt a force pulling him out through the window. Desperately, he grabbed for the windowsill, trying to hold on. Useless. As he was sucked out of the room, an anguished scream echoed in his head: "Fredrik! Don't go! You can't leave me again. Please, let me stay with you."

In a cascade of bubbles and frothy water, Robert continued to spin in the darkness outside the house. He expected to crash into something at any moment—into a streetlight, to get tangled up in power lines, or maybe even to collide with Olav or the army of the dead. However, none of that happened. Eventually, the chaos subsided. Everything calmed down, and he found himself back on Hitra. In the water by the ravine outside Blåskyskjærene. Still descending towards the bottom. Robert could no longer see the Witch, nor could he see Olav, the sea floor, or the wreck. However, in the pitch-black waters, he still felt Olav's hand in his, and he knew what he had to do. He couldn't wait any longer.

I'm sorry, buddy! I really didn't know it would come to this. I probably should go down with you, but I can't. I really can't. I have something I must do. I have to go home. Back to Øyerstad. I hope you find peace. That you find your family.

Robert released his grip and let go of Olav's hand, allowing him to fall further down towards the bottom, towards something unknown. Robert didn't have the strength to fight his way back up either. He too needed a rest. He needed to close his eyes for a bit.

Everything is going to be okay.

Mixed Excerpts from Chapters 53, 54, and 56

Sand and polished stones massaged Robert's body as the waves pushed him ashore, rhythmically, inch by inch. His lungs filled with oxygen as it brightened, and with saltwater as it darkened. Oxygen. Saltwater. Throw up. More oxygen. More saltwater. Throw up. A bit more oxygen. A bit more life. Throw up. Oxygen. Life.

At first, the incoming waves reached his chest, but as he gradually pulled himself further ashore, they soon only reached his stomach, then his hips, knees, and finally barely touched his toes. From warm to cold, and back to warm again.

—

Old fisherman Olderø was the only one who knew they were going to dive near the lagoon by Blåskykøya. When neither of them showed up for work in Karskjær the next day, he set out to sea. He found their boat immediately; resting on the calm sea ripples, it appeared perfectly normal, as if the divers had just left and would return from their excursion at any moment. However, they had been gone for 24 hours. Something was wrong. Olderø gathered several of the local and also alerted the coast guard. Not many hours later, they found Robert, beaten and battered, on a beach between the cliffs on a small island slightly north of where they found the boat. They all hoped that Olav would appear on the same or one of the other nearby islands.

—

Sitting on a plastic crate on board Olderø's fishing cutter, Robert adjusted his bandage. It had come loose, hanging bloody down his forehead.

"You okay?" Olderø scanned the waters around him, studying the reefs and every single wave. He wiped sweat from his brow with his forearm.

"I… I guess I am. I feel better than Olav, I guess."

"We'll find him too. He has to be around here somewhere."

"I don't think he made it to the surface. He... went down with the wreck. I let him go..."

"You did what you could. You could've been gone too."

"Yeah, maybe. If it wasn't for that damn storm…"

"You keep saying that. Talking about that storm."

"It shifted while we were down there. We had no chance to get back up." Olderø glanced at the radio. Silence.

"I was nearby, and the sun was baking like hell itself yesterday. It was calm. Not even a breeze." The radio crackled and Olderø grabbed the microphone. Still nothing. "I don't understand why the hell you had to go down there again," he muttered.

—

The gash in Robert's skull was patched up with thirteen stitches at the infirmary in Fillan. However, the doctor who treated the wound was more worried about other symptoms. Pain in the joints, itching, and rashes were apparently signs of decompression sickness. He mumbled something about hyperbaric treatment at the hospital in Trondheim. Robert, however, defied the warnings and left the hospital as soon as the doctors looked away. "I'm fine. Just tired."

He hoped they didn't see him as he stumbled down the stairs and vomited outside the hospital. Considering what lay ahead of him, a bit of decompression sickness here or there probably didn't matter much. The chances of him getting out of this alive were slim anyway.

—

Robert stood outside the local store, Bunnpris, in Karskjær, after taking the car from the house in Nordbukta for the last time. He placed the keys to the car he got from Olav in the mailbox on the wall by the kiosk. A Tottenham jersey hung on the outside of his backpack, even more worn than when he first came to the island a few years ago. June gave way to July, and Olav had been missing for several days. They had searched around the clock but found nothing. Olderø and Danne would surely keep searching for days and even weeks to come, but Robert kinda knew they would never find him. Olav would remain missing: gone, like his father.

Hitra - 1972

Dad & Co

Kai continued to crack open beers as they navigated through Ramsøysundet. Out of habit, Dad stood at the front of the boat, scouring for treacherous rocks and shoals as they neared the dock. The scent of exposed seaweed and saltwater was reminiscent of the whisky they'd consumed the night before. Kai jumped onto the dock before they'd properly moor the boat. He landed on the iron grating, staggering a few steps to the side before regaining his balance.

Dad secured the boat, and Kai barked as Petter began picking up empty beer cans, chocolate wrappers, and fish remnants from previous trips. "Leave that crap. We're not coming back here anyway."

Petter glanced at Dad, who was using a bucket to wash blood off the deck. Reluctantly, they stopped cleaning and followed Kai up the gangway. The plastic tub, filled with fish remnants and garbage from previous adventures, was left behind on the dock. The cows in the meadow along the path to the house barely reacted when Kai threw a half-empty beer can at them, laughing.

"I hope they gore you in the ass one day," Dad muttered to himself.

Back at the house, Kai insisted on following his newly established rule: leave your shit for someone else to take care of.

"Are you serious?" Dad asked. "We can't just leave it like this. It looks like a bomb has gone off in here. We should at least fix it up a bit."

"If we get complaints, we'll have issues with Old-Gunnar," Petter added.

"I don't give a shit," Kai responded, gathering his belongings into a bag. "We're not coming back here anyway." He peered out of the window, up towards the road. "She might have brought her crazy father. They could be on their way now, and I sure as hell don't intend to be here when they arrive. She can deal with that bun in the oven herself."

"You're really just going to leave?" Dad followed Kai's gaze up the road.

"That kid isn't mine. I can't become a dad anyway. Not now." Kai turned towards them and chugged a beer. "Let's get the hell out of here."

Petter sighed, shook his head, and packed up the box with fishing lures, jigs, and leaders. Kai went to empty the fridge; the leftover beers would come in handy for the drive home.

"We should at least leave some final words in the cabin book," Dad said, settling down with a beer on the sofa. He swept bottles, glasses, cigarette butts, and other remnants of last night's revelry from the coffee table. Then, picking up a pen from the bowl of peanuts and bottle caps, he began to write.

"Beautiful poetry, as usual?" Petter stood in the doorway leading into the living room, offering a wry smile. He was packed and ready.

"Oh yes, we must leave some words of wisdom for those who come after us," he replied. Reading the last line aloud as he wrote, "—get back home to Øyerstad. Fast as…"

"Cut the crap!" Kai emerged from the kitchen.

"Relax, this isn't crap, this is poetry." Dad smiled teasingly. "We have to warn our successors. Don't mess with the local women. They only bring trouble, and…"

"Idiot," Kai snapped.

"You haven't changed your mind yet?" Dad lifted a beer can towards Petter. He smiled and rolled his eyes. "We could still stay a few more days, what do you say?"

"Put that shit away!" Kai first reached for the pen, then for the cabin book.

"Hey, I'm not done!" Dad laughed, resisting the attempt to snatch the book.

Soon, they were tugging at it together—Dad smiling, and Kai with a more serious look. Eventually, Dad released his grip on the book, allowing Kai to hurl it across the room. It struck the ceiling above the pine cabinet with a thud, then tumbled down behind the imposing wooden structure.

"Seriously?" Dad looked at Kai.

“Seriously! The book’s good there.”

“Yeah, well, it probably won’t be read for a while, unless some of the guests decide to rearrange the place,” Dad remarked. He walked over to the cabinet, yanked at it, and jumped a couple of times, trying to see if the book had landed on top. He couldn’t see it.

“No one is going to read your poetry. Not for a long time. And when someone finally does, maybe you’ll become famous. Posthumously. Let it go now. Have another one; it makes your hand steady,” Kai tossed a beer towards Dad. He caught it, glanced at Kai, looked down at the can, opened it, and took a couple of gulps. “So, I’m driving again, am I?”

“As always,” Petter and Kai answered in unison. Dad downed the rest of the beer. The ensuing belch was powerful, but it still couldn’t move the cabinet. Kai handed him another can. Dad took it with him as they headed towards the car, settled in, and drove off.

Part IV

Chicken & Whisky

Øyerstad, August 1999

1

Robert

For as long as I could remember, Dad always had the same old clogs in the hallway at home. Now, as I moved quietly into the hallway after being away for nearly two years, the old worn pair had been replaced with a brand new one. His dirty work shoes were swapped out as well, with a spotless pair of the same brand. He told us a million times while we were growing up that the parquet in the hallway needed a new layer of lacquer. He had finally had it done. The wallpaper in the hallway was new, and even the skirting boards were finally up. I entered the kitchen and the lights reflected off the plastic mats on the floor. The counter was free of bottles and old dishes. Despite all this, the smell of chicken with rosemary and garlic surprised me the most.

I ran a finger over the stove—no dust, not a single hint of old grease. I was about to open the oven door when I realised I could see through the glass. It was no longer covered with a thick layer of burnt fat and oil. The rosemary sprigs, the garlic, and the bubbling skin on the chicken looked fantastic. It smelled amazing. I had underestimated Dad.

A voice from the TV spoke of withdrawing forces from Kosovo. Successful negotiations had resulted in a peaceful solution between the parties. The flowers in the windowsills impressed me just as much as someone actually finding a peaceful solution to anything. Dad had developed a green thumb?

Teletext pages fluttered by with the evening news in the

background. Rosenborg led the Norwegian soccer league, and Haugesund was at risk of relegation, but many matches were still to be played. "It's anyone's game these days..." Dad used to say. Frode Johnsen led the top scorer's table.

He didn't see me standing in the doorway from the kitchen to the living room, the same doorway Fredrik and I had dashed through countless times. We raced around and around, weaving between the living room, kitchen, and hallway on tricycles, scooters, barefoot and with shoes. It was the world's best obstacle course, a war zone, and the ultimate game of tag. The last time we played here was on Christmas Eve, so many years ago, just hours before he passed away.

Once the glass in the doorframe leading to the hallway shattered into a thousand pieces when I slammed the door during our eager play. Fredrik, coming up behind me, flew right through it. Cops and robbers. He had to get stitches at the emergency room, maybe twelve or thirteen, on his right forearm. The glass was never replaced. Not until now. Dad had been busy.

I wanted to shout out, "You replaced the glass in the door!" Or even better, "You're alive!" After my last meeting with Fredrik, I wasn't quite expecting that. Alternatively, a simple "Sorry" might have been an appropriate way to start. But, the first words I spoke in Øyerstad since leaving were simple and cautious: "I've been to Hitra."

He didn't react. Perhaps he had heard my voice many times over the last couple of years, but obviously only in his head. Grown accustomed to it. And now, as it was there in reality, he couldn't distinguish it from the voices in his dreams. "Dad, I've been to..."

It was as if he suddenly woke up, realising the voice was coming from somewhere outside his head.

"'Robert?" he uttered. His small, blue eyes widened, and

his mouth hung open in astonishment.

"Yeah. I'm…"

"You've come home!" he exclaimed, rising effortlessly from his chair by the window and moving towards me. The scent reached me first—Nivea, for men, without alcohol. The deodorant stick he used to pick up from the bargain bin at the store before things started going awry. The bathroom cabinet always housed at least two of them as we grew up. I was expecting a stench of cigarettes and moonshine, but he smelled like before everything fell apart. The hug he gave me was both unexpected and strong.

"I'm sorry," I whispered, the lump in my throat sinking a little deeper.

"It's okay, Robert. You're back now," he responded.

"I guess I am. And you… I thought you might be…"

"Be what? Drunk? Gone? Dead?" he asked.

"I…"

"Listen, I have changed, okay? Things have changed," Dad said, chuckling while still holding me tight. "You know, I feel better now. After you disappeared too, I'd had enough. I had to get some order in my life. To do that, I had to stop lying. I had to come clean. I had to tell everyone. And so I did, and I have been waiting to tell you too."

"Dad, I… tell me what?"

"Hey, son, you are back. Let's enjoy that for a little while first, and I will tell you," he said, then pointed at the bandage on my head. "Did you hurt your head?"

"It looks worse than it is. Diving accident at Hitra. Long story. It's not all cheerful."

Dad tilted his head back and looked at me, his eyes brimming with genuine care and love. It had been a long time since I'd seen anything like that in those eyes.

"I've made your favourite dish," he said, almost jogging

into the kitchen.

It was quite a surprise, as even I didn't know that chicken with rosemary and garlic was my favourite dish before I left Øyerstad.

"It smells good. What happened to beer and pan pizza? You've really gone all out, I see."

"Yeah, it's hard to explain, but something told me it was going to be a good day. I mean, haven't felt like this in a long time, not since before everything went to shit. So, I decided to go the extra mile."

During dinner, which was no less than what the team of cooks made in Karskjær, I told him about Hitra. About the people, I told their stories. Painting boathouses, the kiosk, and fixing rusty boat engines. I talked about cooking, serving, and the gigs in the pub. I described the fishing with great enthusiasm. The diving. My God, diving. It was fantastic.

"And dangerous?" Dad referred to the bandage on my head again.

"Olav…"

"Who?"

"Olav, just someone I met up there, he sends his apologies for the accident." Now I pointed to my head. "It won't happen again if we come to visit one day, he says."

"Really? You think he would have us? We seriously need to go there one day. You, me, and Anders." Dad took a bite of chicken breast. I took a bite as well.

"Yes, one day we will. Olav would certainly take care of us. He'll get us a good price, maybe we can even stay for free. Like I did. He was… is a really great friend now".

We kept eating, laughing, and talking, and after a while Dad said, "You left quickly after Mom's funeral. Not many visit her gravestone anymore. Maybe Anders, once in a while, but otherwise, I make sure a light is burning for her there."

"Shall we go there together tomorrow?" I suggested, not mentioning that I had hopped off the bus by the cemetery hours earlier. As we passed the school, guilt had hit me about never having seen Mom's gravestone. I got off the bus, walked across the parking lot. As I faced the graveyard with the iron gate's handle creaking in my hand, a chilling thought struck me. What if there were more gravestones there now? What if I stumbled upon Dad's or Anders' grave? Or both? If they too were gone, perhaps living in ignorance for a little while longer was better. I never stepped into the graveyard, instead, I turned towards the village centre.

A truck roared past outside on the northbound road. At the same time, an old Chevrolet with a Confederate flag in the rear window passed in the opposite direction. The bass from its trunk sent vibrations through the house as it turned into the gas station. "I see Øyerstad hasn't changed," I said.

"Not much," Dad replied, and although we both referred to the car, his answer was disconcerting.

"How is he doing?" I finally asked.

"Who?"

"Anders."

"We haven't had much contact while you were away." Dad put his fork on the table, looking at me. "I try to stay away."

I looked back at him and there it was, a touch of the Dad I had expected to find here. A more worn-down version. "What kind of bullshit is that, that you have to stay away?" I said, saddened by the fact that he still clung to this strange delusion.

Dad stood up and fetched a bottle from the cabinet. He filled two glasses to the brim. More of the Dad I left in Øyerstad. He lifted the glass and took a hearty gulp.

"Laphroaig? When did you start drinking such fine stuff?" I said, looking at the bottle.

"Cheers," Dad said, avoiding my question and raising his glass. Back when I left Øyerstad, the Dad I knew rarely drank anything other than moonshine, occasionally Bells or Grants. Anything more was, in his eyes, an unnecessary expense for spirits you could distill yourself. Now he sat before me with a glass of one of the finer whiskies the liquor store had to offer. Laphroaig, a name I hadn't even known when I left. Did he buy it to impress me? No, that couldn't be it. He couldn't possibly have known I was coming home.

"I read about you guys in the cabin book." I said.

Dad stiffened. He first looked out the window, then at me. "You found the cabin book? I knew it would turn up one day."

"You tried to hide it? Behind the locker?"

"Robert, listen! Everything that's happened in Øyerstad these last few years. Fredrik, Mom, Anders, and Linn. Kai and all that shit. It started there. On that Island. I mean, at first, it was almost innocent, something that could happen to anyone. But it kept growing, and then everything went to hell here in Øyerstad. I have wanted to tell you this for a long time, son. It's all my fault, and it's not just something I say.

The women up there were wild. And we, some handsome fellas from Øyerstad, we were fresh blood. New opportunities. Maybe you experienced that on Hitra too?" Dad said, his eyes suddenly bloodshot. "So, if you read about it in the book, you've pieced it all together?"

"Well, I have some..."

"The problem wasn't that she was pregnant, but that she accused Kai of being the father."

"He denied it, right?"

"That's right, and I mean, we couldn't be completely sure

either. As I said, those women out there were wild. Rakel was the worst, which suited Kai quite well. She had some issues at home and constantly talked about getting away from the island. She wanted to start a new life where no one knew who she was. She wanted to come with us, and maybe she saw Kai as a ticket out of there.

I guess, we assumed the problem with Rakel would blow over if we turned our backs on it. So we simply left Hitra and never returned. And believe it or not, things were fine for a few years. Jesus, we had almost forgotten all about it when she suddenly showed up. Here! In Øyerstad, with that kid!"

Dad took another sip of whisky. "Kai kept denying he was the father, but he knew, just as well as us, that the kid was his. The boy was the spitting image of his father, except for parts of his face."

"The Elephant Boy," I whispered.

"What?" Dad asked.

"Nothing," I replied.

Dad continued, "We never contradicted Kai. You know how he can be. But we did our part and fixed up a house for them up in the Mørkved Hills. Each of us chipped in; perhaps we felt a bit guilty. Petter and I spent a lot of time there, building. We helped them settle in. Even Kai pitched in at first, though he probably did it mostly to keep her quiet. He gave her an ultimatum of some sort, if she stopped nagging about him being the father, if she stayed away from him, he would help her with a place to live. So she would never have to go back to Hitra.

"You hid them away up there."

"Yes, we did."

"But there must have been some talk?"

"Of course there was, and that was our plan. We poured gasoline on the fire, and went on with one outrageous story after another. The kind that made the town buzz. You should have seen her when she came to the store. You should have heard them. People talking. The things they said. Stories that we planted… I… We… Sometimes she stood outside the chapel. Maybe she was hoping someone would lend her a hand, inviting her in. But for her, the Christians were just glances in the windows. No outstretched hands. We treated her like a monster, and it worked. It didn't take long before she stopped coming."

"So, what did she do? You think she simply locked herself up?"

"We didn't talk about it. Not even when Kai bragged about having been up by her cabin to 'get some of the old fun'. Even after he met Hanne and had Linn. We knew he kept going there, and we didn't say a goddamn word. For fuck sake, we looked the other way. Said nothing."

Dad's trembling hand looked pale in contrast to the whisky in his glass.

"It's incredible what you can put up with if you pretend it doesn't exist. Something really terrible today is just bad tomorrow. The day after tomorrow, it's bearable. A week later, you think it's okay. A month or a year after that, it's the new normal. We adapt. We wanted everything to be okay again."

"And then Death showed up?"

"That damn kid with his helmet and his bike. Pål-Ottar."

"You used to say he was a vampire."

"That too."

"We believed you, you know? We thought…"

"He was simply helping her. With shopping and stuff."

"My God, we ran when he came to the store, Dad! We thought he was going to eat us alive."

"That's what we wanted you to believe. We wanted you

to stay away from him, when all he actually did was hide behind his helmet," Dad sighed, and we sat in silence for a while."

"You remember the night I went hunting with Kai?" Dad continued.

"The night you fought by the road. Everything changed after that."

"That night." Dad coughed and grew paler, almost translucent, as he continued to speak.

When Kai announced that there would be no hunting due to the weather, Dad was relieved. Sitting in a hideout in the forest while the sky tried to swallow him was not his idea of a great night out. However, a party in the hunting cabin was more up his alley.

They had parked their cars up by the lake and ran through the rain to the cabin. Upon entering, they hung their soaking wet clothes on protruding nails in the wall. The cabin, not much larger than the kiosk outside the store back in the day, had one room that served as a living room, bedroom, and kitchen. In the centre of the room stood a long table, flanked by six chairs on each side. The log walls were lined with bunk beds, except for the kitchen corner. There, Kai lit the fireplace, warming both food and people.

Later Kai stuck his knife into a cured ham, and the bottle of liquor landed next to it on the table. The mixers were also brought out, orange juice, apple juice, and sparkling water. Lukewarm. Dad and Kai mixed with tonic water, as it made the spirit taste the most. They cut the ham into thick slices, gobbling them up before the stew cans were heated on the wood-fired stove. Then there were guns. Of course there was an abundance of firearms, and to become a proper hunter, one had to know how to use them. Rain hammered against the tin roof as Dad studied the rifle Kai laid before him. It was heavier than he had thought.

Back home in Øyerstad, so many years later, Dad mimicked Kai. "This, Dad, this is a rifle! A gun-happy gal. Meet Rakel. My lady," he had said. The others laughed.

"That bastard had named his gun after her. It was as if he was waiting for the right occasion," Dad said before continuing the imitation. "Rakel is a Mauser M98. A classic. She's spread fear in these woods for many years, in many ways. She's seen things, and she's shot things. She's never failed me. Always loyal."

Now Dad took another sip. "Kai looked at me first, then at Petter, when he said 'always loyal'. Then he took the gun apart and showed me how to put it back together. If the gun jammed with a moose in the line of fire, you had to be quick. All hunters should be able to disassemble and reassemble their weapon in case of a jam. Quick. Even drunk, Kai did it in seconds.

Jesus! All those damn parts. The alcohol had its effect on me, but after some fiddling and swearing, I managed to put the rifle back together. Or, someone else might have helped me, for all I can remember.

"Once the weapon was assembled, they insisted that I had to test fire it too. Rakel. The gun. 'You weren't a man until you tried her.' The rest of us were fine enough in the cabin, but Kai insisted we go out and give her a go. So I put on the rain jacket, probably upside-down and sideways all at once. It wasn't long before rain ran down the inside of my clothes. We couldn't see a damn thing."

Dad poured himself another glass, and my thoughts briefly turned to Olav. We had shared a few drinks on Hitra and considered ourselves capable of handling a good amount of spirits. But the quantities Dad was downing now, and at that pace—shit, it would have knocked me out in no time.

"Kai waved the floodlight around when I was to fire the rifle. I couldn't see a damn thing, so I fired a shot at random into the forest. The sooner I did it, the sooner we'd be back in the cabin, right? Rain pelteded against my hood like an eternal echo of the shot that raced through the forest. The guys raised their beer cans and cheered. Soon their voices turned into a rhythmic, once more! Once more! Once more! If I'd just thanked them for the applause after the first shot and gone in, everything would be fine today. It was the second shot that should never have been fired."

"What do you mean? The second shot? Did you hit something?"

A tear rolled down Dad's cheek. "The shot itself was like the first one. I still followed Kai's orders. I chased his light with the rifle barrel, swinging it from one side to the other when something flashed down by the meadow beyond the cabin. It all happened so fast, but I had time to think, 'Don't shoot, for God's sake, there's someone there'. But the thought never reached my finger before it pressed the trigger."

Sitting in the living room in Øyerstad, Dad closed his eyes as he recounted how the guys had cheered wildly, once again. Kai even gave Dad a hug. They praised him for how damn accurate he was. They said he probably shot both a pinecone and, with a bit of luck, a squirrel. As a reward, he could sleep with Rakel all night if he wanted, and shoot with her the next day. Hunting leader Kai glowed in the rain. He was proud.

Dad had tried to explain that he saw a light in the direction he shot, but they showed no interest in his ramblings and retreated into the cabin. They didn't want to spend time looking for something he thought he might have seen in the rain so far away. Eventually, Dad managed to persuade Kai that they should take a walk and check. Just to be sure.

They were as wet inside their clothes as on the outside

when they reached the gravel road where Dad thought he had seen something. This was the same road that led up to Lake Mørkved after passing through the dense forest. "The Tunnel of Darkness", or something like that, is what we had called it when we were kids.

"He must have had a breakdown on his moped, because if he had been driving as usual, I would have heard him, or at least seen the lights."

"Moped?"

"That damn thing had to break down at some point, I guess," Dad said.

"What had to break down?"

"The moped."

"You mean…"

"Yep. We... I had shot Death."

Dad's laughter reminded me of Jack Nicholson in The Shining. He smacked his forehead with his hand. "I had shot Death. To death," he repeated.

"For fuck's sake, the bullet had gone through his visor and exploded inside the helmet. Kai had to stop me when I wanted to rip the helmet off to see if he was alive. 'You don't want to see that. Rakel can be a real bitch,' he said, holding me back. If Death wasn't a beauty before the bullet hit his face, he wasn't much better now."

The streetlights along the highway reflected in Dad's eyes, and he continued to tell how the rain eased off while they stood there with Death at their feet. He described how chaos raged in his head, while Kai was cold and calculating.

"We must get rid of this body! Now!" Before Dad even registered the meaning of what Kai was saying, they saw movement further down the road. Someone was approaching, their light sweeping back and forth among the trees and across the meadow. It was barely audible, but whoever it was, they were calling out to someone. Dad's heart was supposedly pounding so hard that he couldn't hear either the rain or the sporadic thunderclaps that roamed the sky. He was sure he was going to have a heart attack. In fact, right there and then, he hoped for it. He wished that everything would just disappear.

"Wait here. I'll handle this," Kai had said before storming towards the stranger approaching. His light bounced between the trees and didn't stop until their two light sources met. They seemed to stand still for a while, shining their lights at each other, like two Jedi warriors ready for battle. One of the two silhouettes appeared to stand more upright than the other.

Even though Dad's heart was still beating excessively, he gradually managed to distinguish layers of sound from each other: the blood rushing through his body, the rain, thunderclaps, and shouts. No, not shouts —it was stronger, more like screams. They were screaming at each other. The stranger was the loudest. It could have been a woman, and she sounded terrified. Then suddenly, one light source, Kai and his torch, charged at the other. They collided. The massive explosion Dad expected did not happen. Instead, the lights sliced through the air in quick, sporadic patterns. It didn't take long before one light source began moving in fast, more determined patterns, while the other seemed to fade. Up and down, up and down. The bearer of the bouncing light was pounding on something. Then it went dark.

After what seemed like an eternity, one of the two lights reappeared. It moved in calmer, more swaying motions back towards Dad, and soon he made out the outline of a person. It was Kai, and he was dragging something heavy with him. Soon, the body of the Witch of Mørkved landed next to Death's in the ditch. Kai stood bent over them with his hands on his knees, gasping for breath. The light from the torch he held towards his knees swung slowly under a filter of red. Blood.

"He had crushed her skull with it. And you know, killing a human being takes its toll. Especially when you have to drag the body a hundred metres through the forest afterward," Dad said without taking his eyes off the lights on the tower up on the hill.

"Why? Why did he have to..."

"You know how Kai gets when those adrenaline surges hit him; he's unstoppable. He was ice cold. 'You wait here,' he commanded, then ran back into the trees towards the cabin. I stood there alone, over the two bodies. And that damn rain."

Kai and Petter had already laid out a plan when they came back. They had poached before, so they had their methods for disposing of unwanted animal carcasses. The Mørkved Lake.

"Forget the sheriff. That tired rat never figures out anything. He won't lift a damn finger." Kai had little trust in the local police authorities, and he did have a point. Øyerstad was not the kind of village where the sheriff lay sleepless at night, worried about unsolved cases on his desk. Days or weeks could pass before anyone even noticed they were missing. By then, the rain would have washed away all traces long ago.

Petter, struggling to stand straight, snivelling, suggested they burn down the house with the bodies inside. Dad remained silent, but Kai was firmly against it.

"So we should attract the sheriff and a bunch of fire trucks now? They're going to have questions. If they find the remains of the bodies in the house, they're likely to find a bullet too. And if they find that, then all hell breaks loose," Kai argued. He then pulled out his knife and turned towards Petter. "Do you want to dig out the bullet from his skull? We can't risk them finding anything that can be traced back to us, right? Go ahead, take off the helmet and dig. Dig!"

Kai was inches away from Petter's nose with the tip of his knife. Petter didn't take it.

"Come on, guys, Rakel hasn't been to the shop in years. And Death? It'll be at least a week before people start to wonder. And when they do, so what? They'll find the house empty. No one home. The Witch and Death disappeared as suddenly as they appeared. The police aren't going to do a damn thing," Kai asserted.

Petter carried Death on his shoulders, and Kai dragged Rakel by the legs. Occasionally, when her arms hit a stump or a rock, they jumped and she seemed to wave at Dad, who was struggling with the moped a few metres behind them. Dad could still have stopped this part of the madness.

On the way through the forest up to the lake, Kai and Petter constructed the story they would live the rest of their lives by. Dad said nothing, neither in agreement or disagreement. Kai was resolute, and Petter spoke encouragingly to them both. "Relax, guys. This never happened. The only difference now is that we won't see Death on the road anymore. That's just as well, right? We'll find some other reason to keep the kids off the road. This will be fine, Dad!"

Up by the lake, Kai's boat swayed ominously between heaven and hell as they dumped the bodies into it. Dad stood on the shore, clinging to Death's moped, while the other two rowed the bodies out towards the raft.

It had stopped raining and soon the sound of oar strokes broke the silence. Petter returned alone to fetch the moped. The two old friends exchanged a long gaze as they realised their lives would never be the same.

"The damage is already done," Petter stated as they lifted the moped into the boat. He then disappeared back towards the raft.

Dad was left alone on the shore yet again. He hoped that none of them would ever return, that the fog would swallow them up, hiding them like a dirty little secret, just as they were about to do. But that would have been too easy. Of course, they came back, and soon they were trudging towards the cabin once more. Kai was seemingly untouched by what had happened. He appeared triumphant, as if he had finally defeated his worst enemy, the Witch of Mørkved, who had made his life miserable. Petter did his best to follow Kai, but his voice sounded a bit shaky, and his laughter carried hints of good old panic and desperation.

Sitting in Øyerstad so many years later, Dad glanced down into his glass. There was one mouthful left.

"Some days, I actually thought I could forget it, that things would return to normal. But most days, I waited. Waited for the cops to come knocking, to take me away. Away from you guys. Sometimes, I even wanted them to. I've dialled the police's number a thousand times and hung up. There were days when I actually thought I had talked to them.

I kept dreaming that I had killed someone and was on the run. No matter how fast I ran, or where I hid, they always found me. But it wasn't the police, no, there was someone in the shadows. Just before I woke, they caught me, tore me to pieces, and when I was about to die, finally get some rest, I woke up. Alive. Not a scratch from their filthy claws. So, I waited for the police to show up, before it was time to dream again."

The whisky swirled in my glass, but it didn't tempt me. I looked back at Dad. Looked at the bottle. It was almost empty. I had barely tasted it. I mean, what was I supposed to think about all this? What was I supposed to feel? Hate? Sympathy? Was he to be pitied?

"Back at the cabin, Karsten was asleep at the dining table. The other guys were deep in a discussion about... about how old Cindy Crawford was, I think. Kai grabbed a glass of liquor and seamlessly joined the drunken discussion, claiming she was sixteen. My God, what an idiot. They argued for a long time, and when they finally settled on an age, Kai stood up to get more beer. 'Shape up! Remember we have a plan,' he hissed at Petter and me, who sat quietly at the other end of the table. 'You make sure to stick to the plan.' Kai grabbed a beer from the bench and sat down with the others again. We were still on his radar as they entered a discussion about analogue or digital radio signals, or something along those lines.

"So, then Kai decided to drive you home before you revealed everything?" Dad suddenly looked small and vulnerable as I asked him.

"I really can't say for sure, but that makes sense. I was sitting by the table, I might have closed my eyes, and when I opened them, I was sitting in the car. It's all blank. The next thing I remember is standing outside the car at home. I might have told him I wanted to talk to the cops. That must have pissed him off." Dad emptied the last of the bottle.

"And then you fought."

"While you stood in the bedroom, watching us."

"Yeah. I did. All the bad stuff, it started that night, and you've known why all along…"

"People began to talk, as Kai said they would. Some had even been up to the house. They claimed it was empty, and we kept fuelling the rumours that were farthest from the truth. The Witch of Mørkved and Death had simply gotten tired of this place and moved on.

Even though things kind of went as we planned, it didn't help me much; my dreams got worse. They felt more real, and the panic didn't go away whether I was sleeping or awake. So, I stopped sleeping. Stopped eating. Food tasted and smelled stale and rancid anyway. I didn't deserve to eat or to be happy. It was like having a wet towel over my face. I couldn't breathe. Every single fucking second, they were there. Lurching in the shadows, under a car, in my rear view mirror, behind a colleague at work, or behind me in the bathroom mirror. Sometimes the shadowy figures converged and formed what I thought of as holes in the world. Anytime, anywhere. Entrances, exits, portals, or whatever the hell they were. They are still there."

"They?"

"You know who."

"The Witch? Death?"

"Yes, them. I heard their voices coming from the holes. At first, they whispered, and I pushed them away. Pretended I didn't hear them. That only worked for so long, as slowly but surely, they seemed to get closer. They spoke more often, louder, and one day I saw them move for the first time. Darker shades formed in the shadows. What looked like a hand would emerge from a hole. A face in another. Swollen and pale. Dirty and foul. They grew stronger and eventually they found a way through to the other side. A way back to us."

"But, seriously, Dad, they're dead! They can't hurt us." My voice cracked.

"Yes, they are dead, at least according to our concept of it. But they're not gone. They want me to feel the same as them. Everyone I love will wither and die. And finally, when all are gone, it's my turn. So, I thought, what if I stopped loving you? What if Mom didn't want to be with me? If I hated her, and she hated me. Then she would live, right? Everyone I love will wither and die..."

"So you pushed us away?"

Dad picked out a handkerchief from his pocket, but didn't use it to dry up his tears.

"They took Fredrik away from us. Linn too. And... Mom... They will never stop. Petter and I decided a few weeks ago that we would talk."

"Tell the..."

"Police. We were going to tell them everything."

"And?"

"Kai must have found out about it, somehow."

"And he shot Petter?" I asked.

"I suppose so," Dad said.

"And where is Kai now?"

"He vanished, and that's why I'm telling you this. He's definitely after me too. Maybe even you and Anders. Maybe more. You must stop him."

"Stop him? I don't even know where he is. Dad?"

"Robert?" Dad's voice was barely audible, his head hanging towards his chest. He was mumbling. "No matter what, you must know that you, Fredrik, Anders, and Mom... Mom... No matter how much I've tried to stop loving you, I failed."

"Dad, I..."

"One bad decision leads to another. A spiral of lies spins deeper and deeper into misery. A spiral you never get out of. So, I tried not to love you. I really did try..."

"I... Dad? It was an accident. You couldn't..." I paused, looking out towards the Shell sign on the neighbouring lot. Up towards the lake. "We can still do something right here. It's not too late," I whispered.

"Mom?" Dad whispered with closed eyes. He was drooling.

"Are you awake?" I asked.

"Is that you?" Dad asked.

"Dad, you couldn't have known that..."

"Mom, is that you? Marianne, you must..."

"You go to Mom," I whispered. "Dad... I forgive you. I love you."

2

The Circus

Rakel, the Witch of Mørkved, seemed to have grown. She stood straighter, her back erect, and her facial expression had hardened, resembling stone and granite. Her sadness was washed away. She had butchered Bingo Bob, the one thing I feared the most, and taken control of the Circus; she was the new Director. Now, she was the one sitting on my throne of terror. As if to prove her power, she wore Bingo Bob's blood-soaked fur like gloves, covering her hands and arms. A heap of sticky fur, entrails, and bones lay on the ground in front of their booth. By her side Pål-Ottar, Death, still wore the cauldron over his head. The chain around his neck. Linn still stood in front of them, eyes on the spinning wheel. Buying new lottery tickets. Her dress had soaked up mud and blood from what once was Bingo-Bob.

A film of damp mud had spread all over, covering everything. It seemed to somehow emanate from the two figures in the booth in front of the fortune wheel. The substance, akin to excrement-like mud oozing from their skin, was spreading out from around their feet. They had found a way through. They now moved between dimensions. Between fantasy and reality. Between life and death. For some inexplicable reason, I had developed a special connection with them.

Olav hung a few metres above me in the same position as when he fell towards the bottom of the ravine. Once again, he stretched a ghostlike hand towards me, his mouth moving slowly. "Don't let go of me, Robert. Please. Don't let go!" A bit above him, something moved in rhythmic motions, methodically, like oars through water. It was the underside of a boat approaching the object from which the chain hung. A raft. That raft. On Lake Mørkved.

The raft swayed slightly as someone from the boat jumped onto it. Vibrations spread through the chain and down to us, making Death swing slowly from side to side. The gurgling sounds coming from under the cauldron were either just air released, or maybe some sort of attempt at communication?

Mom grabbed another box of pills and gulped them down. Some of them fell bloodily into the mud in front of her through the hole in her chin. The remnants of our cat, Jungle-Jim hit me over the legs, Kai sat in his car, Anders, the fakir, Olav, Linn… The chain around Death's neck. Soon his body couldn't take it anymore. Soon it would hit the ground in front of him. Death's head.

Robert

The sky loomed over the Mørkved Hills like a fat black dog. Enormous paws, with powerful claws, tore and ripped at the pine trees swaying wildly. Its maw gaped threateningly over Øyerstad. Soon, it would swallow us all.

I was awake, and the chair beside me was empty. Dad must have gone to bed. I tried to call out to him, but my mouth was so dry that my tongue felt glued to the roof of my mouth. I hardly made a sound. I struggled to get up on my feet and stumbled towards the door.

In my modest twenty-one years on the planet, I couldn't recall ever feeling so ill. Not even after some of the worst drinking binges with Olav. Once outside on the stairs, I vomited until acid burned my throat. I started shaking, and

I saw Fredrik and myself on those cold winter days when we dared each other to stick our tongues to the metal railing I now lay against. Fredrik always tried first. Once, his tongue got really stuck, and he had to be torn away. We stopped playing that game, after that. Still, that memory made me smile, even though I felt like shit.

Eventually, I made my way down the stairs and across the backyard. When I rounded the corner of the house, I stopped against the gutter and left another puddle of spit, acid, and streaks of blood. Then I took Dad's car. The keys were, of course, in the ignition. Good old Øyerstad.

It was early, I think, and I was all alone on the road. Sitting behind the wheel, I retched again and opened the windows wide. What was this about? I had one drink, and I didn't even empty the glass. Dad had practically drunk the whole bottle himself.

Outside Petter and Karianne's house, a single piece of police tape clung to a bush, the wind attempting to drag it away. POLICE LINE DO NOT CROSS.

Bits and pieces from the conversation with Dad spun around in my head. My brain struggled to connect my thoughts again.

What the hell was he on about? Had they killed them? And then hidden them up by the lake? And then said nothing? For all this years? Could Dad really do something like that?

I stopped the car near the elementary school and flung open the door, retching again. When I finally felt ready to continue driving, a nervous tingle spread from my stomach. A girl came jogging in my direction. I leaned back into the car and straightened up as she approached. The jogger, much younger than me, greeted me as she passed. She didn't look much like Guro.

Get a grip, Robert. Guro has moved to Hølland. You don't know everyone in Øyerstad anymore.

It was about three hundred metres from my stop to the campsite, but that didn't stop me from vomitting there as well. The sign for the Elk Safari, now boasting a fresh coat of paint and a money-back guarantee, had been updated since my last visit. A couple of extra cabins had popped up as well. Most guests were still asleep, except for a guy at a plastic table outside one of the caravans, sipping on remnants of red wine from the night before. On the radio, the host was talking calmly with some country artist. He savoured the quiet and peace before his wife and kids woke up to a new day at the campsite, likely filled with more campari and summer pork chops.

It was quite noisy, both when I broke into the shed with the diving gear and when I filled Dad's car with necessary stuff. I didn't care if I woke the owners up. No one could stop me anyway. As I sat back in the car, I waved to the tourist by the caravan. He lazily lifted his glass towards me as I drove away in the same direction I had come from.

Past the school. Towards the village centre. To the right. Past the sawmill. Right at the crossroads on Øyerrunden. Towards the lake.

High-voltage pylons slung across the field, along the roads like a stream of crosses. A warning of impending death. Mine or others, it didn't matter. The time had come to end all this.

I slowed down as I passed the stone quarry and entered the forest, remembering how scared we used to be of the dark woods and the house. The taste of Juicy Fruit settled on my tongue. Bryan Adams sang about Heaven, and the sound of bicycle spokes with beads on them filled my head. Flirting, beer, and sun on the cliffs. The girls on the raft.

I slowed down as I neared the turnoff to the house. I hadn't been up there in ages, and I was unsure if I should even let my eyes wander down that road. It couldn't possibly bring anything good. But, of course, I couldn't help it, and it was actually okay because the house wasn't there anymore. Like the ribs of a carcass, black-burned beams and planks stood up from the ashes. Cremated memories danced a hectic waltz in the wind, skimming the ground, and whirling into the window of Dad's car. It smelled sour, like wet sticks on a bonfire. In a ring above the crater where the house once stood, I saw the sky.

The pungent smell still hung in the car as I parked by the lake and began to pick out the diving gear. The sounds of our mopeds and lowered cars swept past me again. We were so young, laughing, joking, and talking nonsense. Guro. A lump formed in my stomach, and an itch ran through the scar on my hand from that dive under the raft so many years ago.

With the day's first thunderclap, Kai's voice echoed from somewhere inside the forest: "Robert! Stand still, or I'll blow your head off!"

Kai

They never shut up. Whispering and muttering. All the time. Everyone knows that he who talks must die, so I keep quiet. I keep quiet. Petter? Petter! He never saw what hit him. Well, he did see, and I think he saw it coming. He got the point. Dad? Ha! Dad… That bastard. We had a deal, that we'd leave this behind us. Why is it so damn difficult for some to stick to the plan? It's easy, after all. Close your eyes. Stop thinking. Give it time. Everything passes! Just look at me. I'm way past it.

"Robert, stand still!"

What the hell is he doing here? He must know everything.

"You shouldn't have come back home."

Robert must die. It's perfect; he can rest with the others. Come on, Kai, get up, out of the grass. Fuck, it stinks. Mud. MUD! It's stuck to my clothes. How can it be...? I just got here. No, it must have been hours ago. Not hours. Days. Petter! And Dad? Pull yourself together now, Kai. Focus on Robert. He is right over there, and he must rot with the others. The others, they still think they can be saved? That they can get what they want? I mean, Rakel and Pål-Ottar must realise by now that they don't exist anymore! No living person knows about them, not for long anyway, except for Robert, and me. I'll make sure they stay down there, to rot for eternity. I will never talk.

"Kai? Is that you?"

"Rakel and I are hunting." Good one, Kai.

"What have you done? I heard about Petter and I spoke to…"

"Petter! Petter. Petter! Rakel and I liked Petter." Keep talking. Keep talking.

"Dad has told me everything. All of it. We can still fix this. Just put down the gun and come out of the woods. No one needs to know."

"Dad? He lies, we should shoot him. Wait, not here. We have to get him down to the water first."

"How long have you been in the forest? You need help. Getting rid of me won't fix anything. They won't stop until everyone is dead."

"Shut up! Rakel and that damned freak. It was Dad's fault. He started all of this."

"It doesn't matter, we must get them out of there. They are poisoning the water. And us."

Dad started it all. Dad. Hanne and Linn! My loved ones. Love… The Witch and Death took them away from me. No, my gun, we should not shoot him here. In the boat, it's better. On the raft. "Go! Down to the lake. To my boat. Go and sit in it! I'll follow." If I can only get out of this freaking forest.

Finally, my boat. I know this boat—the same one we used to bring them out there. Let Robert row. Rakel, my gun, and I, we'll sit here in the boat. We're on watch. "Row! Faster."

If he does something stupid now, if he jumps at us, then we pull the trigger. Pull it now! Pull it. No, we wait until the raft!

"Kai? You don't have to do this. It's not too late..."

"Keep rowing! Out to the raft." See? He does what we say. He's afraid of us. He doesn't like us.

This is perfect! Here, you can shoot him now. But we do it properly. A shot in the neck. Soon, I'll be the only one who knows what happened. I don't care. Right? We don't care.

"Do you really think Hanne and Linn would want you to do this? To kill me, in cold blood?"

"Can't you see? We're doing this for them. Rakel and I. Now, get down on your knees, and shut up!"

"Rakel and Pål-Ottar will never move on until the truth comes out. Look at yourself, man. You're not well. Jesus, how long did you stay in that forest for?"

"Are you ready to meet your friends in hell?"

Well said! Well said. But now, we shoot. One. Two. …

Robert

So, as I said in the beginning, my return to Øyerstad didn't go quite as planned. I was supposed to save the day for everyone. However, sitting on my knees on the raft, with a shotgun to my head, the idea of being a saviour seemed far-fetched. I couldn't even save myself.

Kai had gone into full reptilian brain mode, doing whatever he could to survive. The problem was that it gave the Witch and Death exactly what they wanted: more death. The raft swayed gently. Judging by the smell, Kai had been lying out in the woods since he shot Petter almost a week ago. Grass seemed to have grown into his pants, and the clusters of ticks resembled half-ripe blueberries growing on his skin.

Right before the shot went off, I saw Fredrik up at the parking lot. An aura surrounded him under the pine trees. Even from this distance, the details on his bike were clear—the blue frame, and stickers with flames. The fastest BMX in Øyerstad. He was healthy and happy back then.

"I cannot join you just yet; I have to clean up this mess first. Besides, I don't want to die. Not now. It can't end here. Not like this."

When I threw myself around, the plan was to grab the rifle and lash out at Kai, but my hand arced through the air without hitting anything. Kai opened his mouth, and I sensed a movement in the finger that no longer just rested on the trigger.

The Circus

If I stopped standing still. If I stopped not moving. If I stopped believing that everything would go away by itself. Maybe then something would happen? I can't be a spectator in here anymore. I can, and I must, do something. No matter what everyone else thinks, I'm in charge here. I must believe that.

There was a squelching sound in the mud as I lifted my

shoe. I took the first step. It felt as if I was doing something illegal. My God, I didn't even know it was possible to move in here. Until now, I had stood still and hoped that no one would see me. The second step was easier, and I set my foot down less cautiously. The third step was decisive. I felt confident as something grew inside me. Something burning. Soon raging. A firestorm. I had to set it free. I couldn't hide any longer. It was up to me now. Step four, five, and six. Soon, I moved more freely. It was my turn to unleash hell.

I swung an arm at the lamppost above Kai's head. There was a loud crash, and it lifted from the ground, flew over the circus tent, and vanished into the darkness. The cardboard car Kai was sitting behind, fell into the mud. He no longer scared me as he sat hunched over on the stool. He was just like Mom said, a little scabby rat. I pushed him out into the darkness too. Then I moved, almost floated towards the truck and Jungle-Jim. I saw myself from the outside —my arm and jaw muscles tensed, veins swelled in my temples, and my face contorted. My eyes burned with flames of fury.

As the truck reappeared to hit Jungle-Jim once again, I stood engulfed in flames fuelled by frustration and rage. It had to come out, and I let it. My scream. It was like a thunderstorm, a hurricane, swirling the truck back to the hell it came from. Forever. I broke the loop and Jungle-Jim made it across the road. Over to the other side.

Parts of Mom's skeleton were exposed, and blood-red foam coated the mud on her body. But the thing is, it wasn't really my mom. It was an illusion created by me, and therefore, I could also destroy it. She… It… hissed when I placed a hand on its shoulder. Despite it clawing and thrashing wildly, I didn't let go. On the contrary, I added another hand and said, "I love you, Mom."

I didn't use any force or push it, but it still sank into the ground. Soon the mud was over its knees, over its stomach, breasts, and face. Even as it seemed to realise it had lost, begging in a voice vaguely resembling my mom's to let go, I didn't move my hands away from it. I followed it all the way down, and soon the figure pretending to be my mom was gone, devoured by the earth. I was the exorcist.

I fell to my knees, overwhelmed, tearing at my hair. This time, my scream was even stronger, a hurricane. The ground beneath me shook, and booths, tents, and installations creaked. Planks, rubbish, and dirt swirled on the ground, while Anders' car shook and sank into the mud. The clown's tricycle stopped in the same muck, and he didn't look so scary anymore as he to begged for mercy. He didn't want to disappear, to be nothing.

I continued to scream, and the cauldron on Death's head began vibrating, swinging back and forth. Could he possibly withstand this too? No, not a chance. Fueled by a power coming from somewhere inside and outside of me, I pushed even harder. Louder. Somehow I knew that this would never be over before that damn cauldron was taken off his head. It swung faster from side to side, but soon, to my horror, I felt my power burning out. And so the cauldron started swinging slower again. As with all things, even my scream came to an end. I had lost my power. I stood panting frantically. Powerless. The cauldron on Death's head had stopped swaying altogether. Seconds of absolute silence followed. The Witch looked expectant, something in her gaze. She wasn't evil, not really. She was scared. Like Mom in front of the mirror so long ago, she came through to me.

Then, at last, the cauldron fell. Death's headless body hung for a brief second before the chain loosened and shot up into the darkness above us. It struck the underside of the raft above me with tremendous force. I felt the pressure in my chest, followed by a terrible boom as the shockwave blasted through the underworld. Something fell into the water, from the raft above and down towards me.

The cauldron lay mud-stained in the... It wasn't a cauldron; it was a helmet, front facing me, in the mud. Through the hole in the visor, I stared into Death's crushed skull.

Robert

I was about to get executed by Dad's friend. More accurately, Dad's *former* friend. Kai had always been something else, but now he had completely lost it. He squeezed the trigger, and after that, things happened both quickly and slowly at the same time. The sound of the shot came like a wave from afar. First almost silently, then growing in strength as it swept towards me. The glow of overheated gases grew out of the barrel, and the bullet followed. The shot was fired. Like the rest of the world, I too moved in slow motion, so it wasn't as if I could dodge the bullet for that reason.

So this is what dying felt like. The very moment before the end came slowly. There was time to think, reflect, and perhaps even see life pass in review. I should have been scared. Death should have frightened me, but it didn't. Instead of seeing a replay of my life, a feeling of relief and security washed over me. Not because I was about to die, but because the bullet was going to miss. The projectile would fly past my head. Why I was so sure of that, was hard to explain. The whole situation, the raft, Kai, the shot. I had seen it before. In a dream, a vision, or whatever. I just knew it. It wasn't my turn to die.

That's why I wasn't surprised when the raft shot up into the air at the same time as the sound started to rise and sparks flew out of the gun's barrel. Like a float dragged under by a fish that eventually fought its way off the hook, the raft shot up out of the water. First, we were both sucked down towards it. Then we flew a metre, maybe two up into the air, and we were weightless for a moment as the raft stopped rising. Along with all this, there was a burning sensation in my left temple, and I smelled gunpowder. Then we fell back towards the water, and with that, the world returned to its normal speed. The edge of the raft hit me hard in the chest and sent me out into the water with a splash. A dive far less elegant than the ones I had performed from the raft earlier.

The blast from the gunshot roared in my ears as the water closed over me. Bubbles crawled like millions of ants over my body as I tried to figure out what was up and what was down. No matter which direction I swam in, I found nothing but water. The breath was knocked out of me when I hit the raft, and I was already desperate for air. My heart raced even though I knew I had to calm down. *Calm down, Robert. Like in the bathtub. Calm down.*

It shouldn't have been possible, but I gained some control over myself. The chaos slowly subsided, and soon all I heard was an underlying beep in my head. A metallic taste of blood and stagnant water spread in my mouth. I should have panicked. Should have fought to get up, but I accepted the situation.

Let it be. It's okay, Robert. It's okay.

My skin contracted as the water grew colder. It was dark, so I reckoned the specks below me were an illusion, like when you see stars after a blow to the head. Fredrik spoke, and I wondered if my life was passing in review after all. For it could be so, that I was about to die. That the bullet had actually hit its mark. That the leaping raft was just a misfire in my brain after it had been shot to pieces. This could be my journey to the other side. I wasn't breathing.

The sparks came closer. Wasn't that how Fredrik described what he saw under the bed up in the haunted house? Like someone shining a light on thousands of glass bottles? Yes, or those I saw in the rusty bathtub that same afternoon? The same ones I saw on Hitra when Olav disappeared? Soon I made out a silhouette around them. A head. A body. Closer. He came closer. Kai. His eyes. They were the ones shining. His mouth gaped wide and black while the tendons in his neck stood out of his skin. His fingers were curved like branches of a tree, and his legs were twisted in unnatural angles. He didn't move. Frozen in a moment of terror.

My fingers responded when I tried to move them. They were relaxed and soft. My legs and my arms also moved. I wasn't paralyzed like Kai. I could move.

He stopped a metre or two below me and hung in the water like a luminous fishing lure. The situation was expectant, as if I was about to watch a theatre with Kai as the main character on a stage.

First, I just sensed them, the shades flickering around him. Around us. A school of fish, or one big one. They came closer and disappeared, only to approach again. More boldly. Black waves grew into the glow, and occasionally bumped into him. Kai spun around his axis, still locked in the same convulsive posture.

It was hard to say exactly what it was that pulsated in and out of the darkness around us. But it sure as hell wasn't fish. Sometimes it formed a solid shape, sometimes more fluid. I wondered again if maybe the bullet had hit its mark, that I was indeed dead, as the shape gained colours. Like someone was painting images or perhaps memories onto a canvas surrounding us. It could also be them, Rakel and Pål-Ottar, trying to show me something.

Something similar to a snake, or more like a rope, sailed past. Tied at the end was a round object, and I jolted when I recognised Linn's head. Her face was pale, with a vacant stare. After the initial shock, I realised that she actually looked kinda peaceful; the vision didn't really scare me. Soon, another face was painted on the canvas. I was dreaming, dying, sleeping, seeing things, living; it was hard to tell. This face was more indistinct, yet it reminded me of Dad. Then Petter appeared, clear and detailed, with his eyes closed and mouth half-open.

Another figure somewhat resembled me, but it was more vague. That one, over there, was it Mom? I hoped to see her, but I wasn't sure if I did. However, I did see the Witch of Mørked, Death, and others I couldn't quite pinpoint. People and figures unknown to me. Maybe it wasn't my life I saw after all, maybe it was someone else's? Maybe what I was seeing was Kai's fear coming to life? What he feared had found him. Everything and everyone at once.

Kai didn't defend himself when the first attack came. Like piranhas. Something tore and pulled at him until the glow around us shifted from white to dark red. A memory of, or a projection of, the Witch clawed out his eyes, and Kai spun around in the water with snakes of blood dancing from his empty eye sockets.

When facing me seconds later, his eyes were back. It didn't last long, though, before another figure appeared and clawed at them again. Another shadow, resembling Death, pressed its filthy fist into his mouth, down his throat, stirring around. A cloud of blood rose from Kai's mouth like smoke from a chimney as the arm was pulled out again. Kai made no resistance, but I am sure he felt the pain. Every single second of it. An unrecognisable figure grabbed one of his arms and pulled until it detached at the shoulder. Someone else grabbed his leg. It continued like that, limb by limb. But no matter what they tore off or how they hurt him, he became whole again. The arm reappeared seconds later, only to be torn off once more. An eternal cycle of pain and mutilation.

I feared this theatre of pain would last forever, but slowly, Kai seemed to diminish in size, drifting further away as the relentlessness of the attacks persisted. Soon, he was nothing but a small, meaningless flicker of light, a trivial object, and then he was gone. I didn't think I would see him again. The first act of the show was resolved, at least for me, and I felt myself sinking down towards the next part.

The chain underneath the raft wasn't there to guide me this time. Nevertheless, I knew I would reach the bottom soon enough, and then the next act would begin. The grand finale.

Seconds later, a new light source appeared underneath. It somewhat resembled a Christmas snow globe with a glow radiating from its core, one of those that had falling snow if you turned it upside down or shook it. Inside, were the main characters of the show's last act, set in a macabre underwater installation, mired in mud. The moped lay on its side, covered in a thick layer of sludge. Yet the one I saw in my head was clean. I heard it. That sound. Outside the kiosk when we were kids.

The form of a body in a clay jumpsuit lay against the front wheel of the moped. It could have belonged to anyone, but I knew it was her, Rakel, the Witch of Mørkved. The other body, presumably Death's, was headless and hung partly over the moped as if he had tried to climb up on it and drive out of their underwater purgatory. He got nowhere. The helmet, lying in the mud next to the body it belonged to, stood out from the other objects. It must have recently fallen off, as both it and the breakpoint in the neck were free of mud. The chain must have ripped the head off when it fell from the raft and landed on them. Again I had a hard time connecting my thoughts. Was it the chain coming loose that made the raft jump into the air? Why did it happen now? Today? The second I needed it. Someone had made it happen. Somehow.

The hole in the visor of Death's helmet sent an itch through old scars. That was where I got stuck when I dived here so long ago. That's what almost tore my hand off. It was no coincidence, for imagine if I hadn't come loose? It wouldn't have taken long before Kjell and the guys on the raft started worrying. First, they would have checked if I had gotten stuck under the raft. Then they would have attempted to dive down to the bottom, but none of them would have made it, no matter how many times they tried. Meanwhile, Guro might have hurried to shore to call for help. There would have been a hell of a commotion up there, but they wouldn't have been able to save me. Half an hour, or even later, the search team would have arrived. They would have taken a boat out to the raft and started diving. Kjell and the guys would still not have given up hope of finding me alive.

When the search team eventually got down to the bottom, they would have found me with my fist driven through the helmet and into Death's skull. They would have called it a freak accident. I had gotten stuck in his helmet, which was stuck to the body, which was stuck to the moped. I drowned. I had to die for them to be found. An eye for an eye.

If I had drowned back then, many others would have been alive, and Øyerstad would have been spared so much misery. But, as it turned out, no one found them, and from their underwater prison, something grew over time. Fuelled by a desperate desire to be found. For the truth to come out. As sorrow turned to rage the water soured. Hatred spread its slimy tentacles from the lake down to Øyerstad, weaving threads between the dead and the living. The Witch of Mørkved and Death found a way back, seeking vengeance against Dad, Petter, and Kai. Everything around them was to wither away and die. And then, finally, when the actual perpetrators had nothing left to love, it would be their turn.

The last thing I remember of the finale show, before all went black, is that I was hovering over their bodies. Perhaps expecting that they would come to life and attack me too, as they had done with Kai. That I too would be torn to pieces. Forever. Nothing happened. Not as I remember anyway. Down there with me, they were no more than what they were. Two bodies dumped in the lake so long ago. Eternally bound to an old moped at the bottom. Hidden away so that no one would have to be held accountable.

I came to on the beach, warmed by the sun. Kai's boat had drifted ashore on the other side, and the raft was slowly moving towards the same side. Light summer clouds, rocks and trees, reflected in the water, which lay still as glass. Birds chirped as they followed me towards the cottage near the parking lot. I hadn't noticed the birds in a while. I needed to borrow a phone.

The local sheriff listened intently to my story while the police force prepared to search for the bodies. "You sure you haven't got any more secrets up there?" He pointed at the stitches I had received when diving at Hitra.

"I've told you everything I know, and those stitches have nothing to do with this. Fishing accident. Alcohol and boats. Dangerous combination."

"Alright." The sheriff turned to leave but stopped. "One more thing…"

"Yes?"

"I might have more questions for you later. It'd be good if you didn't rush off from Øyerstad any time soon. Also, there's an ambulance on the way. You need to get that new wound checked. It was a close call." He pointed towards my right temple.

"Okay," I replied, realising how close Kai had come to blowing my head off.

"Next time you hear stories about dead bodies at the bottom of a lake or something, you call us first, right?" He looked at me, then turned his gaze to the cottage owners with their coffee cups on their terraces. "Like flies to dung," he grunted and walked towards one of the boats on the beach.

When the divers finally arrived, they did not move with the same grace as the divers I met at Hitra. "Welcome to Øyerstad!" I shouted at them from the shore. "Do you know why divers always fall backward into the water?"

"What the hell are you talking about?" The slightly heavier one, clad in a too-small dry suit, stopped, furrowed his brow, and glared at me.

"Why do divers always fall back… no, forget it," I said, turning away. They didn't seem in the mood for a joke.

On the other side, by the "party cliff" where we used to hang out back in the days, a new generation of kids had thrown off their shirts and popped open beers, watching the drama unfold. I wondered if Kjell and Guro were among them. But deep down, I really didn't think so.

A slightly larger boat approached the area where the raft usually lay, now marked by a large square of ropes and white buoys. The sheriff was on deck, waving his arms as he orchestrated what seemed like a total chaos. Soon, they lowered a cage into the water, resembling a giant lobster trap. I could have told them there had been no crayfish in the lake since the plague in the early '90s. One might wonder what caused that plague…

Divers followed the trap down, and soon the surface was still again. The music out by the cliff, Nirvana, had turned silent, and the kids were no longer laughing. A police radio crackled, emitting electronic voices speaking in a foreign language. I wondered if Olderø was still standing on his boat near Blåskykøya, waiting for news via his radio. I could smell the coffee as the locals stood expectantly along the water's edge with their thermoses. Even the crow that passed over my head seemed to respect the moment, remaining silent.

About half an hour later, activity on the radios increased. People on the boat began to move closer to the railing facing the square. The crane swayed lightly and it didn't take long before the trap broke the surface.

What remained of the bodies were washed clean of mud and dirt. They were so small and fragile that I was surprised they didn't fall through the meshes of the net. You could make out bits of skeletons and pieces of clothing. The moped seemed to have fared better than the bodies during its time down there. Death's helmet was also there, and I prayed that they had retrieved every bit of his skull.

Chills ran down my spine as a small boat carrying Kyrre, the church priest, approached them. Soon, he was helped aboard and immediately began gesticulating wildly. He had many prayers and blessings to offer, and I hoped with all my heart that this would be enough.

My hangover was forgotten, and the ants in my brain had ceased their crawling. I felt weightless and dizzy, but in a good way. From the beach, I looked up towards the parking lot where I had seen Fredrik while I was on my knees on the raft, with the gun against my head. He was no longer there, but still I whispered, "Thank you. I think everything will be okay now."

Around afternoon, I slipped away from the circus up by the lake and walked down towards Øyerstad, sporting yet another Band-Aid on my head.

3

Anders

Like the engine on my old '69 Chevrolet Chevelle, my heart stalled when Robert rounded the corner at Dad's house. He was breathing heavily, sweat streaming down his forehead. His eyes jumped between the house, me, and the ambulance. Finally, his gaze settled on mine, and we stood in silence for a while.

When he fled Øyerstad, it broke me. How could he do that to us? How could he be so selfish? When things really went apeshit, he just disappeared. Without a word. I searched for him for a while, not to bring him home, but to give him a taste of the same pain and frustration he left us with. He hadn't even seen Mom's grave. If I saw him again, I'd punch him in the face, and then tell him to fuck off! Go to hell!

I bore a bitterness for quite some time, but eventually, I realised the rage I directed at my brother was simply a vent for the fear inside me. Being angry and bitter was easier than dealing with the fear and sorrow. Truth be told, I didn't take my share of responsibility when Fredrik passed away either. Robert was left alone with Mom and Dad when things really went downhill. I wasn't there for him. We weren't there for each other. Perhaps my problem was that I didn't do like Robert when Mom passed. That I never got away from this place. Now he was back, and I didn't quite know what to do. I wasn't prepared for this.

"You... you look tired." It was only when he uttered those first words to me since Mom's funeral that I dared to believe it was really him, and not an illusion conjured to push me further into despair. The aggression that had once festered within me, directed squarely at him, was gone. My knees felt weak, threatening to buckle under the weight of this very moment. My little brother was back.

"You're not exactly Pamela Anderson either," I replied, smiling with trembling lips. His smile was strained too. Despite the bandage covering half his head, he looked like himself.

Our family wasn't known for being huggers, still, we lifted our arms simultaneously and met in a good old-fashioned bear hug. Part of me still half-expected my arms to pass right through him, as though I was trying to embrace a ghost, a faded memory. His body was solid, and I hugged him tightly. He didn't see the tears that fell behind his back.

Unsure if my voice would hold, I asked, "You've been in a fight?"

"Yeah, that too. It's been some crazy days," Robert replied.

The last few years have been pretty hectic, if you ask me, I thought. But instead of saying that, I remarked, "You've grown a beard too."

We let go of each other, Robert smiled and kicked away a stone in the gravel. "Yeah, life as a fisherman demands its look."

"So you've been fishing?" I asked, as Robert shifted his focus from me to the ambulance.

"I've been to Hitra," he said.

"You went to Dad's island?"

"Yep. It wasn't really planned, but I guess for some reason it was where I was supposed to be."

"Was it as good as Dad said?"

"It was good. Actually, yes, for a while."

"For a while?"

"Yeah, eventually I discovered some things in a cabin book

up there that made me think of this place again. And then there was Olav's accident," Robert said, gesturing towards the bandage on his head. "It turned out better for me than for him."

"He was someone you met up there?"

"Yes, that's a long story, but we'll talk about that later. Those cabin books... they stirred something in me, and they had an effect on Dad too when I told him about them. They got him talking. He finally revealed the truth about why they stopped going to Hitra. He told me stories not many have heard before. About Hitra and everything that happened here in Øyerstad and up at the lake." Wait a minute, you're saying you talked to Dad? Didn't you arrive yesterday?"

"Yes. We had dinner. It's not that many hours since I crawled out and puked on the porch here. There!" Robert pointed to the vomit in the gravel behind me.

"So that was you who..."

"Didn't think I drank that much. Must have been strong stuff he served."

"And you ate sausages, I see."

"Sausages?"

"In the vomit. Sausages..."

"Actually, I ate chicken. I mean, we ate chicken."

"Okay, it's not that important what you ate, I guess. I heard about the chaos up at the lake. Drowning accident?"

"Something like that, yes. Or, whether he actually drowned is debatable," Robert responded.

"I stay far away from that place. You should too. There's something bad going on up there," I said, without mentioning my nightmares.

"I'd say something bad was going on all over the place, that's why I left," Robert said. "But it didn't work. Leaving. The Witch and Death, they..."

“Robert,” I interrupted, “you shouldn’t talk about them.”

Robert paused, shifted his gaze to the forest, up into the sky, and then at me. “I didn’t mean to leave...”

“It’s okay. As long as you don’t talk about the Witch and stuff. It’s as if they are still here. That they hear everything we say. Watching us...”

“Anders! I’ve found them.” Robert grabbed my arm.

“Found who?” I asked.

“The Witch and Death,” Robert replied. “Up in the lake, just like Dad told me.” His hand was warm against mine. “Dad, Petter, and Kai, they did all this. They killed them and sank their bodies beneath the raft. I’ve found them. That’s why the police are up at the lake now.”

I didn’t notice it at first, but as he continued staring at me, I saw something in Robert’s eyes. It was something I hadn’t witnessed in Øyerstad for a long time—a spark, a glimmer of hope, a streak of light. It even made me feel... something.

“You found them? In the lake?”

“Yes, I did. And I think it’s finally over,” he replied.

“You know, about Dad...” My voice trailed off as I followed Robert’s gaze back to the ambulance.

“I kind of figured,” Robert whispered.

“You didn’t talk to Dad yesterday.” I fixed my eyes on him.

“Eh, yes, I did. We talked about Hitra, the hunt, the Witch, and...” He paused.

“Robert?”

“We had dinner. He was like he used to be, before all this mess started. We had a good time, at least until he began that story.”

“Robert!”

“What’s wrong?”

“You came home too late.”

“No.”

"Yes, Dad is dead!"

"What are you talking about?"

"Dad is dead. He's been gone for a while."

"…"

We still stood by the stairs when the ambulance personnel emerged from the house, a stretcher between them. "You can say goodbye to your father..." The burlier of the two stopped mid-sentence, his gaze shifting from me to Robert.

"They are here to pick up Dad," I said. Then, turning to the ambulance team, I added, "This is Robert. He's my little brother, and he's just returned home!"

"I talked to Dad yesterday," Robert whispered, more to himself than to any of us. "You probably didn't talk to him," I whispered. "Maybe you saw him in the bedroom and were shocked?"

"I wasn't in the bedroom, and I wasn't shocked. He was sitting in the chair in the living room, watching TV. We ate chicken."

"If you want, you can say goodbye to your father as well. But be gentle. He's been dead for a while." Robert shivered as one of the ambulance personnel addressed him in a calm manner.

The zipper on the body bag opened like that of an old leather jacket, and Dad's face stood in stark contrast to the bag he lay in. Black against white.

"He's been dead for some time. Probably shot and killed the same evening as Petter. That's almost a week ago," I said to Robert.

"But I was in the house with Dad yesterday… We… I…"

"I don't know what you saw yesterday, Robert, but Dad was gone by then. It's just you and me left."

Robert

Dad's house no longer looked like it did when I arrived from Hitra the day before. Paint was peeling off the walls, resembling sunburnt skin, and out on the lawn grass lay flat under its own weight. The door handle had always been loose, but now it was replaced with a wrench. Dad had, as Anders had said, been dead for quite some time. Not that I was an expert in determining how long a person had been deceased, but Dad had been gone longer than one night. Even I could see that.

But it didn't make any sense, right? If I wasn't here with Dad yesterday, how could I know everything that he told me? About Rakel's arrival in Øyerstad, about what happened up at that cabin? How could I know about the bodies in the lake? He must have told me, and it must have been last night.

Silently, Anders led me up the stairs and into the house.

Inside the hallway stood his wooden clogs. The old and worn ones. The ones we used to borrow when we didn't have time to put on our own shoes before running to the store to buy salty liquorice. *Dad was alive when I came home. I saved him. I saw it myself. We were together. I smelled him, tasted the food, and the liquor.* My brain was spinning again as I noticed his dirty work shoes as well.

Inside the kitchen, we waded through a sea of empty bottles and cans. Dishes were stacked in towers. As we passed the open stove, Anders and I simultaneously pulled our sweaters over our noses. What had once been dinner seemed to move in the frying pan. There hadn't been grilled chicken with rosemary on that stove for a very long time. Probably more like never. The two realities clashed in my head.

"Dad hadn't been himself for a long time, but when Mom died, and you... disappeared, he simply collapsed into himself.

It went downhill from there. I don't think he showed up at work after Mom's funeral. He didn't leave the house much. So, I tried to help him, for a while," Anders said.

"Cleaning and fixing the house. Shopping for groceries. A few times in the beginning, I felt like he actually wanted me to help. But it didn't last. It was like he started to see right through me, like I wasn't there, so I stopped coming. I got angry. I wanted to scream at him, and tell him to go... I never did. I... He was a ghost. Lost within his own reality."

"Thing is, I believe he did it to protect us," I said.

"What?"

"He told me he had to push us away to protect us. From them."

"You think that's why he behaved like that? Because of the Witch and Death?"

"Rakel and Pål-Ottar… No, I don't *think* so. I'm quite sure. He couldn't stop loving us, that's what we were punished for."

I accidentally knocked over a pile of cans and bottles, and the sound, the loud crash, sent me back to the bottle containers under the sun at the campsite in Askim. For a brief moment, I was eight years old again. Dad, Mom, and all the other guests were enjoying themselves with drinks and barbecue. Music and laughter. We went from tent to tent, collecting cans and bottles we could return for a deposit at the kiosk. Too bad that there was no deposit on liquor bottles. We would have been rich.

Numerous dust-clad, half-empty glasses and bottles stood on the table where Dad and I had dinner last night. One bottle, Laphroaig, didn't bear the same coat of dust as the others. The chair at the table, where I sat as he told me everything, stood alone. Anders placed a hand on my shoulder, and that's when I saw them. My family, in a sort of lazy glow, out by the road.

4

Robert

Rakel and Pål-Ottar were buried at Øyerstad Church, on Saturday, August 29th, 1999. Olav's mother asked for a quiet funeral, and both the press and the locals respected her wish. Only the closest family members were present, and there weren't many of them left. Despite everything I had told her, Olav's mother insisted I should be there. She believed that Rakel and Pål-Ottar had now found peace, that it was over, and she was sure I was forgiven, Dad too.

"Thank you," I said, as she gave me a hug that seemed to last an eternity.

I was standing outside the church, engaged in conversation with Olav's mother, Danne, and Olderø, when Kjell and the guys approached on foot. Their arrival reminded me of a TV commercial, walking casually with their jackets draped over their arms and shirt sleeves rolled up, as if in slow motion. Two things hit me at that moment: first, we were all getting older; second, my friends were actually quite handsome.

"There he is. For fuck's sake, we've been looking for you all over Øyerstad!" Kjell almost shouted.

"It didn't take long," Rune added.

Kjell gave me a hard glare. "After about half an hour, we realised you were M.I.A."

"We looked for you in Skjønnsund too, you know. That took us about an hour, and thankfully you weren't there either," Tony chimed in.

"People run *away* from Skjønnsund, not *to* that damn place," Kjell said, as he gave me a hug.

The others joined in. For a moment, we stood there, outside the church, in a group hug that could match any moderately directed Hollywood feel-good drama.

"Hold your head high today. You got this," Kjell whispered, placing a hand on my shoulder.

"Tomorrow there'll be beer and storytelling at my place. I believe you have a lot to contribute." We broke the hug, and together we entered the church, Kjell with his arm still around me.

Had Dad passed away earlier, while he was still the Dad he used to be, the mood in the church would have been heavier. Nonetheless, you couldn't have squeezed another soul onto the benches with a shoehorn. People stood along the walls, spilled through the main entrance, and down the stairs. I didn't recognise half of them. Many, having followed the case in the news, probably hoped to hear Anders or me speak about it for the first time. A journalist from VG, Dagfinn I think his name was, stood at the back of the church, hoping for a scoop, despite our request for the press to stay away, like Olav's mother did. He likely wasn't the only journalist who ignored our request that day.

What really happened up by the lake? Who was involved, and how was it connected to the murders of Petter and Dad? Were the rumours about the Witch of Mørkved, Rakel, true? Why had I gone to Hitra and then returned? How did I know where they were? And Olav, did I know anything about what happened to him? And what about Kai? He was never found, and the police had stopped searching. Some of the sheriff's questions even suggested they doubted that he was there in the first place.

Once again, I stood before the crowd, up at the altar, with a white coffin by my side. A picture of Dad in a thin gold frame balanced on the lid. It was taken just over ten years ago.

Right before everything really went to hell. In the picture, he stood by his Beetle, strong, maybe just a little overweight, laughing, with a bottle of beer in hand. Work clothes. Blue overalls. Clogs. That's how he should be remembered. Dad—man, he really did look like Bud Spencer.

Guro, she was there as well. I saw her, and she saw me. My hand was steady, and my heart beat calmly. All eyes on me.

Eulogy for Knut-Erik "Dad" Baastad by Robert Baastad. Øyerstad Church, Saturday, August 29, 1999, 3:00 PM

"You should have seen those eggs! The ones Ringåsen sold cheap at the farm. Now, surely many here remember them better than me. But my goodness, they were something else. Some had no shells, they were like soft bags, barely holding together. And those that did have shells were so fragile, they cracked and fell apart at the slightest touch. But it didn't matter, because they tasted exactly how eggs should taste, and mom glowed with joy when we came home with our 'catch'. Dad, you and Mom, making pancakes in the kitchen, while we played Nintendo in the living room. You served them with homemade strawberry jam. To this day, I can still taste them—the best pancakes in the world. Made for me and my brothers.

We had bought crazy-eggs, as Dad once called them, and eaten pancakes on the day we went to the circus. It was a Saturday and you had just gotten paid. The locals were buzzing with excitement and pride. A circus coming to Øyerstad: wow, that was something special. Out on the Haugen Fields. You and Mom wanted us to go, the whole family. That's why I didn't tell you that the circus scared the shit out of me. Especially at night when I lay in bed and heard all the sounds. Saw all the lights. God knows what was going on over there at night.

In the daytime, it wasn't as scary, and of course, I was curious about all the exotic animals, clowns, and acrobats. At the store, they said the circus had both bears and elephants. And the poster on the wall by the kiosk, it was… I couldn't take my eyes off it. The colourful drawing showcased the toughest of them all—the circus director with a whip in his hand, surrounded by lions.

We had just bought entrance tickets, and I begged you for some coupons for the Wheel of Fortune. The teddy bears were huge—imagine winning one of those! They were larger than me, and I considered myself quite big for being so small. Of course, I didn't win. So, I wanted to try again, but you were set on buying soda and popcorn and going inside for the show. You started walking away as I drifted off into some teddy bear fantasy world for a second, and then you were gone.

I couldn't see you anywhere, so I turned my attention to The Wheel of Fortune yet again. This time it spun faster. Grew larger. Louder. Majestic and beautiful. The music and the organ. The smell of popcorn and cotton candy, mixed with animal manure. Laughter, children crying... Crying. Why were they crying? Suddenly, I couldn't move. I tried to call out for you. As the wheel slowed down and finally stopped, the surrounding noise faded into a sudden silence. Soon, in that stillness, a tiny squeak escaped my lips: 'Dad, where are you?'

At that very moment, even though the place was packed with people, I felt like the only person left in the world. The circus changed, turning into an episode from one of Mom's 'Creepshow' movies, a circus of horrors from outer space. Even though it was all over in minutes, and I could literally see our house from where I stood, I was sure I would never see any of you again.

A juggling clown on a unicycle was the first to stop. His face was pale, and his eyes burned with yellow flames deep within his skull. As he spoke, his mouth opened wide. Way too wide. "Hey, little friend. Are you lost? Come, let me help you." His voice slithered past dirty teeth, making me think of a fakir's snakes. He was a monster. He didn't want to help me, but rather kidnap me and make me a part of their late-night freak show, behind closed doors, for eternity. All over the world and beyond.

As I stand here today, I realise that he was just a clown, probably a nice one, maybe even funny. A man with a job, and make-up, seeing a scared kid and wanting to help. When he took my hand, it was actually with a large, white, soft cloth glove, but all I saw was a huge crab claw.

The clown was a hissing and sizzling sea-monster, hell-clown, and vampire. And you, Dad, were a cross, holy water, and garlic when you came back. From nowhere, you reached into my fantasy, took my hand, and pulled me out. You told me everything was going to be ok and didn't let go of my hand. Later, inside the circus, when the clown appeared in the ring as part of the circus act, I wasn't scared. He could never do anything to me, not as long as I sat with you, still holding your hand. Because you were bigger and stronger than him, than any clown. I was safe there. For a very long time.

Oh, and we need to talk about Christmas trees. At our place, they came in all sorts of shapes. In the days leading up to Christmas, everyone wanted to play at our place, just to see what our tree looked like. You ventured out into the forest as usual, saw under your arm, trudging around to find the perfect... or, well, to find a tree. "We're not paying two hundred and fifty kroner for some twigs at the market when

I can find a tree just as nice, if not nicer, in the woods, for free," you'd say. If it lacked branches on one side, it was better against the wall, you argued. And there was more room for gifts if the branches didn't start until halfway up the tree. I will never forget the trees, and how proud you were of them.

You and Mom. You were proud, and we all understood the real reason you didn't want to pay for 'some twigs at the store." Money was tight. But that never stopped you. You never hung your heads. Dad, I need you to know that a hundred trees from the store wouldn't have made us happier than the ones you found in the forest. We loved your Christmas trees, Dad, just as they were. We still talk about them, laugh at the stories, and we will continue to do so for a long time to come.

Our last Christmas with Fredrik, the tree was especially crooked, and we liked it even more. It was that Christmas we got our jerseys, those two special presents under the tree, Manchester United and Tottenham. Fredrik wore his jersey only once, before his time was up. But that evening… It was one of the best evenings of his life. The shield on his jersey, the colours, they gave him superpowers. You should have seen him, Fredrik, before the light went out.

After that, things got tough. For you. For Mom. For us. Things fell apart, and I feared it would stay like that forever. That we would be in pain forever. But it didn't last. Somehow, despite all that happened, we found our way back to each other. For a very brief moment.

You know, they say that energy never dies, it only moves and changes composition. If so, maybe we can touch each other in ways that go beyond our physical and psychological limitations. Across borders, time, and space. Across emotions. Can we, if we want it enough, shake the seemingly constant boundaries between life and death? For what is death, if not just another state of being? Back to where we came from.

I'm not standing here shattered because I've lost you. No, I stand here relieved, because somehow you came back. You gave me a chance to say goodbye. And you got a chance to finally tell someone the truth. And with that, you gave me hope. You gave *us* hope. A belief that we can still turn bad into good. That we always can and should make amends. We always have a choice.

You are a part of me, and I am a part of you. We are also a part of them—our family. So go to them, and we'll see each other later. I forgive you. I love you. Dad. Rest in peace."

We moved slowly, with his coffin between us, to the melody of "Wish You Were Here" floating from the church organ. "So, so you think you can tell heaven from hell..." I cried and didn't care if anyone saw it.

We passed the main entrance, stepped out onto the stone stairs, and continued down the narrow pathway. After crossing the main road and the parking lot, we entered through the cemetery gates and passed all the other graves.

Down by Dad's grave, I stood admiring Anders while the priest completed his rites. Anders had put on a good deal of weight since we met outside Dad's house a week ago. A banner, "Live to Ride", waved over the Confederate flag behind the motorcycles on his t-shirt. His jeans were holey. With his rockabilly hairstyle he kinda looked like he used to, and it added to the sense of hope I had felt lately. My big brother was back.

"Do you see them?" he asked after the priest had finished mumbling, and people started moving towards their cars, to go on with their lives. He wiped sweat from his forehead.

"She's back, the Witch!"

"What?"

"The Witch of Mørkved, do you see her too?"

"What the hell are you talking about?" I asked, a tingle building in my stomach.

"Over by the old graves! Can't you smell her?" Anders pointed towards the older part of the cemetery.

"What? Wait, did you...? Goddammit, did you just release the badger (a term we often used in the old days to refer to someone breaking wind)?"

"Well, maybe..."

"Darn..., well, that's the smell of death, but it's not Rakel," I blurted out, covering my nose."

"No, I guess you're right. I… I shouldn't have had that second bowl of cornflakes this morning."

"With jam, bananas, and sugar?"

"Yeah, and…"

"A spoon of chocolate spread to top it off."

"Hey, you remember." He grinned widely, lifted his butt cheek, and let another one rip.

"Jesus, are you serious? You and Fredrik, man, you could have run your own nuclear power plant." I waved my hand under my nose, taking two steps backward.

Anders laughed so hard he almost lost his balance. We both laughed.

Whether it was time passing or Anders' farts that made everyone disappear, I'm not sure, but soon we stood alone, in silence by Dad's grave. Just as outside the house in Øyerstad the day we found Dad dead, I saw them again. Like a mirage, they stood on the edge of the cemetery. Mom, Dad, and Fredrik. Air shimmered around them, as they almost blended into the background. Yet, there was no doubt they were there. I lifted my arm to shield my eyes from the sun to see them better. Behind us, Dad's grave still lay open with three shovels of dirt and a pile of roses on the lid.

"Do you think this is the last time we'll see them?" I asked, not taking my eyes off them.

"Yeah, it might be," Anders replied, barely audible.

"So this is the final goodbye then?"

"Robert..."

"Do you think this is goodbye?"

"Yeah, I think so. We all know what happened, the truth. They should be able to move on, do what dead people should do."

"And Rakel and Pål-Ottar?"

"I think they can move on too. I think they got what they needed."

"I guess that only leaves Kai? Where the heck did he go?"

"I don't know. But if it's like you say, I don't think we'll see more of him. If hell is really a thing, there's a risk he'll end up there," Anders whispered.

"Or maybe everyone goes to the same place, and it doesn't matter much what you've done in your short time here. You're kind of reset at the final station, once you get there," I said.

"He's hopefully better off now than he was while he was here," Anders replied.

Behind a film of what could best be described as heat-waves, Fredrik bent down and picked up Jungle-Jim, who rubbed against his legs. The joy in his face at the sight of our four-legged friend was a picture of unconditional and heartfelt love. I cried again.

"They're together now, all of them," I said, watching our family slowly dissolve into thin air.

From the top of Sandåsen, I could see all of Øyerstad. From the old store to the campground. I saw the fields and the forest, separating this little oasis from the rest of the world. All of this under a sun that hung like an overripe blood orange in the evening sky. Despite being well into August, it was still shorts and t-shirt weather. "This is my hometown," I whispered, taking a breath. It smelled of warm asphalt and grass. I turned towards the door. Took a breath again. Was about to knock. Paused briefly. Exhaled. Inhaled. Thought about getting the hell out of there, but then I pressed the doorbell. For hope.

A small window in the door revealed her as she appeared in the hallway. Again, I considered getting the hell outta there. I still had time to hide, but I didn't move. When Guro finally opened the door, I prayed my knees wouldn't fail me. She wore black sweatpants and a short top. Her parents, the sumo wrestlers up in the other hill, were probably still eating most of her food. She wasn't skinny, but she looked healthy. Her hair hung night-black in waves down to her stomach. Her eyes were larger and darker in reality than in the pictures in my head. *Brown.* Cocker Spaniel. Her glasses with thick frames were the, "If I'm going to wear glasses, they're going to be real glasses" kind. I had not seen her with glasses before. She wore them well.

I wavered a half step backward before finding the courage to take a full step forward. "Hi, and sorry," my voice sounded as if it were going through a belated change. "I'm sorry, for absolutely everything." My voice grew a little stronger. "Listen, you probably don't remember this, but when Terminator bit Fredrik... that terrified me. I mean, that darn mutt has been haunting me in my nightmares ever since. Shit, I even tried renaming that damn monster to make him less intimidating. I... I called him Bingo-Bo... You know, never mind. I'm not afraid of him anymore."

Guro looked at me, those eyes, but remained silent.

"The thing is, that day, when you took my hand, you saved me. At that very moment, I really needed someone to care for me. You… I… Since that day, I haven't really known how to act around you. Seriously, just talking has been a pain in the butt. What if I said something wrong, or did something you didn't like? What if you stopped liking me? Jesus, I…"

Guro seemed to loosen up a bit, but her arms were still crossed over her chest. Still silent.

"Sorry, I'm rambling. Wait, I have to show you something," I said, rummaging through my backpack. "Last time I saw this movie, I seriously didn't understand a thing about anything."

On the cover of the DVD I held out to her, Leonardo DiCaprio and Kate Winslet spread their arms in the air at the front of a ship that couldn't sink. My hands didn't shake as badly as I feared they would. "That trip to Oslo has haunted me a million times. I still don't understand—"

"How dumb you were?" Guro interrupted. She took a step towards me and stopped at arm's length.

"Remember, I was just a simple guy from Øyerstad." I tried a smile.

"Listen, you've been gone for an eternity, Robert. You left us. Things haven't stood still just because you disappeared."

"No, I get that. Even in Øyerstad, something must happen every year or two."

"Remember the guy from Hølland? The one I told you about on the train?" Guro looked at me seriously.

"Yes, I do. He kissed you."

"Good."

"Good?"

"That you remember him, because I don't."

I swallowed hard to keep from floating off the ground. *Come on, Robert. Do it! Ask her.*

"Would you like to watch it again?"

"Watch what?" She pretended to not get my message, but I thought I sensed a smile, so I said it outright. "Do you want to watch *Titanic* with me again? I promise to try to hold your hand, but just once. Very gently. Then you can decide whether you will hold on to it or not."

She took another step towards me. It was a smile. I could have kissed her. Fortunately, I didn't try. Strawberries. She smelled like strawberries.

"You're silly, you know," she said, leaning towards me. She whispered, "Cheese puffs."

"Cheese puffs?"

"And champagne." Now she smiled, there was no doubt about it, and the world I stood on spun. *Stay on your feet now. Stay on your feet.*

"Okay, cheese puffs and champagne." I impressed myself. I managed to talk.

"Today?" I asked, suddenly afraid I had been too eager.

"Today doesn't work."

"Tomorrow?"

"Tomorrow is fine."

"At my place?"

"Okay," she said.

"Okay," I replied.

She glowed as she leaned forward. I cautiously opened my mouth to meet her lips when she said, "Could you move aside so I can close the door?" Her hand was on the doorknob. I lost my balance as I stepped back and missed a step. Fortunately, I managed to stay on my feet and blurted out, "You know, I guess I'm falling for you." She paused in the doorway. Oh my God, That smile.

"See you tomorrow," she said and closed the door.

"Yeah, see you tomorrow," I whispered, alone outside her apartment, my heart aflame.

Epilogue

The Circus

Familiar, yet more joyful tones from the steam calliope surround me. The music isn't as slow and sneaky as it used to be. It lifts me up instead of pushing me down. Although the night still paints the sky black, the tent, glowing dimly, no longer scares me. No, I believe there's something nice in there now. Something warm and genuine. Something loving. Laughter and joy. A whiff reminiscent of smoked whisky makes me think of the last night with Dad. The one that was or wasn't. Goosebumps. I'm no longer afraid. And the phantoms? They're gone. There's no one else here. Just me and the tent. I think.

It doesn't take long before I realise I am not entirely alone after all. Fear washes over me again as I hear him growling. He is right over there, a few metres away. Slowly. He comes closer. Bingo-Bob observes me with milky white eyes and open jaws.

My breath becomes shorter, choppy like an old LP record. The air stops at the top of my lungs. He's no more than two metres away. Fuck, it's not over after all. In the end, everyone except Bingo-Bob has gotten what they wanted. With the Witch of Mørkved and Death out of the way, it's his turn to reclaim his throne.

Soon, in seconds or minutes, depending on how long he wants me to suffer, he will leap at me. He'll sink his teeth into my face and tear it off my skull. He floats closer.

After the Witch tore him to shreds, someone had stitched him back together, like Frankenstein's dog. Whoever it was, they didn't do a particularly good job. Wide-open wounds gape, while shreds of skin and flesh dangle from patched fur. No wonder he's vicious.

"We haven't been kind to you." My voice feels foreign with a strange echo. "Actually, we're quite alike, you and me."

I want to step back, but instead, I step forward. I do not freeze. I do not flee. Not this time. The ground is rough against my knees as I kneel down. I refuse to be scared. I extend a hand and whisper, "We don't have to hate each other." The cur snaps at the air, splattering saliva and something dark, like blood. He is close now. I consider retreating again but don't. Instead, I crawl closer, crouching. Hand still extended. Bingo-Bob continues to chew the air. I move even closer. And closer. Wait a second, did he just lean back? He did. A small step backward.

"Calm down, boy. No one's going to hurt you. See, I'm not dangerous." I expose my palms to show him I don't have a stone or anything else I could hurt him with. "Can I pat you?" Surprisingly, his lips lower over his teeth. Then he sinks down with his front body. He whimpers as his hind legs also give way. "Relax, boy. Take it easy. Good boy. Lie down. I won't hurt you."

Suddenly, he doesn't look so threatening anymore, and he kind of shrinks as I lay a hand on his head. He shivers. "We need to stop treating each other like this, right? We need to be better friends, you and I."

As I stroke his fur, the wounds, blood, and dirt seem to stick to my hands, like I have some sort of magical powers. I pull the wounds with me. I pat him more eagerly, wiping away blood, and bone splinters as if they're makeup from a Halloween party. His eyes slowly change colour, from white with floating blue irises, to brown.

"You like that, don't you? Feeling better now?" He looks at me and the tongue that licks my hand is pink and healthy. His gums are black and his teeth white.

Soon the mist around us lifts, and I hear people approaching. Laughter. Adults and kids. Rakel is as young as she was when she ran away from Hitra, or maybe even younger. She has a warm glow about her. Pål-Ottar is a child, his face still disfigured, but he is smiling, revealing two missing front teeth. It appears they can't see me or Bingo-Bob as they walk hand in hand towards the tent. Pål-Ottar has a giant candy-cane lollipop, and Rakel holds a paper cup with a straw. Then they turn towards me. I light up. They laugh. They wave. But no, not at me. Olav jogs towards them with a teddy bear. He gives it to Pål-Ottar, who is too small to hold it. More laughter.

A younger me holds the world's largest bucket of popcorn, and Anders has a huge bag of mixed candy. Fredrik carries his special assignment under his arm while balancing cotton candy and soda. Mom and Dad hold each other's hands right behind us. We follow the crowd into the circus. A whole and happy family. Just before Fredrik disappears into the portal of joy and excitement, he turns towards me and waves. He can see me. I wink back at him. A tear trickles down my chin. "Thank you. See you again someday."

Bingo-Bob sits beside me, and soon we're alone again, outside. Laughter and cheer filter out to us through the tent fabric. The show has begun. "It'll be alright now," I whisper to my four-legged friend. "Everything's okay. Perhaps we should go in too?" Bingo-Bob gets up, and together we move towards the entrance.

Robert

"Robert?" It's a woman's voice, so sincere I get goosebumps.
"Everything will be fine," I answer softly.
"You're talking in your sleep again."
"Bingo-Bob?"
"Hey, are you awake?"
"I... yes, I think so. I am now."
"You okay?"
"You know what, I actually am. Everything's just fine."
"That's good. Good night, sleep well."
"Good night. Love you…"

abattleagainstdemons.com

Printed in Great Britain
by Amazon

42780348R00205